"Carefully plotted...EMINENCE is a strong novel that follows Kienzle's gritty MARKED FOR MURDER, excellently combining the rituals of religion with page-turning suspense. Kienzle never fails to faithfully entertain; his sharp ear for dialogue and his image-filled flair for detail shine through like a beacon for other aspiring mystery authors."
Lansing State Journal

"Kienzle has perfected his art....Crime and the clergy provide an intriguing combination for mystery."
Daily Herald (Elk Grove, IL)

"Koesler performs wonders....Proving that faith does move mountains, the author entertains and educates."
Publishers Weekly

"Engrossing...Another spiritually sinister mystery...An intriguing blend of crime and religion."
Booklist

EMINENCE

A Father Koesler Mystery

WILLIAM X. KIENZLE

BALLANTINE BOOKS • NEW YORK

Library of Congress Catalog Card Number: 88–35007

ISBN 0–345–35395–1

This edition published by arrangement with Andrews and McMeel, a Universal Press Syndicate Company

This is a work of fiction and, as such, events described herein are creations of the author's imagination. Any relation to real people, living or dead, is purely coincidental and accidental.

Manufactured in the United States of America

First Ballantine Books Edition: May 1990

FOR JAVAN

IN MEMORY OF

CARDINAL JOHN F. DEARDEN AND MAY O'KRAY

Grey Eminence. The name given to François Leclerc du
Tremblay (1577–1638), or Père Joseph, as he was called,
the CAPUCHIN agent and trusty counsellor of
Cardinal Richelieu. It was inspired by his influence
over Cardinal Richelieu's policies: he was, as it were,
a shadowy CARDINAL in the background.
—BREWER'S DICTIONARY OF PHRASE AND FABLE

gray eminence *n* [trans. of F. *Éminence Grise*,
nickname of Père Joseph (François Joseph du Tremblay)
†1638 F monk and diplomat who was confidant of
Cardinal Richelieu, styled *Éminence Rouge* (red eminence);
fr. the colors of their respective habits]:
a person who exercises power behind the scenes.
—WEBSTER'S NEW COLLEGIATE DICTIONARY

ACKNOWLEDGMENTS

Gratitude for technical advice to:

Mary Alfano, Archdiocesan secretary
Roy Awe, Sergeant, Retired, Homicide Section, Detroit
      Police Department
Ramon Betanzos, Professor of Humanities, Wayne State
      University
Detroit Free Press
      Patricia Chargot, Staff Writer
      Neal Shine, Senior Managing Editor
Detroit News
      Robert Ankeny, Staff Writer
      Judy Diebolt, Staff Writer
Detroit Police Department
      James Bannon, Executive Deputy Chief
      Sergeant Mary Marcantonio, Office of Executive
      Deputy Chief
      Barbara Weide, Lieutenant, Homicide Section
Jim Grace, Detective, Kalamazoo Police Department
Sister Bernadelle Grimm, R.S.M., Samaritan Health Care
      Center, Detroit
Philip D. Head, Vice President, Manufacturers National
      Bank of Detroit
Margaret Hershey, R.N., Pulmonary Care Unit, Detroit
      Receiving Hospital
Timothy Kenny, attorney-at-law, Larson, Harms &
      Wright, P.C.

James McIntyre, Manager, The Clamdiggers Restaurant
Thomas J. Petinga, Jr., D.O., FACEP, Chairman,
    Department of Emergency Medicine, Mt. Carmel
    Mercy Hospital, Detroit
Walter D. Pool, M.D., Medical Consultant
Rudy Reinhard, World Wide Travel Bureau, Inc.
Werner U. Spitz, M.D., Professor of Forensic Pathology,
    Wayne State University
Robbie Timmons, Anchorperson, WXYZ-TV, Detroit

With special gratitude to Dr. Liam Bannan, Durrow,
Laois, Ireland; The Most Reverend Thomas J.
Gumbleton, Auxiliary Bishop of Detroit; Lynn Lloyd;
Rosemarie Lubienski.

Paraphrased excerpts from *Medicolegal Investigation of
Death* (Second Edition; Charles C. Thomas), by Werner
U. Spitz, M.D., and Russell S. Fisher, M.D., used by
permission of Werner U. Spitz, M.D.

Any technical error is the author's.

SATURDAY
JULY 22

CHAPTER
1

He killed the first guy he ever shot.

Dumb luck, expertise, or a finely tuned reflex response? It didn't make a damn bit of difference to David Powell. He was dead.

David Powell, fifteen years old, grade school dropout, with a prodigious arrest record; purveyor of just about every manner of controlled substance, from the relatively innocuous marijuana to the current drug of choice, crack cocaine.

The essence of David Powell—soul or whatever—was gone now. What remained had been dropped on a slab in the morgue. How had Shakespeare expressed it—"Shrunk to this little measure . . . a bleeding piece of earth."

Alonzo Tully was not particularly strong on Shakespeare, but he was pretty sure of those phrases from *Julius Caesar*.

Zoo, as he was known to just about everyone, had been a Detroit police officer for twenty-two years, thirteen of them in Homicide. He dealt in death. He could not count the times he had stood in this dank, gray room in the Wayne County Medical Examiner's building, attending an autopsy.

Certainly he had been here for each and every murder case he'd investigated.

Tully believed that each investigation needed all the help it could get. And, after the murder scene itself, the next best place to build one's case, chronologically and every other way, was the morgue. The autopsy process, and the morgue's boss, Dr. Wilhelm Moellmann, were instructive teachers.

However, Tully needed little enlightening with regard to the death of David Powell. The case, as Hollywood was wont to put it, was open and shut. Or, in the jargon of the police, a platter case, i.e., presented on a silver platter.

Tully had killed Powell. It was as simple as that—on paper. It was far more momentous to Tully.

In his twenty-two-year career as a police officer, Tully had had to draw his gun numerous times. But outside of a firing range, he had never pulled the trigger. A record by no means unique in the department.

He had told no one, but, last night, after it was over and the details were wrapped up, he had wept. It was the first time since his childhood. And it hadn't happened that often even then. However, last night, at home, in Alice's arms, he had wept.

Tully dealt in death, but this was the first time he had ever killed anyone. And it had to be a kid!

Moellmann removed Powell's clothing meticulously. More than once, the M.E. had found bullets among the deceased's garments. Bullets that had plowed through a body, exiting to lie among the clothing. Once a bullet entered the body there was just no telling where it might go. The course and extent of damage depended on such variables as the angle of entry, the distance between weapon and target, the class of weapon, the type of bullet, and the path it took inside the body. Bullets had been known to ricochet off bones. Bullets had been known to penetrate the aorta and be transported via the bloodstream elsewhere in the body.

It was not unheard-of for Moellmann to wisecrack during autopsies. Today, out of deference to Tully, whom he re-

4

spected, the M.E. merely made factual observations as he conducted his examination. And, due to his Prussian demeanor, which dictated that his subordinates follow his lead, the morgue was uncharacteristically quiet this morning as the other doctors mumbled through their respective autopsies.

The clothing was removed and packed away for subsequent examination by the police crime laboratory. Powell's body lay naked on the shiny metal tray. Firm, young flesh. A kid.

Memory transported Tully to the events of last evening that had led to this. He could remember every detail. Indeed, would he ever forget?

Actually, Tully's squad had been investigating another crime entirely. As happened so frequently in Detroit these days, it was a multiple homicide connected with the drug traffic. Three dismembered male bodies had been found in plastic garbage bags in an alley in the north-central section of the city. All three were known drug dealers. Drugs— the most common current cause of gang war in this and many other cities in America.

There followed some intense investigation, calling in of markers, and clandestine meetings with snitches. Everything pointed to a crack house on Curtis not far from Livernois in the vicinity of the University of Detroit.

Tully and five of his squad placed the house under surveillance. This was not a drug bust, nor did they want it to become one. They were looking for David Powell. According to their information, it was Powell who had shot the victims, execution-style, before they were dismembered.

The weather had been pleasant enough for an evening in late July. A clear sky, a gentle breeze, not oppressively hot.

The six officers were in three unmarked cars, cruising the streets, occasionally parking, but making sure that at least one of them was keeping the house in sight at all times. The sort of duty that too often seemed unending. As it had last night.

There were times, as traffic in and out of the house was

fairly steady, that the officers strongly suspected the information given them was, intentionally or not, incorrect. Maybe David Powell was not in the house. Perhaps he had never been there.

Then it happened. At about half-past nine, just as it was getting dark, Powell was sighted at the door talking with three young people who had just arrived.

In a matter of seconds, all three cars drew up in front of the house. Sergeant Mangiapane, first on the sidewalk, was approaching Powell.

Tully cursed silently. Of all the officers on this detail, Mangiapane most resembled the stereotypical cop. Large, and a good target, he was walking too quickly, too purposefully.

Tully was out of his car only seconds behind Mangiapane.

Everything happened quickly, too quickly to be assimilated at that moment. Only later, in retrospect, could events be pieced together.

Tully saw the flash of the nickel-plated pistol as it emerged from Powell's cardigan. Evidently Powell had no doubt or hesitation. In one motion the gun was in his hand and aimed at Mangiapane, who was only then going for his own weapon.

But Tully's .38 was out as he shouted at Powell. Later, it seemed it had been the shout that had momentarily distracted Powell. He wavered for a split second, unsure as to whether he should fire at the big white cop in front of him or at the guy who was yelling.

At that instant of indecision, Powell opted for what should have been a sure kill directly ahead: he fired point-blank. Mangiapane spun and fell heavily to the pavement. Was Mangiapane dead or alive? Tully's presumption was that he was dead. How could Powell have missed the kill at that distance?

No time to speculate; the next shot would be at him. But it was a shot that would never come. Tully, aiming almost instinctively, fired once. Afterward, he remembered the look of almost childlike surprise on Powell's face—as if he had but a moment to wonder that his life was over so soon. Then he tumbled down the porch steps.

Pandemonium.

One of the other cars called for backup. In no time, the street was overflowing with cops keeping order and bystanders attempting to upset order.

Tully was numb. Of the numbers of dead and dying he had seen in the course of duty, this one alone belonged to him. Once in his career as a police officer, once in his entire life thus far, had he fired at anyone. And he had fired only once. One bullet, one dead person.

Absently, he wondered about that bullet. Where had it hit Powell? Before he could check out the dead man, Tully had been whisked from the scene. With all the ensuing commotion, no telling what might have happened next.

It seemed an unspoken consensus that it was essential to get two people out of there. Mangiapane needed medical attention and Tully needed protection from the crowd.

Two EMS vans had arrived only minutes after the shootings. Mangiapane and Tully were packed into one and Powell in the other. Powell had no vital signs. But the technicians worked on him feverishly just in case.

Mt. Carmel Mercy Hospital pronounced him dead on arrival.

Mangiapane's was a shoulder wound. He was rushed from Mt. Carmel's emergency room to the operating room. His condition was now listed as stable. That announcement was for the media's benefit; Tully had more detailed information. Powell's bullet had lodged in Mangiapane's right shoulder. The bullet had been removed during a relatively brief operation. The prognosis was complete recovery. After an indeterminate time for rehabilitation, Mangiapane should be as good as new.

The fact that Mangiapane had caught the slug in his right shoulder interested Tully. Since he himself had come from Powell's left, Tully reasoned, his shout had distracted the kid just enough that he had shifted the gun ever so slightly toward

7

the sound. Thus the bullet caught Mangiapane in the shoulder rather than inflicting a more serious wound to the chest.

Tully's stream of consciousness led him back to the question of his own bullet, the fatal shot. He returned his attention to Doc Moellmann and the autopsy.

The M.E. had finished checking the body for bullet wounds, either entering or exiting. There was but one wound. The bullet had entered and stayed.

Tully stole a glance at the body chart Moellmann and the other doctors used to diagram wounds and marks. There was a notation that the wound's shape was oval, which indicated that the bullet had struck Powell's body at an angle. Only natural since Tully had fired from ground level up toward the porch. There were no powder burns; Tully had fired from a distance.

Moellmann continued his examination. Tully had to admit his interest was marginal. Unlike any other autopsy he'd ever attended, he knew exactly what had happened, who had done what to whom and, in all probability, what the conclusion would be. About the only question left to be determined was the path the bullet had taken and where it had finally lodged. Moellmann would take his time tracking its course.

There were, Tully supposed, medical examiners who cut and hacked their way through bodies in search of bullets. But not Moellmann nor his associates. Moellmann's creed was to describe the wound path in anatomical order and to document the path of the bullet by following the track of the hemorrhage through the organs before they were removed from the body. This saved the time and trouble of relying on X rays to locate the bullet.

While Moellmann measured and probed, Tully's interest strayed to a body on an adjacent table. The dead man seemed to have been elderly. Quite obviously his throat had been cut. Another straight-forward probable cause of death.

Dr. Thomas Litka noted Tully's interest. Catching Tully's eye, he nodded toward the corpse. "Zoo, meet John Doe Number 26."

"Only 26?"

Litka shrugged as he placed an abbreviated ruler alongside a gaping wound in John Doe's neck. "That's about par for this time of year."

Tully knew it was almost miraculous that the doctors, even with all their technology, managed to identify as many John and Jane Does as they did. From experience Tully knew that every avenue to identifying Number 26 had been explored with the probable exception of fingerprints.

"How about the prints?"

"Being processed." Dr. Litka did not look up. "But I've seen this kind of pickup too many times. They aren't going to find his prints. No sir, I got a hunch we'll keep him a month, then they'll bury him as Number 26."

Tully was willing to defer to Litka's experience. "Where'd they find him?"

"In an alley; northwest side, near Eight Mile."

"Last night?"

"Uh-huh."

"How long'd he been dead?"

"They made it sometime yesterday afternoon. Found him about 9:00 or 10:00 last night."

About the same time David Powell got his, thought Tully. Two exits: one old, one young.

"A bum," Litka continued, nodding toward the dead man's clothing, now in a neat pile. "No identification at all. Filthy. No labels. But all there. They didn't even take his shoes."

Tully wondered at it. So senseless. There ought to be a motive for something so violent, so cataclysmic as murder. Yet, not infrequently, there was none, or at least no detectable one.

And it was murder. He knew the telltale signs. Suicides seldom slit their own throats; they usually open a vein in their wrists. And when they did go for their own throats, there were usually several cuts. Tentative, perhaps, at first, until one slash was deep enough to cause death. Or else the cumulative effect of the cuts was eventually fatal.

Tully studied the ruler Dr. Litka had placed near the cut. A technician was photographing the area for the records. The cut looked to be a couple of inches in length—considerable for a knife wound. And deep. Not the sort expected in a suicide.

Of course Doc Litka knew that.

"What are those scratches along the cut?" Tully asked.

"Look to be the high points of a serrated weapon," Litka replied.

"Hunting knife."

"Maybe."

"But you'd know it from those marks if it ever turned up."

"Probably; one of the teeth is missing. Not likely to turn up, though."

From the first moment he saw the body, Tully had been aware of other marks—none, of course, as arresting as the slit throat. "On the trunk, Doc: those insect bites?"

"I thought so, too, at first. But they look more like he got hit with something. A beating of some kind. Happened before his throat got cut. They probably tortured him. Beats me why. A real mean killer, I suppose."

Some cop at this very moment was pondering the same questions, thought Tully. And whoever the cop was, he undoubtedly knew it was not likely he'd find any good answers. A bum in an alley, probably sleeping off a cheap wine drunk. Some kids, maybe, or perhaps another bum with a sadistic turn of mind. Whatever, they beat him up, slit his throat, don't even steal anything. Just for the hell of it. How you gonna find someone like that? Unless he or they do it again. Next time, maybe a mistake, or somebody'll see something. But not much chance on this one.

Doc Litka was wrapping up his examination. "Well, that does it. Bled to death. Exsanguination due to cutting of throat." To Tully: "At least the poor guy went fast. The knife penetrated the large vein. An air embolism formed and got sucked in, causing foam, which produced a valve lock in the heart. One or two gasps and he was done."

A mercy . . . I guess, thought Tully.

As he turned back to Doc Moellmann and the autopsy of David Powell, Tully noticed John Doe's knees. Scarred. Probably reduced to crawling around the alley. What a life! Maybe somebody did him a favor by putting him out of his misery. And, as Litka had observed, quickly. Still, it *was* murder.

Which was considerably more than one could say about David Powell. Justifiable homicide in the line of duty. Of course that verdict was not in yet. But it was a lead-pipe cinch.

The Powell case was already in the hands of, and being investigated by, two agencies. Because it involved a killing, the investigation would stay within the Homicide Division, which had processed the scene of the shooting and would continue investigating until they reached a conclusion. Independent of this investigation, the board of review would conduct its own hearings.

The potential consequences of a cop-committed killing were so fraught that it seemed imperative that the investigation leave no doubt whatsoever. If it was a cop who got killed, an unspoken vendetta was sworn. Over and above the manifestation of grief over a fallen comrade, it was necessary to remind the criminal community that cop-killers get caught and are punished. If it was a cop who killed, there had to be no hint or semblance of a whitewash. The police were the only nonmilitary who were not only empowered but required to carry guns. That explicit power carried a heavy responsibility. The department was more eager than even the civilian populace to determine whether it was a case of justifiable homicide.

In addition, one thing was certain when a cop killed anyone for any reason: Somebody was going to sue the department and/or the city. So, for this reason also, the investigation had to be thorough and objective and complete.

Tully had witnessed such investigations too many times. He could write the script. Some witnesses—especially suppliers, pushers, and users of drugs—would cry, "police brutality.'' They would swear that Powell never carried a weapon and certainly hadn't had one last night. Others— neighbors who wanted that troublesome dope house closed down—would recall that Powell had come at the police with a blazing Uzi. Still others would advance that most frequently heard charge: racism. This type of individual would not be bothered in the slightest by the fact that Tully as well as Powell was black. For some Detroiters, racism was so automatically cited as the cause of all urban evil that the attitude itself had become colorblind.

But the authorities had the slug from Mangiapane's shoulder that had been fired from Powell's gun. Ballistics would confirm that. And in a little while, Doc Moellmann would find the bullet Tully had fired. Those pieces of evidence, plus the testimony of credible witnesses, would exonerate him.

Meanwhile, Tully had been assigned to restricted duty for the duration of the investigation. The official term for this assignment was ''minimal duty.'' In effect, it was a sort of benign suspension or a brief vacation. At the conclusion of the investigation, the findings would be announced by the board of review.

Then the official decree of justifiable homicide in the course of duty would be rendered. That verdict was, Tully felt, inevitable.

Moellmann was mumbling again. As was his custom, he wrote nothing during the examination, merely making cryptic notations on the body chart. Afterward—immediately afterward—back in his office he would write a complete report.

''. . . uh-huh,'' Moellmann murmured, ''twenty-one and one-half inches below the top of the head, one-half inch to the right of the midline, and five inches above the navel is located the entrance bullet wound. The wound measures one-quarter inch in diameter surrounded by the narrow rim of abrasion. There is no evidence of close-range fire on skin surrounding the injury.''

Following the trail of dried blood, the M.E. began to trace the path of the bullet as it had passed from one internal organ to another. "The wound track passes from front to back, from right to left and slightly upward. . . ." There was a pause as Moellmann removed the affected organs. ". . . ah, here it is!" This intonation as if he had just successfully panned for gold.

Tully assumed the bullet had been located and that he was being invited to view the discovery. Both assumptions were correct. He moved closer to the body and studied the small area defined by Moellmann. There it was, lodged in one of Powell's ribs. Now somewhat misshapen, nonetheless the slug would carry the distinctive markings made by whichever gun barrel it had exited. In this case, unquestionably, Tully's gun.

Moellmann carefully excised the segment of bone containing the bullet. Then with strong fingers, he bent and flexed the specimen until the slug fell free. He was careful not to handle it with forceps or a hemostat for fear of destroying the bullet's distinguishing markings.

So, there it was. Powell's remains would be examined further. Moellmann would know more about David Powell in death than anyone had known in life.

Ordinarily, at this point in the autopsy, Tully would leave. Ordinarily he couldn't get out quickly enough. The autopsy in which he was involved was, for his purposes, concluded. But for some reason that he could not identify, he lingered.

An autopsy was just beginning at an adjoining table. Automatically, from force of habit, Tully began mentally ticking off the evident clues this body presented.

Hispanic woman, maybe in her late thirties, wearing an ordinary housedress, which was being carefully removed. From the condition of the clothing, Tully was fairly certain what had happened. The dress was stained with grease and tire marks. Fragments of glass tinkled onto the metal table and were carefully collected. There'd probably be paint stains on the dress too, though from this distance Tully couldn't distinguish them. She'd been hit by a car. How seriously she had been hit by that car was about to be revealed.

Briefly, she was placed face-down, nude. There were

bumper injuries on the back of her legs. Hit from behind. But the bumper marks were at different levels on each leg. An indication that she had been walking, or, judging from the discrepancy of the marks—much higher on the left than on the right leg—more probably she had been running. The scenario was getting clearer.

Why would she run from a car? In the case of an accident, if the victim isn't aware of the approach of a vehicle, he or she is usually hit from the side. Or, if there is some apprehension, the victim may turn toward the oncoming vehicle and be hit from the front.

But if someone is running away from the car when struck, the probability is that the driver is chasing the victim. And if that is the case, the charge is battery with a motor vehicle. Or, in this case, homicide—probably Murder One.

The deceased was turned over onto her back. Suspicion confirmed. There was a deep gouge in the groin. Tully was certain this one was a homicide. Not only had she been struck from behind, but the car was being driven at high speed.

There were lacerations all over her head. Easily to be expected, since a pedestrian hit at high speed tends to be thrown high in the air, perhaps landing briefly on the car's roof or trunk, and then falling into the street. Frequently, the victim then may be struck by one or more of the following cars.

To top it off, there were multiple parallel tears over the victim's trunk and upper legs. These were injuries caused by overstretching of the skin under the great weight of a car.

Where this case broke through the mold was in the pattern of the tire tracks across the victim's body. To Tully's experienced eye, the tracks appeared startlingly similar. He bet it wouldn't take the technicians long to establish that all these injuries had been caused by one and the same vehicle. As frequently happens in such cases, when this woman had been run over repeatedly, the edges of the tire's grooves between the tread were imprinted on her body. Something similar to a rubber-stamp effect.

If the police ever found the right guy with the right car, they'd be able to match the actual tires with these treadmarks, which were at this moment being carefully recorded by the morgue's technicians. In this case, the tire treads would prove almost as helpful as fingerprints.

And, thought Tully, the cops very possibly would catch up with the guy who did this. Whoever the perp was, he had certainly been motivated.

Killing somebody was so easy. Or was it because Tully had become so inured to violent death that the act seemed so simple? In any case, one could kill quickly with little or no expense or trouble—as with that bum who'd had his throat slit. Or one could kill from a distance with little effort with a gun, as he himself had done with the late David Powell.

But to take the trouble to chase down a defenseless woman with a car, deliberately hit her at high speed, then run over her again and again—that required a good bit of intensity and dedication. There was little doubt, thought Tully, if they get this guy it would be murder in the first degree. For some reason he did not think of the driver of the death car as a woman.

And because there seemed to be such intense motivation in this killing, it seemed likely the good guys would win this one. But, experience stepped in to wag a finger, you never could tell.

With a deep sigh, Tully turned away from the autopsy tables. Idle speculation about homicide was a waste of time. And so was everything else he could think of doing just now.

Investigations into murder had substantially become his life. His dedication to the Homicide Division had cost him his first and, to date, only marriage. His wife long ago had decided that she had no chance in competition with his job. So, after a reluctant but finally amicable no-fault divorce, she had moved to Chicago with their five children. He visited the kids four or five times a year. He would have done so more often but he couldn't tear himself away from all these cases that begged for his attention. She had remarried. He had not.

For a little more than a year after the divorce he had lived alone in their now-too-large home in northwest Detroit.

Then he met Alice Balcom, a Wayne County social worker assigned to juvenile court. They were attracted to each other immediately and began dating. Soon they had mutually decided that the drive between the far reaches of the east and west sides of Detroit was silly. She moved in with him. It was Tully's first miscegenational union and, until recently, it had worked more smoothly than he could have hoped.

Al, as Tully called his "significant other," knew from the outset that he could not compromise his total dedication to his job. She had seemed content to finish a close second.

However, for the past several months, Al had not been well. And no one seemed able to diagnose her ailment. Her doctor, a renowned internist, had attended her carefully, but had not been able to stem the tide of symptoms that kept popping up like the buttons on a blender.

Most men would be grateful, even if they would not admit it, to have some time off to spend at home. Tully was not one of them.

Al was ill and there was nothing he could do about it. That was frustrating. Everyone would expect him to stay home with her. He expected it of himself. But he was confused. He was uncomfortable with a situation wherein he was surrounded by a problem, a problem that he could not solve.

For that was the whole kick of homicide. Tully thrived on real-life whodunits. The puzzle, the challenge of solving it, that was the entire enchilada.

Now the only challenge was how to deal with and what to do for Al. And he had no clue as to an answer.

Otherwise, he was on the shelf. And he didn't like it one little bit. But there was nothing he could do about it. And that, as he pulled his shapeless rain hat on, was that. But he didn't like it.

**SUNDAY
JULY 23**

CHAPTER
2

Following an afternoon of dodging raindrops on the golf course, four priests met for dinner at the Wine Barrel, one of Father Robert Koesler's favorite downtown restaurants. After being served drinks, they ordered, then got down to the serious business of clerical gab.

Father Patrick McNiff stirred his Manhattan on the rocks. He used his right index finger. He always had. But then, almost everything he did he always had done. "I heard that Al McNeeley is getting St. Al's. Anybody else hear that?"

Father Jim Tracy tilted his head to look through his bifocals. "St. Al's? St. Aloysius down here?"

"The same," McNiff affirmed.

St. Aloysius was a famous tri-level church in the heart of what had once been the hub of downtown Detroit. Its building housed a myriad of archdiocesan bureaucracies, including the Tribunal, the Chancery, and the offices of the Cardinal Archbishop of Detroit, Mark Boyle.

Tracy shook his head. "By me."

"So what?" Father Darin O'Day said. "What's so hot about St. Al's? Anymore, I mean."

He had a point. Once, the J. L. Hudson department store had anchored the commercial downtown. And St. Aloysius Church, only a few blocks removed from Hudson's, had profited in every imaginable way from its nearness. Even though its congregation was heavily transient, the people who flowed through its doors all day, every day, had been among the genuine celebrities of the city, the country, even the world.

Now, the core of Detroit's downtown, such as it was, had shifted several long blocks to the riverfront. And what a difference those blocks made in terms of commerce, population, traffic, interest, special events and, by no means last, safety!

"St. Al's is St. Al's, and I think McNeeley's lucky to get it," McNiff stated with a touch of infallibility.

"Pat's got a point," Koesler said. "The history of that church and parish is special, even unique. It still serves a goodly group of interesting people. And it's still the hub of the archdiocese if not the city."

"Sounds good to me, Bob, especially if you don't mind staying inside your fortress for protection every night." O'Day seldom gave any thought to downtown Detroit anymore so involved was he with his Novi parish.

Koesler smiled. "I know how you feel, Darin. We're all part of the suburbs now. But Detroit's not an alien planet. We all grew up in this city. This is our town."

"Then why are we all out in the 'burbs?" O'Day commented.

Koesler winced inwardly. "Because that's where we were sent. Because that's where a good bit of what used to go on in Detroit has moved."

"Along with a good percentage of the Catholic population," said Tracy.

It was all true, thought Koesler. But that didn't make him feel any less uneasy. Actually, he had attempted more than once to return to a city parish. But the assignment board that ruled on such matters was forced to juggle a Catholic population that was constantly shifting further out of the city against an ever-diminishing number of available priests. In a word, Koesler had been unsuccessful in his attempts to return to the city. But the fact that he'd tried did not make him feel any less guilty.

"I don't care what you say," O'Day said, "it's different than it was. It's not safe down here. I don't care if the mayor does have most of his cops downtown; I won't feel comfortable until I—and my car—get out of here in one piece tonight."

"Come on, Darin," said Tracy, "are you trying to make us believe there's no crime in Novi?"

"Not like Detroit. Not anything like Detroit. God! The last time it was safe in this city was when the Pope was here."

"Who could forget that?" McNiff said with a fervor bordering on veneration.

"I guess I can't," said Koesler. "I dreamed about it the other night."

"Dreamed about it?" McNiff pursued.

"Uh-huh. It was weird. I dreamed that the Pope was appearing in Hart Plaza on the riverfront, just like he did when he was actually here a couple of years ago.

"And just like it was then, everybody was worrying about security and afraid that some nut would seize this opportunity to settle an imaginary score or make a name for himself by assaulting the Pope.

"In my dream, the police, the FBI, the Secret Service, everybody had the downtown area pretty well secure. The Coast Guard was even able to control the river and all the boats that would be there to get a good look at the Pope. Just like when he was here in real life, everything in the immediate vicinity of Hart Plaza was taken care of. The only chink in the armor was Windsor, across the river. They weren't able to secure that, but, on the other hand, they weren't too concerned about it either. Downtown Windsor is a fair distance from downtown Detroit across the river."

Koesler studied his companions. "Did any of you see that movie about an assassination attempt on General de Gaulle—*Day of the Jackal*?"

All three nodded and smiled at the recollection of a memorable movie.

"Okay," Koesler continued, "I must have been influenced by that movie. Because in my dream, an assassin was taking advantage of the lack of complete security in Windsor. He rented a room in a hotel directly across the river from Hart Plaza. He was an expert marksman. He even looked like Edward Fox . . . the actor who played the assassin in *Day of the Jackal*.

"Anyway, he set up his tripod and attached his high-powered rifle to it—so there would be a minimum of movement when he pulled the trigger. And—oh, yes—he had a telescopic sight attached to the rifle.

"He was taking no chances. Even so, that's a hell of a long distance. And there are variables like the wind factor. I don't know if someone could actually do it in real life, but it was, all in all, even in my dream, a chancy shot."

The waiter brought their entrées. It was a testament to the captivating quality of Koesler's recital that none of them reached for a fork. They simply sat and gazed at him.

"Come on," Koesler invited, "eat up."

They proceeded to dig in, McNiff, however, exhorting, "Go on with the dream, damn it!"

"Oh, well, where was I? Oh, yes. The assassin was ready. He had the stand, the rifle, the telescopic sight. Still, it would have to be a fantastic shot to hit his target."

"We know that," said McNiff. "What happened then? And if you say you woke up, there are three of us priests here . . . just enough to give you a solemn high funeral."

"No, I didn't wake up . . . not just then, anyway. What happened next was that the procession of priests and bishops and Cardinals filed onto the raised stage in Hart Plaza. Just about every ecclesiastical dignitary in the country was there. Then, the Pope, in his white cassock and red cape, stepped up to the microphone and began reading his speech.

"Meanwhile, in Windsor, the assassin was ready. He took very careful aim. He inhaled deeply. Then, as he partially exhaled, he very carefully squeezed, rather than pulled, the trigger."

Koesler paused. His companions once again put their dinners on hold, McNiff with a forkful of vegetables poised between plate and mouth.

"And there on the stage of Hart Plaza," resumed Koesler, "shock registered on the face of the Bishop of Flint as he tumbled from his chair onto the stage. There was a neat bullet hole in his forehead. He was dead."

McNiff frowned. "Bishop of Flint? Flint's not a diocese. There isn't any Bishop of Flint!"

"It was a dream, for Pete's sake," Koesler said.

"You mean to tell us the son-of-a-bitch missed the Pope?" O'Day asked. "What the hell kind of dream was that, anyway?"

"That's when I woke up."

"Woke up?" McNiff almost shouted. "Woke up! You mean that's it?"

"Well, not exactly. I was so interested in how this dream would work out, I tried to get back to sleep and take up where I left off. Occasionally it works out that way."

"And . . . ?"

"When I got back to sleep—in, for me, record-quick time—the same dream continued.

"The police started with the theory that the assassin had missed. Obviously, the intended target had to have been the Pope. He was the one all the law enforcement agencies were protecting. The one area of total protection they could not guarantee—at least in my dream—was Windsor. And that's where the lethal shot came from.

"But then, a smart detective came up with a different premise. Suppose—was the way his premise started—just suppose the assassin hadn't missed. Suppose the assassin's real target was not the Pope but the Bishop of Flint."

"Makes sense," said Tracy. "Doesn't make much difference which one you're talking about. To lots of people, one bishop is as good or bad as another.''

"Right," Koesler said. "That's what this detective figured. The target could have been the Pope. In which case the motive probably would have been some insane desire for notoriety. But since the shot came from across the river, presumably it was a professional assassin. Why hire a professional assassin? Any idiot who hungers for notoriety gets close to the target and does the dirty work himself. One hires an assassin when one wants the job done neatly and professionally and with anonymity for the employer.''

Tracy gestured at Koesler with his fork. "But who would do that? Who would contract for the murder of a bishop? Who cares enough?''

"That's where the dream culminated." Koesler grinned. "It seems that there was a meeting of the Flint diocesan priests—all of them sworn to secrecy—and during the meeting, this plot was outlined for them. And one hundred of them consented to it and chipped in to pay for the hit man. It would have cost them between fifty dollars and one hundred dollars per priest, depending on the stipend for the assassin.''

"I love it!" said Tracy.

"Sacrilegious!" growled McNiff.

"Hey, it was just a dream!" Koesler protested.

At this point, Moe Blair, the proprietor of the restaurant, approached the table. Moe made it a practice to circulate among his guests. And he scarcely could have overlooked a table not only filled with priests, but priests who looked the part, wearing black suits and Roman collars. Beyond that, he was concerned that the reverend gentlemen did not appear to be eating. He could not know that their abstemiousness was the product of Father Koesler's dream. Indeed, Koesler was the only one at the table whom Blair knew.

"How's everything, Fathers?"

"Fine," Koesler said.

But Tracy was still engrossed in Koesler's dream. "Can

you imagine that? What in God's green world would a prosecuting attorney do with one hundred priests accused of conspiracy to murder!''

"I beg your pardon?" Blair was nonplussed.

"It's nothing, Moe. Just a dream I was telling my friends about." Koesler realized how bizarre Tracy's statement must sound to anyone coming upon the conversation at just that point. He immediately made the introductions.

"Enjoying yourselves?" Blair was still concerned that the food be satisfactory, even though since his arrival at their table the priests had proceeded to eat with evident appreciation.

"Excellent," said Tracy. The others nodded agreement.

"One thing, though," O'Day said. "We haven't got any water."

Koesler looked embarrassed. "Darin, why do you suppose this place is called the *Wine* Barrel!"

"Oh," Blair smiled, "we'll get you some water. Sorry about that. As a rule, we don't serve water unless someone requests it."

"No, no," O'Day said. "Wine sounds great, now that you mention it. Much better than water. What would you recommend?"

Blair quickly evaluated their meals. "I think a nice cabernet sauvignon . . . compliments of the house."

O'Day flashed his most engaging Irish smile. "Thank you very much, Moe."

Amazing, thought Koesler, how quickly a priest can make himself comfortable on a first-name basis with someone he has just met, while the new acquaintance feels compelled to continue using the priest's title of "Father." Amazing, too, how priestly perks never quit. Had this table been occupied by four laymen, Moe Blair surely would have seen that they were served water. Or, if they had decided to go with the restaurant's motif and order wine, the proprietor might merely have taken the order. Or called the waiter to take the order. Under no circumstances would he have offered a complimentary bottle. But, because they were priests . . .

As it happened, Blair asked their waiter to bring the wine.

Koesler looked about. ''Where's Betsy?'' The reference was to Mrs. Blair.

A worried look flitted across Moe's face. ''She's not feeling just right.''

''Oh,'' Koesler said, ''I'm sorry. Not serious, I pray.''

''I don't think so.'' But his worried look returned. ''It's just that whatever it is doesn't seem to want to go away.''

''Whatever it is'' sounded odd to Koesler. ''Doesn't the doctor know what it is?''

''Hasn't been able to pin it down. I'm sure he will, though . . . just a matter of time.'' Blair laughed nervously. ''She's even considering going to see Father Robert.''

''Father Robert?''

''Yes, you know: the faith healer. He's been in the papers . . .''

''Oh, sure. I should've known. I guess I just haven't paid much attention to that.''

There was an intensity in Blair's eyes. This matter of a faith healer bothered him more than he was willing to admit. ''Then you don't think it would do any good?''

Koesler stopped himself from giving a typically flip response. ''Frankly, Moe, I don't know enough about Father Robert to have an informed opinion. I don't suppose it would do any harm though. If you'd like, I'll ask around and get back to you.''

''I'd appreciate that.'' Blair seemed relieved that he had tossed the theological ball to a professional. With the expressed hope that the priests would enjoy the remainder of their dinner, he left to circulate among the other customers.

''What's this about a Father Robert?'' O'Day asked.

''You haven't read about him?'' McNiff responded.

''I've got more important things to do than read every item in the papers.''

''He's been getting a bit of coverage, Darin,'' said Tracy.

"So, what about him?" O'Day tasted and approved the wine the waiter presented.

There was a moment's hesitation. Evidently none of the others knew anything appreciable about the subject.

"I don't know where he came from. And," Tracy held up his palm toward O'Day, "before you say anything, I know how important it is to know something about his background. But in what little I've read about him so far, there's been no reference to that."

McNiff gulped down a mouthful of food prematurely in order to get in the next word. "Isn't that typical! Nobody from the news media knows how important that is. They just tell you what's going on. They don't give you any perspective."

"So, what does he do?" O'Day was growing impatient.

"Well, apparently his prayers have been pretty effective . . ." Koesler appeared hesitant.

"Effective prayers!" O'Day stopped eating. "You mean cures? Like Lourdes?"

"Maybe," Tracy said, "maybe not miracles." He made a vacillating gesture with his hand, indicating uncertainty. "Certainly not like Lourdes."

"More like Father Solanus," Koesler contributed.

O'Day looked from one to the other. " 'Not like Lourdes'? 'Like Father Solanus'? What in hell does that mean?"

"For one thing," said Tracy, "Lourdes is big, and popular, and public. Almost everybody has heard of Lourdes. Nearly everyone has seen the pictures of the grotto where the Blessed Mother appeared to Bernadette Soubirous with the miraculous spring water and all the crutches and canes hanging from the walls of the cave."

"Yes," O'Day readily agreed, "there was even a book and a movie . . . *Song of Bernadette*. So?"

"So," Koesler responded, "what's going on in Detroit at the moment is not like Lourdes. There's no grotto and there aren't any implements of the lame and the halt hanging from any walls. And there's no claim of any kind of miraculous water or anything like that.''

"So it's not like Lourdes," O'Day said. "That much I've got. It's like Solanus Casey?"

Koesler, having dropped the name, almost blushed. "Well, not exactly. It's something like Casey. You remember him?"

"Not intimately."

Koesler grinned. "Okay, Casey *was* a little before our time. At least, we were kids when he was operating. But we've surely heard enough about him to know what he did . . . or what he was supposed to have done."

"Okay," O'Day admitted. "Bernie Casey had a lot of careers before he became a priest. He was a lumberman, a streetcar conductor, a jail guard, and a farm worker."

"I didn't know that!" Koesler said.

"See!" O'Day crowed. "But then he finally got what he wanted: to be a Franciscan. Right?"

"Right," Tracy affirmed. "Or pretty close to right. He was an OFM Cap . . . a member of the Order of Friars Minor Capuchin."

"Or, as we know and love them, the Caps," McNiff added.

"But he was that really odd number, a 'simple priest,' " Koesler said. "He was a priest, okay, but about all he could do was say Mass. He couldn't preach or hear confessions."

"I heard it was because the poor guy was sort of slow," McNiff offered.

"Maybe," said Tracy, "but more likely it was just because he never learned Latin. Oh, he knew enough to get through Mass, because that was pretty much the same day after day. But he wouldn't know enough to get through the Latin texts we had to wade through in Theology."

"Well, that's history," O'Day said. "And I'm familiar with it . . . or most of it. A lot of people claimed to be cured by him. And he's on his way to being named a saint. Now, what's that got to do with this Father Robert?"

"Just that it's what some people are saying about *him*,"

Koesler said. "According to the papers—and this really hasn't gotten that much play just yet, but a few accounts have appeared, mostly on the Saturday 'religious' pages—there are a few people who claim that they've gotten the answer to their prayers through him. Something like the way Solanus used to function, mostly through prayer."

"What's wrong with that?" a belligerent McNiff challenged.

"There's nothing wrong with that, Pat," said Tracy.

"Well," Koesler hedged, "there might be something wrong with it."

"What!"

"Don't get me wrong. There's nothing wrong with prayer. But suppose someone needs chemotherapy for cancer. And instead of getting medical treatment, that person is just told to pray."

"What is this, Koesler: You don't believe in the power of prayer anymore?" McNiff was definitely becoming combative.

"Of course I do, Pat. But I also believe there's a time and a purpose for prayer and a very definite and vital importance for medicine."

"Do you believe in miracles or not?" McNiff demanded.

"Yeah, I believe in miracles. But I also think—and this, as a matter of fact, if you'll recall, is what we learned in Theology—that God does not multiply miracles."

"Well, I think we oughta be open-minded about it." McNiff exuded conviction. "I think, as priests, we ought to tip the balance in favor of the miraculous."

"McNiff," said O'Day, "how in hell does that figure to be open-minded? Open-minded is 'maybe it is, maybe it ain't.' Open-minded is fifty percent says there's miracles going on; fifty percent says it's all in the mind."

"There's such a thing as presumptions, O'Day," McNiff insisted. "The accused is presumed innocent until proven guilty. Well enough for the laity to toss the conclusion up for grabs; priests have to presume that God involves Himself in our lives."

"She does?"

"Koesler!"

"I couldn't resist."

"Just the same," Tracy said, "I'd like to know where this guy comes from."

"He's not a Detroiter, is he?" O'Day asked.

"That much seems certain." Koesler was thoughtful. "He's not one of us. As far as I've read, the papers have not been clear about just what he is."

"That's right," Tracy added, "it's some kind of religious order. But which one . . . apparently not one of the mainliners. Not Dominican, not Redemptorist, not even Franciscan . . ."

"Not Jesuit." O'Day was grinning.

"Are you kidding?" McNiff said.

He was.

"Well, if we don't know *who* he is, do we know *where* he is?" O'Day asked.

"Uh-huh," Koesler said. "He's set up shop in a former bank building on the southwest side, near St. Hedwig's. And, while we're at it, he's not alone. There are four or five with him."

"Monks?"

"I suppose."

"Well," O'Day said, "they can't just walk in here and start operating as a Catholic religious community, can they?"

"I don't think so," Koesler said.

"Not on your life!" Tracy echoed. "There'd be no accountability. The Catholic Church hates no accountability like nature abhors a vacuum."

"You're right," Koesler said. "But do any of you know the rigmarole for that?"

There was a unanimous shaking of heads.

"I mean," Koesler continued, "there's got to be some kind of protocol for this sort of thing. Remember when some years back the Little Brothers of Jesus came into town and set themselves up in a rundown apartment in Cass Corridor? Now, they've been here for ages. But they have to have had some dealings with the archdiocese, with the Chancery."

"Right," Tracy agreed. "If they had gotten into any kind of trouble, the archdiocese would have had to take the heat. And certainly the Chancery knows they're here. There had to have been some contact between the Brothers and the Chancery. They'd never let these guys function without knowing something about them and, I suppose, exercising some form of control . . . would they?"

"I'd have to agree," said Koesler.

"Didn't I hear you tell the owner here that you were going to find out about Father Robert for him?" McNiff said.

Koesler reflected a moment. He had forgotten. "I guess I did. I'll have to ask around."

"Okay," Tracy said as he finished dessert, "now let's get back to your dream. A bishop gets killed in Hart Plaza and a hundred of his finest priests have paid for the contract on him. Fantastic! Let's develop that theme."

"You're joking," McNiff said, ". . . aren't you?"

CHAPTER
3

Joe Cox was pedaling diligently, but he wasn't going anywhere. He was aboard the Schwinn Air-Dyne. It had only one wheel and that was set off the floor. Intended for exercise and nothing more, it measured the speed and distance one would travel if riding an actual bicycle.

He had a choice of views. He could gaze through the window-wall of the twenty-fourth floor apartment in the downtown Lafayette Towers. That provided a breathtaking vista of Detroit's northeast as far as the eye could see, including the Detroit River and a fair view of Windsor as well. The scene drew exclamations from visitors, while even residents rarely tired of it.

Cox's alternative was to study Patricia Lennon, his paramour, significant other, or roomie, depending on one's vintage.

Pat, seated on the couch, legs crossed, was wearing white shorts and a halter. She was, without qualification, the most beautiful woman Cox had ever encountered. And Cox was—or at least had been, prior to the advent of Pat—a dedicated connoisseur of beautiful women. During their decade-long relationship, he had strayed on occasion, but on the whole he had been—for him—as faithful as a bird dog.

He had even surprised himself several years back by actually proposing marriage. Both had been previously married and divorced. But Pat was a Catholic, who, while not a regular churchgoer, felt that any marriage ceremony for her must be Catholic or forget it. After a disastrous attempt to secure a Church annulment from the Tribunal of the Archdiocese of Detroit, she had vowed never to try that again. As a result, she and Joe were now quite content merely to live together.

Professionally, the two were competitors. Cox was a reporter for the *Detroit Free Press*. Lennon had worked at the Freep, as it was popularly known, but several years ago she had moved to the *Detroit News*. Each had the reputation of being among the very best journalists in town. Word was that they shared everything but their bylines.

Faced with a choice between these views—a panorama of Detroit and environs or the smashing Lennon—Cox had to conclude he might just have the best of all possible worlds. His actual problem: an announcement he had to make sooner or later. He had concluded that his news should be postponed as long as possible. He did not know how Pat would react to it. Or, rather, he was fairly certain of her reaction and was loath to experience it.

At the moment he was midway through his half-hour on the exercise bike and perspiring profusely. Fortunately, it was a rather pleasant evening easily survivable without air-conditioning.

"Anyway," Lennon was saying brightly, "I think it will make a neat story. I should be able to clean it up in a day or so and be ready for our trip."

Cox moaned inwardly. Might this be the right time? No; it would have to be brought up eventually, but not now. Instead, he said, "How did you ever come up with that assignment? The Freep considers it a dead-ender. About on a par with Jesus's head on the side of an oil-storage tank, or a weeping statue of Mary in some church, or my all-time favorite, the face of Jesus in a fried tortilla.''

Lennon chuckled. "A story is what you make it, Joe. I convinced the assistant editor it would make an interesting feature. And, by God, it's going to be an interesting feature for a total of two days. At which time I will solve the mystery and we'll be off to a terrific month in Vancouver and points north.''

Now? No, not yet. Instead, Cox said, "It never fails to amaze me, with all the blockbuster stories in this town, how they waste somebody like you on a fluff piece.''

"That's because you never worked at the *News*, sweets.''

"Never worked there! With all that security, I can't even get in the place.''

"More horses, honey; the *News* has lots more horses. I can remember the Freep: when you got there in the morning, you hit the ground running. You'd be surprised what you can do with more than a skeleton staff. For one thing, you can afford to work on a story and develop it. And this will be a good one—at least for a couple of days.''

Cox had no doubt Pat could put some meat on this thin story line. She had the knack of making even an obituary interesting.

Lennon was leafing through some notes she had taken earlier in the day. "Besides, it's about time this town had a new wonder-worker. It's been—what?—about forty years since Solanus Casey was operating out of St. Bonaventure Monastery—check that," she corrected herself from her notes, "St. Bonaventure *Friary* on Mt. Elliott. And before him . . . who? Nobody from a first-run church like the Catholics or Lutherans.

"Too bad Gabriel Richard didn't dabble in miracles," she reflected. "But then, he was having too much trouble with the cholera epidemic.''

"That's part of it," Cox said. "Who the hell is this 'Father Robert'? He may be a Catholic and he may be a priest, but then what? My Catholic colleagues at the Freep tell me he is definitely a minor leaguer. He doesn't belong to any of the—what?—big orders . . . does he? Name some.''

She smiled. Religion was not Cox's long suit. "Jesuits, Dominicans, Franciscans, Redemptorists, Passionists . . . no, he doesn't belong to any of the more established orders. But that's part of the story: where he came from and whether he's real or a fake.''

"Real or a fake! Do you mean to tell me you actually believe he could be for real?''

"I don't know. But it doesn't much matter. Say he is real. In that case, I bequeath my story to the religion department while you and I head for vacationland. If he's a fake, he's either funny or dangerous.''

"Funny? Like the tortilla caper?''

"Exactly. And don't forget that the tortilla was a good enough story so that people remember it. Just listen to some of the stuff I got from our library this afternoon—all from the *News* files. Here's one datelined May 13, 1977: *Spiritual leader Cushing Smith, 'doctor of metaphysics,' author of the book, 'I Can Heal Myself and I Will,' is not feeling well these days.*

"Or, how about this one from '73: *Faith Healer 'Sister' Katherine Wayne swindled Flat Rock man and his wife out of $105,000 by telling them that 'purifying' their money might cure his terminal illness.*''

"So the Nixon gang were not the only ones 'laundering' money.''

"Not hardly. But there are others. Datelined 1947, Vandalia, Illinois: *Faith healer talked to by a tree when he was eleven.*

"Or, here's one of my favorites. Datelined 1960, UPI: *Faith healer Kivado Nti, who said he could vanish into air, was arrested and taken to jail on fraud charges yesterday.*''

"That's it?''

"The entire story.''

"It took a lot of guts for old Kivado to hang around and go to jail when he could just as easily have gone up in smoke." Cox checked the odometer. "God! Ten minutes to go on this wheel of torture and I'm already exhausted."

"It's good for you. It'll take those love handles off your middle. Besides, I'll do my half-hour after you're finished."

Cox looked appreciatively at all those curves so clearly defined by a minimum of covering. Everything was just where it should be according to God's best plan. "Honey, you need this machine like Dolly Parton needs an additional size bust."

"It couldn't hurt." But she smiled as she continued to page through her notes.

"Don't you have anything there about my favorite healer?"

"Lemmee see; that would be Oral Roberts, wouldn't it? Yeah, here's a clip about Oral's facing a deadline by God to raise eight million bucks or die. According to this item, he got 1.3 mill from a Jerry Collins from Florida who owned two greyhound racetracks. For a while, Oral was undecided about accepting money from a gambler."

"A very brief while."

"And then he took the money and ran."

Five minutes to go. Cox figured there was hope. "But what did you say before: something about if the healer were a fake, he'd be funny or what . . . dangerous?"

"You bet. Here's a 1945 story about a guy who was killed by a rattlesnake that was used as part of the religious practice of the Dolly Pond Church of God in Chattanooga, Tennessee. Says he was struck in the hand by the snake he was lifting from a box at one of their religious ceremonies. Says he continued to preach for ten minutes. Then he complained of feeling ill. He died an hour later."

The high-pitched beep signaled an end to Joe Cox's self-inflicted torture. "Poor guy just didn't have enough faith. That, or the snake didn't believe.

"Remember the one about the guy who falls off a cliff? About fifty yards down he grabs onto a bush growing out of the side of the cliff. So he's fifty yards from the top with no way of getting back up, and with a thousand-foot drop beneath him.

"He yells, 'Help! Help! Is there anybody up there who can help me?'

"And a deep voice says, 'Yes, I can help you. I'm God and I can save you. All you have to do is believe and then let go of that bush. Then I can save you.'

"The guy thinks this over. Then he yells, 'Is there anybody else up there?' "

" 'O ye of little faith,' eh? But this faith-healing stuff can be pretty brutal, especially when kids get involved. Here's a 1973 story about an eleven-year-old diabetic boy who died a painful, lingering death after his supply of insulin was thrown out and the kid was treated by a faith healer. And here's another one—goes back to 1959—datelined Hagerstown, Maryland. This Bible-quoting father claimed he was doing the Lord's will in not letting modern medicine step in to try to save his five-month-old daughter. She died of pneumonia."

"Good God, his own kid!"

"It can get pretty dicey. But, would you believe this UPI story from 1976? It says that witch doctors and other traditional healers play a crucial role in caring for the sick in poor countries. Then it quotes a report, 'Health professionals have much to learn from traditional healers regarding their practice of psychotherapy.' "

Cox, dripping perspiration, slowly dismounted from the exercise machine. "Did I ever tell you about this buddy of mine in the army? He was stationed in southeast Asia with not a hell of a lot to do. So he drank . . . a lot . . . sometimes a very lot. After one such historic night, Ralph ended up with the emperor of all hangovers. He tried everything short of suicide . . . and he was close to that.

"Then, someone mentioned the local witch doctor. Ordinarily, Ralph would have been insulted that anyone would even suggest anything so bizarre. But—and this is a testament to how awful he felt—he decided to give it a whirl.

"The witch doctor put him in a hammock near a deep

precipice. First the doc put on a huge cape. Then he hid something under the cape—but he wouldn't let Ralph see what it was. Then he approached Ralph, who was taking this in with all the attention he could muster.

"The doc came right up to Ralph, and three times he flashed him with the object under the cape. Well, it turned out to be a cage containing a creature the doc had sewn together. It was half mongoose and half chicken. After flashing Ralph three times, the doc went over to the edge and threw the cage and its contents off the cliff.

"The idea was that the evil spirit who was inhabiting Ralph would get so curious and intrigued by the weird creature the doc had created that the spirit would leave Ralph's body and follow the goblin over the cliff.

"And you know what? Ralph was cured. He felt great right away. Can you believe that?"

"In a word, no."

"No?" Cox paused in his toweling.

"That's about the tenth time you've told me that tale." She held up her hand to forestall a herniated disclaimer. "Oh, it's a great story and I certainly don't mind hearing it again. It's just that I've grown accustomed to your buddy, Ralph, even though I've never met him.

"He is not the type of guy to have a psychosomatic ailment. You know what I mean? If he were a woman, he'd never have a hysterical pregnancy. So when he complained about a hangover, he had a hangover. And in this case a world-class hangover. So when the witch doctor threw his bizarre little creation off the cliff, well, whatever happened, it wasn't a psychosomatic cure. Ralph's hangover was not in his mind; it was all over his gut."

Lennon slipped on a sweatshirt and headband. She was serious about her exercising. She set the timer, adjusted the seat, and prepared to ride nowhere in particular.

She continued. "I don't know what the hell you'd call whatever it was the witch doctor did for Ralph. I'm a little reluctant to call it a miracle. But maybe that's my Roman Catholic background coming out. We Catholics tend to believe we've got a corner on the miracle market . . ." but she smiled her disbelief at the statement. "I was looking through a book this afternoon called *The Faith Healers*, by James Randi."

" 'The Amazing Randi,' the magician? You really have been busy."

"Gotta." Lennon picked up her pedaling. "I've got a time frame on this story. Got to get it done by vacation time."

Cox winced. Now? Almost; wait till she really gets going on the bike.

"Anyway," she continued, "Randi pretty well dismisses all faith healers and, for that matter, all faith healing. He's got some pretty good arguments, although it's hardly a definitive work. For instance, there's Lourdes."

"Back to the Catholics."

"What did you expect the bottom line would be? Even Randi treads a little cautiously with Lourdes. And for good reason. Everything I've read about Lourdes tells me the people there are very slow to acknowledge miracles."

"With all those canes and crutches hanging from the walls?"

"Exactly. The religious authorities were very hesitant right from the beginning to stamp what went on in that cave with little Bernadette as miraculous.

"And that's the way it's been ever since. There've been hundreds of claimed cures at Lourdes, but very, very few are recognized by the Church. Every once in a while, though, something happens that can't be explained by any rational argument."

"Like?"

"Like somebody who has terminal cancer. Maybe goes to Lourdes, gets X-rayed so that the doctors can see the affected internal organs.

"Then, something happens. The person gets dipped in the stream or gets blessed during the benediction. And that person suddenly feels something fantastic has happened—

maybe gets out of a wheelchair or rises up from a gurney. Maybe jumps around.

"Now, mind you, apparently a lot of this sort of thing goes on at Lourdes. But every once in a while there'll be that documentary evidence that the person has been eaten up by cancer. Then, the next set of X rays shows nothing but healthy organs. Every trace of the disease that was evident on the X rays yesterday is now gone.

"Even then, they don't document it as a miracle at Lourdes. Not unless years later the person has suffered no return of the illness."

"Now, what could be more fair?"

"Not bad, I must admit. But, playing devil's advocate, we are just beginning to learn the miracles that nature can perform. Who's to say that a phenomenon even like that might not be another psychosomatic reaction? Or that the overwhelming emotional reaction triggers as yet undiscovered natural resources to heal?

"The opposite argument is that while we don't yet know everything that nature is capable of, we do know the outside limitations of nature. And nature can't heal itself permanently, suddenly, with no more outside intervention than some water or a blessing, or the touch of some unique person," Pat concluded.

"But—"

"Whatever. In any case, I'm going into this story with an open mind. Even though I know that ninety-nine chances out of a hundred it's going to end up either a fake or, more likely, a few well-intentioned psychosomatic cures. Anyway," Lennon began to increase her stationary speed, "it looked like the perfect story to work on for a couple of days before we head for Canada."

"Uh . . ."

"What?" Something was wrong. She knew it.

All during dinner—all evening—Joe had seemed somewhat inhibited, reacting awkwardly each time the subject of their vacation was mentioned. For one thing, every reference to the vacation had been made by Lennon. For weeks they had made meticulous plans to use every day in Canada to the best combination of pleasure and relaxation. Somehow, Joe had been out of it throughout this entire evening. It was like waiting for the other shoe to drop. And, she sensed, the other shoe was heading for the floor.

"Uh . . ." Cox repeated, "you're not the only one who came up with an interesting assignment."

"Oh?"

"Yeah. This afternoon our good old city editor came up with one for me."

"Nelson Kane? Oh, I know: you've got to be on the Father Robert story too!" Lennon felt a rush of relief. Perhaps her worst fears would not be realized. "Kane almost lives for these 'miracles.' He even sent me to Toledo once to check out the image of Jesus on a tabernacle veil. Joe, you sandbagger! You're on the same story and you've been milking me for all my research. Son of a gun!"

"That's not exactly it."

"Oh?" Her pedaling grew less enthusiastic.

"Actually, it's more a reward than an assignment."

"Oh?" She was traveling nowhere at less than one mile an hour.

"It's a cushy story. Things haven't been too great between me and Kane lately, as you know."

"You've mentioned that."

"But in the last few weeks, things have improved."

"You didn't mention that."

"Well, they have. So Nellie gave me this assignment as a sort of peace offering. He made no bones about that. It was definitely a peace offering."

She stopped cycling altogether. "Joe, cut the bullshit and spit it out."

She was right. Damn the torpedoes, full speed ahead. "I'm going to cover the Port Huron to Mackinac Race."

Her mouth opened but nothing came out for a moment. Then, "What?"

"The race. The sailboat race."

"You're not in Sports. That's sports."

"It's not going to be a sports angle."

"What . . . ? What the hell else is there to a boat race?"

"Human interest."

"Human interest! Wait a minute. Before I operate completely on intuition, let's get some basics settled. Okay, so you're going to cover the race from a human interest angle. That means a couple of days of preparation before the thing starts. What the Sunday sailors and their hangers-on are doing to get ready for the race. Good grief, Port Huron is only an hour-and-a-half—two at the outside—from here. You can commute, for God's sake.

"So you get a peace settlement with Kane and a sweetheart assignment. There's no problem. We can finish these stories at about the same time and head off for vacation." She paused. "Then why do I have this awful, sinking feeling?"

"There's something to be said for intuition."

In a low, ominous tone, she said, "Go on."

"Well," he took a deep breath, "Sports found this one crew that enters the race every year, but not only have they never won, sometimes they don't even finish. Or they finally get there, but two or three days late."

"Hmmm." She fixed him with a baleful gaze.

"The point is, why do they do it every year? And how do they manage to botch it so badly? See, almost everybody else is very serious about this race. . . ."

"At least after it gets started."

". . . but what are these guys? Misfits? Clouseaux? The living embodiment of Murphy's Law? That's the hook."

"And you? Your part in all this?"

"I'm going to be one of the crew on this tub. Do the story from their rather relaxed point of view. It'll make a good story. We're all convinced of that."

"We are, are we?"

Cox had seen her like this before. She was angry; indeed, furious. It was still all just below the surface. But it would erupt any minute.

42

"So," she continued, "you're going to leave for Port Huron tomorrow. . . ."

He nodded. "But to the Black River, not Lake Huron."

"Uh-huh, the Black River. And you're going to take up residence aboard the I-Don't-Give-a-Damn frigate." Her emphasis on the last word clearly bristled with allusion to a similar sounding phrase. ". . . and you will stay aboard the goddam boat until your particular race is concluded."

He nodded.

"And that should be a matter of a week or more—including the parties on Mackinac Island."

He nodded, without ebullience.

"Then what, *dearest*, of our vacation!"

"I haven't forgotten that."

"I don't believe I've let you. That's what we've been talking about these past several weeks."

"So what's so awful about postponing it a week, ten days, two weeks at the outside? Canada is not going to disappear."

"No, but you are. Do you think I can switch my vacation at the last minute because you want to play sailor?"

"You don't have to tell them that. You could be sick."

"Then I take sick leave, stupid, not a vacation. But you're right about one thing: I am sick—of you. And what about all those dates we've made? Reservations? All carefully planned and coordinated!"

"We can rebook them."

"Like hell we can. *You wanted this story!*"

"I told you: It was a peace offering from Nellie Kane. How could I turn it down?"

"How about, 'Thanks, Nellie. I appreciate your giving me this nice piece of fluff. But, as you already know—because you pay attention to these things—I'm up for a vacation in a couple of days. And my live-in, Pat Lennon—you know her, she used to work here—she and I have been planning this trip. We've got all our reservations and we're ready to leave. So, again, while I appreciate your thoughtfulness, I'm afraid I must decline your kind offer. I'll just

43

go on my vacation. If I were to change it at this late date, it would screw up a whole bunch of other people's vacation schedules. And the International Newspaper Guild would not be happy about that.' . . . Would you like me to write you an idiot card so you can deliver the message to Kane?''

"You're not trying to understand."

"Oh, I understand, all right. You just can't resist a party, can you? You'll never grow up, Joe Cox, *never*."

"Pat, be reasonable."

"You've got a choice, Joe. Take the couch tonight or, if you prefer, I'll move out."

"Oh, okay; have it your way. But you'll be sorry. What are we gonna do about our trip?"

"The couch and no conversation. As General MacArthur once said, 'These proceedings are concluded.' ''

"He was accepting the articles of surrender from the Japanese."

"So am I. In case you haven't tumbled to it, you are in a position of unconditional surrender. Good night!''

The remainder of the evening passed in a protracted pregnant silence.

Lennon aborted her bike ride. She made a salad for one, which she ate in the privacy of the bedroom. The sound of slamming doors was the extent of any significant noise made that evening.

Cox wished that Lennon were not wearing white shorts. She might have changed into anything else. Her legs looked so great. And, for no discernible reason, he had always felt a superfluous stimulation at the sight of white shorts.

For both of them, bedtime was early, but sleep came late. Cox tossed and turned in a mixture of anger, embarrassment, frustration, righteous indignation, and a lumpy couch. In Lennon's case, it was simply fury and resentment.

But sleep came, eventually, for both.

Fitful dreams punctuated Lennon's night. Each had a sameness. Cox would be aboard a series of boats—yachts, actually. Not one of them resembled a craft that had not or could not have easily won the Mackinac Race. There had

44

to be some internal reason for a constant and infamous failure. Perhaps it was because, in her dreams, Lennon found the crews, such as they were, composed entirely of women—extraordinarily voluptuous women. There was not much sailing. There was a lot of tanning. As a centerpiece of each dream, there was a sated and ecstatic Cox, smiling blissfully and attended hand and foot by nubile beauties. Years later, Pat would recall this series of dreams as her Night of Nightmares.

Oddly, Cox was having the same sort of dreams. However, for him, they were far from nightmarish.

**MONDAY
JULY 24**

CHAPTER
4

Beverly Hills Cop was a movie about a Detroit policeman. Nine-tenths of the picture was filmed in California, but the opening scenes were in Detroit. It featured some of the Motor City's seediest neighborhoods. Citizens staggered across sidewalks. If they weren't sitting on curbs, they were tumbling into gutters.

This image of their city did not amuse Detroiters. But they could scarcely deny that such neighborhoods existed. There they were, on the big screen, in living color.

Their argument was that the decaying locales that appeared on the screen were not the only neighborhoods in town. Some were better. A few were considerably better.

One such livable area could be found in the southwest part of the city. It was identified with and by its Catholic church and parish.

St. Hedwig's, a monster in red brick and stained glass, was the hub around which a very ethnic Polish community had gathered. Now, in the final years of the twentieth century, the neighborhood was holding up well under the steady gaze of the life-sized statues of the four evangelists mounted near the steps leading to St. Hedwig's Church.

Once, the neighborhood had been so predominantly inhabited by Polish-Americans that it merited the title "Polonia," their word to describe a Polish community outside of Poland. In effect, it was a little Poland.

But time, very hard work, and a touch of upward mobility had seen many, especially the young, leave for the suburbs, particularly Warren and Sterling Heights. Still, St. Hedwig's boasted a solid nucleus of Poles as well as a functioning parochial grade and high school—rare now in the city.

Even though the neighborhood, centered at Junction and Michigan Avenue, was changing, the homes, by and large, still exhibited the tidiness and cleanliness that so exemplified the Poles. Traveling through the neighborhood one was impressed with the mint condition of most of the houses. Large two-, even three-storied homes; wood and brick; lots of whites, yellows, greens, and browns. Large porches, furnished—even featuring that monument to summertime conversation, the porch swing.

The only readily perceivable fly in this ointment was the closeness of these immense houses. One could visualize residents shaking hands—or fists—from one living room to the one next door. Even more maddening was the concomitant lack of privacy. It was difficult to keep conversations, not to mention loud quarrels, all in the family.

It was into this predominantly quiet neighborhood about nine months previously that a tiny religious community had moved.

There were five of them—a priest and four religious Brothers. They called themselves the Congregation of St. Stephen. They dressed in dark gray habits that covered the body from shoulders to feet. They wore sandals, a cincture, or cord, tied about the waist, and a scapular that covered their shoulders and fell to the ground fore and aft. Affixed to the neck of their habit was a cowl, which they often pulled over their heads like a hood. In the spectrum of post–

Vatican Council II ecclesial theology, they were viewed as extremely conservative.

Before even considering converting anyone to their way of life, they first had to convert an abandoned bank building into a quasi-monastery.

The bank, an obsolete branch of First Standard Bank and Trust, had become an anachronistic eyesore to its parent company. So, in a gesture rich in spiritual generosity, First Standard gave the old building to Sacred Heart Seminary and took a seventy-five-thousand-dollar tax write-off. In time, Sacred Heart was happy and relieved to lease the place to the Congregation of St. Stephen for next to nothing.

Father Robert, the leader of this little group, presented himself and his papers to the chancellor of the Archdiocese of Detroit, who, after giving the matter a modicum of thought, could find no earthly or celestial use in the diocese for either Father Robert or his band. The diocese was already sufficiently torn between liberal and conservative factions without introducing another polarizing group into parish life. However, he wished Father Robert well, and forgot about him.

That is, until the first soundings of the possibility of miraculous goings-on at the new monastery were heard. That began in about the fifth month of the monastery's existence. Thus it had been going on for about four months now. Nothing for the local hierarchy to be unduly alarmed over, but something to watch and monitor.

The hierarchy were not the only ones watching and monitoring. The former bank, the present monastery, was located on the southeast corner of Bushey and Michigan, only four blocks from St. Hedwig's. At first, the priests of St. Hedwig's Conventual Franciscans—OFM Conv., or Black Franciscans—paid little mind to the ragtag band in the bank building. The Franks had enough to occupy their time in the parish. But, as the months passed, the Congregation of St. Stephen began to grow in popularity and, more threateningly, in the size of its flock. And there were those rumors of miracles. Or, at least, miraculous answers to the prayers of this Father Robert.

Distressing.

The monks were not much given to external works of charity, nor, for that matter, did they seem to have much of anything to do with the outside world. Those curious enough to wonder about the purpose of the Congregation were compelled to conclude that their principal concern was contemplation and prayer.

As a contemplative, prayer-oriented religious order, the Congregation of St. Stephen was not alone in the Archdiocese of Detroit. Not counting various rather informal houses of prayer, there were the Monasteries of the Blessed Sacrament and St. Therese of the Child Jesus, Sisters Disciples of the Divine Master and Sisters of the Cross of the Good Shepherd.

To date, the monks of the Congregation had spent most of their time making the considerable alterations necessary to turn a bank into a monastery. The principal obstacle, of course, was poverty. For them, poverty was not only a vow, it was a way of life. But things were improving financially. Freewill donations that had trickled in at the beginning were increasing markedly. This was particularly true with regard to the people who found Father Robert's prayers effective.

Now, the building, at least the interior, no longer so clearly denoted its previous function. Simple cells for the monks had been constructed at the rear of the building. Naturally, the Congregation could not afford stained glass, but the windows were heavily tinted in dusky colors. This, plus extremely inadequate lighting, created a rather grim atmosphere.

A modest altar for Mass and reservation of the Blessed Sacrament was built. The altar, on a raised platform, was flanked by what had to pass as chair stalls. Three chairs on one side, one on the other.

Mass was offered each day at noon. Three monks, who, being approximately the same size, and with cowls pulled over their heads, seemed clones of one another, took their places to the altar's right. The fourth Brother was alone at the altar's left. He seemed not to fit with the rest. Taller, ~~more~~ more athletically built, he cut a decidedly impressive figure.

The congregation was left to shift for itself. There were no pews and few chairs. Many simply stood for the length of the services.

But most, in keeping with the generally conservative tone of the entire enterprise, knelt throughout. This was no easy venture on the rock-hard uneven terrazzo floor.

Today's Mass was nearing conclusion.

Father Robert, assisted by Brother Paul, the tall one, was distributing Communion. The congregation numbered well in excess of two hundred—phenomenal, especially for a weekday. Many were attending on their lunch hour.

Toward the rear of the chapel, two women who had managed to find chairs conversed in whispers.

"Have you been here before?"

"Oh, yes, many times." She seemed somewhat uncomfortable talking in church, but reluctantly willing to help this obvious neophyte.

"It's so dark!"

"That's the way they want it, I guess. They painted the windows."

"That's bad enough, but the lighting is so poor."

"So are they. Very poor. They can't afford much."

The first woman wondered about that. She had observed people before and even during the service stuffing money— mostly folding money—into collection boxes conspicuously placed around the chapel. But who knew what they did with the money? They certainly seemed to be poor. "Father Robert is the only one who hasn't pulled that hood over his head. And I still can't quite tell what he looks like."

"That is strange, isn't it?" the second woman responded. "Actually, this is the only time that he doesn't wear his cowl—when he says Mass. The rest of the time, as far as I can tell, all of them wear the cowl all the time . . . at least when there's anyone around."

"So, this is the only time you get a look at Father Robert . . ." The first woman squinted. "I wish the light were better."

"It's not just the light. Father Robert always keeps his head down, sort of bowed. Very humble." She nodded authoritatively. "Yes, a very humble man. That must be why it's so difficult to see what he looks like. Very humble."

Father Robert traced a sign of the cross in the air, intoning, *"Benedicat vos, Omnipotens Deus, Pater et Filius et Spiritus Sanctus."*

The Mass was over.

Mass at this monastery was always offered in Latin. In itself that was not necessarily significant. But the Latin liturgy had come to connote a conservative presence. However, that connotation was mostly in the mind of the worshiper.

Popularly, the Latin rite was equated with the entire Catholic Church, which was termed the Roman Catholic Church. Historically, this was most inaccurate.

The Church of the Apostles was, of course, entirely Jewish. But as it centered and grew in Rome, the language of the early Church became Latin.

Then, as the Church spread to other countries, worship was expressed in the language of each local region. Thus, rites other than Latin were established, most of which exist today—rites such as Chaldean, Greek, Coptic, Maronite, Russian, and so on.

Nonetheless, it is true that the Latin rite is, by far, the most widespread.

The Council of Trent, which rambled off and on from 1545 to 1563, authorized a formula for worship in the Latin rite. It was known as the Tridentine—from Trent—Mass. That ritual continued unbroken for close to four hundred years. So one might easily understand why Latin-rite Catholics got used to it.

It was not until the Second Vatican Council in the early 1960s that permission was granted for the vernacular to be substituted for Latin in the Latin rite. The Council made it most clear that Latin remained the official language of the Latin rite and that any vernacular version had to be approved by Rome before permission to use it was granted.

Thus, the language of priority throughout the Latin rite of the Catholic Church remained Latin. English, in the eyes of the Church, was the equivalent of a poor cousin, a substitute at best.

When English was introduced in the United States Mass, there was enormous opposition to it. Now, some twenty years later, the English liturgy was taken, generally, as the norm in the English-speaking world. When the new liturgy was offered in its original Latin form—the Tridentine had been phased out—people tended to interpret this not as a return to their roots, but as an expression of a conservative or rightist philosophy and theology.

The Congregation of St. Stephen, by its unswerving use of the Latin Mass, thus told whoever was interested that a pre–Vatican II spirit could be found here. And the majority of attending Catholics understood that clearly.

There was a good deal of stirring in the Chapel of St. Stephen as the Mass ended. Many in the congregation had to return to work, perhaps picking up a sandwich or a Coney Island on the way.

But some remained. There was more to come.

The three Brothers who had been kneeling to the right of the altar made their way through the chapel, emptying the collection boxes. Father Robert, assisted by Brother Paul, removed his Mass vestments, while a line of people formed down the center of the chapel.

The two women who had been whispering to each other remained in the chapel, but only one of them knew what was going on.

"What's going on?" the first woman asked.

"Blessings. Father Robert blesses people after the Mass."

"What's the big black bag for?" The first woman pointed

to a black grip Brother Paul was holding. It was about the size of a valise or the satchel a doctor might carry on calls.

"That's where they keep the relics that he blesses the people with."

"Relics? What relics?"

"Relics! Don't you know what relics are? Say, are you a Catholic?"

"Of course I'm a Catholic. I just never heard of relics."

Some Catholic! the second woman thought. But, with a sigh, she explained, "There's three kinds. The first kind is a piece of bone from the saint."

"How gross!"

"Do you want to know or not?" Her patience was running short.

The other nodded, with some reluctance.

"Well, then, the second class is something the saint owned—like a rosary or a prayer book. And the third kind is something that was touched to the body of a saint."

"Oh."

They watched while Father Robert blessed several people.

"Those things he's using to bless those people," the first woman observed, "they're so little . . . are you sure they're relics?"

"Yes," in an exasperated tone, "those are the first-class relics. There's only a tiny sliver of the bone."

"That makes sense." Pause. "One more question . . ."

"Yes?" Plainly irritated.

"Why does the Brother keep handing him a different relic every time he blesses somebody?"

"Because different saints are better at different things."

"Huh?"

"How come you don't know about all this? Everybody knows what you say when you lose something: 'Dear St. Anthony, please come around; something is lost and can't be found.'"

"Really!"

"And St. Matthew is the patron saint of tax collectors.

And St. Valentine is for lovers. And Cecilia is for singers. And Mary Magdalen is for prostitutes."

"That figures. And St. Nicholas is for Christmas?"

"No, that's the baby Jesus!"

"Sorry."

"Actually," the second woman added thoughtfully, "there isn't any first-class relic for Jesus. He ascended into heaven, you see. Maybe a relic of the True Cross . . . no; that would be Easter, wouldn't it? Or Good Friday—oh, never mind."

By this time, the two women had worked themselves close enough to the front of the chapel to see more clearly and hear what was going on. While over half of the original congregation had long since departed, the remainder seemed determined to stay with this paraliturgical ceremony to the end.

A young man, whose turn it was, knelt on the floor near Father Robert, who was seated on an uncomfortable-looking straight-back chair. Seated so close to Father Robert that their knees were touching was Brother Paul.

The kneeling man, perhaps in his early twenties, and whose tattered clothing was in desperate need of cleaning and repair, was saying, just loudly enough to be heard by those nearby, ". . . and so, Father, everything depends on my book. I've poured my life into it. I could have gotten a job in a factory and been much better off than I am. I could have done lots of things and made some money or, at least, I could have qualified for unemployment compensation. But I didn't. I fasted and prayed and wrote. But it's a good book, Father. It will help people, and if it's published, I'll be able to make a living by writing. Everything depends on that book."

"What kind of book is it, my son?" Father Robert's voice was muffled, coming from deep within the cowl he'd pulled far over his head, completely concealing his face.

"It's a spiritual book, Father. I know you'd like it. It's about the miracles of Garabandal, where the Blessed Mother appeared. I have eyewitness accounts of the miracles and the apparitions of Our Lady. And photos—not very close, I must admit—but photos of the children in ecstasy while they see Our Lady and the Sacred Host floating through the air, snatched right out of the hands of the priest as Our Lady herself gives Communion to the children.''

Father Robert nodded. ''Very impressive, my son. You have done good work.''

''But it won't mean anything if it doesn't get published.''

''It is at a publishing house?''

''Yes. I'm waiting to hear from them.''

''Very good. We will do what we can.''

As if actuated by an unseen sign, Brother Paul rummaged through the black bag. He handed the priest a small round container, which appeared to be painted or gold-plated. A tiny white fragment was mounted therein on a red background. The container bore some sort of identifying tag. It was impossible to know what was there without the leisure to study it and that opportunity was not afforded the young man.

Father Robert read silently from a document handed him by Brother Paul. Then, ''My son, this which I hold in my hand is from the bones of St. Francis of Sales. He lived on this earth hundreds of years ago. He was a great bishop and a doctor of the Church. He converted many, especially those trapped in the heresy of Calvinism, to the one true Church. And, most important for you, he too was a writer. He wrote *Introduction to the Devout Life*, a book much prized and read even today. I will bless you with these remains of the great St. Francis and I will pray for you. Dispose yourself, my son, to receive the blessing of Almighty God through the intercession of St. Francis of Sales.''

In silence, the priest traced with the relic a sign of the cross over the young man. Then the priest leaned back as if tired. The movement also indicated that the interview, as well as the blessing, was concluded.

The young man did not rise. ''But Father, won't you pray for me and my book now?''

From within the cowl worn by Brother Paul came a voice

rampant with authority, a tone which, indeed, in other surroundings, might almost be taken for menace. "Father will pray for you later. Now, go."

The young man seemed stunned as much by the tone as by the finality of the message. Without another word, he struggled to his feet and backed away from the two monks until he was lost in the congregation. Then he turned and hurried out of the chapel.

Though a substantial crowd remained, not many more were in line to talk with Father Robert.

The next suppliant was a woman, who might have been in her sixties. She was well-dressed and well-groomed. She wore dark glasses and was accompanied and led by a woman who might have been her daughter.

Some solicitous soul brought over a chair so the woman would not be forced to kneel on the hard floor. The young woman, who would remain standing, thanked the anonymous Samaritan.

The cowl moved almost imperceptibly as Father Robert appraised his latest client. Neither spoke, as if expecting the other to begin.

Finally, the woman cleared her throat. "I am Mrs. Anne Whitehead, Father. And . . . I . . . I don't exactly know what's expected . . ."

The cowled head tipped to one side as if asking what the problem might be.

She couldn't see the gesture but the lack of verbal response suggested she continue. "I cannot see. I've been to doctors—many, many doctors. Hospitals. I've had many treatments. Nothing has helped—at least not much and not for very long. I'm desperate, Father. Is there anything you can do?"

"How long have you had this condition?" Robert asked.

"For the past five years." She hesitated. "I'm sixty-six years old. The doctors tell me I'm healthy otherwise. I feel good enough. From all indications, I may have many more years. Father, I don't want to spend them sightless. I've heard that you pray . . . that your prayers are answered . . .

often." She bowed her head. "Can you do anything for me?"

Brother Paul had been rummaging through the black bag. He now handed Father Robert a small relic, at a distance indistinguishable from the previous relic, along with an identifying note.

Father Robert cupped the relic in his right palm while he held the card in his left hand and read from it. "This is the relic of St. Lucy—a fragment of her bone. She died a martyr in the fourth century. She was a noble Christian woman who was condemned to death by the Emperor Diocletian. They tried to have her burned at the stake, but failed. They tore out her eyes, but her sight was miraculously restored. Finally, she died by the sword. St. Lucy is the patroness of the blind. She is a very powerful saint and, through all these centuries, she has interceded with the good God for all those who trust in her power.

"Can you trust in her power, my child?"

"I . . . I want to believe. Oh, God, I want to see again." Tears appeared on her cheeks, escaping from beneath the dark glasses.

"Then receive the blessing of God through the intercession of St. Lucy." Robert, relic in his fingers, traced the sign of the cross over the woman. *"Per intercessionem Sanctae Luciae benedicat te Omnipotens Deus, Pater, et Filius, et Spiritus Sanctus."*

At these words, the woman made the sign of the cross upon herself.

There had been little sound in the chapel from the moment the blind woman had been presented to Father Robert. Now the silence was profound. There was a sense of expectancy. Yet no one could be sure what anyone was expecting. Even regulars at these Masses and ceremonies could not recall having anyone bring to Father Robert a problem as challenging as blindness. The atmosphere was not unlike that in some of the scenes described in the Gospels when the blind and the cripples were brought to Jesus. The onlookers then and now didn't know, but were eagerly caught up in what might take place.

No one moved. The woman made no attempt to rise from the chair, nor did her companion offer to help her leave.

Father Robert started to extend his hand, then withdrew it. Now, suddenly, he reached out and with delicacy removed the woman's glasses.

"Wha—?" She was startled.

"Believe!" he whispered, just loudly enough to be heard by those very near. "Believe!" There was urgency in his voice.

"I . . . I do believe. Oh, yes, I do believe!"

Brother Paul moved forward abruptly, as if he were going to intervene, perhaps assist.

Father Robert bent toward the woman and pressed both his palms against her eyes, gently at first, then with greater pressure.

She felt the coolness of his hands. It was a refreshing sensation. But there was something else. She became aware of some sort of energy field surrounding her. With the pressure of his hands it was as if that energy field had been compressed around and into her eyes. Though she never revealed the feeling to anyone, the sensation was that of an orgasm brought about by protracted, gentle foreplay. And the expression of that eruption was much the same.

It was a prolonged, even frightening, moan.

There were gasps from the crowd, unsure of what had happened. Father Robert seemed stunned. He fell back against his chair, hands raised as if to protect himself.

The woman turned her head from side to side with a look of incredulity. She kept moving her head as if she could not get enough of whatever it was she was experiencing.

"I . . . I . . . I can see! I can see! Oh, God Almighty, I can see!" She cried over and over, and threw herself to the floor on her knees.

Chaos, tumult.

It was difficult to tell who was more electrified. Those in the chapel were caught up in the madness of the moment.

Some surrounded the woman. Some ran out onto Michigan Avenue, shouting news of the miracle.

The woman, nearly crushed by well-wishers, could not stop weeping nor control her desire to see everything at once.

In the midst of this bedlam, Brother Paul, clearly the only composed person in the chapel, led Father Robert back behind the altar into the residence area, away from the crowd.

They would not be missed until much later.

CHAPTER
5

Cute. Trite as it was, it seemed the appropriate word to describe Pringle McPhee. Bangs, eyes, ears, nose, mouth, breasts, waist, bottom—even her attire was cute. Her legs alone were in exception to the descriptive term. They were magnificent.

Pringle, a recent acquisition of the *News,* had the rudiments of a brilliant and talented reporter. Examining her application test scores, the personnel manager couldn't believe his luck.

Fortunately for everyone involved, Pringle McPhee had spontaneously drifted toward Pat Lennon. Exactly the course the city editor had hoped for.

Pat was too young to be Pringle's mother. More like the ideal age for an older sister. That more or less described their relationship. Pringle confided in Pat and Pat tried to guide her around the professional and personal pitfalls of life. The two, about the same size, could easily have been taken for sisters.

It was midafternoon and in the city room of the *News*

less than half the staff writers were at their desks, or anywhere in the building, for that matter. Most were out digging up stories, researching, interviewing and/or finding themselves frustrated up one of the many blind alleys of journalism.

Lennon was putting the finishing touches on a story about a boating accident on the Detroit River near Belle Isle. She checked her watch. Slightly less than an hour before her appointment to interview Father Robert. It would take only fifteen or twenty minutes to get there, so there was no great hurry. At least that's what she'd thought until she became aware that someone was sitting at the adjoining desk. And it was not the occupant assigned to that desk.

"Pat," said Pringle McPhee, "have you got the deputy mayor's private phone number?"

Hardly breaking stride in her attack on the computer terminal, Lennon flipped open her listings pad and indicated the desired number. If she had hoped that was the extent of McPhee's interruption—and she had—she was going to be disappointed.

"Have you got a minute?" McPhee asked.

"I'm on deadline, Pringle." Lennon was the only one in the office who called Pringle by her given name. Everyone else called her Mac. Lennon called her Pringle because, well, because it was a cute name.

"It'll take just a minute or two," McPhee coaxed.

Out of the corner of her mouth, Lennon blew a stray hair back off her face. "Well, all right, Pringle, but this is a little tight. Okay if I finish this piece while we talk?"

McPhee was in awe of Lennon's ability to do well more than one thing at a time. Even so, she would have preferred Lennon's complete, undivided attention. But . . . "I suppose." And then, without further preamble: "It's about Fred."

Lennon shook her head. The stray hair bounced back onto her forehead.

"I know you don't care for him, Pat, but he's important to me."

"Pringle, I don't give a damn one way or another about Fred. I just think as far as you're concerned he's a dead end."

"Just because he's married with a couple of kids?"

"Yeah, that's not bad for starters."

"That's a problem, I'll grant you. But we're in love. I love him. And I know—I *know*," she emphasized, "that he loves me."

"He has a great love capacity. There's you and his wife and his kids. Do they have any pets?"

"I wish you wouldn't make fun of him."

"Sorry. I don't mean to. It's hard to avoid it." Lennon noticed a typo and ran the processor back through the little green words to correct it.

"I didn't tell you what happened last night."

"But you're going to. Just for the sake of clarification, what does he tell his wife all these evenings he spends with you?"

"Executive meetings. After all, he is senior vice president of the most prestigious PR firm in town."

She was not breaking new ground with Lennon, who was professionally aware of just about all the movers and shakers in the Detroit area.

"And his wife swallows that? All those evenings!"

McPhee nodded, but the motion was lost on Lennon, whose eyes were fixed on the screen as she wrapped up the story.

"Anyway, I want to tell you what happened last night."

"Ah, yes." Lennon could guess what was coming. One of the things she desired least in life was to listen to others' sexual adventures. That ranked down there with sexually explicit films and novels. She fervently believed sex not to be a spectator sport.

But McPhee confided, often. Having lived almost her entire life in Battle Creek, Michigan, she was somewhat overwhelmed by metropolitan Detroit. Not that wheeling-dealing, vice, corruption, and life in the fast lane were totally alien to a smaller city, but she was befuddled by the volume and intensity of all this in the mega-city milieu.

There were many people McPhee could talk to, but no one she trusted more than Lennon when it came to confidentiality. Thus, regularly, Lennon was bombarded by McPhee's "sexperiences." And because she understood that she was McPhee's only receptacle for confidences, Lennon was resigned to her role.

Sometimes McPhee's affairs were tender, even engaging. Sometimes they bordered on slapstick. And, at times, they were genuinely unconventional.

McPhee edged closer to Lennon. Yes, this seemed certain to become sisterly.

"You know," McPhee said, "Fred doesn't like to use a condom. He says they offend his esthetic taste."

There were times when Lennon wondered whether public relations work caused brain damage. "So . . ."

"So, last night, he—"

"—just happened not to have a condom handy?"

"Well, no . . . uh, well, yes . . . um, I mean, yes, that's right, he didn't."

"And you couldn't supply him with one."

"He says that condoms inhibit him. He calls them anti-erotic."

"A more popular word for them is 'safe.' "

"Safe?"

"Someplace along the line, Pringle, didn't you have a class in something called 'hygiene'?"

McPhee blushed. "I know what condoms are and what they're for."

Lennon, having wrapped up the boating accident story, turned to McPhee. "Pringle, the last thing in the world you want right now is to get pregnant." Unbidden, her thought continued: *Pregnant Pringle*. It had a ring.

"I'm not going to get pregnant, Pat."

"How do you know? Fred's fertile, isn't he? I mean, he's got two kids. And did you say anything about pets?"

Pregnant Pringle and Fertile Freddy. It had an ominous ring.

"I'm not going to get pregnant because this is my safe time."

"Rhythm? On top of everything else, you're relying on rhythm!"

"It never hurts to have a fail-safe method to fall back on."

"Not a bad thought—if only the fail-safe method were more dependable."

Something was nudging at Lennon's consciousness, something she should be doing, something she should have done. But she was so distracted by her conversation with McPhee, that whatever it was would not come to the fore. On top of that, she was getting a headache that promised to develop into a migraine.

"Anyway," McPhee said, "that's not what I really wanted to talk to you about."

"What!" Lennon glanced at her watch. Only a half-hour until her appointment with Father Robert. "Look, Pringle, I'm on a tight schedule. Could you get to the point?"

"Sure. See, Fred's going to New York next week and he wants me to go with him. What do you think?"

"Is he taking the wife and kids? Maybe you could go as the au pair girl."

"Pat, get serious."

"Who says I'm not? Where would you stay?"

"His company has a suite at the Waldorf."

Lennon whistled softly. "Not bad. But isn't that sort of public? I mean flagrant?"

"He says not. He says we can pull it off easily."

Lennon tended to agree. Old Fred probably had done this any number of times with pre-Pringle mistresses. "My gut feeling says don't do it. Or, at least, take a rain check. But somehow I feel this is one you're gonna have to learn in the school of hard knocks." She looked meaningfully at Pringle. "Just one thing."

"What?"

"You'd better at least be wearing a diaphragm."

Pringle giggled. "You know, it'll be kind of nice being in New York and thinking of the fun you and Joe are having in Canada."

Lennon considered that for a moment. It didn't pay to go into too much detail when confiding one's plans. It was one thing to let others know your vacation dates. That, after all, was public knowledge. But telling Pringle the particulars of that vacation had been a mistake. Ordinarily, Lennon did not make such blunders. But this had been so certain. Nothing could go wrong. Nothing but Cox's lust for a happy-hour story.

"We're not going."

"But all your plans are made."

"Yeah, but we've had to put it off. Maybe we'll be able to go later on."

McPhee shook her head. "What a shame! You were looking forward to it so."

One of the many nice things about McPhee was her heartfelt empathy. It was particularly touching at a time like this. "Thanks, Pringle, but I'd just as soon not talk about it."

"Whatever you say."

Another of the many nice things about McPhee: that rare gift of not prying when someone wished to close a subject.

Suddenly, Lennon remembered what it was she had been forgetting to do all afternoon. "Excuse me, Pringle, I've got to punch up this State wire. I should check out this story before I leave here. Just in case."

She pressed several keys on the computer until the STWIRE basket appeared on the screen. She requested information under the heading "healer."

Rapidly, the message was spelled out on the tube.

"Damn!"

"What is it, Pat?"

"Damn! Damn! Damn!" Lennon grabbed her tote bag and started down the aisle. "There's been a real miracle. An alleged, reported, goddam miracle! And I spent all afternoon writing about a goddam boat accident!"

McPhee felt guilty for having bent Lennon's ear for so long. On the other hand, it wasn't her fault that Lennon had not checked the AP/UPI wire. She returned to her desk to phone the deputy mayor at the number she'd gotten from Pat. There were lots of stories to cover before fun time in the Big Apple.

As Lennon turned the corner of the L-shaped city room, she spotted Bob Ankenazy, the assistant editor.

"Dammit, Bob!" She was almost shouting. "Why didn't you tell me about the miracle?"

"What miracle?"

"What do you mean, 'what miracle'? How many miracles happened today? The one over at the monastery! The one by Father Robert."

"Oh, that. Well, while we're at it, why the hell didn't you check the State wire?"

She reacted defensively while maintaining her anger. "What do you expect, that I'm going to sit all afternoon watching the terminal?"

"I saw it. You could have seen it. Besides, I tried to find you."

"I disappeared by sitting behind my desk."

"Never mind; I sent Tim Sullivan to cover it. That's not the important thing. What's important is that this can be your story. This *is* your story. You've done all the research on it, which puts you a few blocks ahead of everybody else. What we want you to do is get on this thing in depth. Sullivan will bring in the nuts and bolts. You get in touch with the woman who got cured. Or says she's cured. Do an interview with her, then get to the priest—what's his name?—Robert. You already got a contact with him. Use it and get everything you can from that outfit."

As Ankenazy enumerated the steps that she'd known she was going to take when she first saw the item on the State wire, Lennon remained silent. She had little choice; his monologue allowed for no interruption.

"Okay," Lennon said, finally, "I got her name from the wire. But who is she?"

"The reason you didn't recognize her is that they misspelled the name."

Lennon checked her notes: "Not W-E-I-T-H-E-A-D?"

"W-H-I-T-E-H-E-A-D."

Lennon nodded appreciatively. "Not *the* Mrs. Anne Whitehead, wife of H. Emery Whitehead, the architect?"

"That's the lady."

Lennon winked at Ankenazy. "He could scarcely have picked a better subject. Emery is Old Money."

"And rolling in it. If the Congregation of St. Stephen has had any financial problems—and I'm sure they have—they're gone now."

Lennon figuratively rubbed her hands together; she could see her story building. She started back to her desk to begin setting up her interviews.

"Hey!" Ankenazy called after her, "aren't you glad you're not taking your vacation now?"

"God works in mysterious ways His wonders to perform," she proclaimed, and added under her breath, "But I'll never forgive that son-of-a-bitch as long as I live...."

CHAPTER
6

It was almost time for his guests to arrive, so Father Koesler was doing what he could to prepare for them. Which was not much.

Ordinarily, when it came to dinner he would fend for himself. On the rare occasion when he entertained, he could call on, and pay for, the services of a professional cook who lived in the parish. But tonight that gentleman was busy catering a Knights of Columbus testimonial.

Thank God for Mary O'Connor, thought Koesler, not for the first time. Mary was a widow, a secretary, and much more—general factotum at St. Anselm's parish in suburban Dearborn Heights. When Koesler had mentioned his dilemma—dinner party and no cook—Mary had volunteered to do the cooking. He accepted readily, with the proviso that she dine with him and his guests. In this, he thought he was being considerate, whereas in actuality Mary would have much preferred to merely prepare and serve the meal and then leave. But, over the years, she had come to understand Koesler about as well as anyone. She knew he was only thinking of her and so accepted his invitation, which in reality was an inconvenience.

Koesler's guests this evening were Inspector and Mrs. Walter Koznicki, whom he numbered among his dearest friends. Koznicki, head of the Homicide section of the Detroit Police Department, had met Koesler many years before in connection with a murder investigation. And, as it happened, the two had been involved in several such subsequent inquiries over the years. By odd coincidence it seemed that whenever an element of Catholicism became ineluctably intertwined in a homicide, often Father Koesler was not far removed either.

At the moment, Koesler was making sure the appropriate potables were at hand. That would be a white wine for Wanda, a touch of port for the Inspector, a Manhattan for the dealer and, come to think of it, he wasn't sure what Mrs. O'Connor preferred.

The first of the evening news telecasts was beginning. For Koesler it was no more than background noise. In fact, he had just about decided to turn it off and find some soothing classical music among his records and tapes. Perhaps Mozart's "eine kleine Nachtmusik"—"a little night music." Yes, he thought, the Inspector would like that.

As he turned to the TV set, the voice of anchorperson Robbie Timmons caused him to give her his full attention. "Earlier this afternoon, there were reports of a miracle right here in the city of Detroit."

Koesler, holding the bottle of port, turned toward the set, his mouth ajar as it usually was when he was bored or thinking. "Miracle" was a buzzword sure to grab his attention, especially when used by the news media.

"Reportedly," Robbie continued, "a woman, blind for years, was cured, her eyesight restored by a controversial Roman Catholic priest. It all happened on Detroit's southwest side. Our Rosanna Kelly has the story."

Funny, thought Koesler, Father Robert must be the priest they're referring to. He hadn't been considered controversial until just this minute when television deigned to call him that. A celebrity becomes a celebrity whenever the media christen a celebrity.

The TV scene was captioned "live." It showed the exterior of what was unmistakably a bank building. Or, rather, what had been a bank building. Also in the picture was a gorgeous blonde identified as Rosanna Kelly.

"A few months ago," began Ms. Kelly, "this building was empty and all but abandoned. Before that it was a branch of First Standard Bank & Trust. Now it is the unlikely home of a monastery. This afternoon it became a full-fledged tourist attraction. The people you see milling about the building are sightseers, neighbors mostly. The reason for all this attention is that after the noon Mass today, a blind woman reportedly was cured.

"The woman, Anne Whitehead, wife of architect and philanthropist H. Emery Whitehead, asked for a miracle and, it seems, got one. A priest—a Father Robert—touched her eyes and, like that, Mrs. Whitehead declared she could see again.

"Yesterday, hardly anyone knew what went on inside this building. Today, all metropolitan Detroit knows. Tomorrow—who knows—maybe the world.

"This is Rosanna Kelly, Channel 7 News, reporting."

On the screen, Robbie Timmons reappeared with Rosanna and the bank facade as an inset. "Rosanna, what's going on inside the bank—or, rather, the monastery—now?"

"Robbie, everything's locked up. Not unusual at this time of day, local people tell me. But somewhat odd, I think, in view of what happened here earlier."

"Okay. Thank you, Rosanna." She turned back to the camera. "Well, that looks like the beginning, not the end of this story. And you can be sure we'll be following it as it develops . . . Bill?" She turned to her co-anchor.

Koesler snapped the set off.

Now that was strange, he thought. That bank was no more than a few miles at most from the neighborhood of his youth. He had passed that corner hundreds of times. Yet he had never been aware of its existence. And now look:

that unpretentious corner and its neighborhood could become a famous landmark.

He found the tape of "eine kleine Nachtmusik" and inserted it in the player. No sooner did the music begin than the doorbell rang. *How's that for timing?* he thought.

He greeted the Koznickis and ushered them into the rectory living room. They knew Mary O'Connor, so introductions were unnecessary. Koesler served drinks and learned that Mary, like Wanda, favored white wine.

"Have you heard about the miracle in Detroit, Father?" Wanda opened. "We heard about it on the radio on the way over."

Koznicki tentatively tasted the port. "I doubt that it is recognized as such just because the media says it is so, dear . . . Father?" The small wine glass appeared particularly insignificant in the Inspector's meaty paw. He was perhaps an inch taller than Koesler's six-foot-three, but with the added bulk, he resembled an amicable bear.

"Right you are, Inspector. The mills of the Church grind slowly and exceedingly fine." There was a touch of old-worldliness about the two men that precluded their ever being on a first-name basis. They would forever address each other by title.

"Oh," Wanda waved in impatience ". . . we're not waiting for the Church to put her seal of approval on it. A woman was blind and now she can see. Sounds like a miracle to me."

"The Church must be cautious, dear."

"I agree," Koesler said. "There is something to be said for waiting until three hundred years after death before canonizing someone."

"Well, for one thing," said Mary O'Connor, "everybody who knew the candidate, including his enemies, would be dead." Mary said little, but what she said was pithy.

Koznicki placed his glass on the end table and clasped his hands over his paunch. "Now that the subject has been raised, Father, what is the procedure? What will happen now?"

"Your guess is as good as mine. I've never been around a real—or alleged"—he glanced in Wanda's direction and smiled—"miracle. The word I used earlier may be applicable."

"What was that?"

" 'Slowly.' In a situation like this, the one who can outlast everyone else wins—if I can put it that way." Koesler nodded at Koznicki. "It's like that saying in baseball: A tie favors the runner. In this case, time favors the winner. I suppose there will be a medical examination. Well, that surely must be the case. Her doctor will want to examine her. He knew her as blind; now she can see. Undoubtedly, her doctor will have evidence—records; proof of her deficiency, illness, whatever it was that caused her to lose her sight. He'll probably release his findings since this situation has become so public."

"And then?" Wanda said.

"And then, my guess is that the Church will take the whole thing under advisement."

"That's all?"

Koesler shrugged. "What else can the Church do? Suppose the Cardinal were to proclaim this a miracle and then, someplace down the line—months or years—the woman were to become blind again? What then? What happened to the miracle?"

"Men!" said Wanda with a breeziness possible among friends even when one of them is a priest. "You have to have everything etched in granite. I say if she was blind and she was blessed, or touched, by a saintly priest, and was cured, that's a miracle. And that doesn't mean that the poor woman must be put under a microscope to see if she contracts an illness in the next hundred years."

"She's got a point," said Koesler, always willing to learn. "This singular experience, at least to that woman—and maybe to the others who witnessed it—was a miracle. There is no other possible way a person affected in this way could understand it. If I put myself in her shoes—if I were blind and then, in an intense religious experience, I was cured—what word could I possibly use to describe my experience other than'miracle'?"

"But, Father . . ." Koznicki protested.

"Yes, I know," responded Koesler, "I just contradicted myself. But what I was getting at is the necessity of defining our terms. What's a miracle?"

"A miracle," said Mary O'Connor, "is the possibility of our eating dinner if I don't get things going in the kitchen."

"I'll help." Wanda left the living room with Mary.

Koesler made as if to rise from his chair. "A little more port, Inspector?"

Koznicki placed a protective hand over the small glass. "No, thank you, Father. You were saying something about defining the word 'miracle.' That interests me."

Koesler rose, freshened his own drink, and resumed his chair. "Well . . ." He paused. "There's the definition we learned in our Dogmatic Theology course way back in the fifties. Almost everything we learned back then, particularly in moral theology, has changed. But, for some reason, I'll bet the thinking on miracles hasn't changed."

"And what might that be? Do you remember?" Koznicki enjoyed the priest's periodic excursions into his theological past.

Koesler smiled. "Strange. I can see in my mind's eye our professor when he taught us that. Father Genovese— he missed his calling when he did not become an actor. *'Miraculum,'* he declared, *'est factum sensibile extraordinarium et divinum.'* " Koesler quickly translated: " 'A miracle is a sensible fact, extraordinary and divine.' I think the reason I remember it so clearly," he added, "besides the fact that the prof was so instinctively dramatizing it, was his emphasis on the divine element. *'. . . factum sensibile extraordinarium et divinum, divinum, divinum!'* "

They laughed.

"So," Koznicki asked, "what does it all mean, Father?"

"It means that for a miraculous—in the loose sense— event to be a genuine miracle, there must be a sensible fact;

76

that is, something has to have actually happened, an event that is perceived by the senses. In other words, not an exclusively spiritual phenomenon, a spiritual conversion, something like that. It must be a material happening, if you will. Something that can be seen, smelled, touched, heard, and/or tasted—perceived by the senses.

"Then, it has to be extraordinary; that is, completely beyond the power of nature to accomplish. This came up in a conversation I had recently with some of my confreres. Something like the instantaneous healing of a wound, or an inner bodily organ, or a diseased condition like cancer.

"Finally, the last criterion, and the toughest of all to substantiate: The sensible extraordinary fact must be caused by God."

Koznicki made a palms-up questioning gesture: "But how could anyone know?"

"A good question. The essential question. And the simplest answer I can think of is that the Church decides."

Koznicki smiled. "I must confess that is a simple solution. Too simple?"

"Maybe. I don't know. There are people who just don't believe in miracles, period. Rationalists, we used to call them. But, if you believe in miracles as an authentic reality, then by almost anyone's definition, a miracle is granted or brought about by God."

"That makes eminent good sense, Father. But how could anyone possibly tell that God is, indeed, involved?"

"Now we're in virgin territory as far as I'm concerned, Inspector. But let me try to think it through." He sipped his drink as he pondered.

"Obviously, when I say, 'the Church' decides these things, I don't mean that the entire Catholic Church, all six hundred million of us, assembles in one place to straighten something out. Usually, it seems, it's left to local authorities: A local bishop makes the examination and determination. Again, I don't think the bishop himself gets personally involved—bishops seldom do; bishops send other people—priests, I suppose.

"This sort of thing usually happens when something unusual takes place, like a weeping statue or a moving statue or a cure—or a whole bunch of cures. Then there's a lot of publicity, which is usually followed by an 'official' denial of the miraculous claim. And nine times out of ten, the reason for the disclaimer is that the 'sensible fact' is not 'extraordinary.' There's a leak in the ceiling and rain water is dripping down the statue, not teardrops. Or the foundation of the building shifted and that—not God—is the reason the statue moved. In other words, ordinarily, the matter never gets to a consideration of whether God is involved."

Mary and Wanda, conversing in low tones, set steaming dishes on the dining room table.

"And," Koznicki said, "the woman who was cured this afternoon?"

"Well . . ." Koesler, aware dinner was almost ready, finished his drink, ". . . there again, before we ever get to the question of God's intervention, there's the consideration of whether or not it was an extraordinary event."

Koznicki raised his eyebrows. "Not an extraordinary event? A blind woman having her eyesight restored?"

"Then comes the question: Was she really blind? Was there a discernible, physical cause of her blindness? Is it possible that this might have been a hysterical cure? That the blindness might have had a psychosomatic cause and thus a psychosomatic cure?

"There hasn't been time yet, by any means, to get answers to those questions. So, if I had a last buck, I would put it on the following scenario: When, eventually, they get around to asking for an authoritative response, the spokesperson for the Archdiocese of Detroit will say the matter is 'under investigation.'"

"And," said Wanda, as she entered the living room, "the matter of dinner is served."

Everyone gathered around the table. Koesler pronounced the traditional blessing before meals: "Bless us, O Lord, and these Thy gifts which we are about to receive from Thy bounty, through Christ our Lord."

Before anyone could utter a concluding "Amen," Wanda added, "And God bless air-conditioning."

They all laughed as they sat down. Koesler experienced one of those positive/negative vectors that often occurred in his life. He was grateful for the rectory's central air-conditioning so his friends could dine in comfort on this hot and very humid day. At the same time, he could not block out the countless millions who had no relief from heat. To keep them in mind and in some way unite himself with them, he hardly ever used the cooling system when he was home alone.

"While we are thanking God for the air-conditioning," Koznicki said, "it reminds me that Father was just at the point in our conversation of speaking on how God alone is—what?—the ultimate cause of a miracle."

"Well, that certainly makes sense," said Wanda, in her direct way.

Koznicki smiled. "Of course it does, dear. We were speaking of how one can tell whether God is truly involved in a wondrous event."

"So," Wanda said, "how?"

"Won't you continue, Father?" Koznicki invited.

"I think this is a fiendish conspiracy," Koesler said, "to keep me from eating this beautiful dinner."

Mary O'Connor nodded and smiled in acknowledgment of the compliment.

Koesler began with the salad and his explanation. "Let's start with the notion I've already explored with the Inspector: When a miracle, in the technical sense, happens, it is God suspending His own laws, as it were. For instance, nature abides by its own law—the natural law. As far as we're concerned, the law of nature—natural law—is God's law.

"That there are laws of nature seems self-evident. We depend on them for everything from simple math to landing on the moon. Now, there are people who see no need for an intelligent cause for all these laws. But," he smiled at his dinner companions, "we are not of that number.

"We believe that the Creator, the First Cause of everything, is the author of nature's laws. Now, a miracle—again in the technical sense—involves a suspension of this law. Levitation, for example, is the suspension of the law of gravity. And an instantaneous cure is similar. Say almost the entire interior of a person's body is eaten away by cancer. Something happens and immediately the body is completely sound and healthy. There is no vestige of cancer.

"Now, nature, as we know it, does not operate at that level. Oh, there are times, of course, when the body heals itself of various infirmities, but not that radically, and certainly not that abruptly.

"When such a thing happens, we believe that God has intervened, that God has, for the moment, in that specific instance, shelved His own law, the law of nature."

"Then the question," said Koznicki, "is why. Is that what you are coming to, Father? Why does God grant the miracle."

"Exactly. Beside the unquestioned favor he grants to the individual beneficiary of the miracle, there is usually, if not always, a secondary reason. And that usually is to give a reason for others to believe—to strengthen the faith of others.

"There's one gospel incident that best illustrates this idea. Let me paraphrase the story, if you will."

The others smiled permission as they continued to eat. Ordinarily, Koesler was a rapid eater, a penchant he attributed to his days in the seminary with limited fare for hungry growing boys. In that setting there was a direct correlation between speed-eating and survival. But, because he was now so wrapped up in this explication—an endeavor he enjoyed quite as much as eating—he was falling behind the others in their progress through the meal.

"The incident I'm thinking of took place when Jesus was teaching in a small, private home. There was a wall-to-wall crowd of people listening to Him. But not all His listeners were friendly. Sometimes it seems that His enemies—Pharisees, Scribes, Sadducees—were always in attendance, trying to trip Him up, trying to trick Him.

"Anyway, this incident occurred at the close of a very busy day. And as Jesus was finishing His teaching, there was a disturbance in the crowd. It seems that four men were determined to present a friend of theirs to Jesus no matter how big the crowd or how many obstacles.

"So they opened a trapdoor in the roof of the single-story house. Then, after placing their sick friend on a sheet, and raising him to the roof, with each of them holding a corner of the sheet, they gently lowered him through the open trapdoor.

"The crowd had no choice but to give way; otherwise, the sick man would land right on top of some of them.

"I often imagine this scene. The people who got there early to be close to Jesus as He taught, now have to back away. I can just hear them grumble, complain, and possibly even get a bit nasty.

"To go to all that trouble required a great deal of faith. This man was so sick he couldn't get out of bed. There were times in the Gospels where people were too sick to get out of bed and ask Jesus for help. Sometimes a relative or a friend would come alone and ask. Like the centurion whose servant was sick with palsy—the same illness, by the way, that afflicted the man whose friends now brought him to Jesus.

"Jesus told the centurion he would come and heal the servant. Then the centurion said the words that are so familiar to us. 'Lord, I am not worthy to have you come to my home. Say the word and my servant will be healed.' And because the centurion had such great faith, at that very moment his servant was healed.

"But the man who was carried to Jesus was a very different case. Obviously, his friends had brought this desperately sick man for a cure. Instead, Jesus told him his sins were forgiven. Kind of surprising because the man didn't ask for forgiveness and that doesn't seem to be the reason he came in the first place.

"But the enemies hopped on the statement. The Scribes

asked the crowd just who this guy thought he was, forgiving sin: Only God can forgive sin.

"This turned out to be a setup. Because Jesus then said, 'What is easier to say: "Your sins are forgiven," or "Get up, pick up your mattress and go home"? But,' Jesus said to the Scribes and the crowd, 'so that you will understand that I have the power to forgive sins'—then he turned to the sick man and told him, 'Get up and go home, because now you can walk, now you are even strong enough to carry the mattress that your friends have used to bring you here.'

"And, of course, that's what happened. The crowd, and especially the enemies, probably were bug-eyed—but the sick man was cured."

"I think I see what you are driving at," Koznicki said. He launched into his clarification as much as anything else to give the priest a chance to partake and catch up in the meal.

"The point being," Koznicki proceeded, "that forgiveness of sin is something that can happen only interiorly, in a person's soul. So that when Jesus told the sick man his sins were forgiven, no one, not even the man himself, could know whether that had actually happened. Some questioned that it had. But when Jesus cured the man's physical illness, he intended that as proof that he had the power to forgive sin."

"Exactly," Koesler said. " 'I claim to have healed this man's soul. You can't tell whether I have done it or not. But, what if I heal the man's body? That you can see. Now, see: This sick man can walk. He's cured. And I have done it. It was at my word that this man who had to be carried to me is able to walk away using his own power. If I cured his body, and I offered this as visible proof that I have the power to heal his soul, then you can confidently believe I actually forgave his sin.'

"And that's what I meant," Koesler concluded, "when I said that God generally has more than one thing in mind when He bestows a miracle on us. It is, obviously, a gift to the one who receives it. But it also is a statement on behalf of the cause for which it was given.

"Take Lourdes, for instance. A young girl, Bernadette Soubirous, claimed that she had a vision of a lady who professed to be 'the Immaculate Conception.' At the very least, if you wanted to believe in the reality of Lourdes, you would believe in an afterlife, since the 'lady' whom Bernadette claims to have seen and talked to lived a couple of thousand years ago. It would also be an added incentive to believe the entire Gospel message wherein Jesus promises eternal life.

"Then, once again, if you wish to accept at least some of the cures, the physical cures, that have taken place at Lourdes, then those miracles are motives of credibility; they are proofs offered by God that what Bernadette claims to have seen and heard really happened."

"A wonderful thing happened within the soul of the sick man brought to Jesus," Koznicki summed up. "And to prove that this spiritual healing actually occurred, Jesus performed an external, physical wonder—a miracle. Just as no one else could see what Bernadette saw. But, to prove that what she claimed was true, God granted external, physical miracles. A miracle is God's ultimate proof. Would that be a fair appraisal, Father?"

"I think so." Koesler was eating steadily now and gaining on the others. His ancient seminary experience was coming to the fore. "This has hardly been a theological treatise. But I think it is a pretty good basic way to understand the various implications of miracles."

Koznicki grew thoughtful. "Then that casts a new light on this priest who seems to have worked a miracle today. This 'Father Robert.' "

"Yes, I think it indeed does," Koesler agreed.

"It would pay to check out what this priest is selling," said Wanda.

"Absolutely," said Koesler. "Apparently, a woman's sight was restored. Was it a miracle or not? If it was a miracle, then why did God grant it? Does it have anything to do with this priest's mission? And what is his mission?''

"And if it is not a miracle . . . ?" said Koznicki.

"That would be a horse of a different color," said Koesler. "One thing for sure: If it goes much further than this, the archdiocese is going to have to get involved, make some sort of decision, issue some kind of directive. Which means that one of our priests will have to get out on the firing line, administer the investigation, conduct the examination. If it comes to that, I certainly would hate to be in his shoes."

"Amen," said Mary O'Connor.

She had a premonition.

CHAPTER
7

They rode in silence. It was not the easy quiet achieved perhaps only by extremely good friends or lovers during which communication continues wordlessly. This was the sort of stillness wherein people turn inward and become oblivious to others.

Lieutenant Alonzo Tully was driving. Alice Balcom was the passenger.

She had taken a taxi to get to the doctor's office. She had a car but had not driven for many months.

She had phoned Tully when she was finished at the clinic. He had driven from Headquarters to the far east side to get her. Now they were taking Eight Mile Road to the far west side and home. East side, west side, all around the town. The fact that this was rush-hour traffic only intensified the pressure. The car windows were open. There was enough of a late afternoon breeze to make them feel barely comfortable, but just barely.

Alice was first to feel the need to break the silence. "How did it go today, honey?"

Tully shrugged, not taking his eyes from the heavy traffic. "Not a day to write home about. Spent a thrilling hour or so at the morgue watching Willie Moellmann carve up David Powell." He paused, searching for something—anything—that might prove diverting in this grinding day. "Two other homicide autopsies going on while I was there. One by knife, the other by car. Kind of odd having all three be homicides. Figure accidental death would be more common. But three killings all together . . . that's different."

He didn't wish to amplify. Things with Alice were bleak enough without detailing violent deaths. But what else was there in his work?

They fell silent again. Again it was a strained quiet. There was the feeling that each had something in mind, something that should be discussed. But for their own reasons neither wanted to broach a serious subject.

"How about the investigation?" Alice asked finally. "The Powell kid?"

"By the numbers. The board of review figures to come in with a decision tonight—tomorrow at the latest."

"That's pretty fast, isn't it?"

"Uh-huh. They can drag on. Especially if there's the slightest complication. A day is about as fast as it can go. I'll get my gun back tomorrow morning. Lucky I thought to bring the spare with me this morning while they were testing the .38."

That gave Alice something to think about. Before getting to know Tully as well as she did now, she had been only vaguely aware of how virtually inseparable are a police officer and his gun. She'd read about off-duty officers intervening in a crime scene and invariably having their guns ready whether they used them or not. Now she knew that had Tully gone to work this morning with only his regular revolver and had the officials taken it from him to test, he would have been considered more helpless than a blind man without a guide dog.

If he had been rendered gunless, it would not have been for long. One of his buddies would have driven him home to pick up the spare. If he had not had another gun, the buddy would have taken him to the practice range to borrow one. That he might drive himself either home or to the practice range would never enter the mind of anyone in the Department. There was always the outside chance that at any moment he might be called upon to function as a police officer and in that instance there always was the possibility that he might need a gun. And he would not have one.

Try as she might, Alice could not think of many occupations that required an implement as much as a police officer seemed to need a gun.

"Outside of that," Tully continued, "it's been a day of answering phones and chewing the fat. I never knew a day could be this long."

"And I didn't make it any easier for you, did I?"

Tully glanced briefly at her. "It's not your fault, Al. God knows it's not your fault. In fact, I've wanted all day to apologize about Saturday night. I shouldn't have come crying on your shoulder. You got enough on your mind."

She reflected her surprise as she turned toward him. "My God, Zoo, you'd just killed somebody! If you didn't need to get that off your chest, you wouldn't be human. It's about time I could do something for you. The rest of the time, you've had to take care of me like a baby."

"Men don't cry."

"Of course not. Just human beings do."

His only response was a grunt.

Alice was quite sure she knew how he felt and why he felt as he did. Zoo was a strong man, almost the quintessential strong silent type. But much of this macho exterior was no more than skin-deep. He was in a tough profession. Cops stereotypically were impervious to emotions that came quite naturally to most other people. If an officer had to kill someone in the line of duty, the public expected the cop to shrug it off, have a beer, forget about it. No matter that if such a calamity happened in anyone else's life, everyone would understand—even expect—some ensuing emotional breakdown.

But, dammit, she knew her man. She knew how precious life was to Tully, even though he regularly dealt in death. He would live up to the public's expectation, but he had to let go somewhere, to someone. She could handle his vulnerability. It was between them.

She was grateful she'd had the temporary stamina to absorb the deep emotion that poured out of him Saturday night.

Alice had never been a mother, but as a woman she sensed what it is to not have the latitude to be ill. If the family is down with the flu, mother has to nurse them no matter how rotten she herself feels. No matter how sick she was and had been for some time now, Alice had to rely on what was left of some inexplicable inner resource in order to be Tully's needed reservoir.

And God knows she had been and was sick. Though what ailed her, again, God only knew.

Tully didn't want to ask, but it was inevitable. "How'd it go with the Doc?"

He couldn't see her eyes tear, but they did. "Not so good. He still doesn't know what it is."

"The tests?"

"I can only tell you that an upper and lower GI are no fun."

The sound that came from deep in his throat was an affirmation. "Nothing?"

"Apparently not. Let's see: that makes a chest X ray, the GI studies, cardiogram, blood tests, CAT scan, and sigmoidoscope . . . and they haven't found what's wrong with me."

"You forget the gallbladder."

"Oh, yes, the gallbladder. It's getting so I can't remember them all. But nothing, nothing, nothing. I'm beginning to wonder if the doctor thinks I'm a kook."

"Just because your illness might be in your head doesn't make you a kook"

"Now you?"

"I'm just supposing. Hey, babe, I'm on your team."

"Oh, I know you are, Zoo. But it's all so discouraging. Dammit, it's *not* just in my head. I can feel the spasm in my throat and I know there's a lump there whether anybody else can detect it or not. I *know* it's hard for me to swallow. This is how I feel. I don't need anybody to tell me I'm imagining it all."

"That's not what the Doc is getting at, Al. He believes you when you tell him about not being able to swallow and having indigestion and nausea. And it's a fact that your bowels have been acting up something fierce."

"The pain is unbelievable." The mere memory made Alice tense her muscles.

"It's just that he can't find any organic disease in your stomach. He can't find any physical cause for all your pain and misery."

The tears were flowing freely but still silently. She was able to stifle any sobbing. "So, we're back to it's all in my head."

"Maybe not. Personally—and I don't claim to be any doctor—but I think it's your sleep—or your lack of sleep."

"Zoo, I can't help that!"

"Honey, that's a form of torture. You keep somebody from sleep long enough and that person's gonna break down, no matter how strong he or she is. They do it in those dictatorships all the time. Keep people in a cell with a light that's never turned off. Make sure the person can hear screams of others being tortured. Having to listen to it is worse than getting it yourself. But, most of all, what they want to do is keep you from sleeping. If they can, you're gonna end up one sorry person. And one real sick prisoner.

"And that's what you've been going through: one long, sleepless torture. No wonder your insides are all out of whack."

"It's not that I can't get to sleep."

"I know, I know. . . ." He almost smiled. "It's something like that old saying: You can sleep okay all day and into the evening; it's just the wee hours of the morning that throw you."

"Don't make fun of me, Zoo."

"I'm not pokin' fun, honey. But why can't you turn it around like most folks do? You don't get real good sleep in those naps in the daytime and it seems to me you're robbing yourself of good restful stuff by staying up most of the night."

"Don't you think I *want* to sleep at night? You don't think I *like* to be awake while nearly everybody else is asleep?"

"Then?"

"It's the depression. That's at the bottom of the whole thing. I don't know what causes it, but it's scary. It's like dying or going to die. It's like the lights are out all over the world. It's like the light is going out for me."

"But you turn the lights on. You read. Sometimes you even turn on the TV."

"You don't understand. God, I can't blame you. How could you understand? It doesn't matter that I turn on a light or pick up a book or turn on the TV. It's a feeling. I can't explain it or even express it very well. I just feel rotten all over. And one feeling leads to another. Pretty soon I'm near panic and there isn't anything I can do about it . . . and . . . and . . ." She began to sob softly.

"Want to stop someplace, babe?"

"No, no; keep going. I don't want anybody staring at me. Let's go home."

They drove on in that complicated silence.

Then Tully spoke. "But what can it be that depresses you? Is it me?"

"Of course not. Don't be silly."

"Then what? Your job? I know Wayne County social work is no picnic."

"I . . . I don't think so. After all, I've been doing this for years. And it's what I always wanted to do."

"Still, it can crowd in on you."

"But I've been on medical leave for months. If that's what was depressing me, I should be over it by now."

"Except that you've got to get back to it someday. That

is, unless we can find a different way for you to use your M.S.W.''

"Oh, Zoo, I—"

"Hold it, babe," he interrupted. There was an urgency in his voice that halted not only her sentence but also her thought.

He apparently was aware of something that had slipped by her. Was something wrong with the car? No, it was running; she could detect no sound of trouble. She tried to more carefully observe what was going on around them, but she could discover nothing untoward.

Tully eased the car two lanes to the right until he was driving next to the curb. Alice swiveled to look through the back window. An old, rusted-out wreck of a car was parked at the curb behind them. At this time of day it was an obvious illegal park. But why would that so interest a member of the Homicide section? Why was he stopping when she had already asked to go directly home?

At the corner, Tully made a right turn onto a side street, pulled to the curb, and turned off the engine. "Stupid," he muttered, then said to her, "This ain't gonna take long, honey. You just stay in the car. I'll be back in just a little bit." He got out of the car and hastened back to the corner they'd just turned. She saw him give his jacket a familiar pat in the area of his shoulder holster, as if reassuring himself the contents were there.

She adjusted the rearview mirror so she could watch him without turning around. After reaching the corner, he turned in a casual fashion in the direction of the parked car.

She just couldn't stay in the car while her man was facing probable danger of some sort. The familiar phenomenon of self-hypnosis overrode her depression, pain, the whole thing. In effect, she totally forgot herself in this tense moment and concentrated all her attention on Tully.

She hurried to the corner and peered around it in time to see Tully reach the spot where the clunker was parked. For the first time she noticed the young white man slouched next to the open doorway of the liquor store. He was shabbily dressed. He and the car made a matched pair.

Tully sauntered past the rumpled youth. But when he was one step beyond the young man, Tully whirled. As if by magic, Tully's gun was in his hand. And the hand with the gun was only inches from the man's head.

As he passed the store's open front door, it had taken Tully only a fraction of a second to confirm what he suspected. There was a robbery going on. Even with heavy traffic buzzing by, he could hear the shouts of the confederate inside. He was ordering the owner to lie on the floor. *Please don't shoot him*, Tully prayed. And, he thought, with just a little luck he could get through this whole mess without any shooting.

Tully was now leaning so close to the lookout that it would be difficult if not impossible for those driving by to see the gun, which was now tightly pressed to the man's head.

"Don't move. I'm a police officer." Tully spoke at a conversational level but with a good measure of authority packed in. "Don't move anything. Just pretend you're a statue and if you pretend good enough you may live to get some supper."

Ordinarily, Tully economized on words. But in a situation such as this, he preferred to keep up a steady chatter. He would rather the suspect reflect on what he was saying than try to think of some means of escape or counterattack.

"This whole thing is gonna be over in just a couple of minutes and you are gonna be one happy dude 'cause you did just exactly what I told you to do. Just stand perfectly still. Don't even take that butt out of your mouth. That's a good fella."

As he talked, Tully was able to reach an approximately five-foot-long aluminum pole that was used to raise and lower the awning over the store's plate-glass window.

The young man, now perspiring freely, started to move, but stopped abruptly at the ominous sound of the gun's hammer being cocked.

"You don't want to do that, my man. You don't want

to do anything. This is just too nice a day to get wasted. That's a good boy.''

The inside man backed out of the doorway, shouting at his victim. "Okay, old man. Kiss that floor for another five minutes or you're dead meat.'' He turned and stepped quickly onto the sidewalk. "Come on, Bobby, let's—''

As the thief rushed past them toward the car, Tully threw the aluminum pole between his legs. The youth fell heavily to the sidewalk; his gun skittered out of his hand, slid over the curb, and disappeared under the car. For all the good it would do him, he managed to hold on to the bag containing the loot.

"Okay, turkey!'' Tully shouted, "That's a good spot. Stay right where you are and don't move. And Bobby,'' now that Tully had been given the lookout's name, "you get down on the ground and join your buddy.''

It took Tully several moments to coax the owner off the floor, which he was fervently kissing, and to the doorway. But when the man was finally convinced that the voice he heard was that of a police officer—after all, Tully reassured, why would the thief call him outside when it would've been so easy to shoot a prostrate victim—the owner hesitantly made it to the doorway. There he saw two thieves lying immobile on the sidewalk, a black man watching them carefully, holding a gun in one hand and displaying with the other his badge and identification, and a lot of backed-up traffic that had come to a halt on Eight Mile Road.

At Tully's instruction, the owner dialed 911, told the operator he had just been robbed and that an officer needed help.

It was the officer in need of help that did it. Even through rush-hour traffic, it took only minutes for two blue-and-white Detroit police cars to pull to the curb at either end of the clunker. Two uniformed officers exited each car. Once they had handcuffed the suspects, read them the Miranda rights, and had the situation in hand, Tully stole a glance up the street. He saw Alice's frightened face peering around the corner. He sighed deeply. Of course he couldn't have expected her to remain in the car all this time. But she was in no condition to absorb all this excitement. He knew what was about to happen.

He gave the necessary information to the other officers, told them he would be in touch with their commander, and left the two sorry perpetrators in their hands. But before leaving the scene, he asked the store owner for a plain paper bag. The owner felt, in a bewildered way, it was the least he could do.

Tully escorted Alice back to the car. He decided to cut down to Seven Mile Road. By now, Eight Mile was congealed by gawkers who would embellish the story of the robbery they had witnessed on the way home. It would provide some unusually stimulating dinnertime conversation.

"How did you know?" Alice asked.

"Know? What was going down back there? I don't know. Vibes. It just didn't look right. The car's motor was running. Then there's the guy standing outside the liquor store. His head is moving back and forth like a toy dog in the rear window of a car. Does the car belong to him? Then why isn't he in it? If the car isn't his, it probably belongs to someone who's gone into the store. If the two of them aren't together, why did the guy who went inside leave the motor running? With a stranger just standing there, it doesn't figure. He leaves the car running so a stranger can just get in and drive away? If they are together, why didn't the guy stay inside the car while his buddy was getting some booze? And why is the guy outside giving every indication that he's a lookout? It just didn't look right."

"All of that went through your mind? In just a few seconds?"

Tully smiled. "Well, not in all that detail. That comes up when I try to explain it to you. In this job you get used to noticing little things that somehow don't fit. After a while you tend to get sort of suspicious by habit."

"But there was a chance there was nothing wrong, wasn't there?"

"Sure, babe. That's why I wanted to find out what was going on inside the store before I did anything. Lucky the lookout was standing on the right-hand side of the open door. Gave me a chance to case the inside as I passed by. The guy was just winding up the hold-up. He had the bag and was backing away from the counter. I figured if he was going to shoot the owner, he would have already done it. So there was a chance of getting through the thing without anybody getting hurt. The luck held. We made it."

Alice was rubbing her hands together. Peripherally, Tully noticed the gesture.

"You know, Zoo," Alice said, "that's the first time I ever saw you in action. On your job, I mean. God, that was scary!"

"Hey, babe, don't worry. That was the exception that proves the rule. My job is investigating homicides. I go for years on end without ever drawing this gun. So, okay, there was the shooting Saturday night, then this business just now. Odds are I go right up to retirement with the gun in its holster from now till then."

Alice was rubbing her feet against the floor and shaking her hands as if trying to dry them.

"Tingling, eh?" said Tully.

"Yeah. Maybe it'll go away."

But Tully knew better.

"What happens now?" Alice asked. "Do you have to do anything more?"

"About those dudes? Uh-huh. I'm the arresting officer. The guys who took them in are going to book them at the precinct. They'll take their prints, process 'em. But 'specially 'cause this is robbery—armed—they'll take 'em down to Headquarters, seventh floor. I gotta go downtown and do some paperwork on them . . . after I get home, that is."

True enough, there was paperwork to be done. But, given the time of day, he could easily have taken care of it tomorrow morning. This merely gave him the opportunity to get out of the house tonight. He was ashamed to take advantage of this situation, but he was going to do it nonetheless.

Even though he gave every indication that foiling a robbery and apprehending crooks was a routine matter, it wasn't. Tully was keyed up, bubbling internally. It was uncharacteristic for him to want to avoid Alice's almost constant depressed state. But this was one evening when he and Alice would mix about as well as oil and water.

The nearer they got to home, the more Alice's symptoms intensified. By the time they pulled into the driveway, she was hyperventilating.

Tully took the paper bag he'd gotten from the store owner, cupped the open end over his lips and blew into the bag, inflating it almost to the point of explosion. He handed it to Alice. "Here, babe; breathe into this."

For an instant she wondered where in the world he'd come up with the bag. But she took it gratefully and began breathing into it. Ever so gradually she became more composed. Her breathing took on a relaxed, normal regularity.

Tully had to admit that these anxiety attacks were recurring less frequently than when her illness had begun months before. And, while there was still a frightening aspect to them, he and Alice had become better able to manage the manifestations.

In the beginning they had been scared stiff. Tully was afraid she would die. She was convinced of it. But after a few panicky runs to the hospital emergency room and an informative explanation by a doctor, at least they knew what to do about hyperventilation even if the cause eluded detection.

As the doctor had explained it, hyperventilation, or overbreathing, is one of the manifestations of an anxiety attack. The panic breathing causes a rapid loss of carbon dioxide from the blood. Among the symptoms are tingling in the arms and legs, faintness, numbness, blurred vision, headaches, and even chest pains. All of these physical manifestations are the result of breathing too quickly or too deeply.

And the overbreathing is caused by—what?—that catch-all phrase, an anxiety attack. But if these problems are caused by nothing more than anxiety, they can be relieved simply by breathing into a paper bag. This allows the exhaled carbon dioxide to be reinhaled until the proper balance of blood gases is restored.

A milestone was passed when Tully and Alice found the remedy for this specific manifestation of anxiety.

Henry Higgins in *My Fair Lady* describes the utter naturalness of having Eliza Doolittle around as "breathing out and breathing in." Imagine the terror, then, if breathing—this most natural of all functions—becomes life-threatening. At least now they knew what to do about it.

They both remained seated in the car until Alice was breathing normally without help.

"Come on," Tully said, finally, "let's get you inside."

Once in the house, Tully investigated the contents of the refrigerator. He took a carton from the freezer compartment. "This okay for you, honey? Chicken Oriental?"

"Sure." She hesitated. "You're not going to stay for dinner?"

"I told you, babe, I got paperwork to do downtown."

"I could wait dinner for you to get home."

"Better not, honey. I got no idea how long it's gonna take."

"I'll wait up for you."

"No, don't do that." The guilt he could not entirely suppress was causing him to lose patience. That, plus he was beginning to feel circumscribed, fenced in. He knew that was a fatal feeling. As much as any other contributing factor, it had caused the death of his marriage. Then he softened slightly. He couldn't help feeling sorry that he was deserting her this evening. But, he insisted to himself, he needed the break.

"I mean," he said, "there's just no telling how late I'm gonna be. You know how that works. I can't tell you when—or even if—I'm comin' home tonight. It goes with the job. You know that."

Alice nodded. She knew well enough. Going into their relationship she knew that being a cop and trying to solve real-life murders was his top priority. She had come to know and appreciate the fact that she had become an extremely close second. But second nonetheless.

However, things were different now. They surely were different for her. And she'd hoped they might be different for him, at least for the duration of her illness.

In the beginning, when she had been entirely well, she had been able to sublimate her need. His work came first for him, so it came first for her too. It hadn't been all that difficult. She had an interesting job that she found fulfilling. She had a full life and both she and he were free of any lasting commitment. Most of all, though she didn't in any way appreciate it until it was gone, she had her health.

Alice moved close to him. "Zoo, you know we don't make love much anymore."

He looked at her with some surprise. "You've been sick. You have noticed that."

"I know . . . but . . . you could make love. I'm never, or hardly ever, too sick for that. Even if I couldn't . . ."

Tully interrupted her. "I thought we had an understanding on that, Al. I just can't think of you as a seminal waste-basket. I don't intend to use you. I couldn't just use you. I love you."

That brought tears. "I love you too. But what can I do? What can *we* do?"

Tully shook his head. "Wait it out, I guess."

"But we'll lose our . . . spontaneity. God, we were good in bed."

"Maybe we will be again. Sure we will. Besides, bed isn't everything."

"It comes close. You're still a young man."

"Babe, we have to wait until you're feeling better."

"Zoo, you want me to see a psychotherapist, don't you?"

"I never said that."

"But you do, don't you?"

"There are times . . ." He sighed. "But you don't see a shrink until you really believe it will help."

"You understand why I don't want to go for psycho-therapy, don't you?"

Tully could easily understand why he would not want to subject himself to that sort of treatment and he simply projected his attitudes onto Alice. "You don't want that notation on your record. You don't want that in your history. Or, from this time on, people will tend to dismiss you as someone who is . . . who has only one oar in the water." He did not add that, with few exceptions, he did not care for the entire profession. After all, in a way, Alice was a shrink. But Tully did allow for exceptions.

"That's part of it," Alice agreed. "Also, I know the rules for the games they'd play. I know what I'm supposed to see in the Rorschach Test. I know all about transference and I'd gum up the process, even subconsciously. It just wouldn't work, I'm afraid."

Tully held her. "It's up to you, honey. It's just that the doc can't find anything physical causing all this trouble. So the, next place you turn, I guess—"

She pulled away from him. "It's not that the doctor can't find . . . it's that the doctor hasn't found. It still could be something physical. I'm sure it is. Medical science just hasn't solved all the riddles."

"But—"

"Zoo," she became defensively earnest, as if expecting strong opposition, "there's something else I want to try."

"Something else? Sure, honey. But what's left?"

"Prayer."

"Prayer!"

"There's a Catholic priest—"

"A priest! You've been to one of the very best doctors in this area. You've been to the best clinics, the best hospitals. We can go through the whole thing again if you want. Maybe they missed something. But a priest? Prayer? We aren't stuck on Haiti where we gotta go to some voodoo *Houngan* or *Mambo*."

"It's been in the papers. People have gone to him, been blessed by him. It seems like his prayers get answered . . . not all the time, but some of the time anyway." She had not yet heard about today's "miracle." "Haven't you read about him?"

"If he hasn't committed a crime, I probably haven't read about him."

"Zoo, I want to try it. If it doesn't work, I'll try psychotherapy. I promise."

Tully paced the large kitchen area. Absently he picked up the Chicken Oriental and set it back down on the counter. "Well, hell, I suppose we can give it a try. I don't suppose it could hurt . . ." Then, quickly reflecting, ". . . could it?"

"No, dear, it couldn't hurt. And it might be the answer."

"What do you want me to do?"

"Take me there."

"A church? Me in a church?"

"If it'll help, he doesn't operate out of a real church. He's using an old bank building. It's close to Michigan and Junction."

"Not a church? That's a slight improvement. What do we have to do? We don't have to be Catholic, do we?"

"Just go. Just give it a chance. How about it, Zoo?"

There was no possible way he could deny her, even though he thought it a foolish waste of time. But he remained wary. He didn't really accept her protestations that there was no possibility of anything hurtful. It had been a very long time since he'd trusted any religion, organized or not. And it had been his experience that one could not completely rely on every reverend in the world. And that went double for the so-called miracle workers.

"Okay, babe, we go. But nobody plays fast and loose with you without answering to me." He hugged her and was hugged in return. "Now, I gotta get downtown. And don't you wait up . . . okay?"

"Okay."

Alice watched him head down the driveway and out onto

100

the street. She continued watching until the car disappeared from view.

She returned the chicken carton to the freezer. She wasn't hungry. She made a cup of instant coffee, sat down at the kitchen table, and surrendered to misery.

What had happened to her life? Everything had fallen into place so well. She had grown up secure, a member of a tightly knit family in Minneapolis. She enjoyed her family and her city. She'd earned her Master of Social Work degree at the University of Minnesota. She had recognized the prime challenge to that degree not in the Twin Cities but in Detroit. The Motor City couldn't possibly be as bad as its image, she'd thought, but it was undoubtedly a more fertile field for an M.S.W. than any other city she'd read about.

So, in the face of her parents' serious misgivings and, in truth, some qualms of her own, she had accepted the offer of a job with the Wayne County Juvenile Court. And she'd gotten very busy very quickly.

It was every bit the venture she had anticipated, and more. One crisis followed closely on the heels of the previous calamity. Most of the problems were so deeply imbedded and of such long standing that, frankly, they were insoluble. However, every once in a while there appeared a glint of hope. When that happened, it was enough.

Then Alonzo Tully had come into her life.

They had met at a Coney Island. He was divorced; she had never married. The casual atmosphere of the eatery belied the depth of relationship that would build from that point.

Alonzo was such an awkward name to her. She had begun calling him Al. The problem was that he did not look or act like an "Al." (Besides, he frequently called her Al.) Then she discovered the nickname that his friends had bestowed. "Zoo" was perfect. It was familiar and fun.

They'd liked each other from the start. The friendship evolved into affection and love. She would have married him without a great deal of pondering. Then he had explained his one and only attempt at marriage. He was clear about the demands of his job, his commitment to that job, and the disastrous effect it had had on his marriage. He did not want to put either of them through such a turmoil.

So she had moved into his home in northwest Detroit. It was far too large for two people. But, then, it had housed seven when Zoo, his wife, and their five children had lived there. It was a better than average neighborhood and satisfied the edict that, as a police officer, he had to live within the corporate limits of the city of Detroit.

Her parents, who had yet to meet Tully, were hesitant at first, as would be any concerned parents anxious about their daughter's welfare. When they became convinced of her happiness in the relationship, they simply shared her joy.

It did not matter to her parents, or to any of the couple's friends or relatives, that they were racially mixed. Both Zoo and especially Alice were grateful that the time was ripe for more understanding and acceptance than prejudice regarding miscegenation.

Before falling in love and living with Zoo, Alice had had no notion of how natural, healing, and complementary a relationship such as theirs could be. They both worked long, hard hours. They were totally understanding of the demands their jobs made on each of them for lots of overtime. They prized and used tenderly the time they could be together. Their lovemaking was a natural expression of the affection and respect they had for each other.

Everything was about as perfect as it could be. Until, that is, she had fallen ill.

It happened without warning. Suddenly. She was well. Better, in fact, than she'd been at almost any time in her life. Then, abruptly, wiped out. In time, gradually improving, but locked into expecting the unexpected. Two steps forward, one back. At other times, one step forward, two back.

And no one had a name for it—or could ascribe it. There were times she fervently wished she had the flu, diabetes, a tumor, even cancer. She longed to be well, of course.

But, short of that, she would accept being sick like normal people, with an illness that had a name, that could be found in a book, *that could be treated*.

She was especially close to despair each time she underwent uncomfortable, prolonged medical tests that indicated, in the end, nothing.

Normally, she wouldn't have looked twice at a religious item in the paper. That she would be drawn to reports of a local faith healer was a measure of her desperation.

From what she could learn from the news accounts, this Father Robert operated on prayer. Sometimes it worked, sometimes not.

Not much to go on. But, at this point, any port in this unrelenting storm.

From what she could remember from Sunday School, almost everything hinged on the faith one brought to such an enterprise. She assumed Father Robert's faith was plenty strong. And hers? It was almost nonexistent. She was going to have to work with great diligence before she gave this remote possibility a shot.

But how does one get faith? By prayer? And how does one pray? Through faith? It seemed a classic Catch 22.

She decided to spend the evening searching through her books. Maybe she would find something on prayer or faith that would prove helpful.

But first, she'd get the latest news on the radio. She was about to hear the consensus number one story, an item that was being picked up—mostly as a curiosity—by the wire services and the networks.

She was about to feel much better. If Father Robert could cure a blind woman, he might be able to do wonders for someone who couldn't even tell him what was wrong.

Her spirits were about to rise. She was about to wish fervently that Zoo could be there to share her hope.

There was never a cop around when you needed one.

CHAPTER
8

At this time of day, Pat Lennon decided, it made more sense to drive directly out East Jefferson. Not only was it shorter, Jefferson being the straightest line between Detroit and the Pointes, but with the dregs of rush-hour traffic, it was faster.

There are five Grosse Pointes. In geographical order, they are Grosse Pointe Park, Grosse Pointe, Grosse Pointe Farms, Grosse Pointe Shores, and Grosse Pointe Woods. Pat was headed toward the simple unassuming suburb of Grosse Pointe, toward one of those prestigious addresses: "One"—which would put the house practically in Lake St. Clair.

The Pointes were, by and large, synonymous with money—old money. The Fords, of course, and the Dodges, as well as many extremely wealthy families who were household words mostly in Michigan.

At Jefferson and East Grand Boulevard, the intersection that led to the MacArthur Bridge to Belle Isle, Pat could get her first unimpeded glimpse of the Detroit River. From that point and moving upstream, one sailed that narrow river whence Detroit got its French name, "the straits," into Lake St. Clair, to the St. Clair River, and into majestic Lake Huron. That would be the present location of her erstwhile amour, Joe Cox.

Strange: If Cox had not caused the cancellation—or postponement, in whichever way it would work out—of their vacation, she probably would have. There was no way of predicting how this faith healer thing was going to work out. At present, it had moved from a piece of fluff to a major news story. And, as in any important story, there was no way of predicting which direction this might take. Would Father Robert turn out to be a fake? Probably. Might he be genuine? Possibly.

In any case, her reason for shelving the vacation clearly was more valid than Joe's. She was involved in a breaking story, with national—even international—implications. He was involved in covering a race aboard a boat that, at worst, hardly ever finished the course, and, at best, didn't really give a damn about who won what.

Her mind's eye took her over the familiar lakes and rivers to Port Huron's busy piers, clogged as they never were at any other time of year, the basins, marinas, and docks filled with serious sailors, dedicated if bumbling amateurs, lots of good old boys out in search of the ultimate party and, for want of a better term, naughty nautical groupies.

She knew where Joe was. And this time it wasn't his fault; it was all Nelson Kane's idea. But the SOB didn't have to accept the assignment—the assignment that had steered him aboard the S.S. Snafu. She could envision that happy crew cramming the boat with Cutty Sark, Beefeater's gin, Canadian Club, Jack Daniels. Then, out in the middle of Lake Huron they would discover they'd forgotten the battery for their ship-to-shore radio. And then they would have a good laugh. One of the jokers would say, "We're lost in the middle of Lake Huron and there's a storm coming up." And another jerk would respond, "I'll drink to that."

And Joe—God, he barely knew how to swim! She was verging on feeling sorry for him when she remembered what he was most likely doing at this very minute. The vision was so clear she had to shake her head to refocus on the traffic in which she was channeled.

There was Cox in swim trunks—no, make that Bermuda shorts, and a tank top. He was getting just a bit paunchy and he wouldn't chance turning off the girls by revealing those generous love handles. So, not trunks. But stretched out on deck picking up the sun, absorbing just enough sailing jargon to make his story sound authentic. He probably had filed his first installment already. It would be in the Freep tomorrow.

And what tonight, Joe? Yeah, tonight. Tell me again, Joe, why you couldn't come home for the night. Sixty goddam miles! What big breakthrough are you going to uncover tonight that'll keep you in Port Huron right through to the start of the race? She bit her lip. She shouldn't use words like "uncover." It too graphically described what she suspected he would be doing with those bimbos tonight.

Damn him anyway! It was no longer a matter of the vacation. At first, all she could think of was the time they had spent preparing for their trip through and around Canada. And not only the time, but the fun they'd had with travel brochures, consulting the travel writers for both the Freep and the *News*. The anticipation of a really relaxing holiday.

When Cox had broached the subject of his assignment, her first and overpowering reaction was anger over that carefully planned vacation going down the drain. With the story she was pursuing now, she saw that that wasn't the point. The demands of this job they had could supersede just about any previously made plans. If, that is, the story was worth it.

The real villain of this piece was not the postponement of a vacation. It was the type of assignment Cox had accepted that had torpedoed their plans. That he would dare so bitterly disappoint her for a garbage story: that's what infuriated her.

When this whole thing was finally over—her investigation

of the miracle worker, his trip to Mackinac, or however the hell far they got on their voyage of the damned—this relationship would have to be reevaluated.

She could hear him now—protesting her "overly emotional" reaction to a vacation that could be taken "any time." She would have to make him see the point. That it was not the fluff story nor even the squashed vacation.

It was his attitude toward her. That he would so grievously disappoint her for such a flimsy reason! And, while they were at it, for some frosting on the cake, there was his probable conduct with the women in his every port of call.

It's true they weren't married, but both of them understood that was a technicality. What right had he to expect her to remain faithful in view of his track record even now after all these years?

So engrossed was she with the hanging, drawing, and quartering of Joe Cox that she almost missed her turnoff. At the last moment, she flipped on her right-turn signal and cut sharply into the narrow side street. Behind her, horns honked; some fingers were raised, and not in salute. She would have returned the gesture but she had to zigzag carefully around the parked cars that made this by-road a constricted slalom.

To give the street its due, there were far more than the usual number of vehicles parked there this day. She was not surprised. After all, this was where the action was. Oh, not that the people who lived here were unused to the spotlight. They were, indeed, among the shakers and movers of the city—in some cases, the nation and even the world. But this was where they lived, not where they worked. Under ordinary circumstances, this was where they partied, played bridge, swam, gardened, met socially and, occasionally, made a baby or two.

These were not ordinary circumstances. Today these massive Colonial and Tudor homes served as a backdrop for the "miracle lady." And, the media had gathered to record the event.

Pat surveyed the scene as she slid her subcompact into

the only available curb space. She expected the three major TV stations, at the very least, to have crews on hand. But only Channel 7, the ABC affiliate, was present. Their crew had assembled on the lawn of the relevant home. She recognized the reporter as well as the rest of the team. They exchanged greetings as she approached the house.

"What is it, Guy," she said, "an opener, a closer, or a bridge?"

The reporter looked a trifle embarrassed. "None of the above. This is a straight standup."

Lennon lifted an eyebrow. "What happened?"

"Nothing. That's the problem. They're not letting anybody in. None of the media people anyway—except Cynthia and Robbin."

"Cynthia and Robbin!" The society writers for the *News* and the *Free Press*. "What have we got here—a miracle lady or a cotillion?"

"Damned if I know . . . obviously. They've got muscle at the door. Guess it's a Miracle by Invitation Only. They turned away 2 and 4 earlier, so they're not playing favorites, at least with TV. None of us could get in. They turned the print guys away too—that is, with the exception of the high-society mavens. So, all the viewers are going to get tonight is a bunch of guys and gals standing in front of that splendid house, saying, 'This is so-and-so, Channel Whatever, from the armed camp otherwise known as the Whitehead residence, reporting—nothing.'"

"Back to the 'talking heads,' eh?"

" 'Fraid so."

"Well," Lennon took a deep breath, "wish me luck."

"You're going to try it?"

"In the best tradition of *The Front Page*."

The entire crew, as a Greek chorus, sang out, "Good luck, Patricia!"

She grinned and headed toward the house as they continued to pack up.

Pat did not move directly toward the front door. Rather, she walked about the property briefly to get the feeling of the place. The house was no more nor less opulent than any of the nearby homes. The difference, at least the most obvious difference, was its site. The property, not deep by neighborhood standards, abutted the shoreline of Lake St. Clair. What a beautiful sight, she thought—and then she thought further: Either they know more about the tides and weather conditions than meets the unpracticed eye, or else they have serious problems when a storm hits. She guessed the former was true; this place exuded an aura of simply not abiding inconvenience.

Ultimately, it seemed intended as a monument to its owner, one of the Midwest's best-known and most successful architects.

Be that as it may. Pat squared her shoulders. She would return to the *News* with her story or on it.

She was about to ring the doorbell, when the door opened, not by magic, but by the hand of one of the largest persons she had ever seen up close.

She gulped. "I'm here to see—"

"Your name?" It was an understated growl.

"Lennon. Pat Lennon with the Detroit—"

"Come in."

She entered without hesitation.

From the Channel 7 van, the TV crew watched open-mouthed. "Well, I'll be . . ." said the reporter.

"You probably will," concluded his cameraman.

In her relatively brief time on earth, Pat had lived a lot. She'd been everywhere, from the reflective depths of a cloistered Carmelite convent to the raunchy interior of a coed massage parlor. Buoyed by substantial and well-placed self-confidence, she usually took charge of whatever situation in which she found herself.

This was a whit different.

The house, at least what she could see of it, was packed. The men appeared to have come directly from work, but definitely not the assembly line. Three-piece suits—blues, grays, soft summer colors—abounded. And seemingly all complete—in the middle of the summer—with French cuffs. But, why not? From home to car to business to lunch to business to car to home, they never left the genteel comfort of air-conditioning. Even now, with all the body heat abounding, she estimated the room temperature at about seventy degrees. Very pleasant.

Most of the women appeared to have come directly from the beauty salon. In some cases that would undoubtedly be true. Evidently, they had more preparation than their menfolk, since they were attired for—what this was—a cocktail party. An *après*-miracle cocktail party!

With her parochial school background, Pat was more than familiar with the Bible, particularly the New Testament. Try as she might, she could not come up with a Biblical scene to compare to this. Jesus seemed to travel in the company of the poor. So, after a major miracle no one would expect a bash at the "Top of the Temple" revolving restaurant.

Wait a minute. Now that she thought of it, there was a rich guy . . . Gamaliel? No, that wasn't it. Ah: Zacchaeus, that's the one. The priest who had taught her class had said that from that text it was impossible to tell whether it was Zacchaeus or Jesus who was short. Jesus had come into town and was surrounded by a crowd. Zacchaeus wanted to see Jesus but couldn't because one of the two of them was not tall enough either to see or be seen over the crowd.

And . . . oh, yeah: Zacchaeus was a tax collector—not a popular guy even back then. But Jesus singled him out and stayed at his house. At which time, Zacchaeus got religion and said he'd give half of his fortune to the poor and pay up all his long-standing debts. Whereupon Jesus announced that salvation had come to that house that day.

A miracle? A rich guy unloading half his fortune on the poor and making good on all the graft? No strings? Yes, indeed; that qualified as a genuine, first-class miracle. And since he was rich and hadn't yet paid his debt to society, he must have still been loaded when he threw the party, so it must have been pretty extravagant.

110

Somehow she felt slightly more at ease having established some sort of precedent.

Wandering through the assemblage, Lennon spotted both Cynthia and Robbin, each working a different section of the crowd. Pat was not a devotee of the society section. She had only a mild interest in who was doing what with whom. But she promised herself to catch tomorrow's accounts of this party, "What to Wear to a Miracle."

Several times, while wending her way through the throng, she motioned away uniformed waiters or waitresses bearing trays with glasses of white wine, or hors d'oeuvres. She was, after all, on the job. Or supposed to be.

Someone touched her elbow. She drew back. She detested being handled.

"I beg your pardon," he said. "You must be Pat Lennon of the *News*."

"That's right."

He smiled. "I'm Emery Whitehead. Please call me Hank."

She stepped back and took stock as she offered her hand. He smiled again as they shook hands.

She estimated his height at slightly less than six feet. A comfortable build . . . probably had been an amateur athlete. Now gone to seed and pot, not drastically, only slightly—yet decidedly. His dark thinning hair was parted down the middle and plastered against his scalp. His glasses were trifocals. It was a peculiar characteristic, but he seemed in a constant state of apology. Maybe the expression his mouth conveyed. She guessed his age in the late sixties or early seventies, but trying very hard to stay in the fifties.

"Would you like to see the house?"

Now that's extraneous, thought Lennon. "Maybe later. I'd like to see your wife."

"She's not well."

Lennon almost snickered. The standard line men offered when philandering. "I was given to understand she's better . . . cured, in fact."

"Oh, oh, yes, of course. Her sight. Yes, of course. Well,

she's upstairs. Would you like to go up? Of course you would. Well, then, follow me, please."

Obviously, the nagging question was why she seemingly was the only media representative allowed in his home. Of course, Cynthia and Robbin would argue that they were media people. But Lennon tended to discount everyone but staff writers who reported or commented on the news. Society was a thing apart. In any case, it did not seem the appropriate time to question her unique presence in the house. All in good time.

As they climbed the open spiral staircase, Lennon observed, "That's quite a group you've got downstairs."

"Some of our friends."

"One or two hundred of your closest friends," she murmured.

"What was that?"

"Nothing. I was just surprised at the size of the crowd."

Whitehead was walking almost sideways ahead of Lennon so he could converse with her. "There would have been more"—he seemed to apologize—"many more. Our secretaries weren't able to reach everyone at such short notice."

Inconsiderate of the priest, thought Lennon, not to have cured her earlier in the day so *all* their friends could have been invited to the party. "Given the time frame, your secretaries seem to have done a commendable job."

"Oh, you think so? Very good, then. Thank you."

They approached a closed door on the second floor. "The doctor and the nurse are with her," Whitehead said. "I'll just see if they're through." He knocked on the door.

The door opened a crack. Low whispers passed between Whitehead and someone in the room.

He turned back to Lennon. "The doctor's almost finished. It'll be just a couple of minutes. Would you care to return downstairs, have something to eat—or drink?"

"No, I'll wait here if you don't mind." This seemed as good an opportunity as any to discover why she alone, of all the journalists, was to be granted this exclusive interview. "I was going to ask you, Mr. Whitehead—"

"Hank, please."

She considered his invitation inappropriate. "If you don't mind, I'll stick with 'Mr. Whitehead' for the moment."

The door opened. They were invited into the room.

Lennon shelved the question for later.

It was like walking into a darkened theater. She stood in the doorway while her eyes became accustomed to the gloom.

The blinds were drawn and draperies pulled, effectively muting the early evening sun. From what she could make out, it seemed an attractive bedroom, tastefully decorated in basic whites and pinks. A bit too feminine. Separate bedrooms? Germane to the story? Time would tell.

Lennon was introduced to Mrs. Whitehead, her doctor, and his nurse.

Lennon flipped her notepad and clicked the point on her pen, grateful that her eyes were adjusting to the semidarkness.

"May I get you anything, Ms. Lennon?" the nurse asked.

"I could use more light."

"I'd prefer things the way they are," the doctor said. "Protect the eyes. A precaution."

"Whatever you say, Doctor." Lennon turned toward him. "May I ask you a few questions?"

"Certainly."

"First, then, what kind of doctor are you?"

"I'm an ophthalmologist."

"The best," Whitehead added.

The doctor cleared his throat, indicating humble acceptance of the accolade.

"You've been Mrs. Whitehead's doctor for . . . ?"

"The past . . . oh . . . twenty years or so."

"And she's had this . . . problem how long?"

"The past five years."

"Did it come on gradually?"

"No, actually it was quite sudden. Oh, there was a touch of astigmatism, a little nearsightedness. But, then, out of the blue—"

"Did you diagnose a cause?"

"We performed every conceivable test. She's seen specialists at the Mayo Clinic, several of the best men in Europe. We—all of us—were unable to find a somatic cause."

"Does that mean it was psychosomatic? Emotional? In her head?"

"No, it does not." He was a bit testy. "It means we were unable to find a physical cause, not that one did not exist."

She flipped a page. The previous page wasn't filled, but she was beginning a new thought. "What happened this afternoon?"

"I have no idea," the doctor replied.

"She went to a priest. He blessed her and touched her eyes and she could see."

"I'm acquainted with those details." He was a bit testier.

"So, what happened? Was it a miracle?"

"A miracle?" he repeated. "What is a miracle? There are miracles of human endeavor. There is the miracle of a sunset. People do miraculous things daily."

He's being cute, she thought. She hated that. Blind people don't receive their sight daily! "She can see again, can't she?" Lennon indicated the devices the nurse was packing. "I mean, your tests do indicate she can see again?"

The doctor glanced at the equipment. "She can see as well as she did before."

"How's that?"

"She's still an astigmatic and she's still nearsighted. But, yes, she can see."

Interesting, thought Lennon. She didn't know much about miracles but she would have assumed that miracles weren't limited. She would have guessed the woman would have gone from blindness to perfect vision. She persisted in pushing the doctor toward a conclusion. "Even then, doctor, the readers will want to know: Was it or was it not a miracle?"

"Ask a theologian. As I indicated earlier, I think the word is ambiguous. If by miracle, you mean some wonder God performs, I simply don't believe in miracles."

She was tempted to ask if he believed in God. But—who cared? "What is the prognosis for Mrs. Whitehead, Doctor?"

Obviously, as far as he was concerned, the interview was over. He rose, nodded to the nurse and prepared to leave. "We will monitor her condition very carefully. We hope that her present condition, whatever its cause, will prove lasting. We'll just be guarded and cautious. If that's all . . . ?"

"Thank you, Doctor."

Whitehead ushered the doctor and the nurse out of the room, suggesting they mingle, for a while at least, with the guests . . . partake of the buffet and bar. He suggested the doctor would know many of the people present. The doctor allowed as how that might very well be true.

Doctor to the Stars, thought Lennon. She turned her attention to the miracle lady. This, after all, was the star of the show.

Having consulted the *News* files before setting out, Pat knew Mrs. Whitehead's age. She was an extremely well-kept sixty-six. Artificially strawberry blonde, lots of makeup—impeccably applied—attractive features, a once probably stunning figure—but no more. What had happened to the figure, Lennon wondered. What came first? Was it too many self-indulgent society breakfasts, luncheons, dinners, along with minimal—or less—exercise? Or was it spousal disinterest? None of these observations was material, but, as a backdrop, they would render the story three-dimensional.

Mrs. Whitehead looked radiant—one might even say beatific. After all, she was on the receiving end of a reputed miracle. Could anyone blame her for playing St. Bernadette?

Unlike "Hank," this lady would be quite content to be addressed as Mrs. Whitehead. In great detail and with obvious relish, she narrated the events that had surrounded her cure in St. Stephen's chapel earlier in the day. Lennon scribbled copious notes, the while "Hank" sat by looking happily apologetic.

Mrs. Whitehead told of the young man who had preceded her and the blessing he had received. And then her moment in history. The surge of faith, the aura of some kind that seemed to enfold her; about being blessed with some relic or other, then wanting something more; about the holy priest's sensing the supercharged moment, touching her eyes, at first gently, then with greater pressure.

Then, it had happened.

"What was it like, Mrs. Whitehead?"

"Well, when he removed his hands, there was some pain. But—can you believe it?—a strangely welcome pain. Then there was a sort of light. Not a bright white. A sort of off-white. It was . . . frightening. This may sound ridiculous, but I'd grown accustomed to the darkness, to not being able to see anything. This was the first thing I'd actually seen in five years. I didn't know what was happening and I was afraid to hope.

"Then, gradually, forms began to take shape. The first thing I actually saw was that blessed man, Father Robert. Oh, not clearly by any means, just a fuzzy, shadowy outline. Then, little by little, the images became sharper. I could see! I coud see! At first, I was afraid it was some sort of momentary abberation. But then, I knew. I could see!

"But do you know, my dear," Mrs. Whitehead touched Lennon's arm, "I still don't know what that dear priest looks like."

"You don't?"

"No. He had this cowl pulled over his head. All I could see was his simple monk's habit and his delicate, healing hands!"

Quite a recitation, thought Lennon. Should make a hell of a story. But it was not quite in the bag. "Mrs. Whitehead, how were you dressed this afternoon?"

"Dressed? What do you mean?"

"What were you wearing when you went . . . when you were taken to St. Stephen's?"

"Why, what I'm wearing now."

"In other words, when you were presented to Father Robert you looked pretty much the way you do now."

"Yes, of course. I haven't had a chance to change . . . what with all the hubbub and all." Mrs. Whitehead touched her hair self-consciously. Until this moment, she'd had no opportunity—nor had she thought of it—to check her appearance. She wondered, now that Lennon had called it to her attention, whether she was at all disheveled. "Is there something the matter?"

"No, nothing. I was just trying to recreate the scene for myself and I wondered if you had changed clothes since you returned from the chapel. You look fine. Don't give it another thought."

Lennon naturally was familiar with the area of the city where St. Stephen's was. She knew it comprised the poor, many unemployed, blue-collar and, at most, a few lower middle-income families. In the group in that chapel, Mrs. Whitehead must have stood out like a sore thumb.

In addition to her well-kept person, her accoutrements, including the triple strand of pearls, dripped money. She and whoever had escorted her to that neighborhood must have sorely tempted the local muggers. Vaguely, Lennon wondered if their car still had its hubcaps.

But the holy monks—particularly Father Robert—had to have been well aware that this lady proclaimed where the money was.

Which brought to mind an extremely relevant question: Why Mrs. Whitehead? Of all the people in the chapel, why had Father Robert selected her to be the beneficiary of what would seem to be his first significant miracle?

Mrs. Whitehead claimed it was her faith that had inspired Father Robert to act. Maybe. Did that mean that none of the other suppliants had a like faith? Did it mean Father Robert could not recognize a belief as strong as Mrs. Whitehead's in others?

Or did it mean he went for the money?

Possibly an unworthy inference, Lennon reflected; but it

was from such unworthy questions that the best investigative stories sprang.

"I'm sure you must be exhausted, Mrs. Whitehead," Lennon said, "and I don't want to tire you any more. Just one final question: Was today the first time you attended services at St. Stephen's?"

"Why, no, dear. This must be—Hank, where is Phyllis?" Without waiting for an answer, she continued. "That's the way it is these days: You can never depend on people when you want them. Phyllis would know. She took me there each time we went. Well, at any rate, I believe we went three or four times."

"Successively?"

"Success—oh, you mean without missing a Mass. No, as I recall, we attended Mass there the first couple of times with several days in between. Then we went yesterday . . . and of course today." She nodded self-assuredly. "Yes, I'm certain that's the way it was."

Under normal circumstances, Mrs. Whitehead would not have deigned to answer the question. But, then, under normal circumstances, she would not have granted this interview. These were not normal circumstances. For one, she was still stupefied by the maelstrom that had swept over her within just the past few hours. Also, Hank could be surprisingly forceful when he demanded something. And, without explanation, he had demanded that she give this—and no other—interview.

In any case, she hoped the interrogation was now ended.

It was. There were only a couple more immediate questions to be directed to Mr. Whitehead—"Hank." Lennon bade good-bye to Mrs. Whitehead and thanked her for her time.

Hank closed the bedroom door. He and Lennon stood alone in the hallway. They could hear the downstairs mingle of voices and clinking glasses.

"I've got just a couple more questions," Lennon said. "May I have a few more minutes of your time?" Glancing down the staircase and realizing the futility of trying to hold a conversation amid the din, she added, "Alone?"

Whitehead reacted as if she'd given him a Christmas present. "Of course." He led the way down the hall, ushered her through a door, and closed it behind them.

Her antennae vibrated. Another bedroom. Very masculine. His. Thus answering the separate bedroom question. And raising another question: Would he be stupid enough to attempt a pass?

She chose the chair near the door. He moved the other chair closer—so close that their knees were almost touching.

She opened her notepad. "Have you had any contact with this St. Stephen's Monastery?"

"Before today, no."

"But you knew your wife was attending services there?"

"Not really. We don't talk about things like that."

Lennon wondered what, if anything, they did talk about.

"Well," Lennon proceeded, "I've asked her doctor, I've asked her; now I'll ask you: What do you think of it . . . of your wife's restored sight?"

He hesitated, realizing he hadn't actually given it any thought. His secretary had notified him at the restaurant at lunch. From that time until now, he had been consumed by details: the party; postponing some appointments, cancelling others; checking particulars such as the notification of relatives; and, after reviewing the list of reporters who had phoned for an appointment, issuing the stipulation that Pat Lennon alone be granted an interview.

Now, confronted by the question, he was uncertain of his reaction to the cure. He was in slight awe of it, he supposed. Until now, he had only heard about miracles. And he'd never believed any of them. As far as he was concerned, there had to be a rational explanation for everything. He was an architect. His work was based on immutable laws of physics and math. He couldn't erect a building suspended in air with no support. No power would or could operate against or above nature.

Yet there was no denying it: His wife had been blind. Oh, she could fake some things, such as an orgasm, but she couldn't have acted blind for five years. Besides, doctors he trusted had confirmed the blindness. And just now a doctor whom he both trusted and paid very well had affirmed that she had recovered her sight.

What was he to think of it? He hadn't had time to puzzle that out.

However, he would have to answer the question. "There isn't much to say. I'm grateful."

She tapped the pen against her lips. "How grateful?"

He smiled. "You mean, have I responded in a concrete way?"

"Okay."

"I've sent a check to help defray the cost of their ministry—in gratitude for the wonderful gift my wife has received."

"The amount?"

"I'd rather not say."

"Substantial?"

He smiled. "Quite substantial."

"The check is in the mail?"

He seemed mildly offended. "It has already been delivered by messenger."

"Nice. Then, one final question: Why me? Why did you exclude every reporter but me?"

Looking less apologetic than at any time since she'd been with him, he hitched his chair even closer. Her antennae were quivering.

"Because I've watched you work. Because I've watched you. You're good. And I wanted to get to know you better." He leaned forward. "I think we can get together on lots of things. I think we can have fun together."

"Mr. Whitehead—"

"Hank."

"Hank, your propensity for womanizing precedes you. It's no secret."

He smiled, gratified at the recognition.

"My problem with what I'm sure you're proposing is that I don't fit the profile. Your preference," she continued, "seems to be kids, girls in their late teens. The type who plans on becoming 'either a brain surgeon or a pompon girl.' Hank, I simply don't fit the pattern." Gershwin's "What You Want with Bess?" sprang to mind. Except Lennon knew very well what Hank wanted with Bess.

He gave her knee, which by this time was virtually an extension of his own, an intimate pat. "All the more a tribute to yourself, dear girl. I've wanted you for a long while. And now—"

Pat swung her right leg around, up and over so that it landed in Whitehead's lap. He was now the kid in the candy shop with his hand in the chocolate bin.

"Take a gander at my calf. Feel it."

"Gladly, m'dear."

"Strong, isn't it?"

He nodded in eager agreement.

"I build it up along with the rest of my body with lots of exercise."

His tongue caught the saliva at the corner of his mouth before he could be accused of drooling.

"Hank, you know how your leg jerks up in a reflex action when the doctor raps your kneecap with his little rubber hammer?"

He nodded again.

"Well, if you move your hand another fraction of an inch, my leg will jerk up and take your head off."

He scowled.

"And," she continued, "should you even think of removing your trousers, I will kick your balls so hard that you'll wish you'd been castrated."

She delivered all this in a calm, unemotional tone.

His mood had deteriorated from that of sheer anticipatory glee to near apoplectic anger. "You . . . you can't do this!" he stammered. "I . . . I gave you . . . I gave you an exclusive interview. I'm going to take a bath . . . I say I'm going to take a bath with the rest of the news media because of this. You . . . you owe me. Dammit! You owe me!"

"And I'm going to pay that debt, Hank: I'm not going

to tell the other boys and girls of the media why you wouldn't let them in. This way, they'll just be puzzled—instead of laughing their heads off over a middle-aged fool. Now, if you'll excuse me . . ." She rose so abruptly that he almost toppled over backward in his chair. ". . . I'll show myself out," she said, as she opened the door. As she left the room, she added, over her shoulder, "Oh, and thanks for the exclusive."

As she briskly descended the stairway, she scanned the main floor crowd. She spotted the doctor in animated conversation with an attractive chic blonde. He was holding a drink. It was not wine. He appeared to be feeling no pain. Lennon hoped the nurse was driving.

She made her way to the door, departed without ceremony, climbed into her car, and headed back downtown.

It had been a worthwhile interview. Of particular interest was the fact that Mrs. Whitehead had not been totally cured, but only restored to her prior condition. Could that mean a psychosomatic cause and "cure"?

Interesting, too, was the fact that Mrs. Whitehead had attended services at the chapel several times previously. Plenty of opportunity for the monks to note her obvious social status, and, possibly capitalize on it.

Capitalize . . . capitalism. She wondered about Whitehead's check. How much had he given them? What would it mean to them? Was that their game? Were they for real?

At this point, there were just lots of questions and very few answers.

She would go back to the *News* and file her story. And then? She couldn't go back to the apartment. Not right away. Not with Joe living it up in Port Huron. She didn't know what she would do.

CHAPTER
9

"This wine seems an extravagance," Brother Dominic commented.

"But it is awfully good," Brother Francis said.

"Sinfully good," Brother Bernard contributed.

"Now, Bernard," Father Robert spoke in a conciliatory tone, "there is nothing sinful about wine. Our blessed Lord changed water into wine at Cana of Galilee for His very first public miracle. And then He used it again at the Last Supper when He changed wine into His sacred blood. And we use wine in the holy sacrifice of the Mass. Of course, there is always the possibility of the misusing of wine that leads to drunkenness. But sinful man can always find a way to pervert God's good gifts."

"All very good," Bernard replied, "but there is a world of difference between Mass wine and an expensive cabernet sauvignon."

"Slow down," Brother Paul ordered. "We deserve a treat tonight. We made a killing this afternoon."

"What does he mean by that?" Brother Francis asked of no one in particular.

"Just an expression of speech," Dominic replied. "It means something very good happened this afternoon."

Francis glowed. "Oh, the miracle!"

Paul smiled. He seldom smiled. "I guess you could say it was a miracle."

"Giving sight to the blind! I'd say that was a miracle!" Francis enthused.

"Other than that," Father Robert said, "someone made a . . . significant contribution."

"Oh," said Bernard, "*causa celebrandi.*"

"That's right," Paul said, "that good old catchall, 'a reason to celebrate.' Drink up." An order to be obeyed without question. Even his casual suggestions had the ring of authority.

The five religious were seated in what they called their refectory. Actually, it was simply one of the roomier spaces created by the plasterboard partitions they had erected in converting the building into a quasi-monastery. This compartment happened to be located in an area where sufficient plumbing and electrical outlets existed to create a kind of kitchen.

They were at their evening meal. They sat on plain wooden benches at either side of a long rectangular table. Each still wore his habit, but all had pushed back their cowls, as was their custom when they were by themselves.

Even with their faces revealed, it was remarkable how much Brothers Dominic, Francis, and Bernard resembled each other. Each was within an inch or so of five feet seven. Each was of average build; each wore his hair cut almost to skin level. Brother Francis, who acted as barber, gave periodic haircuts to the others—except for Brother Paul; he got a professional cut once a month.

The three lookalike Brothers differed from each other most visibly in the expressions conveyed by their facial features, accented by their eyes—mirrors of their souls.

Brother Dominic was blue-collar to his roots. Carpentry

was the common denominator of his family. His ancestors in Poland had been woodworkers. They had passed the trade through most of the male descendants down to and including Thaddeus Kukulski—Brother Dominic's name before entering religious life. He performed much of the hardest manual labor in this tiny band. Assisted, to be fair, by Francis and Bernard, Dominic had created the plasterboard partitions that formed the cells, offices, chapel, refectory, and common john that made up St. Stephen's Monastery— such as it was. He, again assisted in some small degree by the other two, had built the altar and the kneeling benches. Although he was not an expert in the field, by default he became the electrician. He also cut Brother Francis's hair, since Francis, the group's barber, could not operate on himself. And Dominic continued to learn. Of all his virtues, the strongest was probably obedience.

Brother Francis quite naturally followed in the footsteps of his namesake, Francis of Assisi. A simple soul, more apt than the others to take literally nearly all he heard, Francis was the gullible one. He was not talented in any discernible way. In the world—before he'd entered religious life—he had held one menial job after another, frequently being hoodwinked by the unscrupulous who reveled in taking advantage of simple trusting individuals.

Among the jobs he'd held before joining the Congregation of St. Stephen, he had been a waiter at a Coney Island restaurant; deliverer of pizzas; dishwasher at a greasy spoon; laundry worker at a public hospital; and garbage collector for a suburban municipality. There had been other jobs as well, all comparable, all low on the totem pole of life, all nondescript, none upwardly mobile.

It never took his fellow workers long to discover his trusting simplicity. After which discovery, most of the pack would capitalize on what they considered his weakness. As a result, almost everyone he knew was in his debt and almost no one would ever repay. But Henry Horkan—his real name—would go on perpetually expecting to find redeeming features in people whom the rest of society had dismissed as refuse.

Henry Horkan counted the moment he had been accepted into the Congregation of St. Stephen the luckiest day of his life. Finally he amounted to something. If the Congregation was not yet as missionary and actively involved in its community as he had been led to believe it would be, he remained confident that one day all the promises would be fulfilled. But then Henry—Brother Francis—did tend to believe in people.

Of the three look-alikes—whom Brother Paul occasionally referred to as Ping, Pang, and Pong, after the characters in the opera "Turandot"—the one who did not belong in this Congregation was Brother Bernard. Before entering religious life, his name had been John Smith—or so he now said. Besides being such a stock name, it had humor glued to it; he always gave his name with an air of irony that made people think he was joking.

From youth onward he had been a difficult person to know. He had always been intelligent, yet his intelligence was compromised by an exceptionally suspicious nature. For example, at the college level, he had entered a Jesuit seminary. Intellectually and spiritually he might have been able to pass the necessary tests of mind and spirit, but his imagination built impossible scenarios. He came to suspect the Jesuit Society of planning to overthrow the Catholic Church as well as the Pope whom Jesuits vow to obey and serve in a unique manner. He also discerned "The Plot" behind the Second Vatican Council and was sure he saw through the deceit of the so-called experts—the *periti*—at the Council, who deliberately misled the bishops. Thus, instead of offering the bishops good advice and sound direction, the experts led their masters into heresy and near schism.

It just seemed that throughout his life, things had gone steadily downhill. There appeared to be no suitable place for him anywhere. Certainly not in "the world," where, he perceived, people ridiculed him and his values to his face as well as behind his back. Nor was there a home for him in the Church that he had once purposed to serve as a Jesuit.

Then, through a friend—who later lost interest in it—he'd heard of the new Congregation of St. Stephen. The strong pre–Vatican II spirit of this small group, while holding to the letter of the current law, attracted him. The decisive factor was the Congregation's size—just a few members of presumably like-minded men. Within such a limited group, he felt he could have some effective impact.

To date, he had achieved none of his goals. But the Congregation was young. Time was on his side.

Father Robert was, obstensibly, the leader of this little group. He was considerably older than the others. Like the others, he'd been in ''the world'' for the major part of his life thus far. As a parochial high schooler in Detroit, he'd joined the Third Order of St. Francis. In simple terms, the First Order consists of priests, the Second Order is for religious Brothers and nuns. The Third Order offers lay people the opportunity of joining with those dedicated to religious life while the lay person remains in ''the world.''

As a member of the Third Order, Hugh Wier—his name before he entered religious life—wore a knotted cord around his waist and a special scapular around his neck. Both were worn under his ordinary clothing. The cord and scapular were designed to remind him of his special dedication to the ideals of St. Francis of Assisi. Others could not, and were not supposed to be able to, detect this miniature religious habit. But it, as well as the special daily prayers he recited, were supposed to inspire him to influence others by the sanctity of his life.

He was, in childhood, and continued to be as an adult, a person of simple faith. Like the others now in the Congregation of St. Stephen, he had been surprised and overwhelmed by what he and they considered the profane novelties and profound nonsense of the Second Vatican Council. Like the others, he had dedicated himself to stemming the tide of sabotage being conducted within the Church—the Mystical Body of Christ—before that body destroyed itself.

And like the others, he lived in abject fear of Brother Paul.

John Reid, Brother Paul, was the latest, hopefully not the last, to join the Congregation of St. Stephen. He too had once been a seminarian. His seminary training had been in Chicago, and fairly recent. Thus he had been in the seminary during the present era when, instead of being inclined to dismiss students for less than significant cause, the tendency was to hold on to the desperately needed bodies.

Nonetheless, despite the drastic priest shortage, the Chicago faculty had expelled John Reid. In a relatively brief time, he had managed to terrify, disgust, intimidate, and/or dominate many of his fellow seminarians and even a few faculty members.

Before taking the drastic step of sacking him, the seminary rector had him tested and treated—as it turned out, all too briefly—by a psychiatrist. The psychological evaluation was that John Reid was a psychopath. While Reid was furious over his dismissal from the seminary, he found the diagnosis amusing. He had no idea why some shrink would find his personality psychopathic.

It was the psychiatrist's conclusion that John Reid was a classic textbook case. Nor was the good doctor's diagnosis precipitate. He had studied young Reid for several months. The psychiatrist was fascinated with the student. The doctor yearned to bottle the essence of John Reid to illustrate to future students the ingredients of a pathology.

Reid, a darkly handsome man with chiseled features, was attractive, impressive, and intelligent. He appeared to be free of anxiety and of feelings of insecurity. He found headaches intolerable, so he gave them to others. To the casual observer, he seemed a person of force and character; a competent, perhaps superior, man. The preponderant and overpowering flaw was his consistent pattern of failure. He never learned from his failures because he seemed subconsciously to be seeking disaster.

With remarkable ease and seeming sincerity he would promise the doctor—anyone, for that matter—whatever he—or they—wanted from him. Time after time he would break his word. Yet he would be able to look the doctor—or anyone—straight in the eye and promise again and again, as if he should be taken seriously.

To Reid, emotions—love, ambition, regret, shame—had always been little more than words, with little or no influence on his conduct. All of which left him with an absent dimension.

On the surface at least, his sexual life was almost perfectly suited to the seminary. He did not have a particularly strong sex drive and he was nearly incapable of forming any lasting attachment or any strong, vivid personal relationship. On the other hand, any time he felt like indulging his sexual inclinations he did so, even under conditions where a normal person might reasonably refrain. Finally, his sexual life invariably showed abnormality.

It was this latter inclination that had been the beginning of the end in the seminary. Ordinarily, with his easily distracted sex drive, there was no problem in a milieu that discouraged any sexual expression whatever. But when the mood was on him, he did whatever he felt like doing to whomever he felt like doing it. And this with little or no regard for the likelihood of being caught. With his moth-to-flame gravitation to failure, he was an odds-on favorite to be apprehended *in flagrante delicto*.

It was during the probing of his peculiar sexual appetites and attitudes that the rest of his fragmented personality emerged. He was a latent bomb waiting to explode. The doctor tried every trick of his strategem-laden profession to keep John Reid in therapy. But Reid was having none of it. It is, indeed, difficult to involve someone in therapy who is quite satisfied with himself.

It was with all this baggage that John Reid came to the doorstep of the toddling Congregation of St. Stephen. Of course, none of the charter members knew anything of Reid's peculiar past or bizarre disorder. They knew that he had been in and out of a seminary. But then so had Brother Bernard. The Congregation did not feel that it enjoyed the luxury of carefully screening candidates. Nor did it have the capability, personnel, or expertise to do so. It was a *causa celebrandi* whenever anyone even inquired about membership in the Congregation.

So they welcomed John Reid with open arms and joyous hearts. They were even somewhat embarrassed that so many names of the really big guns of monasticism—Dominic, Francis, and Bernard—had already been taken. And they were gratified when Reid seemed uninterested in the naming process and was content with becoming Brother Paul.

It did not take the charter members long to realize they had opened the door to a massive dose of trouble. By which time it was too late. For all practical purposes, Brother Paul quickly took charge, setting goals and restrictions, meting out occasional rewards but chiefly punishments, often quite severe. He lied to them so regularly and so matter-of-factly that they came to know they never could trust him.

Above all, they could not escape him. So dominating was his character and so comparatively submissive were their personalities that an unwonted style of life emerged from their interaction. They lived subject to the capricious whims and psychotic swings of Brother Paul. None of them knew how to deal with him nor what to expect of him. This uncertainty—that they never knew what to expect—kept them in line most effectively.

Brother Francis circled the table, pouring in each glass just enough wine so that by the time he had served everyone the bottle was empty.

"Someone made a 'significant contribution,'" said Brother Bernard, repeating Father Robert's phrase. "I'd like to know how significant."

Father Robert glanced at Brother Paul, who lowered his head and shook it slowly.

Robert did not look at anyone as he said, "It is enough for us to know that it was a generous gift."

"What are we going to do with it?" asked Dominic.

"Bank it," said Paul.

Francis choked on a sip of wine and had his back pounded by the considerable hand of Dominic. When he had regained composure, Francis said, "Bank it! But that's all we ever do. And the collections have been increasing all the time."

There was an audible collective gasp. Francis seemed to be challenging Paul.

"Calm yourself," Robert cautioned. "Brother Paul knows what he's doing."

"It's okay," Paul said composedly. He always seemed to extend his patience further with Francis, as if indulging Francis's unfailing simplicity. "Francis," Paul proceeded, "you want that nice big monastery we've been talking about all this time, don't you?"

"Well, yes, but—"

"Yes, but, nothing. It's going to cost a bundle. Lots more than we've got in the exchequer even now. But it's growing. We're going to get there soon, don't worry."

"And the wine tonight?" Dominic returned to his original theme. "If we need all this money in the bank, why was so much spent on wine?"

Father Robert glanced nervously around the table. So far, Brother Paul had been in an unusually good humor. Robert was anxious that this benign mood not evaporate—as everyone knew it quickly could.

But Paul maintained an unruffled course. "It never pays to pinch too many pennies, Dominic. The monastery we're going to put up isn't going to be the kind that's built with pennies, or even with the dollar bills of sweet little old ladies. We haven't got a few centuries to build another Monte Cassino. We want to see this monument to the Congregation of St. Stephen and to the memory of the Church's Golden Age in our own time, don't we? Then the only way we're going to get there is with these . . . generous gifts.

"As for the wine . . . just a few pennies. Today is, as Brother Bernard put it, a *causa celebrandi*. *Haec dies quam fecit Dominus. Exultemus et laetemur in ea*. This is the day the Lord has made. Let us rejoice and be glad in it. Trust me. I'll get us through to the promised land." Paul looked

131

intently at Dominic. "You do . . . trust me, don't you?"

Dominic did not respond immediately. But then, in not much more than a whisper, he replied, "Yes."

An unspoken and unexpressed challenge had existed from the very beginning between Dominic and Paul. While Paul was a large and, physically as well as psychologically, intimidating man, Dominic undoubtedly was the more powerful. A manual laborer all his life, Dominic, in his voluminous habit, might be considered overweight. But there were few ounces of fat on his muscular body. The conflict between the two had never reached the physical level. From time to time, Paul considered his options. It was just barely possible that, given his agility and greater intelligence, he could have taken Dominic in what—Paul would make certain—would not be a fair fight. But why risk it? As long as he could dominate Dominic with subtle menace and threat, Paul could achieve his goals. And that was all that mattered.

The clash between Paul and Dominic was momentary but intense nonetheless, and tension increased.

More to relieve the pressure than in genuine interest, Bernard asked, "So, Robert, what was it like? I don't think any of us have gotten around to asking you how it felt to work a miracle. I, for one, have never met a miracle worker in person." Bernard's smile fixed a light touch to the question.

"Oh . . ." Robert was taken aback. "There's nothing much to explain. It was an impulse. Something happened. I trust it was the Holy Ghost working in our midst."

"Come now," Bernard urged, "you can be more specific than that."

"Well, I just don't know what to say . . . how to explain it." Father Robert reflected a moment. "It was as if some kind of force field built up between the woman and me. *Some*thing I could feel anyway. But there was nothing visible, nothing I could see. Maybe it was her faith working.

"Whatever was there, I couldn't overcome it. My hands

went to her eyes sort of automatically. It was an urge I just couldn't resist."

Brother Paul made a clucking sound. "Shame on you, Robert. I thought one of the things our spiritual life expected from us was the control of impulses."

"Oh, for—this was not a sinful impulse!" Dominic said. "One that—"

"That will be enough!" Paul did not raise his voice. But his tone silenced the room. Only the sound of the clock could be heard above the background street noise from Michigan Avenue.

The color rose in Dominic's cheeks. He clenched and unclenched his huge fists. But he said no more.

After what he considered an appropriate period of silence, Brother Paul spoke again. He addressed Father Robert. "Why do you think I stay so close to you when you're functioning in the chapel, old man? We've been over this a dozen times. It's to *stop* you from acting on any impulse. I have to know what you're going to do at every moment. You've got to know what I want you to do at every moment."

"But this . . ." Robert began.

"Listen! Don't talk!" Brother Paul again let the silence settle in for a few moments. Then he continued. "Every step we take, everything we do, I have carefully planned. So far, it's working just as I want it to. We were lucky today—damn lucky. Do you realize what could have happened if you had made your grandstand play and the old bat had stayed blind? You'd have been a laughingstock! We've spent months building this operation as a prayer mill. We're never going to run out of people with troubles. They come here and tell us their woes and their afflictions. I hand you the proper relic along with enough information to show the connection between the goddam saint and the person's complaint. Most people walk out of here just as sick as when they came in. Oh, maybe they feel a 'spiritual lift' "— his tone evidenced his sarcasm—"but they leave with the same headache they had before.

"Once in a while, we get a cure. Or, more likely, some-one who thinks he got cured. And the reputation begins to spread. More people come. The collections grow. Pretty soon, we'll have enough to . . . do the things we've planned.

"You risked the whole enchilada this afternoon, old man. You could have blown us out of the water.

"As it is," Brother Paul's mood seemed to lighten some-what, although not enough to reduce the room's oppressive atmosphere, "we lucked out. But, I emphasize, it was luck. Blind luck." He smiled, but it was out of place. "That was a pun. Not intended, but a pun, I guess.

"Because it worked, we have taken an unexpected short-cut. I don't know why it worked. I don't give a damn why it worked. It just worked. The old broad is getting us just the attention we need. The kind of publicity we only might just possibly have gotten on a cumulative basis months—maybe a year or more—from now.

"So, *causa celebrandi*, but also *causa cavendi*. From now on, we've got to play it close to the vest. Retreat, as it were. It worked this time. But, by God, we can't count on that luck to repeat itself. No more chances. Got that? No more indulging a passing urge."

Dominic didn't trust himself to speak. He was too angry. Bernard pondered the possible consequences of an inter-vention. Robert had been programmed into virtual servitude to Paul. It was Francis who spoke. "But Brother Paul: It was a miracle! We all saw it. We're all witnesses to what happened this afternoon. Who are we to oppose a miracle? Couldn't this be a sign of what our true work should be? We all thought—at least all of us who formed this Con-gregation from the beginning—we all thought that we should be of service to others. We planned on using our prayer life as our opening ministry to the community. Maybe this is God's way of telling us this is what we should be doing—not staying inside all the time just praying, medi-tating, working, repairing, cleaning."

Once again, for reasons known only to himself, Paul indulged the simple, and, by Paul's lights, naive Francis.

134

"Look, in a little while, you'll—we'll—be in a position to do the kinds of things you're talking about, Francis. But, not yet. Trust me."

Dominic almost snorted.

"Low profile," Paul continued. "That's what we're going to cultivate now. A return to the low profile. With this 'miracle' this afternoon, we built ourselves a better mousetrap. So it's reasonable to expect the world to beat a path to our doorstep.

"Low profile. Remember that. We've got to be very careful to maintain the right image. That's why I had you three stay back here out of sight this afternoon when the media people showed up. Robert did okay with me feeding him lines, but that sort of thing can't continue. You three are going to have to be out front. Now I can't be everywhere at once. Keep the cowls pulled over, the heads bowed in humility. Yeah, that's it: humble.

"This thing humbles us. That we should be selected by God to be the pipeline for His grace humbles us. We haven't got any statement for the press. We don't give explanations to the curious. We just go about our duties and pray for those who come to us for help. Nothing is changed. We are the same humble, serving people of God we were yesterday. We'll have Mass at the same time. Nothing will have changed. After Mass, Robert and I will go through the relic routine just as usual. And you three circulate, get the lines organized, be of help and keep emptying those donation boxes. We're not doing all this just so some smartass kid can rip us off.

"Got it?" Brother Paul looked intently at each of them in turn.

Somewhat more forcefully, he repeated, "Got it?"

Each nodded and mumbled something assentive.

"Okay," Brother Paul said. Then he turned to Father Robert. "Now, you and I are going to go over the Bible quotes. They're more important now than ever. You're going to be asked lots of questions. Whenever possible, words from the Bible are going to be the way to handle whatever they throw at us. Besides, it makes more sense for a guy who relies on prayer like you do to have an impressive command of Scripture. Yeah, right in character."

Brother Paul paused for a moment, then continued addressing Father Robert. "Then after our Scripture rehearsal you'd better use the discipline. In fact, I will assist you."

Father Robert looked stunned and fearful. "I can do it myself."

"I'll help," Paul said firmly.

"B . . . but why?"

"To strengthen your willpower to resist these sudden urges."

"But you said . . . you said it worked. You said we gained time. You said it was a reason for celebrating." Father Robert's pleading was not unlike a child's begging when being threatened with punishment such as bed without dinner. The others were embarrassed that an adult was being shamed by a childlike groveling.

"Now, Robert," Brother Paul said, "remember what happened before? It could happen again." He spoke slowly, deliberately, separating each word from the next. He spoke quietly but with maximum emphasis.

Father Robert bowed his head in abject submission. He would need no special lessons in appearing to be humble.

CHAPTER
10

This is the life a cop leads. At least that's what the general public thinks. Killing someone in the line of duty one night, followed by breaking up an armed robbery in progress the next week.

Alonzo Tully, like most police officers, was stuck with the image. The shoot-em-up cop. In actuality, this violent image was the almost exclusive creation of Hollywood. But it had a touch of the romantic, so the public preferred the image to the reality, no matter how often real cops said it wasn't so.

Of all the TV and movie cops, "Barney Miller," in Tully's opinion, probably came closest to reality, in that Miller's 12th Precinct detective squad hardly ever drew their guns and almost never fired them. Police work consisted mostly of helping people, acting as human traffic lights during power failures, issuing tickets, controlling crowds, and enduring infinite frustration. If anything, the Miller series featured more consistently bizarre characters in one day than a real cop encounters in an average week.

Tully's job, as a homicide detective, was to untangle puzzles, to solve whodunits—with one hell of a lot of paperwork thrown in. But over the past approximately twenty-four hours, Tully's tightly organized world had turned topsy-turvy. His equilibrium was jolted and he was on a palpable high.

Consequently, after completing his report on the attempted robbery, he found himself not ready to go home. He particularly was not eager to return to Alice, who undoubtedly would be in her depressed state. He was not proud of his attitude, but neither could he deny its truth.

And that was why, he told himself, he was in this singles bar.

Located in the Renaissance Center, or as the towering complex was better known, the Ren Cen, Murray's Pub had become a favorite after-business watering hole for downtown office workers. Most of the tables were alongside the outer wall, which provided an arresting view of the Detroit River, the working ships and pleasure craft, and Windsor, on the opposite, Canadian shore.

But the real attraction, particularly at this time of day, was the oval bar. There the singles gathered.

Chris Murray, the proprietor, was wont to shake his head over Murray's being designated a singles bar. He had come to know most of the regulars. He knew that they were singles only because their mates were home waiting for them. But, Murray moralized, what the hell; if they wanted to think of themselves as singles, who cared? Not he. The money they spent on drinks was legal tender and as long as they didn't drink too much at his pub, their lives were theirs to live, not his.

Tully occasionally ate lunch at Murray's. He seldom if ever frequented the place at this hour. So why was he there now? He didn't delve for an answer. He wanted to unwind, have a couple of relaxing drinks before going home. There were dozens of taverns from neighborhood bars to nightclubs between downtown and his home. So why a singles bar? What was he looking for? Someone? He rejected the question and its implications.

"There you go now, Lieutenant," Chris Murray said as he served Tully a tall gin-and-tonic. Murray, with his shock of graying red hair, his bog features, and a brogue as thick as fog from the Irish Sea, was an innkeep nearly impossible not to like.

Tully nodded and took a sip.

Murray sensed his customer's mood. "I'll just leave ya with yer drink and come back a bit later, then."

Squinting against the late summer sun, Tully peered over his glass, taking in the detail he was trained to observe.

The piano player was a large black man whose hair was generously sprinkled with gray. His right foot pumped the sustaining pedal, his left was buried beneath the bench. He perceived no need for a muted sound. His eyes roamed the room as his fingers, from habit, found the right keys. He nodded and smiled at the regulars and added warmth whenever a bill was tucked in the snifter on the Baldwin grand.

The room held a good racial mix, reflecting the cosmopolitan makeup of the city's business, professional, and government workers, at least at that otherwise isolated riverfront area.

The women, predominantly office workers, were mostly young, with a sprinkling of forty- and even fifty-year-olds. Orientals with raven-black hair. Blacks, some with cornrows, a few with Afros, some with do's. The whites were all blow-dried or moussed, but blonde, blonde, blonde.

Girls—women—in clusters, eyes searching for someone—a man? Clearly not focused on anyone in their immediate group.

Men in threes and fours with beer in hand. Glancing at the TV sets mounted high on the wall above either end of the bar, showing nonstop sports. Gestures told stories: last weekend's golf game here, a tennis match there; what had gone on in court today; what I told the mayor just after he fired me.

A couple halfway around the bar are seated on bar stools

as closely as possible without being on the other side of each other. They are involved in a mildly erotic dance without steps. Her knee is in his crotch. They nibble on each other's lips. She gets up: to go to the ladies' room? He doesn't back off to give her room to leave. She has to squeeze past him. He doesn't seem to mind; neither does she.

The piano player is fingering, "The Lady Is a Tramp."

Tully's eyes are attracted to and held by a woman who has just entered the pub. His immediate impression is that she doesn't belong here. Not that there is anything specifically wrong with Murray's Pub, but this lady is an alien element in a singles bar. She doesn't need it. She could have just about any man she wanted. She certainly doesn't need to go looking for companionship—or trouble—in a singles bar. Tully can't take his eyes from her.

Pat Lennon is questioning herself. Why a singles bar? Why not home, for that matter?

The answer to both questions is Joe Cox. He, definitely, is the reason she has not returned to the very comfortable apartment the two maintain high above the city in the Lafayette Towers.

It wasn't by any means the gushy sentiment of the "Show Boat" song, "Home without him ain't no home for me." It was more the lingering anger that still percolated through her, and the uneasiness at being alone tonight with the inescapable images of the faithless fun he must be having.

Thus, the singles bar.

She was chagrined even as she admitted it. She could count on one hand the number of times she'd been in a singles bar. And all of them had occurred in her college years. As a student at a Catholic all-girls school, going to a singles bar then held out the forbidden-fruit aura of "sinfulness." She and her classmates had behaved not much differently than most of the women at this bar tonight. The only saving grace was that she and her girlfriends had been much younger—and less experienced—than most of these women.

Before committing herself to the bar, Pat paused and looked the place over more carefully. From her vantage, she could see no man who looked particularly interesting. Lots of young bodies, lots of three-piece suits. Here and there a few cherubs complete with baby fat carrying themselves as if they were *Cosmo*'s ideal. One wearing a letter sweater looked as if he should be in the bleachers. Many were smoking. Fortunately, the pub had a more than adequate ventilation system; the smoke did not hang in the air. A young woman returned to her bar stool. From the ladies' room? She had to squeeze by her companion. Neither of them seemed to mind. They turned to each other. They couldn't have been closer. She planted her knee in his crotch. They nibbled on each other's lips. The piano player was wrapping up, "The Lady Is a Tramp."

Pat shrugged. Stay or leave; she could have flipped a coin. The determining consideration was the valet parking to which she had committed her car. It was expensive and would cost as much whether she left now or stayed for a drink. That thought plus her self-assurance that she could take care of herself tipped the scales.

As she moved toward a just-vacated bar stool, she encountered small knots of men who, for the most part, were reluctant to make room for her to pass. She knew why. It was touchy-feely time in the singles bar. In her most ladylike tone, she tried excusing herself. When that didn't work, a well-aimed sharp elbow got results. By the time she reached the bar, she was no longer in the running for the Fellowship of Christians and Jews Award.

"What can I getcha, miss?"

She was so angry she'd forgotten where she was. She focused on the questioner. Of course the bartender would want her drink order. Pat gave it a moment's thought. She didn't want anything potent. That, along with her foul mood, would have rendered the short ride home hazardous. "A gin-and-tonic, long on the tonic, short on the gin."

Chris Murray smiled as he wiped the ever-present glass

with the ever-present bar towel. "Y're new in here, now, aren'tcha? Do ya work downtown, then?"

"Remember, long on the tonic, short on the gin." Pat wanted a drink and some time to think things out. She didn't need an invitation to an autobiography. Men! Why didn't they just do their job? And this one an obvious leprechaun to boot!

Murray maintained his warm smile, raised one eyebrow, and went about fixing her drink. Long tonic, short gin.

Pat selected one lone peanut from the dish in front of her. She studied it, then carefully placed it in her mouth. She tried to hold a happy thought. The weather was nice, she had a good job, she was healthy, and maybe she'd take a swim in the pool tonight.

She became conscious of someone not only sitting down next to her, but pulling the bar stool too close.

"Hi there, doll. I haven't seen you here before . . . and believe me, I wouldn't have forgotten you!"

She turned her head just enough to see to whom the voice belonged. A young man, several years her junior, she guessed. She couldn't establish eye contact because he was doing his best to peer down her comfortably low-cut summer dress. She returned her gaze straight ahead. "This is my first and perhaps last time here."

"I don't blame you, toots. This barn is a bit of a drag. Whaddya say we split? We could go to my pad. I've got a splashy place at the Riverview."

Nice address; too bad they weren't more selective about their tenants. She did not look at him, merely frowned. "Here's a better idea: Why don't you get lost?"

"Hey, toots, maybe you don't know who I am." His hand was on her arm. She recoiled as if stung.

"Beat it!" The voice was low, calm, authoritative, and packed a thinly veiled threat.

Both Pat and the young man turned to see the source. It was a black man in sunglasses. The sunglasses were looking at the young man.

Pat could not put her finger on it, but there was something

about this man; something in his demeanor, his bearing, his carriage; something in his voice, the tone, the assumption of compliance, that she had never encountered before. At least she could not remember having done so.

"Who you talkin' to?" It was blurted with more bravado than confidence.

"Beat it!" The command was repeated.

"Obviously you don't know who you're talking to. If you think for one minute that I'm going to—"

The black man shook his head almost imperceptibly, as if regretting what he was about to do.

"Wait," the young man said, motioning with his hand. "There's no need to get upset about any of this. There's more than one fish in this ocean." He slid off the stool. "I was just leaving anyway." He almost stumbled as he beat a retreat, then made his way out.

Alonzo Tully moved the bar stool back to its previous position and seated himself. "Sorry about that, miss. The yuppies aren't usually that pushy."

Pat was smiling almost in spite of herself. She had been about to clear the deck of that offensive young man. But she was grateful that this stranger had done it for her.

She turned her head toward him. A five o'clock shadow, close-cropped, gray-flecked hair, a Poitier profile, a manner of lightly clenching his teeth that made his facial muscles dance. No Rambo or Carl Weathers. But there was something—something that set him apart. Something that wanted him on your side in a fight.

"How did you know?"

He shrugged. "The look on his face. The look on your face. You were like a butterfly and he had a net. That's what brought me over. Then, when he put his hand on you, your reaction told me you'd prefer it if he left. So, I invited him to leave."

She continued to smile. "What would you have done?"

"If he hadn't left? I would have been very disappointed."

A sense of humor to boot. She was beginning to feel

143

comfortable. She extended her hand. "Patricia Lennon, in your debt, sir."

He took her hand in his. She had a good grip, worthy of note in such a feminine woman. "Patricia Lennon . . ." He was searching. "Lennon—Pat Lennon. Reporter, isn't it? The *News*?"

"Uh-huh. And you?" He moved his sunglasses. Her response was one of dawning recognition. "I've seen you— or your picture. But . . . I'm sorry, I just can't put an ident on it."

"Tully. Alonzo Tully. I'm—"

". . . a cop. Sure: Homicide. Yes, that's it: Homicide. That's where I've seen your picture. You catch the bad guys." She shook her head in amusement. "I'm glad my yuppie didn't hang around. I'm sure he would've hated disappointing you."

They laughed easily together.

"Matter of fact," Pat said thoughtfully, "You were just in the news. Saturday, wasn't it? Some dope house. You . . . uh, shot . . . somebody."

Lennon was all too conversant with the extraordinary violence of this city. It was part of her job. She reported it. She had interviewed any number of people who had shot or been shot by somebody. It happened all the time in this gun-crazy town. It was not improbable or even unusual for her to be speaking with someone who had killed somebody. What did give her pause was the abruptness of it all. One moment laughing and exchanging light conversation, the next moment running head-on into the ultimate fact of death.

Tully sipped his drink. There were a few moments of silence—awkward silence. Then, "It wasn't drugs, although it was a drug house. We wanted the kid for questioning in a murder case. The only place we could find him, by our best information, was the drug pad." He gazed out the huge window at the river with its deceptively slow-seeming swift current. "We just wanted to question him."

Lennon began to call up the story. "He was the one who started shooting."

"He got one of my men. Lucky he wasn't hurt bad."

"So, you had to—"

"I killed him." There was the slightest catch in his voice.

Lennon perceived how deeply affected the man was. She wanted to offer solace, put an arm around his shoulders—something. But not here, not now. The wrong place, the wrong time. "Sorry." It was a woefully weak word, but she meant it deeply. And she managed to communicate her sincerity.

Tully shrugged and replaced the steel curtain that concealed the inner man. "That's okay. That's my job. I'm a cop."

Lennon caught the calculated change of pace. "Uh-huh. Like Joe Friday and 'Dragnet.'"

"Right."

"Speaking of Joe, what do I call you? Al?"

"That's all right."

"No . . . wait; I remember now: they call you Zoo, don't they?"

"Some."

"That's it, then: Zoo. Cute."

Tully could not abide the word cute, particularly in reference to a man. But for some reason, coming from her made it tolerable.

The tendency was to ask, "So how does it feel to kill somebody?"

That was consciously rejected by Lennon. Instead, she said, "So, Zoo, have you heard about the new Afro-French bar that opened near the Detroit Club?"

That was unexpected. He did not follow the shift in this conversation. And as familiar as he was with all that went on in this city, he was not aware of this new bar. If it was near the prestigious Detroit Club he surely should have known. Deeply puzzled, he shook his head.

"It's called *Chez What?*"

It took a moment. Then, drumming his fist lightly on the bar, he broke into a low but appreciative laugh.

Chris Murray, thinking he was being summoned, materialized. "Can I get ya both another drink? I remember, miss: long on the tonic, short on the gin."

They looked at each other and mutually decided they'd had enough. Still laughing, they shook their heads.

Murray left them, pleased that both were feeling better about things. Sure and wasn't it wondrous what companionship could do for people. He'd tried to explain that many a time to his pure and holy parish priest. But the good man simply couldn't grasp it.

For Lennon, the mild racial joke had constituted a test. She wanted to see how far his sense of humor would stretch and whether he was comfortable enough with her to laugh even at a delicate and, for some, an explosive subject. If he passed—and he had, with flying colors—it would mean one less barrier between them.

Although she seldom did this, she found herself checking his ring finger. Nope. Of course, that didn't tell much. Men were not as apt to wear a wedding ring.

Long ago, before he had disposed of the yuppie, Tully had noted that her ring finger was bare. Probably that meant she was unmarried. He would have guessed divorced, though he was open to whatever other possibility existed. She might be living with someone. She might be lesbian. But if he were down to his last dollar, he would bet against that.

And then he wondered why he was wondering. Alice was waiting for him at home. So why was he concerned about the sexual status of Pat Lennon? Rhetorical. He knew why. Alice was ill and had been for months. Despite his efforts at sublimation, he was getting horny. And he was with an extremely desirable woman. Not only was Pat Lennon invitingly attractive but he was enjoying himself just in conversation with her. All of this he had had with Al, but not for a long while now. So pervasive was Al's depression that it permeated nearly their entire relationship. This evening was becoming the remedy and release he needed. And he needed it much more than he would have cared to admit.

Where was this relationship headed? Neither knew. Both

felt satisfied with what was going on at this moment, and content to trust the future.

As the time passed, they moved from the bar to a table. Laurie, their waitress, served them decaf, then brought countless refills.

They talked of journalism and police business. How they had gotten into their respective fields, and events that had influenced their careers. Neither mentioned a marriage and divorce. Both almost completely forgot the persons with whom they lived. So, while their conversation was pleasant and informative and the repartee amusing, their relationship remained comparatively superficial.

As shadows lengthened and night approached, their conversation took on an awkwardness. What to do and where to go from here?

There was no point in migrating to another bar. They had munched on more than sufficient snack food to make dinner superfluous. There was no way Tully could invite Lennon to join him and Alice. Lennon, for her part, could easily have invited him to the apartment. Joe was otherwise occupied in Port Huron. But it was, for want of a better explanation, too soon. They'd met only hours ago. In itself, that would not have deterred Pat. But nothing they'd talked about came close to being described as personal. Was he married or not, living with someone or not? There wasn't enough foundation to justify hopping into bed. But who knew what might develop?

They exchanged business cards bearing phone numbers. Neither added a home number. That told each of them something, something neither of them particularly liked.

After a brief discussion, they decided to split the tab. Because the bill was so small and they had lingered so long, they left Laurie a generous tip.

They left the pub together. Tully would see Lennon to the building entrance where the valet would retrieve her car.

During their final forty-five minutes in the pub they had been observed by a man neither of them had ever met. He sat by himself across the room from them until about two minutes before they left. Then the man was joined by a young woman—blonde like most of the other women there.

He was young, tall, and well-built, with attractive features; deep blue eyes, a full head of jet black hair. He was not observing Tully and Lennon exclusively by any means. He was on the make in a singles bar.

His interest was not in them as a couple per se, but because one was black while the other was white. He found that reprehensible; potentially mongrelizing the human race. But he was not there to attract attention so he kept his disapproval to himself.

Actually, he could just as easily have gone to a gay bar. It didn't make that much difference. But he'd read about this singles bar and decided to try it. For that matter, it wouldn't make much difference if he didn't score in this bar—although he was quite sure he would; he was that confident of his good looks.

After he'd finished silently excoriating the racially mixed couple, he'd turned his attention to a blonde whose girlfriends had gone, leaving her alone at the bar. The fact that she stayed said a lot to him. She it would be.

In due course, the blonde came over and slid in beside him. "Buy me a drink?"

"Sure." There was plenty in petty cash. He and Brother Bernard alone had access to the money, and Bernard never touched a penny outside of buying necessities for the monastery.

He had come to the bar because he needed to reward himself, and eating a festive meal with those imbeciles just didn't do it. With that crazy "miracle" this afternoon, things were heading rapidly toward a climax. Soon this charade would be over.

He could hardly wait.

Laurie brought their order. A martini "up" for him, a whiskey sour with a tiny umbrella in it for her.

"What's your name, love?" he asked.

"Chesty Plenty." She rubbed against him to drive home her point.

"Of course you are."

"And you?"

He could have replied, John Reid or Brother Paul. However, "John Smith. But you can call me Joe."

"Why not?" With all she had drunk, she was feeling no pain. But she would. This would be a night she'd remember as long as she lived. It would also mark the last time she would ever bring a stranger home. In retrospect, she would conclude that she had been lucky to live through the horror.

But at this moment, she was anticipating nothing more than a roll in the hay with this handsome hunk.

And he was reflecting on the paradox. Ordinarily, if one wishes to be incognito, he wears some sort of costume. But, if one lives in a costume—say a monk's habit with a cowl covering one's head—one can go unrecognized merely by letting everyone see what one really looks like.

Meanwhile, wonder of wonders, just a little while ago he didn't give a damn. However, now John Reid was going to pack Brother Paul in mothballs and have himself a phenomenal night.

TUESDAY
JULY 25

CHAPTER 11

One half-hour before opening time, everyone was about his or her business.

Tellers were counting their money and going through the previous day's mail deposits.

Bill O'Brien, a vice-president of First Standard Bank and Trust, and manager of the Livernois branch, along with a teller, was opening the night depository. Bank rules required that a member of management as well as a regular employee be present at the opening of the night depository to cross-audit each other. Once they completed their task, the tellers would process the envelopes.

The general teller went from cage to cage, making sure the tellers had enough money to at least get them off the ground this morning. The tellers went through the ritual of "buying" and "selling" money from the general teller. Meanwhile, other employees were preparing a shipment of excess funds for downtown.

All of this was a very busy but almost soundless operation. Thus, even in the midst of all this activity, the tapping of keys against the glass front door could be clearly heard.

Bill O'Brien, along with several of the employees, looked up. O'Brien was annoyed. He had enough to do before opening time without being hounded by some impatient customer who couldn't read the banking hours posted on the door right before his eyes.

The manager's vexed look dissolved when he recognized who was at the door. He nodded to an assistant, who unlocked the door, admitting the two monks, then relocked it after them. Their familiar robed figures glided through the lobby directly to O'Brien.

Customers were not supposed to be admitted before banking hours. The monks of St. Stephen's Monastery were an exception to this rule. The practice of admitting them a half-hour or so before time had been instituted by O'Brien as a courtesy to the religious. In time, it had become an advantageous practice as the monks' deposits grew larger. O'Brien liked to get such large amounts in and counted before opening for business.

"Good morning, Father Robert . . . Brother Paul." It was guesswork, as both monks were in full habit with cowls pulled over their heads. They could see out, although the rims of the cowls acted as blinders. But one could not see in without pressing one's face against the cowl and peering in. An indiscretion at the very least.

However, O'Brien's was an educated guess. It was always Robert and Paul who brought in the deposits. At least that was how they identified themselves. And what reason could they have for lying?

It was the much taller, athletically built Brother Paul who responded. "Good morning, Mr. O'Brien. God bless you for extending this courtesy to us. It really helps with our busy days."

It was just about the same thing Brother Paul said nearly every visit. Ordinarily, O'Brien took it with a healthy grain of salt. He could not conceive how these monks kept that busy from day to day. But after what had happened yesterday, he could well imagine they were about to be besieged. And, in keeping with yesterday's events, O'Brien tried to treat Father Robert with enhanced reverence.

"Let me take that bag for you, Father Robert." O'Brien relieved the smaller monk of the black satchel. "That was quite something that happened at the monastery yesterday. You're a celebrity now. And justly so."

As O'Brien relieved him of his burden, Father Robert, with a small, stifled cry, staggered sideways.

O'Brien was instantly concerned. "Here, Father Robert, sit down here in my chair. Is there anything I can get for you?"

"He'll be all right," Brother Paul said. "He's just tired from yesterday. There were so many questions, so many reporters, the TV cameras and their terribly warm lights, on top of the heat of the day. I'm afraid it's been a bit much for him."

Actually, Robert was weak from the punishment inflicted the previous night by Paul. But he—as the others—knew better than to speak out. Robert sank gratefully into the supportive leather chair, bowed his head, and rested for the moment.

"I can well imagine," O'Brien said to Paul. "Is there anything we can do? We've got some aspirin, but that's all; I'm afraid we don't even have any brandy." He gazed concernedly at the seated priest. "I'm worried about him. Are you sure he's all right?"

"He's got the constitution of a horse. He'll be fine. Let's just let him rest. He's got another big day ahead of him."

"Oh?"

"Mass as usual and then all the supplications and prayers and blessings to follow. And after yesterday I'm afraid we are anticipating a larger crowd than usual." In fact, Paul added in thought, I'll be disappointed as hell if it's not S.R.O.

"Oh, I'm sure that's true." O'Brien was not completely at ease. He'd never done business with a miracle worker before. But then, he consoled himself, who had?

"By the way, Mr. O'Brien," Paul said, "there's a check

in this morning's deposit that is somewhat larger than usual.''

"Oh?"

"Yes. It's $200,000."

"That is substantial."

"Yes. The woman who was cured yesterday—Mrs. Whitehead . . ."

"Oh, yes. The wife of the architect."

"That's right. Mr. Whitehead was kind enough to send the check over. It was very thoughtful."

Until now, O'Brien had not given a thought to what the price of a miracle might be. But $200,000, especially from the wealth of an H. Emery Whitehead, seemed equitable. Perhaps a ballpark figure.

"That was quite thoughtful," O'Brien agreed.

"What I mean, Mr. O'Brien, is, now that this has happened, it is undoubtedly the beginning of quite a lot of that sort of thing."

"Oh?"

"Indeed. The account of the miracle, I am told, has been reported far and wide—carried on the wire services and network television. It's even gotten foreign coverage. So, praise God, there may be more cures. Certainly more very substantial contributions."

"I see."

"Mr. O'Brien, this has been quite literally an answer to prayer. You know how much our order has yearned to build a magnificent monastery."

"Yes. We've talked about that."

"Not that there is anything wrong with the building we're in—you know it used to be a branch of your very own First Standard Bank and Trust. I mean, the building is in good shape. I would not want you to think we are not grateful for the home you practically gave us."

"Of course not, Brother, we all knew that it was a temporary facility."

"I just wouldn't want you to get the wrong idea."

"No problem."

"You see, the land we're looking at for the monastery is out in West Bloomfield."

"Hmmm. Land is pretty dear out there."

"We know. At first we were thinking of Duns Scotus—you know, the old Franciscan place in Southfield."

"So big! I thought you had only—what is it, five or six members?—in your whole order."

"Five. Yes, and that's why we didn't pursue Duns Scotus. But now, with all this publicity, we're bound to attract new members. As a result, we're considering erecting something even larger and more spacious than Duns Scotus."

"My, my!" O'Brien was, of course, very impressed by the miracle. But he'd had no idea that one miracle could have that many tendrils. He was not terribly surprised that a man such as H. Emery Whitehead would make a most generous contribution in gratitude for his wife's cure. It just had not occurred to O'Brien that donations of a similar nature might follow. Or that this sort of publicity might attract more members. But, now that Brother Paul had mentioned it, it made sense.

"My point is," Brother Paul continued, "that we are going to be depositing a considerable amount of money in this bank."

O'Brien brightened. "Well, we'll be more than happy to accommodate you. Perhaps even suggest some investments . . . ought to have that much money working for you."

"Yes, yes, that's all very well. But what I'm interested in right now, if I may be blunt, is your security."

"Our security?"

"You don't have any—what?—guard here that I can see."

O'Brien chuckled. "Goodness! The security in banks today is such that the armed guard is almost a thing of the past."

"I'm sure. But the others at the monastery are wondering about this too. Just before Father Robert and I came over this morning, they asked about how safe our deposits would be. I mean, we've never had this much money before."

"Well, you can certainly assure the others that—wait: Would you like a little tour? Then you could report on our security measures to the others."

"If it wouldn't be too much trouble."

O'Brien checked his watch. A few minutes till opening. Time enough.

He began by assuring Brother Paul that no one but authorized personnel was admitted behind the partition where the tellers worked. Brother Paul reminded O'Brien that he had admitted the two monks behind the partition today and just about every day that they brought in a deposit. The two men had a good laugh over that.

O'Brien made much of the scanning monitors that recorded almost all the action in the bank, especially throughout the lobby. Very discouraging, O'Brien averred, to your average bank robber to have his activity on film, subject to playback, stop/action, enlarged photos. Remember the damning shots of Patty Hearst robbing that California bank?

Brother Paul remembered very well.

He did not mention it, but the film wouldn't be all that much help if the perpetrator was wearing an all-encompassing costume such as a religious habit that covered all from the tip of one's head to the tip of one's toes.

The tour was completed quickly.

"Thank you very much, Mr. O'Brien. I'm absolutely convinced. I'll certainly reassure the others. You've been very kind—and helpful. God bless you."

Brother Paul retrieved Father Robert and led the older man from the building.

Father Robert looked to be in pretty bad shape. But then, O'Brien reflected, all he could see was a gray habit shuffling its way through the lobby.

Now that he thought of it, he had been speaking with Brother Paul for a lengthy period—a very long period if one counted all the times the monks had brought in deposits—yet O'Brien had never seen either's face. O'Brien preferred to look people in the eye when he spoke to them. But if asked what these monks looked like, or even the color of their eyes, he could not have described them.

Odd. But that was the way with religious life. As a Catholic, he could understand that.

Father Robert Koesler believed in God and routine, in that order. Thus, for an initial comfortable feeling, he depended on a predictable beginning to each day.

For mornings, Monday through Friday, that meant: Rise at seven o'clock, ablutions, morning prayer, Mass at eight with a two- or three-minute sermon, breakfast at 8:45. That's how it had gone this morning. So, he was content.

Most days, Mary O'Connor was among the few attending daily Mass. Then she would join him for breakfast, such as it was. That's how it had progressed this morning. So he was doubly content.

Over breakfast, the two would go over the day's schedule, with Mary reminding Koesler of his more forgettable upcoming obligations. Koesler would go through the morning editions of the *Free Press* and the *News*, and apprise Mary of the pressing concerns of the city, state, country, and world.

At this moment, Koesler was slicing a banana over cold cereal, while Mary, fortunately for both, brewed coffee.

"Joe Walk claims the air-conditioning is acting up."

Seated at the kitchen table, Koesler opened the paper and spooned some cereal. "It's out? Completely?"

"Not completely just yet—but going. He says he can't get it to stay running dependably."

"Can't he fix it?"

"Too complex a job. He says we have to call the heating and cooling people."

"Again? They charge an arm and a leg."

"Sunday will be here before you know it."

Koesler sighed and turned a page. "These people are spoiled with an air-conditioned church. In the good old days, men perspired, women glowed and the priest melted under all his vestments. Penance—that was the word! Summers you boiled, winters you froze."

Mary smiled and set a cup of black coffee to one side of his papers. "You know how it is, Father: 'How're you gonna keep 'em down on the farm?'"

"I know, I know. They've come to expect a comfortable church. What do you think: Call in the professionals?"

"I don't see any other way."

"Okay." He tasted the coffee and sighed appreciatively. "See? That's just what I was afraid of."

"The parish council meeting tonight? That shouldn't be too bad. It's midsummer. Several of the members are away on vacation."

Koesler looked up from the paper. He never ceased to be amazed at Mary O'Connor's grasp of the parish and insight into its parishioners. She seemed to know where everyone was at any given time. She knew where all the skeletons were buried. And, what argued most for her sainthood, she never had a bad word for anyone. Not even those who deserved a word or two.

"I wasn't really referring to the council meeting—though that's horrendous enough, now that you mention it. No, this piece in the paper . . ." He pointed to a front-page article. "About the miracle yesterday at that . . . uh . . . St. Stephen's Monastery."

"Not jealous, are you?" She smiled. It was as close as Mary O'Connor would ever come to a figurative jab in the ribs. And that only because she knew Koesler so well.

"For the love of Pete, no!" It was said with great conviction. "If I wanted a ministry like that, I would have joined a circus. No, I was sure this was going to happen. It got a big play on local TV last night and even a mention on network news. Of course the network treatment was kind of snide. Like the pet-pig-that-can-sing story. But I'll bet they'll change their attitude right quick when they find out everyone here is taking it seriously. It's already on page one of both papers. Undoubtedly, it's on the wire services and in most of the other papers around the country."

"I beg your pardon," Mary said, "But what's so bad about that? Isn't it about time Detroit made the news for something besides its murder rate? Isn't this a good story for us? Especially for Catholics?"

"That's not what bothers me." As he gestured with his spoon a drop of milk arched through the air, landing on the table just short of Mary's toast. "What troubles me is the effect it's going to have on people everywhere. Sick people, people with problems, people who are old and ill."

"Isn't that the idea?"

"I don't think so. Not exactly. They'll be sending money. People who can't afford anything will be sending much more than they can afford."

"Do you really think so?" Mary asked, taking his meaning while overlooking his Irish bull.

He nodded. "Happens all the time. Look how well those TV evangelists do—or used to until they began ruining it for themselves. They made millions—not from millionaires but from people of modest means sending all, or even more, than they could afford."

"You think people will do the same for this Detroit monastery?"

"Betcha."

"But why?"

He shrugged. "I don't know. Capitalism, maybe. The kind of quid pro quo life we lead in this country. Maybe in the world. Why do people give money to have a Mass offered?"

"Because they have to."

"They don't, really. The stipend—say five dollars in the good old days—for a high Mass was supposed to mark the maximum offering one could make. People could—and did—have the Mass offered free, gratis.

"And what was the stipend for?" he continued. "It was supposed to be for the upkeep of the clergy. But, I ask you, did any people who gave a stipend for a Mass or a baptism or a wedding or a funeral think the money was going to buy food for the clergy?"

"I don't know."

"I don't think so. I think they thought they were paying

161

for the Mass or the ceremony. And as often as we told them—and we told them often—that you can't 'buy' a Mass, they would say, 'Yes, Father, but how much is the Mass?' "

Mary laughed. "I guess you're right. People come to the rectory now to schedule a date for a wedding or to have a Mass said for the departed and they ask how much it is. Except I've never gone into the real purpose of a stipend with them—mostly because till now I didn't know. I just tell them how much it is."

"I know. Who could blame you? That's the way their minds are set and there's nothing really you can do about it. So, mark my words, money by the buckets is going to be pouring into that little monastery, and it's going to be pouring in right away. There won't be any struggle to get money. There'll be a lot of donors pushing and shoving to get the monks to accept the money and work a miracle for them."

"I still can't see what's wrong. Don't you think the monks will put the money to good use?"

"I don't know. I don't really know. There's that adage that power corrupts and absolute power corrupts absolutely. I have a hunch the same sort of thing can happen with money. What did Jesus say about it being easier for a camel to pass through the eye of a needle than for a rich man to enter the kingdom of heaven . . . ?

"But, forget the money for the moment. The big thing is that all those people are going to be expecting their own private miracles through the intercession of this Father Robert. And I don't think they're going to get them."

"You think Father Robert is not for real?"

"I don't know and I've got no way of knowing." He shook his head. "Although I did tell Moe Blair I'd look into it. One thing for sure: I don't know how long the diocese can let this go on without giving some direction to the faithful. Sooner than later, Cardinal Boyle is going to have to make a judgment on this miracle business. I only know

I'd hate to be the one who has to investigate this business. Think of the pressure!''

"Oh, I agree with you completely. I'd hate to have to investigate.''

"Speaking of pressure—and hope and joy and all sorts of positive Christian virtues," Koesler gave Mary a sly smile, ". . . which council members won't be at tonight's meeting?''

"Well," Mary said, with her own version of a sly smile, "I've got good news and bad news. . . .''

"Don't jump.''

Pringle McPhee didn't jump, but she did start. She had been so lost in thought that she hadn't heard Pat Lennon approach.

Pringle had been gazing out the window and paying attention to nothing she was looking at. "I don't think I'll jump," she said. "We're not up high enough; I'd only hurt myself.''

They were in the city room on the second floor of the Detroit News.

Pat looked concerned. "That bad?''

Pringle turned from the uninspiring sight of Lafayette Boulevard to look directly at Pat. "It's the whole damn thing. The weather as much as anything. Looks like it's going to rain.''

Pat knit her brows. "Rain was never that bad.''

"Let's get some coffee." As they left the window, Pringle added, "It's not just the weather, of course.''

"It's Fred.''

"He's not sure he can swing that trip for the two of us to New York.''

"What happened?''

"His wife. She wants to go with him.''

"Does she suspect?''

"I don't think so. She says she just wants to do some shopping. But he can't talk her out of it.''

"I don't blame her. If I were married to somebody with

Fred's money and I wanted to go to New York with him and spend some of that money, by damn I'd go.''

"But we *planned* it. I was counting on it.''

"Pringle, she doesn't know about you . . . remember? She's hardly going to step aside so you and Fred can frolic in the Big Apple.''

"I know. I know. But I was *so* looking forward to it.''

Pat could think of nothing further to say. She felt sorry for Pringle. But that was seemingly forever the fate of the odd person out in a ménage à trois. She got them both some coffee and led the way back to her desk.

"That was a good piece you did on what's-her-name—the miracle lady,'' Pringle said as she pulled up a chair.

"Anne Whitehead? Thanks. The interesting thing was how much of her sight was restored: not the whole shot; just back to where she was before she went blind.''

"Yeah, that is interesting.''

"If this had been Lourdes, she wouldn't have been able to hang her glasses on the wall.''

"Huh?''

"Never mind.''

"Did you get an exclusive on that? I haven't seen any other interviews with her.''

Pat bit her lip to keep from smiling. "Thereby hangs a tale . . . or, almost.''

"Huh?''

"Never mind. How did it go with the deputy mayor?''

Pringle became animated. "I think the mayor's got his ass in a sling this time. You know that money the city got to provide bullet-proof vests for the police department? Well, it's been diverted to a waterfront project that happens to be right at the foot of the Manoogian Mansion—the mayor's residence.''

"You can substantiate that?''

"Almost. One more source and I've got it. I'm waiting for that phone call now.''

Pat fingered her hair thoughtfully. "That's right,'' she said, "you cover the police beat, don't you?''

"Uh-huh. Why?"

"Know anybody named Tully? Alonzo Tully? He's a lieutenant . . . Homicide."

"Zoo? Sure. Everybody knows Zoo. He's one of the best cops in the department."

"How well do you know him?"

Pringle looked slightly offended. "Not that well. There's Fred, you know."

Pat's tone suggested impatience. "I didn't mean *that*. Is he married?"

Pringle gave it a moment's thought. "I don't think so. No, I'm pretty sure not. Maybe he's divorced," she added brightly.

"Hmmm."

"The reason I'm pretty sure he's not married is because he's living with somebody."

"Oh?"

"Yeah. She's a social worker, with the county. I got it from—hey, wait a minute: you and Zoo?"

"Nothing like that. I met him last night for the first time. Seems like a nice guy."

"As far as I know, he is a nice guy. But mostly a take-charge type. If you hang around cops very much, like I do, you get to know what they're like from their reputation with the other cops. Most of them are honest and work hard. A few are showboats. There's even a Dirty Harry or two. But I've never heard a bad word about Zoo Tully. He came up the hard way. And on the way up, he established contacts he can cash in now.

"I mean, what can I tell you? He spent some time in vice and what's he got to show for it but a whole bunch of hookers who have complete trust in him. They'd tell him anything he wanted to know. And that's the way everybody is with him.

"The other night, for instance: He killed a punk who shot one of his men."

"I know about that. I read your story."

"Yes, but then a couple of days later he broke up a

robbery, armed—singled-handed—and nabbed the two guys who did it.''

"Yesterday? He did that yesterday? I hadn't heard about that.''

"I wrote it. It's in today's paper.''

"He didn't even mention it. When did it happen?''

"Yesterday, late afternoon.''

"God! That had to be just a few hours before I met him. And he didn't even mention it.''

"See? I told you. He's different. Even for a tough cop, he's different.''

Pat looked away and twisted a strand of hair.

Pringle watched her for a moment. "You would have been lots happier if I'd said he was unattached, wouldn't you?''

Pat was almost flustered, rare for her. "Don't be silly. I just met the guy last night.''

"I know Joe Cox is a very good reporter, but, honest, I don't think he can hold a candle to Zoo Tully.''

"Who asked him to?''

"There's nothing permanent about an understanding like the one you and Joe have.''

Pat made no response.

"And there's probably nothing written in stone about the relationship Zoo and his live-in have.''

Reflectively, Pat said, "There's nothing permanent about anything.''

"See? If Joe hadn't bugged out on you, you probably wouldn't have given Zoo any more than the time of day. But Joe's not here and you resent it. And, from all I know, the same with Zoo. There must be something shady in his relationship or he wouldn't have 'met' you. Kismet. Fate.''

"Say,'' Pat looked at her, "just who is supposed to be advising whom here?''

"Pat, you're my friend, maybe my best friend. Sometimes an outsider can just see things more clearly than somebody who's involved.''

"Okay, okay. We'll just see what kismet has in store.''

Pringle's phone was ringing. As she hurried to her desk, Pat called after her, "Pringle, what are you doing after work? Maybe we could spend the evening—"

"Can't. I'm seeing Fred. Maybe tomorrow night."

Pat shrugged and smiled. What a crazy world. Pringle's going hell-bent for leather down a dead-end street. Fred has one of those ideal arrangements: the wife, the family, respectability—and a most desirable young woman on the side. Anybody could write the scenario. And at the end, after the fat lady sings, Pringle will be forced to see the light, left with a large share of nothing.

But what of her own status? Pat had to admit that Pringle, even without being privy to the particulars, had been dead on target. If Cox had not pulled that sophomoric stunt, she never would have gone to a singles bar, let alone met and become—admit it, gal—infatuated with this cop.

Not that Zoo Tully was not a captivating, attractive man. He very definitely was. She just wished she could pinpoint what made him so special.

But Pringle was right: Pat was simply not the type to cheat—even without a marriage contract. Hell, she wasn't the type to even flirt. Not when she was in love. So, like it or not, something had happened to her relationship with Joe Cox. Otherwise last night, innocent as it was, would not have happened.

And, damn it, Pringle was probably right in her evaluation of Zoo's behavior. There was nothing about him, nothing Pringle had told her, nothing she could infer, that indicated he was more than a one-woman man. So what was he doing in a singles bar? Why had he made contact with her? It had been a pickup on his part, with total and wholehearted consent on hers. Why? Something must have happened in his relationship with his woman.

If so, something had happened to both of them. Perhaps Pringle was right—kismet. Pat's eyes narrowed. We'll just have to see where this goes.

* * *

Lieutenant Tully had checked with Inspector Koznicki and arranged to take time to bring Alice to St. Stephen's Monastery. Now he was up to his elbows in paperwork. There was so much paper to shuffle on an ordinary work day that when that day was compressed by personal business, things could get out of hand.

Most of his squad was out solving murders, just as they should. Alone in the squad room with Tully was Sergeant Angela Moore. Both were completing routine reports. So procedurally dull were these reports that both Tully and Moore felt free to converse as they worked. Indeed, Tully had already confided that he was taking Alice to a faith healer this afternoon.

Moore knew of Alice's illness, and, while she sympathized, she, like Tully, had little confidence in preachers, especially the type who claimed healing powers.

Without looking up, Tully asked, "Any word on Mangiapane?"

Moore continued to check off boxes in her report. "I called earlier this morning. They're using that 'as well as can be expected' line. But then I talked to the nurse on his floor. Lucky I made friends with her yesterday. He's doin' fine. They got him up and walkin' around. Before you know it, we'll be seein' his ugly Eyetalian face around here."

"Good. Good." At least there was some good news today.

"Just in case you get the false impression that everything today is upbeat," Moore said, "did you hear the latest about those two turkeys you got yesterday?"

"The R.A.? No."

"They're out."

"That fast." It didn't surprise him. For one thing, there was no room in jail. Not that this fact alone would influence a decision to release someone who had just been arrested. Overfilled cells usually squeezed out convicts at the other end of the scale of justice. Due to the lack of room, cons regularly had their sentences commuted to make space for new admissions. However, judges were well aware of the lack of cots. So bail was easier to make than it should be.

"Guess who they came up with for a lawyer?" Without waiting for his answer, she said, "Ken Crockett."

"Crockett." Tully accorded the name a sense of respect. "Where'd they get the retainer?"

"I dunno. Maybe they had better luck robbin' stores before you caught 'em."

Tully smiled. "Maybe. But I don't know how they'd get away with that. Their M.O. yesterday was nothing to write home about."

"Crockett'll probably get them dressed up like college dudes. Their first bath in years."

"Uh-huh. Jury says, 'How could those nice boys do such a thing?' and they walk."

"That's okay. We'll see 'em again. Next time they'll probably be lyin' on a slab."

"Yeah."

"Better to use a shortcut and take 'em out right off the bat. Like Dave Powell." No sooner were the words out of her mouth than she regretted them. Tully was still tender about having killed the young man. Moore knew it. Momentarily it had slipped her mind. "Sorry."

"It's okay."

They worked on their records in silence for a while. Then Tully spoke. "By the way, Angie, do you know a Patricia Lennon?"

Moore let the name roll around her memory. "Doesn't ring a bell, Zoo."

"Reporter at the *News*. Pretty good."

"She ever been on the police beat?"

"I don't know. I don't think so."

"Then, like as not I don't know her. Why? Anything special?"

"No. I met her last night. Just wondered if you knew her."

Moore's intuitive reflexes triggered. She knew Tully. She knew the telltale tones of his voice. She was well aware of the value he placed on privacy. These questions were out of character for Zoo Tully. Moore felt sure she knew what he was driving at. She just didn't know why. He was so completely devoted to Alice. It didn't make sense.

But he was Zoo Tully, her boss, her friend, and one of the most special people she'd ever known. For him she'd find out.

Abruptly, Moore left the squad room. She found an empty office, dialed several times until the number she was calling was free. She talked longer than she had expected. By the time she returned to the squad room, Tully, having wrapped up all the paperwork he would complete this day, was preparing to leave.

"I got the info on Pat Lennon."

"Oh?" He hesitated, then finished pulling on his jacket. But he was going nowhere until he heard what she had to say.

"Lennon is maybe the top reporter at the *News*. Maybe in the whole city. She used to work at the Freep. She left there at a time when a lot of them were moving to the *News*. She's divorced. Happened a long time ago. She never re-married. Like I said, by consensus she may be the best reporter in town. If she's not, then Joe Cox at the Freep is."

"Him I know."

"The funny thing is that not only are they the two best reporters around, they live together. Have for years."

Moore was watching Tully intently. Although he wore his usual prime poker expression, she thought she caught a glimmer of disappointment over the relationship. But she was no longer guessing. She had just learned that Lennon had been asking about Tully.

"This is the kicker: They've had a falling out. Sort of a serious disagreement. At the moment, Cox is covering the Mackinac Race. The way things stand now, it's possible they may never get back together. End of report." She had watched observantly as she told of their tiff. But this time Zoo remained expressionless.

170

"Amazing, Angie. Where'd you get all that in a few minutes?"

"Uh-uh." She shook her head. "I got to protect my sources." Then she laughed. "I talked to Mac—Pringle McPhee. She works the police beat for the *News*."

"Yeah, I know her."

"Well, it just so happens she's a friend of Lennon's. I'll admit I lucked out on this one. I figured Mac had to know Lennon. I hadn't figured they were buddies."

He thanked her and left. He was running a tad behind on his schedule. He had to pick up Alice at home and get her to the church by noon. He had just enough time to accomplish all that if nothing unforeseen happened. He liked to leave a little margin for error.

As he drove through late morning traffic, he had lots to think about.

After meeting Pat, talking to her, getting to know her at least a bit, he was certain she could not be completely unattached. The good news was that she was not married. The bad news, of course, was that she had been living with someone for a long time. But then, a turn for the better: There might be a breakup.

As he arrived at this thought, he forced himself to back away from it. What was he doing? What was he thinking?

He could never do that to Alice. She was ill—and to a significant extent, helpless. She relied on him almost completely. On top of it all he would freely admit that he loved her.

Still, it had been a long time since they'd been intimate. A very long time. Longer for him than any period he could recall in his adult life. And there were no express commitments between them.

The problem they had both anticipated might try their relationship was his symbiotic attachment to his work. That had been the main cause of the termination of his marriage. It had happened once, it could happen again. He had made certain sure at the outset of their life together that Alice understood the preeminence of his work. The understanding was that if she found it impossible to take second place to his job, there would be a parting of the ways, as amicably as possible. And that was why there was no marriage.

They hadn't bargained on an illness as encompassing and sustained as that which she was now suffering. They hadn't bargained on a caretaker relationship. They hadn't foreseen Pat Lennon's wandering into his life at this critical period.

Things were happening a little too fast, even for Zoo Tully. He needed time to think. Thing were verging on getting out of hand. And he liked to be in control.

Well, what the hell, all he had to do for now was get Al to the church on time. Time enough to consider the rest of it later. Maybe this was a juncture when a firm control of destiny might be impossible. Maybe it was up to fate. Maybe leaving it in the hands of fate was not such a bad idea.

CHAPTER
12

It was just five minutes before noon when Tully drove his elderly, battered, but serviceable, Ford into the area of Bushey and Michigan Avenue. He had expected a crowd, but not this. It was difficult to tell whether people were going into or coming out of the old bank building.

Actually, it was both. Some who had come early enough to get a spot inside had been overcome either by the oppressive heat and humidity or by the emotion of the moment. The ill almost equaled the curious as literally hundreds crowded the sidewalk and overflowed into the streets.

George Fielding, the uniformed officer in charge, was managing things as well as possible under so many and such unpredictable demands. He recognized Tully just as another officer began waving the lieutenant away from the building. In short order, Fielding had an officer take the car; then he ushered Tully and Alice through the crowd and, incredibly, to a fairly good location inside the chapel.

"Al," Tully leaned down and spoke loudly enough to be

heard over the steady murmur of the crowd, "you sure you want to go through with this?"

She closed her eyes and gritted her teeth. But she nodded. There was nowhere else for her to go. She had put all her eggs in this basket.

"Okay," Tully said, "but let me know the second you want out."

Tully began to take stock—the surroundings, the people. He couldn't help himself. By now, taking stock was part of his nature.

Obviously, the place had been a bank. Equally as obvious, it had been erected back when they cared how buildings were put together. This place had been built to last. Lots of brick, a good measure of marble, and the genuine terrazzo floor. They just didn't build them like this anymore.

Tully hoped the bank's conversion into a church—a monastery—was a temporary thing. What they'd done to the place made it look like a bordello. The plasterboard definitely did not blend with the building's solid construction. And if they could not afford stained glass windows, they should have left them alone. Painting over the panes succeeded only in creating what seemed an almost purposeful attempt to dull the spirit. It was so dark in here it had taken several minutes for his eyesight to adjust.

He looked around at the people. Nobody here with the Whiteheads' money that he could see. Some of the building's neighbors. Stolid, Slavic faces. Women in babushkas tied tightly about their heads even in this heat. They would never appear in a church without covering their heads. Some of the Michigan Avenue regulars. Bums, drifters, people who lived on and off the street, beggars hoping some part of the ceremony would include a handout. A few middle- to upper-middle-class individuals. Some merely curious but most of them looking, hoping, for something, for their own miracle.

He looked down at Al. Her eyes still tightly closed, tears sliding down her cheeks. She, as much as, or more than

174

anyone else there, desperate for the healing miracle.

Suddenly he was very angry. He was sure this was some sort of bunco scam. For starters, he did not trust any form of organized religion. Experience had taught him that their top priority was to preserve themselves. After which, anywhere from next to one-hundredth on the list, they served their members.

There were plenty of collection baskets in this old bank; Tully could only imagine the unsolicited donations that were pouring in from a wide variety of contributors—everyone from believers who blindly wished to further the cause to people who wanted to buy a miracle.

The pity was in individuals like little Alice here, who was so desperate for help that she was willing to believe today what she hadn't believed yesterday. And so intensely wrapped up in this last-ditch hope that she wept openly.

He promised himself that if this proved to be the fraud he suspected, he would personally make sure that these guys paid.

Then he saw her. He wouldn't have, if someone hadn't shifted position. Tully was not tall enough to see over this crowd, and Pat Lennon was only about Al's size.

But there she was, standing back against the rear wall, undoubtedly covering this event for the *News*. When he caught sight of her, all the thoughts, the speculation about her returned in a flood.

He had to put them, and her, out of his mind, at least for the present. To check out this operation, he would have to pay close attention. And evidently, the event was about to begin.

A bell sounded, as an abbreviated parade of monks made their way from behind the main partition to the homemade altar.

They were covered from head to toe.

Tully had never seen a monk in person before, only pictures. Three of them took positions at one side of the altar. A fourth positioned himself alone at the other side. He didn't fit in. He was so much bigger than the others.

The final person evidently was the priest. He was wearing Mass vestments. He was the only one whose face was visible. Even so, in this abysmal lighting, it was impossible to make out his features.

With the entry of the monks the crowd noise diminished markedly. It grew steadily quieter as several people made shushing sounds.

The priest bowed low and, tracing a sign of the cross on himself, intoned, *"In nomine Patris, et Filii, et Spiritus Sancti."* Almost everyone responded, "Amen."

"Dominus vobiscum," the priest said. To which fewer people responded, *"Et cum spiritu tuo."*

Tully pondered that. He'd thought Catholics got rid of Latin years ago. He knew next to nothing about the religion, but had, in the course of duty and friendship, attended numerous weddings and funerals. Many years ago the priests had used Latin. Then, for the past twenty or so years, everything had been in English. Now they were back to Latin. He wondered why, if only because he wanted to learn all he could about this operation. If the need to bust them arose, he wanted to know what he was doing. He'd have to ask somebody who knew what was going on here.

The priest looked at a card he was holding, and read, *"Fratres, agnoscamus peccata nostra, ut apti simus ad sacra mysteria celebranda."*

As far as she could translate it, leaning on her nearly forgotten courses in Latin, Pat Lennon thought it meant something like: Brothers, let us know our sins so that we can better celebrate these sacred mysteries.

The Latin swept her back many years, to her days in a Catholic girls' college and even further back to her parochial grade and high schools.

Now, outside of select occasions, she no longer attended Mass. But she had followed the proceedings and consequences of Vatican II. Aware of the role of the vernacular in the liturgy, she knew that the use of Latin here was a statement. Undoubtedly, it identified this group as staunchly conservative.

She remembered enough from her days as a faithful Mass-goer to know that the formula being used here was not the one with which she had grown up. In the Old Mass—what did they call it?—the Tridentine, she thought—in that old format there was no invitation to recall sins so as to prepare one for a worthier celebration of the Mass.

All of which indicated that, while the little group was solidly conservative, it was not off-the-wall conservative. They were observing the letter of the law. It was a Latin Mass, but the approved version of the Latin Mass.

Brother Bernard gave the first reading. Bernard was the only one besides Father Robert and Brother Paul who knew Latin. He finished the reading and announced, *"Verbum Domini,"* to which only those in the makeshift sanctuary replied, *"Deo gratias."*

Shortly thereafter, Father Robert read the Gospel, first in Latin, then in English.

It was obvious to Tully that something was wrong. The priest seemed unwell. Tully could not testify to the Latin reading, but when the priest switched to English, he faltered several times, as if it was difficult for him to make out the text.

After the Gospel, those in the sanctuary sat down, as did those few in the congregation who were fortunate enough to have found one of the few chairs. The rest remained standing.

"You sure you're okay?" Tully asked Alice.

Again she nodded. Her eyes remained closed, as if she was concentrating with all her strength on something Tully could not fathom. Prayer?

Father Robert began to speak. Those who had attended Mass here before were familiar with the ritual. This would be a brief homily. But the regulars were puzzled over Father's delivery. He spoke in a halting voice. It required a determined effort to hear him. They wondered about that.

Pat Lennon had flipped open her notepad and was scribbling in her own version of shorthand. Her frown that had appeared when the priest began to speak grew more pronounced as he continued. Not only was he difficult to hear, he seemed to be speaking at best nonsense, at worst gibberish.

Initially, he spoke of St. Stephen, as the patron and model of their order. Stephen the protomartyr, the first martyr of the then brand-new Christian Church. Stephen who challenged those who hated Jesus and had been instrumental in His execution. Stephen who drove the enemies of Jesus mad with his fearless defense of Christianity.

All well and good, thought Pat, but what did that have to do with anything? As far as she could tell, there was no connection between what Father Robert was talking about and today's Scripture readings.

With no segue whatever, the priest shifted into the topic of birth control. Pat, of course, was aware that the topic was near and dear to the hierarchy and to practically no one else. But even for a conservative Catholic priest, this guy was stretching things.

He insisted that married people who limit their family to one or two children are selfish and that there is almost never a serious, positive, valid reason for such a limitation. He questioned how a married couple, whose prime function is the procreation and education of children, could be so selfish and ungrateful to the all-generous God who gave them their responsibility to increase and multiply and fill the earth.

Tully gave up trying to follow Father Robert's train of thought. Catholics might get something out of it; he was more concerned with the priest's unsteadiness.

The lieutenant's restless gaze fell on the monk he thought of as, for want of the actual name, the Big One. The Big One, in a decidedly restrained way, seemed quite concerned about the priest. In consequence of his barely discernible movements, the Big One's cowl would rise slightly, as if the monk were trying to get a better view of the priest. Several times the monk seemed about to rise from his chair and do something. But each time he stayed seated.

Father Robert, in apparent free-flowing association, began to combine his two unrelated themes.

"St. Stephen," the priest said, "laid down his life for Christ, who had just given His life for sinners—for all of us. Sacrifice for sacrifice. And children in a family are a gift from God, just as is martyrdom. And children bring sacrifices, many sacrifices. But that is how a man and wife come ever closer together: through generous sacrifice. You don't see good Christian parents enjoying themselves. They know the importance of sacrifice. St. Stephen watered the fertile ground of the Church with his martyr's blood. And married people should always look upon their marital bed as an altar on which great sacrifices are offered."

Lennon raised an eyebrow in disbelief. She looked about, attempting to gauge the expressions of those whose faces she could see. By and large, most of the congregation seemed to have tuned out this priest and his strange notions of family life. What little emotion she could detect in the crowd seemed to be impatience. They were not here for sermons. They were looking for something else, undoubtedly miracles.

Then she saw Tully. He appeared to be totally engrossed in what was going on. He was staring straight ahead at the sanctuary. His gaze did not waver to one side or the other.

Why was he here? This had nothing to do with Homicide. Could he be with someone? Lennon shifted position as much as the press of the crowd allowed. Gradually she was able to assemble a composite picture of the area immediately around Tully. She could see no one who evidenced any connection with the lieutenant. Having been advised by Pringle that Tully was living with someone, Pat searched specifically for a black woman. But there were few black women or men in the audience, and none of them was anywhere near Tully.

She returned her attention to the pulpit, where the priest seemed to be winding up his rambling, disjointed sermon.

"And so, my dear children, let us pray that we may have the strength of faith that St. Stephen had. That we will welcome sacrifice and that we will welcome children into our families so that sacrifice will mark our daily lives."

With that, he seemed to falter. The crowd, sensing something was wrong, inched forward en masse. However, instantly, Brother Paul was at the priest's side, assisting him and motioning the congregation back.

Brother Paul supported Father Robert while he spoke to him quietly but with obvious intensity.

"You've got to get through this, old man!" Brother Paul spoke only loudly enough to be heard at extremely close range.

"I . . . I don't think I can," Father Robert gasped.

"You've got to. We'll help you." Paul nodded at Brother Bernard, who quickly joined them at the altar.

Bernard was agitated, though it was all but impossible to tell with his face hidden by the cowl. "This is your fault, you know," he said to Paul. "You shouldn't have been so hard on him last night."

"That's enough! Drop it! Now!" Brother Paul bit off the words.

Bernard reacted as if struck. Silently, he took a position opposite Paul at the side of the priest.

A murmur rose from the crowd, but, again, it was effectively shushed.

The Mass proceeded through the offertory ritual, the prayers of the Canon, and on to Communion. Father Robert could not have collapsed had he wished to. Brother Paul and Bernard had positioned themselves as if extensions of the priest.

Throughout Communion the priest slumped in his chair while the Brothers offered a wafer and a sip of the consecrated wine to each of those who came forward.

After Communion, the Mass quickly came to an end.

The crowd moved forward purposefully, with individuals jockeying for position closer to the sanctuary, either to seek favors from Father Robert or to listen in on those who did. Brother Paul's commanding voice stopped them as if they had run into an invisible wall. "There will be no blessings today. Father Robert is not well, as you can see. Come back tomorrow. He will be better then.''

There were angry sounds. They had perspired through a deadly dull sermon and a ceremony that could have been duplicated or surpassed in almost any Catholic church anywhere. This—the time of blessings, the possibility of a circus miracle—this is what they had come for. They were disappointed and angry and primed to demand the show they had been anticipating.

Brother Paul turned fully toward the congregation as the other Brothers assisted the priest from the sanctuary. In his habit, his countenance shrouded in shadow, Paul resembled nothing so much as the Grim Reaper. He pointed to the door and commanded, ''Leave! Now!''

It was a tribute to his bearing that the crowd's movement halted, then reversed. Now, instead of advancing toward the altar, they were retreating toward the exit.

Tully and Alice were singular in not being swept up in the crowd's ebb. As the ceremony drew to a close, it had become clear to Tully that either this priest was ill or he was giving an award-winning performance. The lieutenant was certain there would be no encore to the Mass. So, sometime prior to Brother Paul's announcement, Tully had begun to ease a protesting Alice toward the exit. The two were almost out of the building by the time Paul ordered everyone to leave.

The only notable exceptions to the mass exodus were the media representatives. They moved against the crowd, clamoring for Brother Paul's attention.

Paul stood his ground and dealt with them, so far as he was able, one at a time. Not wishing to alienate the news media—he needed them to spread the news of the miracle worker—he was as mollifying as possible. But placating as his words were, he remained immovably firm: No one was going to talk with Father Robert until he felt better. Very possibly it would be tomorrow, at which time he would try to get each of them some time alone with Father.

One by one, he got rid of them. Ultimately, each was convinced that no matter how abusive their editors would be when they returned with no story, those editors would be easier to face than this implacable monk.

And now, they were gone. All but one.

She stood against the wall, coolly taking in Brother Paul's performance. In all the hubbub between him and the media, she had remained aloof. It was her attitude that piqued Paul's interest and curiosity.

After an extended period of silence between them, the only two people left in the chapel, Brother Paul spoke. "Did you just come in?"

Lennon shook her head.

"Then," Paul said, "you know that Father Robert is not well. Come back tomorrow."

"My name is Lennon . . . Pat Lennon. I'm with the Detroit *News*."

Now he recognized her. She was the one in the singles bar last night. The one with the black boyfriend. So, she's a reporter.

"Look," he spoke with some asperity, "if you've been here all this while, you heard me tell those other reporters to come back tomorrow."

"I heard."

"Wait . . ." He regarded her more intently. "You're the one who had that interview with the Whitehead woman, aren't you?"

"That's right."

"Was that an exclusive? I didn't see any other firsthand interview."

"You're right; it was an exclusive." She tilted her head. "I didn't think monks read papers, watched TV, or listened to radio . . . or otherwise got involved with the outside world."

"We have to know who and what to pray for."

So this knockout broad who fancies black studs got an exclusive chat with the elusive miracle child! He wondered how she had finagled that. Probably seduced somebody—

maybe the old bitch's husband. Then what the hell was she trying for now? Another exclusive? Was she about to offer a quid pro quo? Another definition of fat chance. Oh, it would be fun, no doubt about that. But he was not about to compromise this caper for a quick roll in the hay with anybody, no matter how sexy she looked.

"I'm afraid you're going to have to leave now," he said. "Father Robert is just as indisposed as far as you're concerned as he is for everybody else. Come back tomorrow like the others; I'll see you get some time with him."

"That's nice. And I'll hold you to it. But right now I don't want to interview him."

"I thought—"

"I want to talk to you."

Looking on as the other reporters were being summarily dismissed, she realized she could never get through to the priest today. That's when she had decided to go for an interview with the sergeant-major Brother.

This was an unexpected tack. He studied her more closely. His better judgement, all his finely honed instincts, told him to stonewall this woman. She could be trouble. Lots of it. But other, compelling inner voices made themselves heard.

If she was going to become a problem he'd better be tuned in to what she was doing and what she intended. Better to know what the enemy was up to than be surprised and taken unawares. Besides, it was possible that this broad had a good brain as well as a great body. Matching wits with her might be a worthy game.

"Just a few minutes, then." He gestured toward a couple of nearby chairs.

Pat sat on one of the chairs, crossed her legs, flipped open her notepad, and waited. He took the other chair, moved it further from her, and sat down.

She noted the maneuver. The darkened interior of this building, his cowl, and the angle at which he sat made it impossible for her to see his face. The ploy disturbed her. She had no doubt that he intended to hide from her.

However, there was little she could do about the situation. A complaint would probably terminate the interview and put an end to any chance of progress on the story for today. So, on with what little she had to work with. "You read my story today, so you know that Mrs. Whitehead had her sight restored only to the extent she had before she went blind." She paused, looking for some reaction from the robed figure. There was none.

So she proceeded. "Did you know that that was the case?"

"Before I read your account? No."

"Does it trouble you?"

"That she hasn't got perfect sight? No."

"I would have thought . . . okay, scratch that." Pat looked up at one of the painted windows. It was as useless as looking at the hooded figure opposite her. She would try a different approach. "Was this Father Robert's first miracle?"

"Hard to say. I suppose it depends on what you think a miracle is. He prayed with and for others. Often enough they improved. Sometimes they recovered completely. Some of those prayers were for a job, for health, for family problems. A lot of those prayers were answered: Were they miracles?"

A no-nonsense tone crept into her voice. "I think you know what I mean . . . Brother . . ."

"Paul."

"Brother Paul." She recorded his name in her notepad and her memory. "Mrs. Whitehead's experience was major league. It separates the men from the boys. More: It separates prayers that may have an effect sometime in the future from an instantaneous cure. Did he ever . . . was he ever responsible for anything like this before?"

Brother Paul hesitated. His cowl tipped forward, suggesting that he might be pondering the reply. "To the best of my knowledge," he said finally, "no. This was the first time."

"Then"—her tone indicated that this was what she was

184

getting at—"when do you think the Church is going to get involved in this?"

Even though he was hooded, his body English made it obvious that this question had taken him by surprise. "The Church? What . . . what do you mean?"

"The Roman Catholic Church. You're got a Lourdes-like miracle on your hands. Thanks to the news media, the report of this is going around the country—the world. People will be flocking here in droves. People from around the country, maybe from other countries. I've read enough about events like this to know that eventually the Church puts its Good Housekeeping Seal of Approval on this miracle—these miracles, there's bound to be more—or, more often, the Church withholds its approval. When's it going to happen?"

Had Pat been able to see inside the cowl, she would have noted that Brother Paul's face was bathed in perspiration.

With effort to keep any semblance of agitation out of his voice, he said, "I would have no way of knowing the answer. We have no interest beyond giving witness to the Lord by our lives. Your guess is as good as mine."

"Well, then, how does it take place? All I've ever read is the conclusion of some sort of inquiry, or examination. Who conducts such an examination? Who appoints the presiding official? What are the procedures in such a study?" She paused. Enough questions for the moment.

The pause persisted. Brother Paul was not considering the answers. He was, rather, most concerned that he had given no detailed forethought to these questions. According to his carefully made plans, this affair was to be concluded long before any outside officials entered the picture. In fact, he had not envisioned any meddling on the part of any Church authority. But then, he hadn't anticipated that there might be a spectacular miracle.

However, of more immediacy, he had to respond to Lennon's questions.

He finally spoke. "You must understand, Miss Lennon, that the five of us are not canon lawyers. We are just simple monks. None of us anticipated this kind of event. Quite honestly, we don't know what to expect. But we're here. If the Church wishes to examine what we are doing, I'm sure the Church has the wherewithal to do it.''

Pat considered the matter. "How long have you been in Detroit, Brother Paul?"

"Not long. A matter of months.''

"Then you're not familiar with how this Archdiocese of Detroit functions.''

A bit defensively, "The Congregation knew enough to choose to locate here.''

"And a good choice you made. But what you might not know is that the Archbishop, Cardinal Boyle, doesn't like trouble. He's had enough of it. Vatican II happened here like almost nowhere else in the world, with the possible exception of the Netherlands. When all the changes of the Council hit the fan in Detroit, things turned upside down. The local Church was picketed by dissidents from the right and left wings, but mostly the right.''

She shrugged lightly. "No need to go into all that spun off from the Council. Enough to say that Cardinal Boyle had grown a little gun-shy with all that's gone on in this archdiocese. Typically, if a problem pops up here that does not cry to heaven for a quick decision, the usual Chancery m.o. is to appoint a blue-ribbon committee to study the matter forever. And my guess is that that's what would happen to your miracle—unless something hits the fan and forces the Archdiocese of Detroit to get off the dime and do something about it.''

Brother Paul turned his head just enough to look at her face. She was gazing off into the distance, but even had she been looking at him, she still could not have seen his features.

Her expression telegraphed her thoughts. She was about to make this major story distinctively hers by finding a way to get the investigation started. She would start the avalanche!

His first inclination had been correct. This woman was

trouble. She had intended all along to interview Father Robert. Only when she became convinced that this would be impossible because he, Brother Paul, would not permit it did she change tactics. She'd get her story by interviewing him.

But Brother Paul did not for a moment regret talking to her. As he had concluded earlier, better to know what potential enemies were planning than be surprised by them.

He had thought he had anticipated all eventualities. For the first time in his life, failure would not dog him. It had been such a tidy little scheme, well worth his investment of time and trouble. But he had not anticipated an official investigation for the simple reason that he had no grounds to expect a spectacular miracle.

Even now, there was no clear indication of any sort of investigation looming. This troublesome broad probably was right: This was not the sort of diocese that went around buying trouble pell-mell.

If that was true, then exactly what would make the bishop take some sort of action? His experience in reading news accounts of miracles was the same as Pat Lennon's: Inevitably, after a purported apparition or miracle, there would be some form of study done on it, usually followed by a disclaimer. Yet her questions were his. Who? What? Where? Why? How? The average Catholic, even one who had studied in a seminary, would have no way of knowing the mechanics of such an investigation.

One thing seemed certain: This young woman was going to do her best to make it happen. And if she could bring it about, she'd be near the center of the story. She'd have a beat on every other reporter in town. She'd already stacked up one exclusive with her interview of the Whitehead woman. No, there was more: She had also inveigled this interview with him. While the other reporters would be forced to face fuming editors armed only with a pale account of a simple Latin Mass and a boring sermon enlivened only by an unexpected illness of the miracle worker, Lennon could flesh out her story with quotes "from the inside."

It was, of course, possible that the dread investigation might commence any time now. It was just as possible that, unprovoked by any further incident or agency, it might well remain for the foreseeable future in an inactive file on the Cardinal's desk. And there, in a forgotten folder, was precisely where Brother Paul wanted this matter, if only for a few more days.

It was a case of simple deduction that the most serious threat to his hopes and plans was this Lennon woman. Well, Brother Paul had risen to more than one occasion. Right now, she was the major threat. But threats must be eliminated. Therefore . . .

The most important consideration was not to act rashly or incautiously. That had been one of his principal failings and he could not afford to be precipitate. He'd have to think it out. But he could do it. He knew that. All he needed was a little time. Time to check routines, activities, opportunities. Time to eliminate loose ends. Time to plan a perfect crime.

When he returned to the present from his deliberations, he was startled to find he was alone. Sometime during his absorption, Pat Lennon must have gotten up and left.

Just as well. He'd have a few quiet moments to examine his options. How appropriate that he had been left to himself in the church.

He turned to the tabernacle, a small, gold-plated boxlike structure, where, Catholics believe, Jesus resides under the appearance of the consecrated bread. He knelt before the tabernacle, conscious of the flickering red votive candle that silently indicated the presence of the Lord. He made the sign of the cross and, a smile playing about his lips, began to pray for the success of his plot to kill Pat Lennon.

WEDNESDAY
JULY 26

CHAPTER
13

"I really feel bad taking you away from work."

Alice sat as close to the open window as possible, fanning herself with a small lacy handkerchief.

"No problem." Tully carefully picked his spots, cutting in and out of traffic in an attempt to maintain a speed that would keep as much breeze as possible flowing through the vehicle.

"But two days in a row!"

Tully smiled ever so slightly. "I have a benevolent boss."

"I'm not worried about your boss. Walt Koznicki—and all the rest of us—probably would feel better if you ever took all the vacation time you're entitled to. It's just that I know how you feel about your work, and I'm taking you from it."

Tully sighed. "That's all we need, honey, for you to get all worked up and nervous. You don't want anything more bothering you than you got. So just relax. The squad is covering for me. Everything will be okay. Right now, you come first."

Alice turned her head to look squarely at him. "That's not true. We all know that."

"Right now it is true."

They rode on in silence.

At length, Alice spoke. "I wish it would rain and get it over with."

Tully nodded agreement. "One of those times when I wish we had air in the car."

"It's okay, it's just a little close." She continued waving the hanky, though all it moved was humid air.

More silence.

"Did you notice the *News* had the most complete story on Father Robert?"

"Uh-huh." Tully also noticed that Alice had not mentioned the reporter who wrote the story. It was a common enough occurrence. Readers rarely note bylines. Columnists whose photos run with their work are fairly well-known and recognized. But few readers pay attention to which staff writers author news stories. Tully well knew that the byline on the story to which Alice referred was that of Pat Lennon. But he did not mention this fact.

"I wonder why that is," Alice mused, as she looked idly out the open window. "I mean I, of course, took a more than ordinary interest in this story. So I paid particular attention. All the radio and TV stations and even the *Free Press* had was just the report that Father Robert had been ill. And then maybe a little speculation of what might be wrong. But the *News* ran that interview with the Brother. Plus the *News* raised the possibility of a Church investigation."

Why did he feel guilty? Nothing had happened. Granted, he had trampled all over his usual m.o. It *was* completely out of character for him to have gone to a singles bar and still more wildly out of the ordinary for him to have—face it—made a play for Pat Lennon. Of course, nothing had come of it. Still, he felt guilty.

"I hope they don't do it," Alice said, after a short pause.

"Do what?"

"Have that Church investigation."

Tully glanced briefly at her. "Honey," he said, "they have to."

"Why?"

"Alice, there are a whole bunch of bad guys out there lying, cheating, deceiving people. If I had a nickel for every fake faith healer, we could afford air-conditioning in this car. A better question is: Why not have the investigation?"

Alice was slow to respond. "It's all some of us have to hold on to," she said, finally, seeming to choke on the last couple of words. Abruptly, she pressed the handkerchief to her mouth. She made no further sound, but he could feel the silent sobs telegraphed through the car seat.

One more corner of Alice's world revealed itself to Tully.

Until now, he had not accurately gauged the bottomless reservoir of her despondency. Both he and Alice were practical people, at home with reality. Neither of them could do his or her job outside the realm of reality. He as a homicide detective, she as a social worker, were constantly involved with real people, situations, problems. It would be counterproductive for either of them to mix shadow with the substance of their lives.

But not for her. Not now. She was so depressed that she had made a faith healer her last-ditch straw. Reality would have told her that odds were heavily in favor of this priest's being no better than a pious fraud. Reality would have made her question what right she had to a miracle wrought by faith when she'd depended on faith so little in her life to date. Reality would have warned her of the consequences to her already deeply depressed state if this last-ditch effort were to fail.

She was so desperate that reality no longer mattered. She feared a routine investigation that might reveal the "miracle worker" to have no clothes. If it was all a myth, she'd rather believe in the fantasy than be crushed by reality.

They rode the rest of the way with their own unexpressed thoughts.

If anything, the crowd was larger than it had been yesterday. Today, however, Tully had made preparations. Earlier this morning, he had spoken with the officer in charge. By prearrangement, that officer met Tully's car at the far fringe of the crowd.

Sergeant Lukas smiled and touched his cap. "Mornin', Lieutenant. We got everything set for you."

"Thanks, Luke." Tully looked about. "Looks like rain."

"It'll miss a great chance if it don't."

Lukas had another officer take charge of Tully's car. Then he conducted Tully and Alice through the crowd to a desirable position in the chapel.

Well, thought Tully, we're gonna give this miracle worker every possible shot at Alice's problems. That was the good news. The bad news was that the increased humidity made it even more uncomfortable than it had been yesterday.

Having arrived early, and aided by her press credentials, Pat Lennon also had an advantageous position; she would be in close range of whatever would happen.

Early this morning, when she was preparing to leave for the *News* before heading to St. Stephen's, the possibility of encountering Tully again occurred to her.

She still had no clue as to why he had been at the chapel. While the crowd and then the reporters were being dismissed by Brother Paul, Pat had had no opportunity to check on Tully's whereabouts. She had been far too busy improvising a scheme that would enable her to get by that most determined Brother and come up with a reasonable story for the next upcoming edition. By the time she'd finished questioning Brother Paul, Zoo Tully was apparently long gone.

So, while it was impossible to figure out what he'd been doing there, the distinct possibility existed that whatever had brought him to the chapel yesterday would return him there today.

With that thought bouncing around the outskirts of her consciousness, Pat had gotten ready more for a date than for work. She had very carefully blow-dried her hair. She applied Chloe, her favorite perfume, which she rarely wore to work. She selected a French-made navy blue pleated skirt, a frilly silk blouse and a light, Italian-made cashmere cardigan, and topped it with a long strand of pearls. She had even shaved her legs and donned lace lingerie. One never knew.

She didn't notice Tully and Alice when they entered. But after they had been escorted to their select vantage, Lennon spotted him. Since she had no idea whom to look for, she was unaware that Tully was accompanied. Depending on what transpired here today it was just possible that she and Tully might go somewhere for a late lunch and then . . . well, who could tell. Her imagination painted vivid pictures of the two of them enjoying each other through the evening and night hours.

Her musing were shattered by the bell announcing the brief procession of Brothers and priest to the chapel's altar.

All was as it had been yesterday, including the soporific sermon. Only the commemorated saint du jour was different. And Father Robert's condition seemed considerably improved. The respite, or something, had seemingly done him a world of good.

The place came alive as the Mass ended and a queue began to form. Actually, two groups began to take shape. One group, in a more or less discernible line, formed to present themselves to Father Robert. The other group, by far the larger, pressed in as closely as possible in hopes of becoming spectators. The news media were part of the latter group.

Father Robert and Brother Paul were seated close together before the altar. Paul held the usual bag of relics. The other Brothers mingled with the crowd, trying to instill some measure of order. In this the Brothers were assisted today by several police officers, who, along with maintaining order, maneuvered Tully and Alice toward the head of the line. Only one person preceded them.

Lennon, with two of the sharpest elbows in captivity, and offering no apologies for using them, worked her way to the front of the crowd, the only print reporter to break through the television people, who always managed to garner prime positions.

Tully and Lennon caught sight of each other simultaneously. Each smiled briefly in recognition and then turned away. For no particular reason, Tully felt embarrassed. Perhaps because she would see Alice. He knew he should have told Lennon about Alice. On the other hand, she had not mentioned the *Free Press* reporter . . . what was his name? Cox. They had not been totally candid with each other. Should they have been? He could not decide.

She was frankly surprised to find him in a line of petitioners. He didn't belong there. He was not the type. She was confused.

Priest and Brother were ready. Speculation on the part of Tully and Lennon ended as each focused on the first of the supplicants. Sincere efforts throughout the chapel managed to muffle much of the noise one would expect from a crowd vying to get close to the action. Still, there was enough background sound that it was difficult to hear, even for those in the immediate area of the priest. Pat Lennon was able to get her tape recorder fairly close to the priest and his client.

First in line was an attractive young woman. Tully pondered that. Making the natural association of illness with old age, he'd expected the lame and the halt. He had taken it for granted that Alice would be by far the youngest person to appeal to the priest. Tully glanced at the lineup behind him. With the exception of this first young woman, Alice definitely won the youth sweepstakes.

Tully noted that the priest had pulled the cowl up over his head. Once again, there was no seeing his face. He alone, of all the monks, had not worn the cowl during Mass. But even then the lighting was so poor it was impossible to see his face clearly. And of course the Big One had not once pulled back his cowl. Tully knew only that this one was well-built and, judging from his movements, young and perhaps athletic.

The young woman knelt before the priest.

Father Robert spoke. "What shall we call you?"

"Judith," she replied. "Judith Ryan."

"Then, so, Judith, why have you come?"

Her hands fluttered as if in embarrassment. "My problem probably won't sound very important to you, Father, with all the troubles you hear, but it's a big problem for me."

Father Robert covered her hands with his. Brother Paul shifted abruptly but abortedly. Tully caught the movement but was unable to assess it.

Father Robert spoke softly. Only the young woman could hear; his words appeared to encourage her.

"I'm a dancer," she said, "and a singer. I know that doesn't sound crucial, but it's my living. If I couldn't do that, I'd be washing dishes in some greasy spoon—or worse." She hesitated.

"Yes?" he prodded gently.

"My big break is coming up in the next couple of days. The Michigan Opera Theater is auditioning for 'Kismet' and I've been called to try out for the female lead. This is my chance to get out of the chorus and maybe go places."

"Kismet," is it? thought Lennon. Where have I heard that recently? Ah, yes: Pringle thought that Zoo and I should be guided by kismet—fate. And now, this girl is trying to get some "Kismet" in her future. I wonder.

"I don't know . . ." the priest faltered.

Brother Paul tapped the priest's knee and handed him a small, round, gold-colored object. Tully, who'd been reading up on this ritual, assumed the article was a Catholic reliquary. He was correct.

Father Robert glanced at the reliquary and the card that was handed him as well. "My child, this contains a tiny fragment of the bone of St. Vitus, who lived in the fourth century. He is the patron saint of dancers and actors.

"Think, my dear child: almost seventeen-hundred years have gone by since this holy martyr lived on this earth. The reliquary holds a bit of what he was. Seventeen hundred years! For all this time, actors and dancers have prayed to him, often successfully, I would surmise.

197

"Bow your head now, my child, and pray that through the intercession of St. Vitus, God may grant you the favor you now seek."

With that, and in silence, the priest used the reliquary in tracing the sign of the cross over the young woman, who reacted by making a sign of the cross on herself.

"Go now," the priest said, "and God be with you."

She rose nimbly from her kneeling position. Just as a dancer should.

Alice was next. She started to kneel, but was halted by Tully's hand on her shoulder.

Lennon saw, and barely suppressed a gasp. Instantly she knew. They were together. The woman Tully had touched was his woman. There was no rift between them as existed presently between her and Joe Cox. The problem was that Tully's lover was ill. It was as simple as that. She certainly looked ill. There was a pallor about her face and a frightened, exhausted expression in her eyes. She probably had been very ill for a very long time.

That explained Tully's presence in the singles bar. Yet, in a long evening of extensive and bordering-on-intimate chitchat, Tully had made no move on her.

So, when push came to shove, Tully would remain faithful to his lover who happened to be ill.

Commendable.

And so much for kismet.

And yet . . . and yet . . . something very positive had happened between her and Tully. Lennon had been around too long to misread the signs. Was a relationship between her and Zoo Tully over before it began? Too early. Her instinct told her it was too early to tell.

For now, back to the moment.

When Alice felt Tully's hand on her shoulder, she halted in her attempt to kneel and stood erect again, in effect performing an abbreviated curtsy.

Tully turned to a sound man carrying a backpack and a mike. He was standing on one of the chapel's few chairs.

"Get off that chair!" Tully said.

Brother Paul's head jerked up. He recognized the tone. It was almost identical to his own. Its timbre brooked no compromise or delay, only instant obedience and compliance. Very few people could carry it off. Two such were Brother Paul and this stranger. And Paul recognized that immediately.

But wait: This was no stranger. Brother Paul had seen this man somewhere before. Night before last—at the singles bar. Except the guy had been with the reporter. Now he was with—whom? His wife? Paul smirked. He sensed the inviting odor of blackmail. How much might this black man pay to keep his dalliance a secret from his wife? As quickly as the thought came to mind, Paul dismissed it. Peanuts. He was going for the big bundle.

He had to admit, though: the black man had marvelous taste in white women. Both the reporter and sick woman were gorgeous.

It was a dramatic testament to Tully's inbred ability to command that as soon as he issued the order, the sound man relinquished his perch. In almost any other circumstance, TV technicians would have challenged such a demand.

Tully positioned the chair for Alice, who sat now very near the priest. Still, she could see neither his nor the Brother's face.

Father Robert waited for Alice to compose herself. Then he asked, "What is it that troubles you, child?"

With the near-breathless continuity of a child telling Santa what she wants for Christmas, Alice reeled off the lengthy list of her ailments.

By the time she had stopped for breath, even she was impressed with the quantity and gravity of all that ailed her. Never before had she enumerated all her ills so rapidly or so completely. Taken like this, her condition seemed beyond anyone's capacity to solve and cure. Maybe even God's.

There was a pause while Father Robert and even Brother Paul absorbed all she'd said. At length, Paul scribbled a note and handed it to the priest. Paul's constant intervention did not escape Tully's notice.

The priest scanned the note, then said to Alice, "Does your doctor ever suggest that your mind must be at peace and rest before your body can heal itself?"

"Which of my doctors could you be referring to, Father?" Sarcasm was evident in her voice. "You must mean one of the head doctors, the psychiatrists or the psychologists. Yes, there has been mention of the possibility of a psychosomatic cause for all this. But none of them has ever put it as delicately as you have."

"I did not mean that your illnesses were imaginary."

"Oh, that's all right, Father. I didn't take it as an insult."

"I only meant that with so many ailments your mind must be terribly troubled."

Alice nodded eagerly.

Tully, listening closely, thought the priest deserved no medal for that conclusion. Anyone confronting as many physical blind alleys as Alice would have to be worried sick.

Father Robert accepted a relic from Brother Paul along with the explanatory note.

Tully began to wonder who was running this show, the priest or the Big One. It was a quiet suspicion but one he stored for future reference.

Father Robert held the relic in his outstretched hand, presumably so that Alice could study it. Her mental state was in such confusion and hopeful anticipation that she took little note of the reliquary. Tully, blessed with extremely keen sight, did the studying. He could see nothing mystical about the object—a small, round, filigreed, gold-colored container, enclosing a small patch of red cloth with an extremely tiny white object embedded therein. Tully took the small white object to be the relic. Again he was correct. Each first-class relic allegedly consisted of a fragment of bone in the case of a saint, or a sliver of wood in the case of the True Cross.

"See, child," said Father Robert, "this is the relic of

St. Dymphna, who lived in the seventh century. She died in exile, fleeing from her father, a Celtic king. Six hundred years later, her body was brought back to the British Isles. On that occasion, many mentally and emotionally disturbed people were miraculously cured. And ever since then, people troubled with worry or mental or emotional problems have been healed through her intercession. I will now bless you with the relic of St. Dymphna, my child.''

The priest traced the sign of the cross over Alice, who, uncertain how to react, simply bowed her head.

Brother Paul's voice cut through the moment. "That will be all. You may go now." It was said not loudly but definitively. Tully recognized the immense assurance of authority in the tone.

Almost in reflex to the command, Alice began to stand.

"Wait." Father Robert extended one of his hands and motioned her back into the chair.

Tully noticed the Big One clench his fists, the knuckles whitening.

Eagerly, Pat Lennon moved closer. In the reports she'd read, Mrs. Whitehead had been preparing to leave after being blessed when the priest had called her back. It was then the miracle had taken place. Would lightning strike twice?

"My child," Father Robert said, "a few moments ago, did you not remark that you had not one but many doctors?''

"Yes . . . yes, I did.''

"Child, do you remember the Gospel story of the sick woman who had spent her fortune on doctors? Not only was she not cured, her condition was worse than ever. Ill and tired, worried and weary, she came to Jesus. She abandoned her trust in doctors, and believed—really believed—that Jesus could and would cure her.''

"I think I remember. It sounds awfully familiar.''

"Can you believe like that, child? Can you leave the doctors behind? Can you transfer all the trust you have had in doctors, in worldly medicine, and put that same trust— and more—in Our Savior, Jesus Christ?''

There was an extended moment when the proverbial dropping pin could have been heard.

Falteringly, Alice said, "I . . . I . . . I don't know."

"You must."

Suddenly, something—a feeling of determination?—seemed to come over Alice. "You're right. I must. Yes, I will." She slid from the chair to her knees. "I do believe. Father, I do believe."

Father Robert led her in a natural antiphonal prayer. He prayed, "Come, Lord Jesus!"

"Come, Lord Jesus!" Alice echoed.

"I believe!"

"I believe!"

"I trust!"

"I trust!"

"In you alone!"

"In you alone!"

"Into thy hands . . ."

"Into thy hands . . ."

". . . do I commend my health, my safety, and my life!"

". . . do I commend my health, my safety, and my life!"

As suddenly and unexpectedly as it had begun, it was over.

Tully had been completely taken aback by the fervor of this spontaneous outpouring of prayer. He had never seen Alice look quite like this before. It was like some sort of transfiguration. She now wore a serene smile as if she had no problems whatever.

"That's it!" Lennon said.

Tully heard her but didn't know what she meant.

Brother Paul heard her and in a controlled fury knew exactly what she meant.

"Is this it?" asked the sound man. "Sid, is this it? Is this the miracle?"

"Damned if I know," Sid replied. "Maurie, is this the miracle?"

"It'll have to do," said Maurie. "I think it's the closest we're going to get."

The three TV technicians could be heard only by each other what with the commotion crescendoing throughout the chapel. But what the three men said quite accurately expressed what had happened.

It was by no means as dramatic as what had happened to Mrs. Whitehead. It was not the restoration of sight to a blind person. It was not the instantaneous healing of visible sores. But for a crowd bent on and starved for a miracle, it would do nicely.

Alice was radiant. The media people clustered around her. Tully was separated from her and pushed back by the crush of people trying to get close to her.

The celebration was not without foundation. Something had taken place. Alice felt it, although she was not sure what; it had all happened too fast. One minute she was being blessed with a relic, yet feeling deeply depressed. It was so anticlimatic. All she could think was: Is this all there is?

Then the Brother's command to leave. Strange, his tone so resembled Zoo's when he wanted something done immediately.

She could not explain to her satisfaction, let alone the media's, what had happened next.

When the priest summoned her back, her emotion was something akin to a rebound from despair to hope. She was giddy. The Gospel scene the priest had painted hit home. That was exactly it. Magnified by frustration, she felt as if she had been under the futile care of every doctor in the world. And she felt worse now than she had in the beginning. Just like the woman in the Gospel.

The priest, in just a few inspired words, had made her see how hopeless was her future in the hands of the medical profession. The prospect had drained her. And in that state—empty to the point of being in a vacuum—Father had invited her to turn to the Lord.

Then she came to the part that was confusing, baffling, bewildering, mystifying. She came to what she was willing to believe was her miracle. She felt better. No, that wasn't the word. She felt healed. It was as if a gentle hand had touched her. Had touched not just one spot on her body. Had touched her entire being, body and soul. And she had been healed.

Tully stood back against the wall, taking in the total scene. Alice was all right. As far as he could tell, she had never been better. The transformation was not only perceptible; it was truly remarkable. He stopped well short of terming it a miracle, if only because he did not believe in miracles.

Whatever it was didn't matter. Alice was ebullient in her tentative cure and basking in all the media attention.

Tully turned his attention to the monks, all but forgotten now as everyone pressed in to question and hear the ''miracle lady.'' The three monks who had been grouped together fanned out like well-trained soldiers and harvested all the collection containers. They then re-formed in their traditional procession and silently filed off, disappearing into the inner sanctum behind the chapel partition.

Tully thought it odd that the monks would not remain in the chapel and join the celebration. After all, this was their show. His hat was off, for the moment at least, to Father Robert. However he'd done it, he had pulled it off. Where any number of high-priced and high-ranking doctors had failed, the priest had succeeded. Why, Tully wondered, would the monks so inconspicuously fold their tents and quietly slip away?

As they had marched from the chapel area, Tully thought he detected the priest shying from the Big One. The lieutenant recalled Brother Paul's reaction when the priest called Alice back after the Brother had dismissed her. The Brother had clenched his fists as if he were furious. Why should that be? And why should the priest appear terrified of the Brother?

True, what Tully did not know about Catholicism could fill volumes. Nonetheless he found all this behavior puzzling. He filed these questions away in his busy mind. Chief among the things that rendered Tully restless were unanswered questions. It was part of his job, which, in turn, was part of his personality, to solve puzzles. St. Augustine held that our hearts are restless until they rest in God. In Tully's case, his spirit remained troubled until puzzles were resolved, loose ends were tied, and files were closed.

Others in his position might simply have been grateful for the miraculous event that had cured their loved one. While that sentiment did not entirely escape Tully, he could not forget or disregard the remaining puzzles.

And, finally, he realized that in all this confusion, he had missed the departure of Pat Lennon. For she surely was gone.

In fact, she had left several minutes earlier. Pat needed no statements from Alice to flesh out her story. She knew what the lead and thrust of the story would be as she would write it.

She could not swear to it, but Pat felt reasonably sure that none of the other reporters had caught that singular remark of Father Robert's. No one else had seemed to react to it—with the possible exception of Brother Paul. And, bundled as he was in his habit from head to toe, it was difficult to read his reaction.

The noteworthiness—and her scoop, if she guessed correctly—lay in the priest's counseling the woman to abandon her doctors and to put all her trust in the priest and, through him, God. That, unless she missed her guess—and she was certain she had not—would prove to be the straw that would break the Church's determination to accord the Congregation of St. Stephen hands-off treatment.

The way she figured it, one of the very last things the archdiocese—or any institution, for that matter—wanted, was litigation. In litigation, the worst that could happen would be to lose the case and become liable for an astronomical sum, especially in Wayne County. The best that could happen would be to successfully defend the case. And even then, tons of money would have to be spent on attorneys' fees and court costs. Either way there was a monumental loss of money.

Lately, there had been an increasing amount of litigation over priests charged with pedophilia. On a moral basis, these cases were tragic and needed much understanding, compassion, and healing treatment from all sides. As for litigation, no one could hold the Church directly responsible for these acts. Every relevant tenet of the Church stood in complete opposition to the pedophile. There were times when litigants could and did charge the church with inaction in some cases when remedial action should have been taken. But in no sense could the Church be charged with direct complicity.

Not so with alleged miracles.

She would check it out just to make certain all bases were touched, but she was sure these monks were functioning legitimately in the Archdiocese of Detroit. That would mean, in effect, that the archdiocese endorsed the sacramental functioning of the Congregation of St. Stephen. It also meant that the archdiocese accepted responsibility for what the Congregation did sacramentally.

So, she reasoned, if Father Robert decided to use pizza and Coke at Mass instead of bread and wine, it was the archbishop's responsibility—nay, his duty—to step in and say that that was a no-no.

She further reasoned that if the monks took on faith healing, that would spring from their sacramental ministry. If he wanted to—and apparently he did—the archbishop could look the other way if Father Robert were to pray with people and bless them with relics. If it works, it works. If it doesn't, it doesn't. Simple.

But what happens when the miracle worker counsels a client to tell the doctors and the whole damn medical world to bug off? Suppose the "cure" doesn't work, or works only temporarily? Suppose that without medical attention the person gets worse or dies? Somebody is going to get sued for everything and then some. In this case, the somebody would be Mark Cardinal Boyle, Archbishop of Detroit.

God, they'd probably have to sell the Sistine Ceiling to pay the bills!

Just for one moment, as she drove back to the *News* to research and write her story, she thanked God her daddy had shelled out the dough for her to attend that nice Catholic Mercy College in Detroit. For once, all that education was going to pay off.

It had started with her research into faith healing, followed by her exclusive interview with Mrs. Whitehead. This angle—the archdiocese being forced into an investigation of the matter—would be the frosting on the cake.

This was her story! Her story! And it was a good, newsy, interesting story that could extend through several days—maybe a week or more.

As far as Pat Lennon was concerned, this was what reporting was all about. The thrill of beating everyone else to a story, and then, by dint of diligent hard work, staying on top of it. Nobody could beat her now. It was her story. She knew it.

So did Brother Paul. His caper was fast getting out of hand. That crazy Father Robert and his "miracles"! At this point, there wasn't anything he could do about that. But the girl, the reporter: She had to be stopped. He sensed—he knew—what she wanted to do. He had to stop her no matter what!

Meanwhile, outside the bank converted into a monastery, a Channel 2 reporter was finishing his taping for the 5:30 P.M. newscast.

"... and so the miracles continue at this modest little monastery. We've made repeated attempts to interview Father Robert, Detroit's own miracle worker. But the good father remains in seclusion, unavailable to the public"—pause, grossly sincere expression, zoom in to catch intensity of the sincerity—"except when he steps out of his monastic cell to bring"—eyes up—"the Lord's healing power—Goddam!"

The rain, which had been falling steadily if lightly, abruptly became a cloudburst. The reporter and the technicians, hastily grabbing up their gear, fled pell-mell to the van and dove inside. They were all soaked. The reporter's jacket and tie afforded him little protection.

"Hey, we didn't get your signature on that piece," Sid observed.

"If you think I'm going back out there in this stuff just to say, 'This is Donald Duck, Channel 2 Eyewitness News reporting,' you are as loony as the jerk who insists we wear jackets and ties in the middle of summer."

"Hey," said Maurie, "why don't we go see the priest? Maybe he can make it stop rainin'."

They laughed as Sid dug from the cooler the six-pack he'd picked up earlier. Sid was always thinking.

CHAPTER
14

John Reid sat in the car, a predator, waiting. For this enterprise, he didn't need to be Brother Paul. If anything, the religious identity would hinder him. He needed to be John Reid with no complications. He had a job to do. It had to be done with dispatch. No frills.

It was the way he liked to work. He did not favor the exotic twist, the poetic turn. Do it quickly, efficiently, conclusively.

He could not recall ever having been in a more severe storm. Lightning crackled at incredibly close intervals, the thunder rolled and roared almost continually. The rain fell in sheets. The car, standing idle at curbside, shuddered in the gale.

Reid rarely smoked, but he wanted one now. He was nervous, very nervous. Tense. Keyed up. A cigarette would not have had a relaxing effect. It would have intensified his mood. The more he thought about a cigarette and how good it would taste, the more he wanted one.

But it would have complicated things immeasurably. The

downpour was so heavy, there was no possibility of cracking a window even slightly. The smoke from even one cigarette would have coated the panes and the windshield in an impenetrable film. He would have to wait it out.

Instead of smoking, and to keep his hands busy sans cigarette, he drummed his gloved fingers on the steering wheel and thought the whole thing through for the umpteenth time.

From the very beginning it had been a plan requiring enormous personal involvement on his part, meticulous timing, much cooperation from the fates, plus a healthy dollop of luck.

Neither fate nor luck had been kind to him in the past. But then, what was it that crazy Chicago shrink had written about him in the seminary evaluation? Something about a pattern of failure. Yes, that was it: The idiot said that Reid seemed involuntarily to seek disaster.

What bullshit! Who would seek failure? Certainly not he. Hell, he'd had his share of successes.

That he couldn't offhand think of even one unmitigated success meant nothing. After all, he had to concentrate on the present problem.

Hey, here was a good case in point! Yes, this was an excellent example: Even with all that had gone wrong, everything was still on track. He just had to accelerate the schedule a bit, that's all.

If he lived to be a hundred, which was not likely, he would never figure out what got into that Robert. He was under the strictest orders to follow the script and not deviate from it. A little prayer, a little explanation of why this saint is relevant to this problem, a little blessing with the relic. The odds definitely favored the system to work at least some of the time. There surely were enough psychosomatic disorders around for a psychosomatic cure to work at least occasionally. Add to that the power of suggestion and the odds got better. Going for a job interview? It couldn't hurt to have Saint Whatchamacallit in your corner. The guy goes into the interview if not all that confident of his own abilities at least trusting in the power of the saint and the good Father's prayers to get him the job.

And it had been working well enough, if slowly, before that idiot decided—on the spur of the moment, he claimed—to try an honest-to-God cure.

Reid could have killed the old fool on the spot, but of course that was impossible with all those people around.

Then—incredible but true—it had worked! And along came that fat donation from the old broad's husband. That had pretty well raised their accumulated balance to a satisfactory level all by itself. So what's all this talk about courting failure? Far from that. He had been able to manipulate a potential major setback into a big win.

Of course he did have to keep the monks in line. So he'd had to discipline Robert. Reid shook his head at the memory. Almost went too far; yesterday the old man was next to useless—had to keep telling people that expending all those curative powers had weakened the old man.

Reid wondered now, parenthetically, if that's how it really worked: Does a real faith healer expend his own power when he cures somebody?

He laughed out loud. No one could hear him. He was alone in the car, and there was no one, not a soul that he could see, on the street. Taking faith healing seriously—what a gas! This masquerade must be getting to me.

Reid kept his gaze fixed on the front doors of the Detroit *News*. She would have to exit the building through those doors. Sooner or later, she would have to come through them. From his vantage, he could survey Lafayette Boulevard, east and west. The downpour limited his visibility, but his range was sufficient to see the street was deserted. He expected no less. Ordinarily, no one was on these streets of downtown Detroit in midevening. There was even less chance of passersby in this weather.

His fingers continued to drum a meaningless message on the steering wheel as he continued ruminating.

Even though he had probably gone a bit far in disciplining

the old man, it was all working out. Donations were coming in from all over the country, Canada too.

Yeah, it was all working out—until today. What could have possessed the old man to try it again? And why in the world would he ever advise someone to forget about the doctors?

The only conclusion Reid could reach was that the role must have taken possession of the man. The bullheaded geezer must have come to believe that he actually had the power. Reid chuckled mirthlessly. He stopped abruptly when he recalled the consequences of Father Robert's seeming self-delusion.

Imagine telling someone to have nothing to do with the medical profession! The nerve! He had considered punishing the old man again, but, after some reflection, he had decided not to. The strongest argument against it was that Robert probably couldn't have survived it. And then Reid had had immediate use for the old man.

However, at this point, the way things were working out, Robert was no longer pivotal in Reid's plans.

The focal point now was this damn reporter. From what she'd said, she was hot on this investigation angle. She seemed fixated on triggering an investigation. Why? But then, it didn't matter. The point was to stop her from carrying through with the idea.

He had to admit he didn't particularly like what he was going to do tonight. Of course he didn't give a damn what happened to the girl. She was expendable, as was everyone.

No, the thing he disliked about tonight was that he was deviating from his plan a lot further than he cared to. That bothered him. Oh, not that he feared for a moment he couldn't handle any repercussions that might emerge from tonight's work. Just that he couldn't anticipate what they all might be. He had lingering doubts about that. But he tried to quiet those doubts by covering them with a heavy layer of self-assurance.

He stopped drumming on the steering wheel, fingers poised in midair. He could feel his neck and shoulder muscles tighten. He blinked several times to clear his vision.

There she was. He'd done his homework well, if hurriedly. He knew her raincoat. The hood was pulled up and she held a newspaper with which she attempted to shield her head from the force of the rain as she dashed across Lafayette to the *News* parking lot.

This would be the definitive tip-off. Yes! She did it: She got into her car. He saw the rear lights go on, the white lights indicating the car was in reverse. A puff of smoke escaped the exhaust. The car had started immediately. Good.

She pulled out of the parking lot, checking carefully but needlessly for traffic before turning left and heading east on Lafayette.

Reid turned the ignition key and listened as the motor turned over several times before it caught. He suffered a momentary panic when the car failed to start at once. That his carefully laid plan might miscarry due to some mechanical failure! Well, never mind, the scenario had begun.

He waited until he could barely make out her taillights through the downpour, then he flipped on his headlights, slipped his car into gear, and slowly began to follow.

He had often thought that whoever had laid out downtown Detroit must have been drunk at the time. Either that, or it was the Indians' revenge against Cadillac.

Since there were any number of routes she could have taken, he had to stay on her tail closer than he would have wished. He hoped she wouldn't notice a pair of headlights recurring in her rearview mirror. With the dearth of traffic, he would need some of that elusive luck in order to remain unnoticed.

She zigged, as she had to, when West Lafayette dead-ended at Michigan Avenue. She followed the divided Cadillac Square to Randolph, moved north to Monroe, traveled through colorful Greektown, turned south at the Chrysler service drive, then onto eastbound Lafayette. So far, no surprises.

She turned left at Orleans, heading straight for Lafayette

Towers. Then she came up with her first unlooked-for turn: She drove into the shopping center just short of the Towers. He would have to check this out.

She parked and dashed into Ye Olde Butcher Shoppe. Something for dinner, perhaps.

Should he strike now? It was as good as anywhere.

No. There were too many lights. Too many possibilities of passersby going into or coming out of one of the shops or restaurants. He waited. The next few minutes were crucial. But everything looked as if it was going to work.

She had a difficult time returning to her car. Now, in addition to the purse hanging by its long strap from her left shoulder, she had to carry a large grocery bag. She managed to finally slide into the car after depositing the groceries on the far side of the seat.

He followed her car around into the Towers' drive, making certain she entered the private parking garage. He continued beyond the ramp, circling the building until he reached the drive that separated the car park from the East Towers.

Cars illegally parked on either side of the narrow drive restricted the movement of any vehicle approaching the Towers' entrance. It was like a straightened passageway. Fortunately for him, no car was stopped in the middle of the drive. He had access, even if only in a straight line, to the entire passage. He nodded once sharply. It was sufficient.

His foot tapped the accelerator nervously. He would have to attain maximum speed in a very short distance. He watched the garage's open portal, not daring to blink.

There she was. She paused at the exit. She would have to run from portal to portal in the driving rain, still encumbered with the purse and the grocery bag.

She broke for the shelter of the apartment overhang. Simultaneously, he floored the accelerator. There was a piercing shriek of tires; the engine roared. A couple about to enter the lobby, hearing the raceway sound, turned toward the noise.

214

They saw a young woman frozen in a moment of terror in the rapidly approaching headlights. Then, instinctively, she spun about and tried to run in an attempt to escape.

No sooner had she turned than she was struck.

Later, describing the scene in all its horror for the police, the couple, the only eyewitnesses—or at least the only ones who would come forward—recalled the incident as if it had happened in slow motion.

The wife said she would never forget the look on the victim's face. It was as if the poor woman was hypnotized when she saw the car headed straight for her. She couldn't understand, the witness said, why the woman had not run between the parked cars. She would have been safe there. She had been only a few feet from the cars parked on either side of the drive. Some elemental instinct must have betrayed her. An instinct that urged her to run from the clear and certain danger. At the moment of impact, the female witness had turned away and covered her eyes. She could not bear to see the rest.

At that point, her husband took over the narrative.

He said the car had hit the woman from behind as she was trying to run from it. The impact hurled her into the air like a rag doll. She had somersaulted remarkably gracefully, almost like a circus performer. She came down head-first, her skull hitting a glancing blow on the roof of the car. He was quite sure she also hit the trunk before her body slammed to the pavement.

He recalled every detail because he had never seen anything like this before. Not even in movies.

What happened next, he said, was the most incredible thing of all.

On impact, John Reid thrust himself forward as if to add the weight of his body to that of the car in smashing into the woman. He could see her body as it catapulted from the ground and disappeared from view over the windshield. He felt and heard the thud as her body hit first the roof then the trunk of the car.

He slammed on the brakes, and skidded a few feet before

stopping. He thrust the gear into reverse far more violently than necessary; his adrenaline was racing. As he shot backward, he could feel the satisfying bump as he rolled over her body. Back in drive gear, he ran over her again. Then he drove off, almost demolishing two parked cars as he turned down the drive returning to Orleans.

"That's what I can't understand, officer," the male witness said, "why would he do that? I mean, if a guy has an accident, why would he back up over the victim?"

"It don't look like no accident to me, mister." The officer was taking notes of the witnesses' account in the lobby. "It looks like that guy wanted to get her pretty bad . . . you sure it was a man driving?"

"No, not really. I was sort of watching the action and didn't get a clear view of the driver. I guess I just assumed it must be a man." He brightened. "This might be helpful: He was driving a late model Pontiac. An '86 or '87 Pontiac. One of the 6000 series."

The officer stopped in his note-taking. His quizzical expression telegraphed his question: How in the world could you know all that in that brief a time?

The witness caught the unarticulated query. "I'm an engineer at G.M. It's my business to know the various models."

The officer smiled and entered the information on his notepad. "But you didn't actually see the driver?"

"No. But my wife may have."

The officer turned to the woman, who was approaching a state of shock and being comforted by a friend who had left her own apartment to see what all the commotion was about.

"Ma'am," the officer said as gently as possible to the distraught woman, "your husband says you got a look at the driver. Is that correct?"

"What? Oh, dear. Yes, I guess I did. What I remember most is his expression. It was one of . . . well . . . the kind of look you get when you're enjoying something very, very much. I couldn't believe his expression. It was so . . . so

216

. . . inappropriate.'' She looked up at him. ''Could I be wrong about that expression, officer?''

''I don't think so, ma'am. I think you probably got it right.

''Do you think you would recognize him if you saw him again, ma'am?''

''Oh, dear. Oh . . . I think so. I don't think I'll ever forget him. Even now, I wish I could forget him. But I don't think I ever will.'' A pause. ''Maybe that poor girl—the victim—maybe she'll know who he is.''

The officer closed his notepad and looked at the taillights of the departing EMS van. ''Maybe, ma'am. But I don't think she's going to tell us about it. I don't think she's going to tell anybody anything.''

''You mean . . . oh, dear. That poor woman.''

Her husband, who had been holding her supportively, along with the friend, assisted her from the chair. As the three entered the elevator, the woman wondered if, indeed, she would ever see that man again. As much as she would desperately like to forget him, she vowed to hold his image in her memory. Someone should speak for that poor girl, God have mercy on her soul.

CHAPTER
15

There was an unusual amount of high-intensity activity in Homicide for so late in the evening. In fact, for any time of a normal day or night, the busyness was extraordinary. The reason: It wasn't normal; the brother and sister-in-law of a homicide detective had been murdered. And the brethren had gathered.

Officers, without being called in to duty, had come voluntarily. The phones were in continuous use. Markers were being called in. Whoever had killed those two people either did not know they were related to a homicide officer, or the guy was an idiot. He was going to be caught.

Lieutenant Tully had come back to work even before getting word of this special emergency. He'd been away much of the day with Alice at the Monastery of St. Stephen. After her ''miracle,'' after all the media attention, and after they'd returned home, Tully had stayed with her longer than he had intended.

She had been so agog, he couldn't possibly have left her. She had to talk to someone and she wanted to talk to him.

She had to reassure herself and him that she actually did feel better—much, much better.

In their mutual joy, they had even made love, quite spontaneously, throwing their former caution to the winds. To their grateful surprise, she didn't break.

To some degree, Tully had pretended to be as hopefully confident as Alice was. He did not believe in miracles, he doubted the power of Father Robert, and he suspected the Big One, Brother Paul, of something. Tully wasn't yet able to label it, but his well-honed instincts told him that something in Brother Paul was rotten.

Put it all together and Tully was less than convinced that Alice was completely out of the woods. But, for her sake, he masked his doubts.

In any case, after Alice had expressed every excited thought and fresh emotion she felt, and had calmed down, Tully headed for work. It was what Alice had expected. She knew where she and the Department stood in his life. If anything, she was gratefully surprised that he had accorded her first place, if only for a few hours.

Tully had returned to Headquarters intent only on catching up on the backed-up paperwork. For two consecutive days he had spent an unplanned and unexpected amount of time away from his desk, and the files were piling up.

No sooner had he reached the Department than he was told about the intensified investigation going on. In moments he was brought abreast of the matter and had joined in the hunt.

When Inspector Koznicki passed the open door of the squad room, Tully was seated at his desk massaging the back of his neck and stretching.

Koznicki stepped into the room and approached Tully's desk. "My heartiest congratulations, Alonzo. Everyone has heard of Alice's miraculous improvement."

So like Walt, thought Tully, to carefully choose his words even in informal conversation. Koznicki had dropped the word "miraculous." But because he knew Tully's view on miracles, the inspector had used the word "improvement" rather than "cure."

"Thanks, Walt. She is better, no doubt about that."

"What do you think?"

"Time. We gotta give it time. Plus we gotta get her to the doctor, no matter what the priest said."

Koznicki cocked an eyebrow. "No matter what the priest said?"

For the first time, a more complete grasp of what had happened occurred to Tully. It hadn't been reported, at least not yet, that the priest had advised—no, better, commanded—Alice to substitute faith and trust in him and God for a continued reliance on medical science.

Now Tully recalled the scene before the priest with crisp clarity.

There had been few people close enough to Father Robert to hear everything he said. But Tully remembered. He remembered the priest's saying those words. Alice heard, of course. *He'd* heard. The Big One heard, and reacted— angrily? And Pat Lennon heard—and reacted. If anyone were to report the entire scene and draw the appropriate conclusions, it would be Pat. But it was too early for her story to be in print.

However, Koznicki was entitled to some explanation. "Yeah, Walt, just before Alice got to . . . feeling better, the priest told her she had to trust in God and not in doctors."

"He said that!"

"Uh-huh. Told her some story from the Bible about a woman who spent all her money on doctors and was worse off than in the beginning. But when she believed in Jesus, she was cured. Just like that."

Koznicki shook his head. "Dangerous, dangerous. Well, let us at least hope that in Alice's case, this is the end and that whatever cured her is lasting."

"Amen."

"I will just get out of your way now so you can get back to work."

Tully nodded toward the phone. "Just waiting for a call

from one of my snitches. He says he can ID the house where Morgan's brother was killed. Personally, I think he's blowin' smoke. Probably wants a few honor points against his next bust. We'll see."

Sergeant Angela Moore's head appeared in the doorway. As she leaned into the squad room she first saw Koznicki, registered slight surprise, and nodded to the inspector. Then she turned her attention to Tully. "Zoo, something just came in I thought you'd be interested in."

"On the Morgan case?"

"No, another case."

Tully wondered why Moore was being so vague. It was not like her. Almost as if she were loath to bring the subject up in Koznicki's presence.

"What other case?" Tully asked.

"An attempted murder. It just came in."

"Moore, we're workin' on the Morgan case."

She hesitated. "I thought you'd want to know about this one. It's the one you asked me about yesterday."

Tully drew a blank. "The one yesterday?" He thought a moment. "Lennon? Pat Lennon?"

Moore nodded.

Koznicki took in the exchange with interest. Why had Moore not simply stated that fact in the beginning? She had seemed inhibited by his presence. Why? And now, Tully looked stunned. Koznicki could not recall ever having seen his lieutenant so affected.

Without another word, Tully rose, slipped on his jacket, and left the room.

Koznicki continued to wonder about it, and with the wonder came concern.

Tully scanned the report and then headed out. Before entering traffic from a parking space restricted to authorized vehicles, he placed the flasher on the car's roof. He reached Harper Hospital in record time. After checking at the desk, he took the elevator to the Surgical Intensive Care Unit.

Pat Lennon was standing in the hallway.

He almost ran to her. "What happened? You're supposed to be—"

"When a fella needs a friend!" Lennon cut in. "I don't know what brought you here, but, boy, am I glad to see you!"

"The report said that . . . that you . . ."

"I know. That's the same way I got the information."

"What—"

"I was in the city room wrapping up a story when a call came in from our police beat that I had been hit by a car and was near death at Harper. Well, of course I wasn't. The guy who took the call told the reporter I was alive and well and standing right beside him. So we checked and found the ID was tentative. I was pretty sure I knew who it was, so I got down here right away. I've been here only a few minutes."

"So, who is it? Do you know?"

"Pringle McPhee. She's a friend—works with me at the *News*."

Tully became aware that his heartbeat was stabilizing. His blood pressure probably was returning to normal. He could read the fear in Pat's expression.

"Can you help me find out what happened . . . how she is?" she asked.

His smile tried to provide reassurance. "Sure. Come on."

He led her into the inner sanctum. Pat was used to barging in to restricted places armed only with her press card and a healthy measure of brass. But even she was impressed with Tully's style. For starters, his police badge and the magic word "homicide" drew lots more cooperation than her press pass ever had. Then there was his gift of raw authority in demeanor. He raised brass, gall, and nerve to chutzpah.

This combination got them to the victim's bedside and to the attending physician, who, as they entered the room, was standing with hands in pockets, the ever-present stethoscope draped around his neck. He was just standing there contemplating the victim.

After introductions, Tully and Lennon joined the doctor in the silent study of human life evidently hanging on by several threads.

Tully had seen it all before. But seldom had he seen anyone so plugged with support systems.

She had been extremely attractive before this, although it was impossible to tell now. Her face was distended and discolored. Both eyes were swollen shut. A white sheet loosely covered her body. From his experience in asking doctors the purpose of various medical devices, he knew the tube in her nose was supposed to decompress the stomach.

A ventilator was connected to an endotracheal oral tube. There were multiple IV lines and multiple hanging bottles. Tubes and wires peeked from beneath the sheet. One tube drained blood for her right side. Another, attached to a Foley catheter, drained urine. The wires led to a cardiac monitor. Both her legs were elevated, wrapped, and in traction.

Without being asked, the doctor volunteered, "We've taken X rays of her facial bones, her legs, her skull, the cervical spine, chest, pelvis. And we've done a CAT scan."

There was a pause.

"And?" Tully prompted.

The doctor shook his head. "She has bilateral broken legs, a closed head injury, a skull fracture, a fractured pelvis, fractures of the facial bones, suspicion of abdominal injury, and six broken ribs on the right side."

Tully almost whistled silently. Instead, he exhaled audibly. "The prognosis?"

The doctor shrugged. "She's alive. She must have been in awfully good physical condition. That, and youth and luck, and I don't know what else, is helping. We've got her pretty well stabilized now. It's a matter of watching her extremely carefully. Nature should begin healing something sometime soon. Nature will give us our cue."

"Is . . . is she going to . . . make it?" Pat asked.

The doctor didn't answer immediately. Then, "I don't know. Officially, she is 'very critical.' "

"That's just this side of deceased," Tully said.

The doctor nodded.

Tully took Pat's elbow. "Come on, Pat. We've got to talk."

Slowly, reluctantly, Pat turned and left the room with Tully.

When they reached the hallway, in the glare of the lights Tully saw that Pat had been crying. Tears still flowed freely. He handed her his handkerchief. Over the years he had become inured to so many emotional reactions, tears among them. But his immunity stopped at the threshold of those he very much cared for.

As he saw Pat's tears, he felt his own eyes begin to fill. So, he seated her in the visitors' lounge and returned to the emergency room desk to check the police report on admission. He scanned the report, noted the name of the reporting officer, and phoned the man.

"Hoover!" the officer barked when Tully finally reached him.

"Tully, Homicide."

"Oh . . . yes, Lieutenant." His tone became conciliatory.

"I'm at Harper. It's about that woman you wrote up this evening. Why did you ID her as Patricia Lennon?"

"That ain't her name?"

"No."

"Uh-oh. It's the only thing we had to go on. There were some business cards in her coat pocket. Said 'Patricia Lennon.' Works at one of the papers. I forget which now."

"No purse?"

"Couldn't find one. Somebody probably swiped it."

Nice people, thought Tully. "What happened?"

Hoover cleared his throat for no other reason than that he needed a moment to recall the details. "Subject was walking—no, make that running; heavy rainstorm, still is—"

"Okay, okay."

"Sorry, Lieutenant. Subject was running from the parking garage to admittance doors of Lafayette Towers East.

224

It's a heavily parked area on both sides of a pretty narrow driveway. Just enough room in the center strip for a single car to get through.

"Doorman tells me it was solidly parked tonight 'cause of the storm. Anyway, when the subject reached the open area in the drive, she was struck by a vehicle. It was hit-and-run, Lieutenant."

"The driver?"

"Witness says it was a male caucasian. Says she might be able to ID him. We gave her a chance to calm down a bit, then took her in to look at shots. She's still at it. No luck yet."

"Any possibility this could've been a chance hit? DWI, drugs?"

"Negative, Lieutenant. According to the witness, after the car struck the woman, it stopped dead, then it backed over her, and then drove over her again. We logged it as an assault with intent to commit murder.

"Uh . . . one more thing, Lieutenant: When the woman hit the ground, her momentum carried her partly under one of the parked cars. So when the guy ran over her again, all he could get were her legs. Geez, her legs must be in bad shape!"

"Her whole body's in bad shape."

"Yeah, goddam!" he exclaimed. "Somebody really had it in for her."

"Hoover, keep me informed on this one. Especially if that witness makes somebody." Tully did not wait for a reply.

He returned to Pat Lennon, who was trying, not altogether successfully, to compose herself. He sat beside her and took one of her hands in his. "Tell me what happened, Pat."

She nodded. "Pringle and I were going to get together last night, but she had a date. The date didn't go very well. She was really down when I saw her at work today. So we agreed to get together tonight."

"Wait," Tully said, "this date: who was it?"

She hesitated. It was an occupational hazard. She spent

so much time protecting her sources, her first inclination was to protect everyone's identity. But this was a most serious investigation; she totally trusted Tully; this was not a privileged secret and, finally, she was not the only one who knew about Pringle's affair.

"Fred Parker."

"Fred Parker." He let the name rattle around the computer in his mind. "Fred Parker, the ad guy?"

Pat nodded.

"His picture's in the papers all the time. Society columns. With his wife. They're always together. Got a family, too. So, he and Pringle, eh? Were they having problems?"

Pat shook her head. "They seemed to get along well enough . . . fine, I suppose. Just the normal triangle problems."

"His wife didn't know."

"Apparently not."

"Pringle have any enemies—besides a possible Mrs. Parker?"

"No, none that I know of."

"Okay. We'll put Parker and wife on the back burner for the moment. You agreed to meet tonight. Go on."

"It was Pringle's idea. She didn't want to be alone tonight. So I invited her over to my apartment. I'm alone there now."

She wanted Tully to know that. He caught the implication.

"She was done with her work for today and I had some yet to do," Pat continued. "She offered to go ahead to the apartment. She was going to pick up some groceries and start supper so it would be ready when I got home. She'd taken the bus into work this morning so she didn't have her car. And since she was going to stop for some groceries, we decided she should take mine. Then I would get a taxi later on."

"She took your car?" Tully tensed.

"Yes. And then the ID—well, she hadn't brought her raincoat, so I let her take mine, because I would be picking up a taxi right outside the door and she had to cross the street and go a distance to get to my car. They must have identified her by the business cards I keep in the pocket. But why wouldn't they search through her purse?''

''Somebody stole it after she got hit. Probably the food, too. They searched the area; neither of those items turned up. But lemmee get this straight: She was wearing your coat and driving your car? Was she wearing any headgear?''

''No, just the hood on my raincoat. I watched her from the office window as she crossed the street.'' A pause. ''Poor Pringle, she was . . .'' Pat promptly corrected herself. ''. . . she *is* going to make one hell of a reporter. But she's not good at the simple things—like driving her car in and bringing raingear even on a day when all the forecasters agree there's going to be a monsoon.''

''Who knew you were going to do this? I mean, did anyone know she was going to your place? Or that she'd be driving your car and wearing your coat?''

''I don't see how. She might have told someone she was going to come to my place. I certainly didn't tell anyone. But she couldn't possibly have told anyone about the car and the coat; we decided that on the spur of the moment.''

Tully contemplated all she'd told him. ''The way I see it, we have three possibilities. One, it was a crazy, out for the thrill of wasting someone. Two, it was someone out to kill your friend. Three, someone wanted you.''

Pat felt the hair on the back of her neck rise.

''One is weak,'' Tully continued. ''There certainly are enough crazies to go around out there, but they don't usually stick around after they make their hit. If they're using a car, they hit and run. The longer they stay around, the stronger the possibility that someone will make the license or the driver.

''Two is not much stronger. As you said, someone might have learned that your friend was going to stay with you. But no one knew she was going to wear your coat or drive your car. Which leaves us with . . .'' He stopped short.

''Three,'' she murmured.

''Three. Who would want to do that to you?''

Pat recoiled from the theory. But, as Tully had implied, it was the logical conclusion. She began to roll her private dramatis personae through her mind. Looking for someone that vicious, that malicious, that brutal, tended to tint otherwise bland characters darkly.

She thought of people she'd written about. The mental parade began: state legislators, judges, attorneys, bums, prostitutes, gangsters, cops, housewives, businessmen and -women, the Mafia, dope pushers, users, priests, nuns, ministers, rabbis. With most rare exception, she had felt nothing personal, no particular animosity as she covered their stories. She was doing her job, and doing it well.

Until this moment, she had given little or no thought to her subjects' reaction. Many, if not most of them, seemed to thrive on the coverage. They seemed proud to have someone take seriously their opinion or what they had accomplished. A lot of them, through her, achieved the status of a "celebrity" by getting their names in the paper.

But, now that she was forced to consider it, others had been most unwillingly dragged into print. Without doubt they must have resented what they deemed to be her intrusion on their privacy. There were so many of them!

A new consideration. Whoever it was had bungled it. Tomorrow he will discover he ran down the wrong person. And, whoever he is, he's still out there.

Her thoughts returned to Pringle McPhee. Standing at Pringle's bedside moments ago, all she could think was, "Poor Pringle." Only hours before, they had chatted in the city room. Pringle had had a bad time with Fred. But she was young; she'd get over it.

Then, in an instant of terror, she'd been hit by a car. Over and over again. It must have been horrible. Then, mercifully, unconsciousness. Now, if the best possible thing happens, and she does recover, she will face months, maybe years, of medical treatment, plastic surgery, further operations, rehabilitation therapy.

In keeping with the brutally honest scenario suggested by Tully, Pat now had to put herself in Pringle's place.

If, if, *if*. If Pringle hadn't decided to stay over. If Pringle had driven her own car to work. Even if she hadn't borrowed Pat's coat. Three very simple conditions contrary to fact. Three fortuitous conditions that had been easily changeable—but not reversible. Kismet?

Suddenly Pat had a vision of herself in that hospital bed with all those tubes and wires invading her body. She shuddered.

Tully felt it and put his arm around her shoulder. He held her firmly until the trembling quieted.

At length, Tully said, "Can you think of anybody?"

She was almost able to smile. "Until just a little while ago, no, I couldn't. But now, just about everyone seems to qualify."

"The shock of all this is still too strong. Give it a little while. Your mind will become clearer. Give it a chance."

She nodded, bravely, she hoped.

"Your car is in the parking garage at the apartment," Tully said. "I'll give you a ride home."

Again, she nodded. She was grateful the car wasn't here in the hospital lot. Just now, she didn't trust herself to drive.

Before leaving the hospital, Tully phoned Headquarters. He ordered a guard for Pringle McPhee's room. Pringle's inert body would have police protection until such time as Tully was sure such protection was unnecessary.

They rode the short distance to the Towers in silence. He pulled up at the front door. She stiffened. This is where it had happened. She could almost see Pringle's body—*her* body!—hurtling through the air.

He pulled the car into one of the few open spaces curbside. Neither made a move to leave. "Want to come up for some coffee?" Pat said, finally.

"Sure."

She turned on every light in the entry hall, living room, and kitchen area. For now at least, she feared the darkness. Even though her eyes were open, in the darkness she felt as if they were closed and perhaps she'd never be able to open them again.

None of this was lost on Tully. He was most mindful that she would be alone tonight. He knew she was frightened. He knew she had reason. And he still felt that special spark between them that had ignited just a few evenings ago in a singles bar.

She put the water on. She was overwhelmingly aware of his strong masculine presence. She wanted nothing more than to curl up in his arms, protected from all evil. She was also painfully aware that his woman had been sick and now was well and waiting for him at home. She could not recall a more ambivalent moment in all her experience.

Then he was behind her in the narrow kitchen. She turned and was in his arms. They kissed tenderly. They backed away. They kissed again, each responding more passionately to the other.

Pat pushed herself away from him. There was genuine love in her smile. "You'd better leave now."

"Pat . . ."

"Zoo, we are about to slip over an edge that has no return. It would be so easy, and so easy to explain away later on. But not now. Maybe never. But definitely not now."

"Are you sure?"

"When you showed up at the hospital tonight, I was alone. I was frightened. Remember what I said to you?"

He smiled. " 'When a fella needs a friend.' "

"I still do. I think I just came close to losing my friend."

He wanted to ask once more if she was sure. But he knew she was.

He cautioned her to lock and bolt the door. Just to be certain, he conducted a search of the entire apartment. Both were assured that all was secure.

With one more, very chaste, kiss, he left.

Pat finished making coffee and poured a cup. She remembered she hadn't had dinner. That was to have been with Pringle. She looked in the fridge. Nothing looked appetizing. She just wasn't hungry.

The coffee tasted good. There was no concern about its

keeping her awake; she knew there would be no sleep for her this night.

With that realization, she decided to return to the *News* and write the Pringle McPhee story. Outside of the monster who had tried to kill Pringle, no one knew the story better than Pat did. There would be no further danger to her this night: That maniac didn't know he had failed twice, that he'd hit the wrong person and that the one he'd hit wasn't dead.

Not yet, anyway.

Tomorrow would be a different issue. He would know.

Then what?

She had not felt so alone and vulnerable since she was a small child. And not often then. At this moment, even Joe Cox looked good to her. How's that for desperation, she thought. And, so much for wearing one's best underwear!

As he drove, Tully noticed the rain was letting up. He was headed in the general direction of home, but in a most roundabout route. He needed time to think, and he had to get his thinking done before he walked in the front door.

He was sure Alice would still be on an emotional high. She would want to talk. He'd never be able to give her the attention she deserved unless his mind was clear of the thoughts that were now battering against it.

They'd come so close. It would have been so natural to have made love to Pat Lennon. If it hadn't been for her strong willpower, he would be feeling guilty as hell now as he returned to Alice. Instead, he felt somewhat virtuous. Rare for him.

So where did that leave him and Pat?

They were friends. Another odd situation. The word evoked images of fellow officers, a few lifelong acquaintances. All of them men. No women. Not as friends. A new concept for him: to regard a beautiful, desirable woman as a friend.

He suddenly felt sorry for his friend. Here he was, going home to a woman who loved him and whom, as long as she remained relatively healthy, he could love physically as well as emotionally. He wished for his friend the same good fortune. Then he realized that, in a very short time, he'd come to dislike Joe Cox, even though they'd never met. Now, he knew that he must see Cox through Pat's perspective. If she liked Cox, well, then so would Tully.

Pat Lennon would be dead—or dying—now if the perp hadn't been misled by the unexpected switch in car and rain gear. Or, at best, she would be vegetating in that hospital bed instead of her friend.

Even though the essence of his life was murder and death, Tully reserved particular loathing for perpetrators who tortured and overkilled in their murders. Like this guy tonight. What kind of fiend rolls over his victim with a car, over and over, tearing skin, crushing bones?

With that question, an image, a memory that had been fluttering against his consciousness all evening, began taking shape. It was another woman. A victim of vehicular homicide. In his mind's eye he could see the tread marks on her body.

Of course! The woman on the slab next to David Powell in the morgue, just a few days ago! The same m.o. Coincidence? Not likely. This sort of m.o. doesn't pop up with any frequency. Two identicals in just a few days? Not likely.

What could be the connection?

By damn, he'd find out. First thing tomorrow.

THURSDAY
JULY 27

CHAPTER
16

William O'Brien was ready for them. Until just recently, the before-hours arrival of Father Robert and Brother Paul had always taken O'Brien off guard. But in the last couple of days, their daily deposits had become so substantial that the branch manager of the First Standard Bank and Trust had been anticipating the monks' appearance shortly before opening time.

And here they were. O'Brien checked his pocket watch: 9:10 A.M., twenty minutes before opening; for them, right on time. O'Brien unlocked and opened the front door, greeted them, then relocked the door.

Brother Paul was carrying the large black satchel, which held today's deposit. "Good morning, Mr. O'Brien. God bless you for being so kind to us. It really helps us get through our busy days."

Just about what he said every morning. But with all the media coverage, O'Brien had become a believer in the fact that their days were indeed busy.

O'Brien led them behind the security gate, where a teller

relieved Brother Paul of the satchel and immediately began to process the day's deposit.

As was his custom, O'Brien invited them into his office and offered them coffee. Brother Paul, as usual, did the talking for the pair. He politely refused the coffee. To drink it would be to chance revealing his features within the cowl.

"However," Brother Paul said, "I would like to talk to you just a moment, Mr. O'Brien."

"Surely."

"Suppose we just let Father Robert rest here while we talk. He has another taxing day ahead of him."

Brother Paul propped Father Robert in an upholstered chair off to the side. By this time, the bank employees were accustomed to leaving the old man alone and to revering his presence as some sort of living relic. The Brother followed O'Brien into the manager's office.

"Well, Brother," said O'Brien, when they were seated, "you've been busy."

"Indeed." The cowl shook as Brother Paul nodded.

"You wanted to discuss something?"

"What's been happening to us."

"It's been miraculous."

"Literally. The crowds coming to us now are beyond belief. I fear we are tying up much of Detroit's police force just in directing traffic and helping keep order at the chapel."

"My, my."

"We've been getting letters from young men. Letters from all over the country. Some from Canada. Young men who express interest in joining our group."

O'Brien smiled. "Isn't that quite out of the ordinary?" He was Catholic enough to be aware of the religious vocation shortage that was becoming critical. He could appreciate that this was a reverse phenomenon.

"It is indeed out of the ordinary. And the money keeps pouring in from all over the world."

"Isn't that marvelous!" O'Brien could especially appreciate the financial contributions, particularly since the funds were being deposited in his bank.

"That's what I wanted to talk to you about, Mr. O'Brien. Our funds and our monastery."

"Oh?"

"It is clear we can no longer expect to stay in our present building and do the work the Lord is directing us to do. The time has come to think of a permanent monastery. Things are moving so quickly now, such a move is overdue."

"You had no way of knowing, Brother. These miracles . . ." O'Brien's voice trailed off in the implication that the miracles had happened unexpectedly and had changed everything.

"Nonetheless, it is imperative that we make our move. It is almost a sin to let another day go by without taking practical steps to equip us to provide the service to which God calls us."

"Do you have something specific in mind, Brother?"

"Specifically? Yes, Mr. O'Brien. I thought a loan . . ."

"A loan? That is well within the realm of possibility."

"Could you provide me with a figure? A maximum amount the bank would be comfortable with?"

"Well, let's see. Let me check something." O'Brien contacted the assistant manager on the interoffice line, and requested the balance statement for the Congregation of St. Stephen. In just a few moments he had the amount. He looked particularly pleased as he turned back to Brother Paul. "We haven't been able to check your cash deposits for today as yet, but $750,000 is a good ballpark figure for your balance." His expression grew serious. "But, tell me, Brother, wouldn't you prefer thinking of a mortgage?"

"I've . . . that is, we, have given that serious consideration. But with all these funds coming in steadily, we should need this loan for no more than ninety days to six months."

O'Brien gnawed at his lip. He had no doubt why Brother Paul was the spokesman for this group. He knew what he wanted. Nor could O'Brien fault the Brother's thinking.

The bank would be able to service this loan easily. One fact was incontrovertible: the Congregation of St. Stephen had money pouring in. "I should think we would be able to talk of such a short-term loan as you suggest in terms of, say, $500,000."

"That sounds fine, Mr. O'Brien. Generous, in fact. To whom shall I talk about this? Someone downtown?"

O'Brien smiled. "That won't be necessary, Brother. It's the policy of our bank to make our branch managers—in this case, myself—commercial lending officers with lending authority."

Brother Paul knew this fact well, but he affected to look surprised. "Isn't that marvelous? That will be so convenient for us. Once again, I'm just convinced that we were led to you by the Lord Himself. God bless you! Now, what kind of timetable are we talking about?"

"Would tomorrow be soon enough, Brother?"

Brother Paul was smiling, but no one could tell. "To-morrow . . . tomorrow morning?"

O'Brien nodded.

"That would be perfect, Mr. O'Brien. God bless you. Yes, indeed, God bless you."

It was just 9:30 A.M. The banking day had officially begun. O'Brien ushered the two monks out through the gathering crowd. Both sides promised to do business again tomorrow.

Seldom could the atmosphere of the Homicide Division be described as euphoric. But the mood this morning came close to jubilation. They had solved the Morgans' slaying.

The work was a monument to group dynamics. There were so many officers on this one case—nearly the entire section—that the perpetrator had stood little or no chance of getting away with it. A pity the Department couldn't function that way in all the homicide cases. But with De-troit's hundreds of homicides annually, it was absolutely impossible to invest that sort of manpower on each and every case.

In the Morgan case, there was added incentive. Criminals must understand that if they kill a cop, they have stirred up a very disturbed and fiery hornets' nest. Killing a cop's relative brings comparable consequences. In either case, in all probability the perpetrator is going to get caught.

And get caught he did. By tapping all available resources, calling in markers, squeezing informers, they got the guy. As was too often the case, it was a "friend" of the family.

Zoo Tully was as elated as anyone that the Morgan case was closed. He also felt pleased, if guardedly, that Alice had so far experienced no relapse. He was especially happy that she had agreed to see the doctor and have him check everything. He knew she'd agreed only to please him. Her argument analogized the wheel that was not squeaking: Don't oil it . . . why should she see the doctor if she was feeling well?

Tully's contention was that for many months, actually up to just yesterday, the wheel was about to fall off. It would be prudent to make certain the wheel had somehow repaired itself.

He had won partly because she felt too good to cloud their happiness by disappointing him.

At this moment, there was only one fly spoiling Tully's ointment: the attempted murder of Pat Lennon. A crime that remained very much unsolved. Not only was it an unsolved puzzle—always a burr under his saddle—but the perpetrator was still out there. When he discovered he'd failed—which discovery should take place right about now—presumably he would try again. Not a happy thought.

Tully was in Walt Koznicki's office, going over the Lennon case. From Koznicki's intimate and longstanding association with Tully plus the inspector's acquired knowledge of human behavior, he had convinced himself that Tully was no more than merely Lennon's friend. Koznicki was able to be more relaxed in that belief.

"At that time of night, and with all that rain," Koznicki said, "I suppose we are fortunate to have any eyewitness at all."

"There was at least one more than the two we know of."
Koznicki's expression asked the question.

Tully answered the nonverbal query. "The guy who stole McPhee's purse and, just maybe, her groceries."

Koznicki sighed. In situations like that of last night, in accidents and injuries, it was not unusual to find bystanders who react generously, even heroically, and others who plumbed the bottom of human degradation.

"Do we have anything on her actions last night?" Koznicki asked.

"We canvassed the neighborhood. She stopped at Ye Olde Butcher Shoppe. She picked up a pork roast and some vegetables. She must have planned to eat late; pork takes a while to cook."

"That's it. Far as we know, the market was her only stop between the newspaper and the apartment. The guy must have tailed her from the paper. If anything had been different . . ."

"Anything?"

"If she'd driven her own car, worn her own coat . . ."

Koznicki completed Tully's thought, but not in the direction Tully was headed. "If she had not done all of that, Alonzo, the killer would have known she was not Miss Lennon and would have waited for his victim."

Tully studied his hand. "Yeah."

"And," Koznicki continued, "if anything that happened last night had been changed, it would be Miss Lennon who would be in the hospital—or worse."

"Yeah."

"Any luck on the car?"

Tully shook his head. "I got Willie Moellmann out early this morning to check out that Hispanic woman—Mary Garcia, the one that was mangled by a car a few days ago. The tread marks don't match at all."

"Too bad. How about Mr. Parker . . . his full name escapes me."

"Fred Parker. Nothing. He and his wife were at the Institute of Arts reception. Photos in this morning's paper.

Hundreds of people can testify he was at the DIA all last evening."

Sergeant Moore walked by Koznicki's open door, stopped, did a double take, and backpedaled. "Zoo, I've been looking for you."

Tully tilted his head upward, inviting her reason.

"They found the car," Moore said.

"My hit-and-run?"

"That's it. For once, a witness hit it on the bull's-eye. It was an '87 Pontiac 6000, dark blue."

"How do you know it's the one?"

"When the guy spun out of the driveway last night, he creamed two parked cars. They traded paint. It matches perfectly. The front bumper's dented where he hit the girl, and the top is stove in, probably where she hit headfirst. Forensics has it now."

"Anything?"

"They just got it. And one thing more: It's hot."

Tully smiled at Koznicki. "Hear that, Walt? It's hot. If the guy stole this car to get Lennon, he probably stole another car to get the Garcia woman."

"So there may yet be a connection," Koznicki observed.

Tully nodded once with assurance. "It's the best we've got going for us just now. I'm going to follow it up. Come on, Moore, let's move."

If Koznicki could have given them his blessing, he would have.

Pat Lennon, having finished the basic story of what had happened to Pringle McPhee, had returned to her apartment just long enough to clean up, eat some cereal, and put on a fresh and more workplace-suitable outfit. Then she returned to the *News*.

She now sat at her desk lost in thought. Her most recent conscious visual image was Pringle McPhee's desk and chair. That triggered her musing.

Pat had no idea how many times she had played the mental game of what-if. She'd gone over and over the details of last night. She had looked forward to spending the evening with Pringle. Pringle needed a shoulder and Pat was lonely. Pringle regularly needed a shoulder. Pat was rarely lonely.

Everything else had been settled at the last moment. It had all made sense. Pringle's work was done. No reason she shouldn't get dinner started. No reason she shouldn't borrow Pat's coat and car. It all made sense. Decisions made in an instant would change their lives, maybe forever.

So absorbed was she that it took her several minutes to realize that Bob Ankenazy was standing alongside her desk. Suddenly aware, she looked up, slightly embarrassed. "Oh, I didn't see you."

"It's okay. Any word on Mac?"

"I phoned. She's listed as 'guarded.' That's one step in the right direction."

"Good. That's good. I'll spread the word." He paused, a smile threatening to break through. "You must be dead tired. Sure you don't want to go home? You were here practically all night."

"No. God, no. I've got to stay on this story. I've got to see if they start an investigation into our 'miracle worker.'" She looked at him quizzically. She sensed he had left something unsaid. "Why?" she demanded.

"There's somebody downstairs to see you."

"Who?"

"Why don't you go find out?"

Wearily, she pulled herself to her feet. She didn't care for games, especially in her present state of exhaustion. "Okay." She was too tired to argue or ask any further questions.

Halfway down to the main floor in the elevator it dawned on her who was waiting for her. When she got out of the elevator, she was not disappointed. "Joe."

"Pat! You look terrible!"

"Thanks . . . thanks a lot."

"Oh, God, I blew it! Here I had this great line worked up, and—you must have had a really ugly night."

"What are you doing here, Joe?"

"Ankenazy got in touch. He told me about last night. But I had no idea it was this bad."

"You're really great for a gal's self-image."

"I didn't mean that. You look great, as always. Just tired. More tired than I've ever seen you."

"Back to the beginning: What are you doing here?"

"I told you: When Ankenazy called, I came right in."

She didn't bother to conceal her sarcasm. "What about your *story*?"

"Okay, it's open season on me. I deserve it. I've been a jerk. That fact dawned on me shortly after I got to Port Huron. I should have turned it down and gone on our vacation."

"So why didn't you come home then?"

"It was too late to salvage the vacation by that time. And . . . well, I was sore at you. But if it makes you feel any better, I had a miserable time. Those goons I was with shouldn't be let loose in a pond, let alone Lake Huron. And what you undoubtedly assumed didn't happen. There wasn't any hanky-panky. My intrepid crew was gay."

Maybe it was because she was so exhausted. She started to laugh. As she laughed, she recalled the last few moments she'd spent with Zoo Tully. If she hadn't applied the brakes, they could have made it beautifully last night.

So Joe Cox had experienced some forced chastity. She tended to believe him. It didn't make a bit of difference. She had not resisted her strong emotions out of any sense of fidelity to Joe. She'd done it for Zoo. She had too much respect for Zoo to give him a one-nighter. Which, given the miraculous return to health of his woman, is undoubtedly what it would have been.

"Your adventures in the Mackinac Race don't make me happy or sad, Joe. They don't matter to me at all."

"Don't mention Mackinac. We got as far as Port Sanilac. I was able to convince them they were too sloshed to find Canada, let alone Mackinac." He paused, clearly ill at ease. "Pat, we've got a lot going for us. I knew it when I was out on that crazy lake and I started worrying I'd lost you. I need you, Pat. Can't we build together, again?''

All along, in her heart, she'd known the outcome. Living through his conciliatory speech was almost déjà vu. In her imagination, she'd lived through it already. But she wasn't about to hop into bed just because he'd said the magic word. She merely murmured, ''We can try.''

''Let's go home.''

''I've got a story to cover.''

''Ankenazy told me you could have the rest of the day off.''

''That was nice of Bob, but I've got a story to cover.''

''You're almost dead.''

''The story is very much alive. And it's my story.''

For the first time since she'd gotten off the elevator, he became aware that they were standing in the middle of the lobby. The scene looked, and he felt, awkward. He led her to one of the upholstered benches.

''Look,'' he began, after they'd sat down, ''Ankenazy spelled it out for me. Somebody tried to kill you last night. Whoever he is, he's still out there. It's just possible you're a sitting duck. I can't let you do this.''

''You can't stop me.''

Cox thought for a moment. He was tired of being on the defensive. It was time to turn things around. ''Okay, you're right: I can't stop you. But I can join you. Whoever the son-of-a-bitch is, he's going to have to go through me to get you.''

Once again, her intuition, which she had good reason to trust, told her he was sincere. She believed that there hadn't been any hanky-panky during his Mackinac assignment. She also believed that he would sacrifice himself to protect her. Joe Cox had almost rehabilitated their relationship.

''But it's my story!'' she warned.

Cox smiled. ''I've got a few sick days coming. Nelson Kane agreed I was sick. Of course, as my city editor, he would have done that any time of the year. No, I'm coming along just for the ride. It's your story.''

244

Pat returned the smile. "Okay, lover. Let's get going. Hungry?"

His smile turned into a lecherous grin. "For lots of things."

"All in due time. Right now, I'm famished. Somehow I missed a meal or two. We've got time to get some food and—most of all—a lot of coffee. Then we've got to get over to that chapel and see what miracles our Father Robert can fashion."

"You got it. Give us this day our daily circus!"

Pat returned to the city room to retrieve her tote bag, notes, and pad. Then she and Cox left together, with trust trying hard to reenter their relationship.

"Inspector," Father Koesler said, "you'll never guess what they've got me doing."

"I would not argue with that," Koznicki said. "What do they want you to do? And who is 'they'?"

Koznicki wondered at this call. He did not mind a call from his priest friend at any time. But out of concern for the inspector's extremely demanding work schedule, Koesler's rule of thumb was never to call during business hours unless he had business to conduct. Otherwise Koesler phoned Koznicki at home after hours.

"'They,'" Koesler repeated. "That's an interesting question. 'They,' I suppose, is the Archdiocese of Detroit. More specifically, 'they' is the Cardinal Archbishop of Detroit. And what 'they' want me to do is to conduct an examination into the business that's been going on at St. Stephen's Monastery. The alleged miracles."

Koznicki couldn't help smiling; over the phone, it didn't hurt. "If memory serves, you spoke of that the other evening at dinner at the rectory. Again, if memory serves, it seems you expressed sympathy for whoever among your confreres was selected for that task. Now, it seems that person is yourself. I suppose I should be offering you my condolences."

Left unspoken was Koznicki's persisting puzzlement at

Koesler's call. There was still no clue as to why he had phoned Koznicki at work. Surely not merely to give him this news. It was an interesting bit of information but easily communicable after hours when he would have expected such a call from the priest.

"What I was wondering," Koesler clarified, "is, do you have any suggestions?"

"Suggestions?"

"I've never conducted an investigation. Never been in charge of one. You do this sort of thing all the time. You've done it for years. So, any suggestions?"

Koznicki hesitated. Were there ten simple rules on how to conduct an investigation? Five? "I am at a bit of a loss, Father. What have they told you so far?"

"Nothing much. I got a call from Monsignor Iming, the Cardinal's secretary. He said, 'The boss wants to see you.' "

" 'The boss wants to see you'?"

"This is not the first time I've been summoned downtown. This is the standard way the secretary phrases it. He says the boss wants to see me. I ask why. He says it's been a while since the boss talked to me and he's grown lonesome. I say, 'C'mon, why?' Then he gets down to business.

"This morning, the business was that I was to conduct an investigation into the Congregation of St. Stephen and the so-called miracles." Koesler explained no further. A few moments of silence followed.

"When is your appointment?" Koznicki asked, finally.

"Forty-five minutes from now."

"Then perhaps when you get there, there will be some explanation of what exactly is expected of you."

"Maybe, but I don't think so. It's not the Cardinal's style. Oh, he's likely to explain the relevant law, details, and circumstances. Then he leaves it up to the individual as to how to get the job done."

"That does not sound too distasteful. Many people would be most happy to have a superior who did not interfere with one's work."

"Granted! As long as you know what you're doing. It's

246

not all that comforting when you haven't the slightest idea of how to go about something.

"One last time, Inspector: Now that I've explained my predicament, got any suggestions?"

"Not really, Father. There was one thing you mentioned, however, that may give us something in common. You said something about the Cardinal explaining law. I find that helpful. Whenever I begin an investigation, I am conscious of the relevant law that may be violated in that case. By now, this is almost a reflex action. One measures what has happened in the given situation against the law. Perhaps that will be helpful to you."

"Yes, maybe. I'll give it a lot of thought on my drive downtown. Anyway, thanks for your help, Inspector. And sorry for having interrupted you at work."

"Perfectly all right, Father. I wish I could have helped you more."

"You were a big help. Thanks again." As Koesler hung up, he clumsily brushed his hand over the desk, knocking over his half-filled cup of coffee. He had no time to clean up the mess. Embarrassed, he sheepishly asked Mary O'Connor to clean it up.

Mary reflected that it was Koesler who had made the coffee, so undoubtedly it was better that it had been spilled. But she said only that it would be no bother to sponge it up.

Koesler dragged himself into the garage, meditating on the likelihood that this did not promise to be one of his better days.

CHAPTER
17

Everything about the second floor of the Archdiocese of Detroit's Chancery Building spoke to the personality of its principal occupant, Cardinal Mark Boyle, Archbishop of Detroit. Both the decor and the man were, in a word, classy.

Exiting the elevator on the second floor, possible only if one's name had been given to the operator in advance, one was impressed by soft, indirect lighting and a most quiet, restrained atmosphere. The office space was laid out in an L-shape. The elongated foyer, just off the elevator, led to offices of two secretaries. At the end of the foyer was Monsignor Iming's office. At that point, the office space took a ninety-degree turn to the left. Down that hall lay, first, the archbishop's office and, finally, a meeting room.

Koesler checked in at the reception desk with Mary Alfredo, the vivacious and seemingly ever cheerful secretary to both Iming and Boyle. Brightly, she informed Koesler that there was someone with the Cardinal but that he would be only a few minutes more.

That, thought Koesler, was a safe conclusion. Cardinal

Boyle shared Koesler's obsession with punctuality. When Boyle supervised his schedule, he allocated an appropriate amount of time for each person—not too much, nor too little.

So Koesler had no more than a few minutes in which to cool his heels. He took a seat on one of the two beige leather sectional couches. Everything was pretty much as he remembered it. He'd been here with some frequency while he was editor of the *Detroit Catholic,* but not lately. In fact, until today, he'd expected he would have no reason to be here ever again. On the other hand, he had lived long enough that he had learned never to rule out any possibility.

The long wall he faced bore photos of the present Pope as well as his two immediate predecessors. There was also a tile rendering of Cardinal Boyle's coat of arms. The brilliant red-orange, plus the thirty tassels, unmistakably identified Boyle as a Prince of the Church. Below the photos and the coat of arms was a long credenza on which was displayed a sculpture of the Sermon on the Mount, all in green and mounted on a log. Between the two sections of the couch was a small table holding a lamp. There were no magazines or any reading material whatever—a statement to the visitor that there would be little waiting time.

He sat recalling his previous visits, mostly informational meetings wherein either he or Boyle had something to tell the other.

A door opened, out of sight down the hallway. He could hear Cardinal Boyle's voice, though he could not make out what was being said. Boyle's voice was easily identified. It had a husky quality, possibly from being used in public addresses far more frequently than the Cardinal would have preferred. Yet there was a softness and a lilt that suggested his Irish ancestry.

Koseler remained seated as another priest emerged from the hallway. It was one of the rare young priets Koesler scarcely knew. He thought the man's name was Father Hanley. The two nodded in a friendly but noncommittal way, as Hanley had to walk the length of the foyer, then wait for the elevator. He seemed somewhat embarrassed.

Koesler speculated as to why Hanley had been called downtown. Reasons could range from receiving a special nonparochial assignment to getting raked over the coals. Koesler found it amusing that Hanley was wearing a freshly cleaned and pressed black suit with traditional Roman collar, and even a white shirt whose French cuffs peeked out from beneath his jacket. Koesler guessed that, whatever his business with "the boss," Hanley couldn't wait to get back to the rectory and climb into some sweats.

He didn't have much time for speculation; Mary Alfredo announced that the Cardinal was ready and waiting. Koesler checked his ever-present watch: 10:45. Right on the nose.

As Koesler turned the corner of the hallway, he saw Boyle waiting at the door to his office. As Koesler entered the room, they shook hands. Not too many years ago, Koesler would have genuflected, taken Boyle's right hand and kissed the episcopal ring. That, like myriad minor rituals, was gone forever, at least in Boyle's life and by his wish.

Boyle gestured toward one of the chairs surrounding a circular coffee table just inside the door. "Sit down, won't you, Father. Good of you to come."

As far as Koesler knew, the Cardinal was the only Catholic clergyman in Detroit who invariably used the formal title of "Father." But then, Boyle was courtly to a fault. On his part, Koesler could not have forced himself to address Boyle other than by his title. So, there they were, two remnants of an older world, marching toward the twenty-first century.

They sat opposite each other. Boyle fidgeted, as he always did—alternating between toying with his episcopal ring—ring finger right hand—and adjusting the gold chain that fell across his chest and held the pectoral cross.

Boyle, still handsome as he approached his eightieth year, was a couple of inches over six feet tall and, due to recent health demands, very slender. His once jet black hair now was white and wispy. But his most arresting feature by far was his eyes. Light blue, they were, beneath beetle brows, piercing and most expressive. It was a challenge to meet his gaze. He never had to verbally express anger, or enjoyment for that matter. His eyes said it all.

Now, Boyle's demeanor was disarmingly cheerful, as if to say that what he was about to discuss was of no great moment.

"Father Koesler," he began, "no doubt you've been following the accounts of that new group in the diocese, the . . ."—he cleared his throat; definitely too much talking for such a quiet voice—"the Congregation of St. Stephen."

"Yes, I have, Eminence." Boyle was the only person he knew who in ordinary conversation sounded as if he were writing a scholarly book.

"Well, then, you are undoubtedly aware that over the past few days there have been several . . . uh . . . unusual events that have been reported going on there."

"Uh-huh. Miracles, I believe the media is calling them."

Boyle waved his right hand as if erasing what Koesler had just said, or giving an episcopal triple blessing. "Well, of course, the news media are unconcerned with the technical requirements that underlay a genuine miracle. We would prefer, at this point, to refer to them as unusual events."

"I've got no problem calling them 'unusual events.'"

Boyle narrowed his gaze, puzzling as to whether Koesler was putting him on. It would not be the first time. "Well, Father, be that as it may, let me tell you a little about how the Congregation happens to be established in Detroit. The purpose of all this will become clearer in due time."

From his earlier conversation with Monsignor Iming, Koesler knew damn well what the purpose of all this was: He was going to get stuck with investigating this ecclesial mess. But it certainly wouldn't hurt to perhaps learn something about how he was supposed to accomplish one more task for which he'd never been trained.

Koesler sat back, relaxed, and watched Boyle wind and unwind the gold chain around his index finger. Those restless hands. Boyle should have been a smoker. But in the nearly thirty years he'd been in Detroit, there had never been an ashtray in his office. Insofar as he could control the atmosphere around him, Boyle tried to live in a smoke-free environment.

Boyle cleared his computerlike brain by announcing, "In all that I shall say regarding Church Law, I shall of course have reference to the 1983 Code."

Of course, Koesler thought, what else? Well, there was the 1917 Code. But that was passé.

In all of the nearly two thousand-year history of the Catholic Church, ecclesiastical law for the entire Church had been gathered, codified, and published in a single volume only twice. The 1917 Code of Canon Law contained 2,414 laws. The 1983 Code had 1,752 laws. Outside of the 662 fewer laws, Koesler was unable to find any radical difference between the Codes. Although he had not studied the 1983 version nearly as carefully as the 1917, from random specific research and conversation with students in the field, he was forced to conclude that Church Law was still primarily concerned with "Preserving the Institution."

"The relevant canon," Boyle continued, "is number 589, which has to do with an institute of consecrated life of diocesan right."

Amazing! Koesler knew the Cardinal had not memorized the entire Code. Some local priest with a Canon Law degree had looked all this up for Boyle. But Koesler knew that the Cardinal was such a quick study that he had mastered all the pertinent law and now was going to toss it off as if it were second nature. Besides, Boyle was a teacher by training and temperament and he loved this.

"As you probably know, Father . . ."

Don't bet on it.

". . . an institute of consecrated life may be said to be of pontifical right if it has been either erected or approved by the Holy See. On the other hand, the institute is said to be of diocesan right if it is established by a diocesan bishop and has not obtained a decree of approval from the Apostolic See."

252

Boyle looked intently at Koesler, but, for the life of him, the Cardinal was unable to ascertain whether there was anything going on behind that bland expression. "Have I made myself clear thus far, Father?"

"Uh-huh. I suppose the Congregation of St. Stephen is one of the two. Either pontifical or diocesan." Koesler was indeed interested—far more interested than he appeared—for two reasons: He found the machinations and/or logic of all law inherently intriguing. And he knew beforehand how all this was going to end—in his lap.

"The very point," Boyle said. "The Congregation of St. Stephen is an institute of consecrated life of diocesan right."

Koesler nodded. "Okay, Eminence: which diocese?"

Boyle was gratified that despite his impassive demeanor, Koesler was paying attention. "Pomaria," Boyle said, in answer to Koesler's question. When Koesler's quizzical expression persisted, Boyle clarified: "Pomaria is a very small diocese in southern Italy."

Koesler looked incredulous. "Pomaria! I don't see what that has to do with anything, Eminence. I mean, what's the connection between a little diocese in southern Italy and a monastic group in inner-city Detroit?"

Boyle sighed. "The only relevance, Father, is that the group is canonically correct. As far as we know, each member of this group is a United States citizen. Some time ago . . ."—again, Boyle waved his hand, this time communicating the message that this and many other details were perhaps fodder for the investigation, but, in any case, beyond Boyle's interest—". . . but within the past year, the group traveled to Pomaria and petitioned the bishop there to establish them as an institute of consecrated life. In effect, a new, if presently insignificant, religious order."

"And the bishop there—in Pomaria—did it? He just did it?" Without waiting for Boyle's response, Koesler pursued, "Then I don't understand why they're not in Pomaria. What are they doing in Detroit?"

The question did not please Boyle; his brows almost met over the bridge of his nose. "Bishop Di Giulio, the ordinary of Pomaria, is not what he once was. He has not been well these past few years."

Koesler completed a simultaneous translation: Bishop Di Giulio was a vegetable and had been such for as long as anyone could remember. "If I understand this correctly, Eminence, these Americans—one of them a priest . . . ?"

Boyle nodded.

". . . one of them a priest, and four or five—what— religious Brothers?"

"Any Catholic, with the correct intention who has the qualities required by law, and who has no impediment, can be admitted to an institute of consecrated life." Boyle correctly quoted Canon 597, as Koesler would later find for himself.

"So," Koesler proceeded, "this priest and his companions presented themselves to the Bishop of Pomaria and requested that they be incorporated—no, better—*established* as an institute of consecrated life. And the bishop, who has . . . uh . . . not been himself lately, put his stamp of approval on the enterprise. But he doesn't demand that they operate in Pomaria. He doesn't make any demand on them at all. So, for some reason, they migrate to Detroit. And here we are."

There was a pause. Then Boyle admitted, "That would be a fair assessment."

Koesler considered Boyle to be holding up well for a Prince of the Church who had been screwed.

"I think I see the ploy," Koesler said. "This is something like that maneuver some twenty years ago during the Council when that extremely conservative priest accompanied the retired bishop to Rome as the bishop's expert."

Koesler remembered the event well because, as editor of the *Detroit Catholic*, he had written a satirical essay about that very affair. The point of the essay had been that the more one understands Canon Law, the better one is able to manipulate it to one's own purpose.

Koesler continued. "And while he was in Italy—what was his name, Father Depaul or something like that—while he was there he dropped over to another little Italian diocese and got the bishop there to incardinate, adopt him. Then the priest returned to New York and set up a strong conservative wing of the Church. There was little Cardinal Spellman could do about it because the priest belonged to the Italian bishop—who, like our Bishop Di Giulio, was also 'not what he once was.'

"And the priest was never canonically incardinated into New York as our Congregation of St. Stephen was officially welcomed to Detroit. So, there was nothing Cardinal Spellman could do about it."

Boyle nodded, not happily.

That was the secret to religious life in the Catholic Church, Koesler mused. Everybody belonged to somebody. He belonged to a territory: the Archdiocese of Detroit and to its archbishop. Jesuits, Dominicans, Franciscans, nuns (of all orders)—all belonged to their religious orders and to their religious superiors. The superiors owed their subjects a living, plus anything else their constitutions provided for. The subjects owed their superiors obedience, maybe reverence, and anything else their constitutions called for. And the superiors were responsible for their subjects. Responsible to see that their work was done, that they did not make waves, that they were punished when that was appropriate and muzzled when necessary.

Everybody belonged to somebody. The Congregation of St. Stephen belonged to Bishop Di Giulio, who was going to be of no help controlling the Congregation because the bishop was permanently under the weather. Sometimes a system as time-tested as the Catholic Church can produce a squeaky wheel.

Koesler thought he might have found a solution. But it seemed such an obvious gambit that he could not believe he was the first to have thought of it. "Why not ship the Congregation back to Pomaria?"

"We have considered that . . ." Boyle began.

Koesler wondered whether the "we" was an episcopal plural or if Boyle had actually consulted with others. Whatever the circumstances, Koesler clearly had been neither the first nor the only one to have considered repatriation, or exile, depending on how one wanted to look at it.

"... But," Boyle continued, "we decided against it." He shifted again and resumed toying with the ring and the chain alternately. "On the one hand, don't you see, Father, there is the notoriety or fame they have gained.

"And, on the other hand, they are here legitimately. We accepted their credentials and approved their presence in this archdiocese. They followed all the prescriptions of the law regarding Canons 936, 937, and so on about the reservation of the Eucharist. Until this issue is settled one way or another, it would be suicidal, from the public relations standpoint, to opt for so extreme a solution. At least at the present time," he added, almost as an afterthought.

"And that, Father," Boyle leaned toward Koesler slightly, "is where you enter the picture. In keeping with the spirit of Canon 1717, I am hereby delegating you to cautiously—and I emphasize the element of caution—to cautiously inquire about the facts and circumstances." Anticipating that the priest might interrupt at this point, Boyle continued in an unbroken pattern. "You need not trouble about such things as the lawfulness of what they do in dispensing the Sacraments. The priest has been granted the faculties of the archdiocese and, in accord with Canon 1223, their chapel qualifies as an oratory in which the faithful may lawfully gather." He paused.

Koesler was convinced that any objection he might raise would be dismissed out of hand. But he simply couldn't resist. "Eminence, why me?"

The shadow of a smile passed over Boyle's face. "Whatever else may be at work here, Father, these unusual events have become a media event. It was thought that with your experience at the newspaper, you might be better prepared than anyone else in the Detroit presbyterate to appreciate all the consequences of what we are facing here."

Koesler reacted inwardly. Yes, he thought, my experience in the media began many years ago when then Archbishop Boyle tapped me to be editor of the *Detroit Catholic*. But, for that sublime mystery of selection I would have no media experience whatever.

Boyle continued, "That, Father, and in addition, the Canon expressly states, 'Care must be taken lest anyone's good name be endangered by this investigation.' Some might find it tempting in conducting an investigation of a matter such as this that has an international spotlight of attention on it, to—how shall I put this?—to play to the crowd. And in that way, the reputation of those involved could easily be tarnished.

"It is tempting, Father, to prejudge what is going on here to be of a purely hysterical nature or even an act of fraud. Any unstudied remark or premature conclusion could damage the reputation of those monks. But it would gain a great deal of attention for the investigator.

"It comes down to this, Father: I have confidence that you shall be most circumspect and cautious about all of the reputations involved." He paused. "If there is no further question, Father . . ." Boyle leaned back, giving every indication he considered their meeting concluded.

But Koesler had one final question. And, while he anticipated that it, too, would be waved away, he had to present it. "Your Eminence, I have no experience in this. I will not know what I'm doing." And, Koesler thought, it won't be the first time. When he'd sat in this same office years ago and heard Boyle announce his appointment as editor, Koesler had had the same demurrer. He knew nothing about being an editor, nor had he had any training to prepare for the position. He had objected, but the objection had been airily dismissed. And it was happening again.

Boyle relaxed and tried to communicate a lighter mood to Koesler. "Father, you must understand that your role in all this is largely pro forma; ceremonial, if you will. Whatever your findings, they will be reviewed by our Tribunal—that in accordance with Canons 1717 and 1718."

Koesler had long since tired of the ritualistic march of canons. "Then, why bother, Eminence? Why not just skip over the middleman, get the Tribunal in here, and settle the matter?"

"Every base must be touched, Father."

Odd hearing him use a sports metaphor.

"This is a matter of law," Boyle continued, "and it must proceed accordingly. The Code is very specific on these matters and it must be followed. You see, Father, in the event—and I do not anticipate this, but it is a distinct possibility—in the event that any sort of punitive action need be taken, we must be sure that every procedure has been completed correctly.

"The Code calls for a preliminary investigation to be carried out by myself or by someone I delegate—in this case yourself—and then a more formal investigation by the Tribunal."

So that's it, thought Koesler. There's no getting around it. I've got to do it. "When do you want me to start this, Eminence?"

Boyle lifted a French cuff and consulted his watch. "It's just 11:30. Time enough for you to attend one of their Masses, perhaps observe their procedures in dealing with the people who come to them for special help, and then spend some time interrogating them—any questions that come to your mind."

Koesler was plainly surprised. "So soon! Right now? I'd like some time to collect my thoughts, prepare some questions . . ."

Boyle's blue eyes hardened. "I would prefer that you do it now. Finish it today. Keep in mind that almost certainly your inquiry will be followed by a more formal and definitive investigation. I would like this preliminary inquiry to be concluded quickly."

"May I ask why? Why the hurry?"

Boyle hesitated, apparently mulling whether to explain. His eyes narrowed. "Did you happen to see this morning's edition of the *News*?"

"Not yet, Eminence."

"It contains a detailed description of yesterday's unusual

event at St. Stephen's Chapel. Father Robert is quoted as recommending that the woman who seemed to be cured have nothing more to do with doctors or the medical profession. We have looked into that allegation and found that it was accurate.''

"I'm not sure—"

"Father, were she to follow that advice and because of it to worsen or die because she separated herself from medical help, the liability would be staggering. And there is every indication that this sort of advice might well be given again to others.''

The liability would be staggering. That pretty well explained the necessity for an immediate investigation. It was easy enough to be jaundiced over such a motivation, but the reality was sobering.

It was not all that difficult for an outside group such as the Congregation of St. Stephen to lawfully establish itself in Detroit. Given that, someone with only one oar in the water could cause havoc, to be followed by a multimillion-dollar lawsuit. And before you know it, the Church would be forced to sell St. Peter's Basilica. It made sense then, to get this Church investigation over with as quickly as possible.

Koesler could think of only one further problem. "One thing more, Eminence: Won't it seem odd to those men for me to come riding in asking questions? It seems that they could have reasonable objections to an invasion of their privacy . . . no?''

Boyle smiled. "The necessary papers appointing you to this position are prepared. Monsignor Iming will have them for you as you leave.''

As he left the Cardinal, Koesler recalled the Gospel story of the landowner who sent his son to find out what was going on with the farm. But the malefactors killed the messenger. Koesler fervently hoped the Gospel fiction would not become reality in his case.

CHAPTER
18

Koesler had seen smaller crowds for a Tigers–Yankees game. The fact that he was not far from Tiger Stadium undoubtedly inspired the comparison. There were even vendors around—although he couldn't tell what they were hawking. He was too occupied with trying not to run anyone down.

He hated to be in crowds. Ordinarily, the sight of a crowd was more than enough to turn him around and send him somewhere else, anywhere else.

But he had a mandate. He was trying not to take the mandate too seriously, but it was a commission from his archbishop. So, he felt he really ought to give it an honest try before giving up. The first traffic officer who waved his car away from the scene would get complete and grateful acquiescence.

After all, his task in this was little more than a ritual. The real investigation would follow his inquiry regardless of what form his report would take.

On the other hand, the Tribunal's investigation was waiting until he at least went through the motions. So, he inched forward in the nearly gridlocked traffic.

By craning, he was able to see a Detroit traffic patrolman ahead. The patrolman was doing just what Koesler had been hoping and praying for: He was directing drivers to turn and leave the area.

As Koesler reached the head of the line the oddest thing happened: The patrolman smiled and waved him forward. As he pulled up even with the patrolman, Koesler took note of the name tag.

"Sergeant Lukas," Koesler said, "I was all set to leave."

"No need, Father. We always reserve a little space for people who have legitimate business here."

That stopped Koesler for a moment. Could news of his appointment as petit inquisitor have been made public? Hardly. Besides, what difference would that have made to the police, whose job it was to control the crowd, not be on the lookout for the Cardinal's representative? Then it came to him. The clergyman's uniform! Could it be possible? "Sergeant, by any means might you be a Catholic?"

Big smile. "Yessiree, Father. Holy Rosary Parish. Father Mac's my main man."

How lucky can you get, Koesler thought, as Sergeant Lukas directed a patrolman to take good care of the good Father's car. There aren't all that many black Catholics in the city. It was Koesler's good fortune, when he might now have been driving back to the peace and quiet of St. Anselm's, to have encountered a member in apparent good standing of Father Mac's parish. And a police sergeant to boot.

It was providence—providence with a streak of mean humor.

There was a good bit of pushing and shoving going on, and language inappropriate to a place where miracles were being sought and dispensed. But with the recognition of his clerical status and some assistance from some of the police, he managed to make his way indoors.

Once inside the packed chapel, Koesler did not fare so

well. The police were almost overwhelmed with trying to protect the crowd from harming itself. In addition, self-assertiveness was not Koesler's long suit. So he settled for being pressed against a side wall of the chapel. Fortunately, he was tall enough, and those in his immediate vicinity were short enough, so that he had a fairly good and relatively unobstructed view of the proceedings.

Others might have been unable to look upon this as anything but an old bank building. But he could recognize its value as a chapel. He had experienced churches and chapels in almost every guise imaginable.

There were cathedrals and churchy churches. There were also lots of churches and chapels that were built with the express purpose of later becoming something else. So, many new suburban churches were intended to become a school, a social hall, an all-purpose building, with a permanent church to come. Often the permanent church never got off the drawing board.

Koesler, himself, had been in one of the earliest classes when St. John's Seminary opened in the late 1940s. During his four years of theological study, the students' chapel had been a section slated to become the library reading room. In fact, it had been not unlike this building, with its generous use of brick and marble and hard terrazzo floor. But Koesler's chapel had not been anywhere near as dark as this.

Why would the monks want to paint over these large windows and make things so dour?

No time for further speculation. A bell sounded, there was a good bit of shushing; the crowd quieted markedly.

Koesler watched as the small, solemn procession of monks moved toward the plain table that served as an altar. His attention was riveted on the priest. Father Koesler was experiencing an occupational hazard.

The hazard would be easily understood by anyone, particularly a professional, who watched as someone else performed a job for which the professional had been trained. A police officer, a doctor, a pilot, watching a movie wherein his or her profession was being portrayed could scarcely

262

help being critical: "That's not the way a real cop [doctor, pilot] would do it!"

So it is with priests. Watching another priest function, it is all but impossible not to critique the performer.

So this was Father Robert. They shared the same first name, except that Koesler's was given at birth and the monk probably chose his when he entered religious life. The priest was the only monk whose head was not covered by a cowl. Still, Koesler had great difficulty making out his features. It was so damnably dark!

Koesler's first observation had nothing to do with the man's priestly function. Father Robert appeared to be feeble, maybe very ill. He walked slowly, with the hint of a limp. He seemed to list slightly to the left. But he reached the altar safely. Three of the monks, all pretty much the same size and—covered by their habits—appearing identical, took places to the right. The much larger monk—he must be the one called Brother Paul—stayed close to the priest.

Father Robert bowed low before the crucifix; he would have fallen had Brother Paul not supported him. Koesler began to think that the "miracle worker" needed a miracle, or at least a doctor. But Koesler could provide neither a miracle nor the doctor. With a sigh, he returned to what he couldn't help doing, evaluating another priest's performance of a common function—offering Mass.

Robert was carrying the fully covered chalice. A nice touch, Koesler thought. Not many did that anymore. Usually, nowadays, Mass began with the chalice and wafer plunked on a side table out of the way of the "Liturgy of the Word," the principal feature of which was the reading of Scripture. While that arrangement made sense, it was a nice bit of nostalgia to see it done as in days of yore.

Robert set the chalice to one side, removed the burse, or purselike container, and, in turn, removed from the burse the large linen cloth called a corporal.

As Robert removed the corporal, the cloth opened up fully above the altar, almost as if the priest were shaking it out. Koesler almost gasped. The corporal was the cloth on which rested the chalice and wafers. After Communion, priests—at least priests of the vintage of Robert and Koesler—would scrape the corporal with a flat, gold-plated disc called a paten, and finally fold the corporal a prescribed four times, making sure that not even the smallest fragment of the consecrated bread was spilled on the altar or the floor.

It was a reflection of an ancient theology that Catholic writer Garry Wills referred to as "the war against crumbs" and one of Koesler's friends called "crumby theology." One simply did not allow the cloth to open and possibly spill breadcrumbs after all those precautions. Koesler took it as an indication of how feeble the poor man must be.

The Mass began. When he heard Robert pronounce, *Fratres, agnoscamus peccata nostra, ut apti simus ad sacra mysteria celebranda*, Koesler recognized the Latin of the new Mass formula. All was kosher.

He did not anticipate that his report to the Cardinal and the Tribunal would be at all lengthy. Actually, he would have to pad it. He now knew he would begin by reporting that while the monks used a Latin liturgy, it was not the outlawed Tridentine formula, but one that was current and in good standing. Now, if only he could find a few more particulars to fill out his pro forma investigation.

"Hmmm, that's interesting," Pat Lennon commented with some feeling.

"What? What is?" Joe Cox's voice betrayed a certain nervous anxiety. He was taking his role as protector very seriously.

Lennon had found a heating duct that ran along the wall. By leaning against Cox, she was able to balance atop the duct and get a better view across the crowd.

"Can't you see him, Joe? Over against the side wall."

By standing tiptoed, Cox was able to see over the heads of at least some of his neighbors. The trouble, besides the physical challenge of actually spotting someone in that crowd, was that he didn't know whom he was supposed to identify.

Lennon glanced down to see Cox's head swiveling point-lessly. "Against the wall, Joe; with the Roman collar."

"Uh-huh; okay, I've got him. Don't I know him?"

"It's Koesler. You're darn right you know him. Remember that—"

"Okay, Koesler; yeah, you're right. But what's so note-worthy about a priest's being in church?"

At that, a middle-aged, babushkaed woman standing directly in front of Cox spun around. "Shh!" she spat, as she pulled a fountain-penlike instrument from her purse and shot a spray of something liquid at Cox.

It hit him full in the face. He recoiled as if he'd been struck with acid. His sudden motion almost caused Lennon to lose her balance on the duct. She clutched him to steady herself. Then she began to snicker quietly.

"Joe," Lennon stage-whispered, "it was holy water. It was just water."

Cox blotted the liquid with his handkerchief and examined the wet spot. It seemed to be water. He was embarrassed at having reacted so defensively to a holy water attack. "There oughtta be a law," he growled.

"Whisper," she admonished, "unless you want to get drowned."

"Okay," Cox whispered, "but one more blast from her and Ziggy Zablonski is going to be a widower." He reset himself as Pat's sole means of balance. "So, what's so odd about a priest being in a church?"

"Nothing, except, I wonder . . . I wonder if this could be the beginning of the Church investigation I predicted."

"They'd send one priest?"

"I don't know. I never covered one of these; I don't know how they work. But, maybe. And, you know, Koesler's been involved in investigations before."

"Police. Police investigations. Into murder, not mira-cles."

"How many priests, do you suppose, Detroit's got that have any training in running an investigation like this?"

Cox shrugged.

"Besides, from what I know of Father Koesler, he's not the type who'd come here as a sightseer, out of curiosity. No, there's got to be another reason. I think he may just be the designated Torquemada."

Cox shrugged again, nearly dislodging her from her perch. "Well," he said, "suppose he's what you think he is: What do you want to do about it?"

"Get me over there."

"Huh?"

"When Mass is over, there'll be a crush to get near the altar where the blessings are given. We've got to get over to Koesler so I can talk to him." She looked down at Cox and noted the furrows in his brow. "Think you can do it, lover?"

"Sure," he said, too readily. Actually, he'd never envied the salmon's penchant for swimming against the current. But he was committed to staying at her side and doing all he could to protect her. So, he'd give it a go.

The present Pope would like this guy, thought Koesler, as he listened to Father Robert's sermon. The preacher's theology seemed to date from the early fifties at the very latest, and was extremely conservative for even that era.

From time to time, Protestants get the mistaken notion that Catholics worship Mary, the mother of Jesus, and make of her a deity. And it was confused theologies such as Father Robert's that contributed to groundless disputes between Protestants and Catholics.

Robert's theme was a contorted version of a montage of alleged Marian messages, communicated at a host of reported apparitions. The general idea was that the world was going to hell in a handbasket. The major villain of the piece was Russia. Not with its overkill of missiles but with its exported atheistic doctrine.

In addition to the "Threat from Abroad," there was the internal disease of secular humanism and worse. Youth were turning a blind side to Marianlike virtues, and instead, indulging in immodest attire, premarital sex and, for that matter, a good measure of postmarital sex, and anatomically correct dolls.

In any case, there was a blend of atheism and sex in almost all of its forms, and that meant trouble. Unlike Professor Harold Hill in *The Music Man*, Father Robert managed to make his warnings about "terrible, terrible trouble" dull.

Well, another item for his report, Koesler concluded; prehistoric theology but neither heretical nor unique.

Yet none of this was getting Koesler any closer to the heart of the matter. The Cardinal and the Tribunal were looking for some sort of statement of judgment on the miracles—no, what was the preferred terminology?—the "unusual events." No chance of coming up with anything on that until the blessings after Mass or, perhaps, the conversation he was dreading with the monks. Koesler intensely disliked talking with anyone who didn't wish to talk to him. And he was quite sure the monks would not be crazy about defending themselves to a stranger. Koesler promised himself that he would try to make it as painless as possible for all concerned. And speaking of pain, the sermon, mercifully, was ended.

The Mass proceeded.

During the Offertory and as the Eucharistic prayer began, Brother Paul stayed as close as possible to Father Robert. But, while the priest continued to give evidence of some weakness, he was managing to hold his own.

Relaxing ever so slightly, Brother Paul raised his head a bit and surveyed the crowd. Packed. Good. These contributions, along with the flood of mail donations, were making it possible for him to bring his plan to a conclusion much sooner than he had hoped or anticipated.

Peering out from within the cowl was like looking through a tunnel. One could see only straight on. And looking straight on, Brother Paul did a second take. A priest! Standing back against the wall. A priest, Roman collar and all. What the hell was he doing here?

Of course it was possible he was a sightseer. Maybe he

was looking for a miracle for himself. Cancer, whatever. But Brother Paul doubted it. Maybe it was a premonition, but it was strong. He had a feeling. A powerful feeling that this priest could spell the beginning of the end.

Well, if so, okay. He could handle it. But, dammit, why now!

Maybe he was rushing things. Now that he thought about it, it did seem a bit contrived. Why would the Church send an investigator just now—the day after he'd killed that meddlesome reporter? As far as he knew, she was the only one who intended to write about an investigation and thus, perhaps, push the Church into doing something about it. But she was undoubtedly on a slab in the morgue. He'd been so busy this morning, he hadn't had an opportunity to see or hear the news of her death. But he was certain that her murder—or accident, whatever they called it—would be the major local story, not the suggestion that the little Congregation of St. Stephen deserved an ecclesiastical investigation. In fact, he hoped her death had been labeled what it actually was—murder. Murder would get far more media attention than just a fatal accident.

So, why worry? The reporter was taken care of. And this priest might just be an innocent bystander. And even if he were an investigator, at least Brother Paul would not be hounded by what's-her-name—Lennon—snapping at his heels.

Father Koesler continued to watch the progress of the Mass with far more attention to detail than he would out of mere professional curiosity. He had to admit he enjoyed the Latin, although Father Robert did mispronounce a few words. One should not demand perfection, however, especially from one who was so obviously ill. Besides, Robert more than made up for the few technical gaffes by his reverence. It was so easy over the years to let things slip. The repetition of the same words, the same actions day after day, could blunt one's devotion. Familiarity bred carelessness. As he watched Robert pray, Koesler promised that he would try to freshen his own approach to Mass.

Koesler would mention in his report Father Robert's reverence. While he doubted this observation would be relevant to the investigation, at this point he was more concerned with quantity than quality.

Mass was almost concluded when Brother Paul saw her. Back against the rear wall, standing on something. She had to be standing on something, otherwise he would never have been able to see her.

Stunned, he stared in utter disbelief. It couldn't be! She was dead. In the unlikely possibility he had not killed her, she had to have been all but dead. At best, she'd be in some hospital more dead than alive.

He tried to call back the event, to remember, to visualize it, experience it all once again. He felt the satisfying thud when the car swept into her. He saw her being catapulted off the ground, her body disappearing over the windshield, helpless and disjointed like a rag doll. He could recall the assuring bump when he ran over her body—twice. It was no dream. He'd carefully, if hurriedly, planned it and executed it.

There also was no doubt that she was here, now standing back against the wall.

Whatinhell had happened?

Ohhh . . . now that he thought of it, he had never gotten a close look at her from the time she left the *News* until he left her ground into the pavement at her apartment. . . .

That damned hood! He'd never seen her face. But, damn, she was the right size. And, from all reports, wearing the right raincoat. And the clincher, she drove the car that belonged to Lennon. She worked at the *News*. She . . .

The whole thing was crazy.

But he wasn't. He'd hit somebody. And because God had a peculiar sense of humor, the woman he'd hit was not Lennon.

It was her car. It had to be a friend of hers.

And now, she had to know something had happened to her friend. That somebody had killed her friend.

One thing seemed certain, at this moment, anyway: Lennon did not know he had done it. Otherwise, he'd be under arrest by now.

So, he had some time. How much, he didn't know. But he had a little time. The question was how to use it.

Then he remembered that yesterday, he'd promised Lennon an interview with Father Robert today. Well, that was out. The right question, the wrong answer from the old fool, and it would be the end of the game.

Unfortunately, the Mass was ending; there was little time to formulate any sort of foolproof plan. He would have to wing it. And his recent improvisations were not proving too successful.

With Father Robert, in Latin, telling the congregation to "Go in peace," the Mass concluded. However, it appeared that nobody was going anywhere. This, they anticipated, is when the show would begin. There was the expected push toward the altar. All except Pat Lennon and her escort. They moved in the opposite direction.

And that was duly noted by Brother Paul. God is good! Can she be leaving? That would settle a good part of the problem. Wait, there's somebody with her. He had no idea who the guy was. But . . . they weren't leaving; they were headed toward the priest—who had not moved from his spot against the wall.

Brother Paul had no idea what was going on. But one thing: He had just bought a little more time. He didn't know how he might have handled it had the priest and Lennon descended on Father Robert simultaneously. With this development, that was not going to happen.

Okay, one thing at a time. For now, stick close to Robert and make sure the idiot doesn't try for another miracle.

Koesler quickly decided that remaining exactly where he was gave him the best vantage. To move with the crowd would be to get lost in the crowd. Staying put, he would not be able to hear what was going on—a problem he would have had in any case—but he would be able to see whatever action there might be.

And, speaking of action, there were a couple of people

making their way toward him. He slipped his mind into fast rewind and tried to place them. In his priestly career he had met so many people it was impossible to remember each and every one.

A couple. He'd probably witnessed their wedding. It was as good a guess as any. Where? What parish? It might help if he could place them in the correct parochial setting. But nothing was falling into place.

Wait! The woman pulled a notepad from her bag. Aha! A reporter. Now he remembered. Pat Lennon from the *News*. And, if that be true, then Joe Cox from the *Free Press*.

"Father Koesler."

He nodded and smiled. "Ms. Lennon and Mr. Cox, I presume." Odd, he thought, she was going to take notes, but he was not.

"Pardon me, Father," said Lennon, "but are you investigating this shindig?"

Koesler chuckled. "You don't waste a minute or a breath, do you?"

"No time. Did you read my story in this morning's edition?"

"Now it's my turn. No time."

"Okay." She was all business. "I did a piece on miracles, fairly recent ones in different parts of the world and how they are usually followed by formal Church investigations—at least when the Catholic Church is involved. Then the piece mentioned the alleged miracles here at the Congregation of St. Stephen. The conclusion was that it was likely that such an investigation probably would be conducted very soon here."

"What makes you think that?"

"Because I heard the priest, Father Robert, tell the miracle lady yesterday to forget about doctors and rely on him—and God, I suppose. That's in the story, too."

Koesler, recalling his conversation with the Cardinal earlier today, wondered if this young woman realized her news story had launched the investigation. "Well, you're right,"

271

he said. "I am here to begin an inquiry." He knew that the Archdiocesan Information Office probably would try to put some sort of lid on the story. But he never had agreed with that approach. Particularly, as now, when dealing with top-flight reporters, it was a far better policy to be as open and cooperative as possible. Sooner or later a really good reporter would get the facts, and if the reporter had been led up the garden path, there'd be the devil to pay.

Pat began to take notes. She remembered that while his name was pronounced K-E-S-S-L-E-R, it wasn't spelled that way. "Okay, for openers, I think our readers would like to know how this thing works. So, how does it work? What are you going to do?"

"I wish I knew."

"You don't know?" Cox broke in, not being able to control his professional inquisitiveness.

"You don't know?" Pat echoed. "Now, that's interesting. What do they do, just throw you into this with no preparation or training?"

"It wouldn't be the first time. Actually, it happens frequently. Priests become pastors without any extensive or express training. They supervise the building of churches and rectories, run fundraisers, just about anything and everything. It's known as *ex officio*."

"But this is so . . . special," Lennon protested.

"Well," Koesler said, "you'll be pleased to know that my role in this is not what you'd call vital."

"Oh?"

"In a way, they're starting with the second string. I'm just going to sort of get acquainted, ask a few questions, make a report. Then, if it looks like it would be a good idea at that point, the first string—in the person of someone from the Tribunal—comes in."

"Sounds sort of strange."

"Church Law is frequently strange. But there're a couple of things you might include in your story. I'd appreciate it."

Pat waited, pen poised.

"These monks are here in this archdiocese quite legitimately. They observed all the laws they needed to. So, we're not talking about some people who sneaked in here overnight, gypsies, or anything like that.

"And secondly, the purpose of this investigation is not to prosecute or persecute them. As far as we know, these men have done good work. People have been helped. A couple of people have been helped significantly. The purpose of this inquiry is, as far as I can see, for the guidance of the people. They want to know if these . . . unusual events . . . are real, honest-to-God miracles. And this inquiry, at least as conducted by the Tribunal, is going to try to make a responsible statement on that."

As Lennon continued to ask questions and take notes from Koesler's answers, Brother Paul attempted to keep the priest and the reporter in sight. Let them talk. Not much of a problem could come from that.

While Koesler spoke with Lennon, he glanced as often as possible at the paraliturgical rite that continued near the altar. From what he could see, he was able to establish the routine. Father Robert would listen to the person who sat or knelt near him. Quite obviously the large monk was also listening. For it was the Brother who selected the relic to be used while he handed the priest a card presumably containing information on the relic. Koesler was beginning to wonder who was running this show.

Literally, the ritual could have continued the rest of the day. But, finally, Brother Paul called a halt. His announcement would have been met with considerable hostility had it not been for Paul's no-nonsense authoritative tone.

Brother Paul shepherded Father Robert backstage, as it were, then went directly to Lennon and Koesler. As he neared them, he heard Lennon's question: "When do you suppose the Tribunal's going to get in on this?"

"My guess would be tomorrow," Koesler replied.

"That soon!" Lennon sounded excited. Her story was moving right along.

"I think so. There seemed to be some urgency. They

want my report today. I assume they'll send the first string right in after me."

"Excuse me. . . ." Brother Paul managed to keep what little light came through the painted windows behind him. Once again, his features were hidden in the shadow of the cowl as well as the back lighting. "May I be of some help to you, Father? I'm Brother Paul."

"Yes, Brother. I'm Father Koesler. I'm here on behalf of Cardinal Boyle. He asked me to look in on your group and talk with you about the, uh . . . unusual events you've been experiencing."

"Excuse me, Father, but do you have . . . documentation? Credentials? One never knows. . . ."

"Certainly." Koesler presented the papers Monsignor Iming had given him.

Brother Paul examined the papers for a few moments. He had no idea what he was looking for nor what sort of credentials were appropriate. But these looked official enough. And the final page bore the embossed seal of the Archdiocese of Detroit.

He returned the papers to Koesler. "Welcome to the Congregation of St. Stephen, Father. Did you happen to notice the doorway just behind the altar, where Father Robert just went?"

Koesler looked in that direction and nodded.

"If you would be so kind," Paul continued, "would you wait there for me? I have just a couple of things to do, then I'll join you and we can get started."

As he and Koesler turned to leave, Pat Lennon called out, "Wait!"

They turned back.

"Wait a minute." She was addressing Brother Paul. "Yesterday you promised me an interview with Father Robert today."

"Why don't you go back there, Father," Brother Paul said to Koesler. "I'll handle this."

Koesler left.

There was a biting edge to Brother Paul's voice. "What's

the matter with you!'' he said to Lennon. ''Can't you see that Father Robert is not well? Do you see any other media people making a fuss because they can't interview Father? Why can't you be reasonable?''

''Hey,'' Cox intervened, ''cool down. She just wants an interview. It's her job. And you promised her.''

Paul turned his anger on Cox. ''I don't care what I promised her!'' Subconsciously he was furious that she was alive. Consciously, he was incensed that she, apparently, had triggered this investigation. At every turn she was blocking his plans.

''Wait a minute, buddy....'' Cox was willing to give conciliation a try.

''No!'' Again that tone that brooked no challenge. ''On top of everything else, we have this investigation to deal with now.'' He returned his attention to Pat. ''We have no time. That's all there is to it!''

Pat was reluctantly convinced that she had no chance of interviewing Father Robert. Not short of crashing into what they probably considered their ''cloister.'' And that, even if it were possible, wouldn't get her the sort of interview she wanted.

Besides, she had an interview with Koesler. To all appearances, she was the only reporter, print or broadcast, to have tumbled to Koesler's role in this. She was still way out front. The only thing that didn't fit was Brother Paul's anger. Why was he so teed off at her?

At this moment, she had two problems and they were working at cross-purposes. Brother Paul, for whatever reason, was angry as all hell with her. On the other side, Joe Cox was rapidly becoming steamed at Brother Paul. She would have to try to deactivate both fuses. At this moment, she wished she had a better prayer life.

''Joe,'' she said, ''go get the car.''

''But what about—''

''It's okay. I can finish up here. There's still a lot of traffic. Go get the car ... okay?''

''It's your story.''

"Fine."

Cox left. Now there was no one—at least in that corner of the chapel—but Pat and Brother Paul.

"If you are finally convinced," Paul said, "that you're not going to get an interview here today, why don't you just run back to your high-rise and let us conduct our business in peace."

With his arms folded within his ample sleeves and the gray monk's habit covering all but his toes, Pat had no way of assessing his mood except from the tone of his voice. However, he did sound more relaxed—as if he'd won, or thought he had.

"How about you?" she asked.

"Me?"

"Like yesterday. When I couldn't get to talk to Father Robert, you gave me an interview."

"That was yesterday."

"And now?"

"Now, as you very well can see, we have a visitor." He wanted to add, "Thanks to you," but he thought better of it. "I am going to be very busy. The investigator is waiting for me. I must go."

She quickly added up the score. With her exclusive interview with Koesler, she was well ahead of the game. In fact, she would probably get a follow-up interview with Koesler on his assessment of today's inquiry before the rest of the media caught on to his role as investigator. But even without an additional interview she was sitting pretty. "How about tomorrow?" she said.

If Brother Paul had any intention of being here tomorrow, he might have fudged any commitment. But by the time this woman would be here tomorrow, he had every intention of being long gone. "Tomorrow may be quite hectic," he said, "but I owe you one for today. So you have my solemn promise that you will have your interview tomorrow."

She thanked him and left, reflecting that his solemn promise and about sixty cents would get her a cup of coffee.

Brother Paul joined Father Koesler, who had been obediently waiting at the doorway to the inner sanctum.

"Before I take you in to see the others," Paul said, "perhaps you'd like a short tour of this place. I think it will give you some idea of the kind of life we lead."

"That would be nice," Koesler agreed.

Austere, was Koesler's first impression of the monks' living conditions. He quickly revised his initial assessment to primitive. The last time he had seen such spartan furnishings was in a Trappist monastery. What he was viewing now was almost a duplicate of that earlier monastic setting.

The sleeping quarters were a series of rectangular cells of back-to-back plasterboard. Each cell was identical. Each contained a straight-back chair, a tiny desk with shadeless lamp, and a small metal bed with a lumpy straw mattress. Hanging from a hook on the wall were nightclothes and a spare habit. Draped over the hook was a ritualistic scourge, consisting of a handle and three or four leather straps, called a "discipline."

A number of religious orders, at various times, had as a rule of life for their members the daily self-inflicted use of the discipline. It was intended not as a serious punishment but more as a reminder of the need for penance and self-denial. Few orders continue its use today.

For Koesler, it dated the spirit of this group. So far, it seemed the Congregation of St. Stephen was trying to reclaim whatever the Middle Ages had to offer. Nothing he would see or hear in this displaced monastery would alter this supposition.

Using existing plumbing conduits, they had fashioned a bathroom of sorts: a urinal, three separated commodes, several sinks, and a two-stall shower. A sign over their bathroom door read, LOCUS—Latin for "The Place." Very ancient.

There really wasn't much more to see. The kitchen and dining area were carved from what might be termed the living room. In monastic circles the whole area more than likely would be called the common room.

To one side of the common room, patiently awaiting their visitor, were the other four monks, seated, silent, hooded, looking straight ahead. Living models of such virtues as recollection and custody of the eyes.

Introductions were made by Brother Paul, followed by an awkward—as distinct from a pregnant—silence.

At length, Father Koesler took a chair, without actually being invited to. "Look," he said, "I apologize for this intrusion into your lives and routine. I wouldn't be here if I hadn't been sent. But, Father, Brothers, we are in this together. We are not enemies. In the end, we are doing the same work. The work of the Lord." He sensed a hint of thawing, though there was no visible way to tell.

"Some months ago," Koesler proceeded, "you were welcomed to the Detroit Archdiocese. At that time no one knew that you would attract so much publicity. But you have. You must know you've become famous, nationally and internationally. Which puts the archdiocese on a bit of a spot. Very shortly, Church authorities, on the national and Papal level, are going to want to know what's going on here. Simply, the archdiocese wants to find out, so it can give an informed response. That's why I'm here and that's why you may shortly be visited by someone from the Tribunal. But it's not a new edition of the Spanish Inquisition—just a brotherly attempt to understand what you're doing. The truth behind the headlines, as it were."

Still no response from the monks.

"For starters," Koesler continued, "might I suggest there's no need for you to keep on wearing your cowls. I'd feel more at ease if I could see who I'm talking to."

There was an almost habitual hesitation on everyone's part. Then the four, as one, looked to Brother Paul, who nodded curtly and pulled back his cowl. The others followed his lead.

That's better, thought Koesler. Now they have faces. Now they have personalities.

Brothers Dominic, Francis, and Bernard seemed shy, embarrassed, and confused. Almost as if, instead of simply

278

removing a head covering, they had stripped and were ashamed of their nakedness.

It was difficult to guess Father Robert's age. He gave the impression of looking much older than his actual years, however many that might be. Behind thick glasses, a wispy, gray-white beard, and a thin mustache of the same coloring, his face was heavily tracked with wrinkles. His crown was bald; a fringe of gray running from ear to ear at the back of his head was all that was left of his hair. He seemed very tired. He sat slightly stooped forward as if carrying others' burdens in addition to his own. He looked not unlike some of the pictures of old Father Solanus Casey, Detroit's other famed "miracle worker."

Brother Paul was strikingly handsome with sharp Celtic features. He was clean-shaven, with a full head of black hair, and heavy black eyebrows. His eyes were deep blue; the shade reminded Koesler of Cardinal Boyle's, except that Paul's eyes lacked any trace of warmth. His countenance seemed alert, intelligent, commanding, and humorless. Koesler was certain that Paul's Irish eyes seldom smiled.

"Well," Koesler said, "where shall we start?" Then he had a thought. "Maybe it would be a good idea to get to know each other a bit." Yes, that might be the ticket. "I've lived all my life in Detroit. Thought of joining the Redemptorists because I grew up in Holy Redeemer parish. Instead, I went to the diocesan seminary and became a diocesan priest. But," he smiled encouragingly, "I'll bet each of you has a more interesting background than that. Brother Dominic?"

"La Crosse, Wisconsin." He volunteered nothing further.

Koesler could picture Dominic working on a dairy farm in a rural Wisconsin setting. "Brother Francis?"

"New York City." He seemed apologetic about it.

Koesler could imagine this childlike creature utterly adrift in New York and eager to escape into an obscure religious order. "Brother Bernard?"

"Chicago." He appeared proud of the fact.

Chicago seemed right for Bernard. Of all this group, Bernard, Koesler thought, seemed closest to Paul. "Brother Paul?"

"Boston."

"You've lost that intriguing Eastern accent."

"I lost that early on."

Koesler chuckled in an attempt to lighten these proceedings. He found he laughed alone. Instinct told him here was the hinge. Was Brother Paul, who seemed in charge of everything, the leader of this group or was it Father Robert? It had to be the priest. Koesler turned, finally, to the priest. "Father Robert?"

"Little place. Very little place. Coeur d'Alene."

"Idaho?"

Father Robert brightened. "That's right."

"When were you ordained, Father?"

Robert hesitated—"1949."

"Just five years before my ordination!" Koesler felt a natural chronological affinity. "But tell me: Coeur d'Alene, Boston, New York, Chicago, La Crosse! How did you all manage to get together!"

Brother Francis seemed to leap at the opportunity to provide some information. "Archbishop Marcel Lefebvre."

"Archbishop Lefebvre?" Koesler thought the reply somewhat incomplete.

"The Priestly Society of St. Pius X," Brother Bernard clarified. "It was founded by Archbishop Lefebvre."

"Yes, I know." Koesler was very familiar with the French archbishop who, during the seventies and eighties flirted with suspension, excommunication, and schism in his lopsided war with the Mother Church over whose version of Catholicism was orthodox—the Pope's or his own.

"We," Brother Bernard indicated all but Brother Paul, "attended St. Thomas Seminary out East. As far as the studies and life went, that seminary was all we expected it to be. But we found two things in common: one, we were afraid that the Society would break its ties to the Universal Church. And the second was that we felt unworthy to become priests. We wanted to be religious Brothers in an order that was like the Society in every way except its willingness to break with the Holy Father."

"But . . ." Koesler glanced at the other priest, "Father Robert—he wasn't there at St. Thomas Seminary . . . was he?"

Brother Francis replied. "Anyone who is familiar with the traditional wing of the Catholic Church knows Father Robert."

I guess that tells me I haven't been paying one hell of a lot of attention to our conservatives, thought Koesler. He'd never heard of Father Robert.

Brother Francis, almost as if constrained, continued. "Father Robert has written for all the more popular traditional publications for years."

"So," Brother Bernard broke in, "we were in touch with Father Robert and, together, we founded the Congregation of St. Stephen."

"I see," Koesler said. "And why St. Stephen?"

"The protomartyr," said Francis. "The first martyr."

That made sense, thought Koesler. It had been his experience that Catholic extremists, on the left or the right, had a tendency to equate themselves with the martyrs. "And then what happened? I mean, you all were in a seminary in the East and Father Robert was out in the Northwest?"

"We were all together—except, of course, Brother Paul." Brother Bernard inclined his head toward the oddly silent Paul. "He joined us later, after we arrived in Detroit. The rest of us communicated," he continued, "first by mail, then by phone. Finally, we left the seminary and met Father in Coeur d'Alene. And then we made our plans."

Brother Francis broke in. "Bishop Di Giulio is internationally famous for his opposition to the Second Vatican Council and yet for his fidelity to the Holy Father."

It's happened again, thought Koesler: Another famous conservative I hadn't heard of—before the Cardinal mentioned him this morning.

"Of course," said Brother Dominic, "Bishop Di Giulio is not as well as he used to be."

"So I've heard," said Koesler, whose notion of Bishop Di Giulio was of a living vegetable. "So, that was it."

"That was it," Father Robert acknowledged. "We traveled together to Pomaria, met with the saintly bishop and, at his direction, founded the Congregation of St. Stephen."

"That is really a remarkable story," said Koesler, vaguely troubled by the account. He turned to Robert, "I'll bet when you were ordained in '49 you never thought you'd become a founder of a new religious order."

Robert shook his head almost sadly. "No, I had no inkling."

"But, Father," Koesler said, "the fifties! Wasn't that a marvelous time to be a priest? The last 'age of innocence' for this country?"

"And," Robert added, "the last 'age of innocence' for the Church."

Yes, you would think that, wouldn't you? thought Koesler. The Council happened in the early sixties, leaving, as far as traditional Catholics were concerned, a Catholic Church that had become Protestant, and which was in desperate need of reclamation.

"Well, now," Koesler said, "now that we know each other better, let's get down to the matter at hand. That would be your healing ministry." Another long pause; no one picked up the cue. "So," Koesler plowed on, "how did you get into it?"

"Well," Father Robert cleared his throat, "it started with the relics. The modern Church," his sarcasm was patent, "has little use for the mementos of our heroes of the past. But we and the official Church"—read the Pope—"still believe in the Mystical Body of Christ, the Church Militant, the Church Suffering, and the Church Triumphant. And we believe in the intercession of the saints in our behalf."

"So, while you were in Rome . . ." Koesler nudged.

Robert picked up the thread, ". . . we made the necessary contacts to get the specific relics we felt we would need."

"Then, right from the beginning you used the relics to bless people with . . . that was the origin of your healing ministry?"

"Using the appropriate relic, of course," Robert replied.

"Of course." Koesler did not mention what he had perceived as Brother Paul's directional role in the selection of the relics. But Koesler had noted it. "Lately," he prodded, "it's been more than the relics, more than just a simple blessing."

"It's been a miracle!" Brother Francis exulted.

"Well . . ." Father Robert demurred.

"Look, I know how slowly the Church moves on a matter like this," Koesler said, "and I know that, from my position, I can't refer to these events as miracles in the strict sense. And, after all, that's what this investigation's all about. But they were certainly 'miraculous' in a more popular sense."

The monks seemed content with this accommodation. All except Brother Paul, who seemed on edge, and had not joined in the ice-breaking conversation; indeed, after conducting the brief tour, he had said almost nothing.

Koesler leaned toward Robert, and in a conspiratorial tone, said, "Tell me, Father, just between us, and off the record: What was it like . . . I mean, when that woman received her sight? What was going on inside you at that moment?" It was a long-standing, if seldom expressed, wonder of Koesler's. He was of course familiar with Biblical miraculous cures and had read about the work of mystics through the ages. But he'd always vaguely wondered what it would be like to actually effect a cure.

Father Robert smiled warmly for the first time in this meeting. He rubbed a fist into the palm of his other hand. "It was marvelous! It's something—a sensation—that builds inside. There's a feeling—I would call it a divine urge, to travel outside the boundaries of nature. It starts as a strong—and growing stronger—inclination to take a chance. Eventually—and I think this is essential—the element of chance gives way to faith. A living faith that engenders the most solid confidence I've ever felt." Robert seemed lost in recollection as he recounted his experience. He returned to the present as he noted, "Of course that same sort of faith has to be present in the subject."

"As was the case in the Gospels," Koesler said. "Jesus always seemed to comment on the faith of those he cured."

Robert glanced away from Koesler, to whom he'd been giving his complete attention. He seemed to stiffen. "Of course, as we read in Mark's fifth chapter, when a woman is cured by touching the hem of Jesus's garment, He was conscious that a healing power had gone out from Him. So, it does take something from the intermediary. Not, you know, Father," he said to Koesler, "that I am a particularly holy person."

"I hadn't thought about that before," Koesler said, "but I suppose if one actually were to work a miracle, it probably would fall under the heading of a *gratia gratis data*."

Father Robert inclined his head as if pondering that possibility.

Brother Paul spoke. "A grace given freely . . . a grace given freely for the sake of the grace itself? Excuse me, Father Koesler, but would you say that was true of the miracles Jesus worked?"

"Really, Brother," Koesler said, "I don't think it's comparable. We believe Jesus has a divine as well as a human nature. He is perfection quite apart from the miracles he performed. All *gratia gratis data* implies is that the wonder or miracle worked is not dependent on the holiness of the human agent. Padre Pio, for instance. He was said to bear the marks of the crucifixion on his hands and feet. Now, our theology tells us that the phenomenon of the stigmata is a *gratia gratis data*; that it may support or instill faith in others. But it does nothing to guarantee that Padre Pio is a holy man."

"*Ex opere operantis?*" Brother Bernard's smile said he was playing devil's advocate.

Father Koesler could not suppress an answering smile. Bernard had made it a game. But Koesler did not mind playing. As far as he was concerned, it was a game that led to uncharted waters. *"Ex opere operantis."* He translated for the benefit of Brothers Francis and Dominic, who did not appear to grasp the Latin: "From the work of the worker, or, the effectiveness is the responsibility of the doer. As opposed to *ex opere operato*, or, the deed itself effects the result."

"Huh?" Dominic said.

"It's the classic distinction between a sacrament and a sacramental," Koesler explained. "A sacrament—baptism for example—takes its effect—the infusion of grace and initiation into the Christian family—by the power Christ puts into the deed, the work, the sacrament. So, as long as the minister or the recipient places no impediment or obstacle in its way, baptism works. It works *ex opere operato*. It doesn't matter whether the minister is sinful or holy. As long as the minister has the intention of baptizing, passes water over the recipient, and says the words, 'I baptize you in the name of the Father, the Son and the Holy Spirit,' and as long as the recipient does not intend to refuse the sacrament, it works—or so we believe.

"On the other hand, sacramentals—blessings, like the blessings you perform with the relics—depend very much on the disposition of the minister and the recipient. Because it comes personally from the minister—his blessings, his prayerful wish—it matters very much what sort of person he is. His holiness or lack of it has quite a bit to do with the effectiveness of the blessing. Or, *ex opere operantis*.

"Now," Koesler smiled again, "as to whether a *gratia gratis data* is the result of *ex opere operato* or *ex opere operantis* . . . I'm sure the *gratis data* is linked with *opere operato*. A grace given by God for the sake of others minimizes the human factor. And so does a sacrament that does its work due to its divine institution, rather than because of the holiness or lack of it on the part of the human minister.

"But what do you think of the argument, Father Robert?"

The priest looked up suddenly as if wakened from a nap. His gaze wandered off to the side. He sighed and said, "In

First Corinthians, we read that 'Through the Spirit one receives faith. By the same Spirit another is given the gift of healing and still another, miraculous powers.' "

Damn! All that talk. All those distinctions. All that lovely Latin. And Robert captured it all in a brief Scripture verse from St. Paul. It put Koesler in mind of the countless weddings he'd witnessed, wherein, by the couple's choice, there would be a five-page reading on love by Khalil Gibran when a brief excerpt from one of St. John's Epistles would have said it all so much better.

"Well put, Father Robert," Koesler commended. "I know," he added apologetically, "I'm keeping you all too long. But just a few more questions should take care of my part in this.

"I think the basic question on my mind, Father, is *why*. If we, for sake of argument, accept as a fact that these 'unusual incidents' are real miracles—and I don't believe I'm qualified to judge yes or no—why you? Why do you think God has chosen you to be the medium through which He operates?"

"Faith."

"Faith? That's it? Just faith?"

Father Robert spoke without meeting Koesler's eyes. Robert was looking off to the side. He had not looked directly at Koesler since making his statement on how it felt to work a miracle. " 'The man who has faith in me will do the works I do. Anything you ask in my name I will do.' John, Fourteen."

"That seems to be an open invitation to all Christ's followers, Father," Koesler replied. "I don't understand how that test would serve to single you out."

"It must be an intense faith. It must be a faith that does not hesitate or question or hedge or qualify. You see, Father Koesler, miracles are impossible. One must believe in the impossible. Don't you see, 'If you had faith the size of a mustard seed, you could say to this sycamore, "Be uprooted and transplanted into the sea," and it would obey you.' "

What a remarkable grasp of Scripture the man has!

thought Koesler. An appropriate verse for every question, every subject. He was surprised when Robert rambled on without an additional question to set him off.

"Our battle, Father Koesler, is not against thrones or principalities. It is not against disease or illness. It is against Satan and the Powers of Darkness."

Koesler was startled by the statement. He was uncomfortable with the diabolical. Not that he didn't believe in the devil. But just as he believed that God did not needlessly multiply miracles, so he believed that the devil did not need to get personally involved in human affairs. There was enough disease, illness, and natural disaster, enough evil in the human heart, to preclude the necessity for an enormous personal diabolic presence.

"In Mark, One," Father Robert continued, "we read, 'The kingdom of Satan is being destroyed.' Jesus shows His power over Satan when He commands a possessing evil one, 'Be quiet! Come out of the man' And much more to the point, Father Koesler, in Luke, Seven"—Father Robert closed his eyes as if to read the text on the inside of his eyelids—"'At that time He was curing many of their diseases, afflictions and evil spirits. He also restored sight to many who were blind.'"

Koesler wondered what he was getting at. Did he mean to imply that a devil had to be cast out before that Mrs. Whitehead had her sight returned?

For the first time in many minutes, Father Robert looked directly at Koesler. "What evil have we done, Father? For what wrong deed are we to be investigated? Why are the authorities disrupting our lives? We come here in peace. Why not let us remain at peace?"

Now, in addition to being embarrassed by his role as inquisitor, Koesler began to feel guilty. But not for long; there was a practical purpose to this investigation and a need for it to be concluded.

"With all respect," Koesler said, "I think you've got the shoe on the wrong foot, Father Robert. You came in peace and you were left in peace until your work caused a commotion. People have a right to know what's going on. Like any other organization, religious or secular, if we don't police ourselves, charlatans are bound to mislead people and cause a great deal of harm.''

Father Robert hesitated and looked away from Koesler. For the first time this afternoon Koesler followed the other priest's gaze. He was mildly surprised to find that Brother Paul was giving Robert some sort of signal. Paul, by slightly moving his hands, was transmitting some sign, far more subtle but not unlike that of a third-base coach to a batter. Once again, Koesler could not help wondering who was running this outfit.

Father Robert spoke again. ''Is it necessary for us to get some sort of license from the Archdiocese of Detroit to do the work the Spirit prompts us to do? Is there some obscure law that forbids us to do good? Like the Jewish law of the Sabbath? The chief priests took scandal when Our Lord cured on the Sabbath. But do you not remember what Our Savoir said to them? 'Should not this daughter of Abraham here who has been in the bondage of Satan for eighteen years have been released from her shackles on the Sabbath?' ''

Robert leaned back in his chair, exhausted but triumphant.

Koesler sighed. Despite what he considered to be one of his better efforts, this interview was disintegrating. Father Robert, in less than an hour, had gone from a state of pleasant affability to one of aggressive and aggrieved hostility.

''I think we are no longer communicating the way I hoped we could,'' Koesler said. ''I wish you could understand the need for—or even the inevitability of—this inquiry.'' He sighed. ''But whether you agree with it or not, it will take place. It will go on.''

''Whether we cooperate or not?''

''I'm afraid so.''

''And what if we refuse cooperation? What if we refuse to speak with any representative of the archdiocese?''

''You wouldn't do that!'' Out of the corner of his eye,

Koesler could see Brother Paul sending signals furiously, almost as if he were signing for the deaf.

"We might and we would." The words were more forceful than Father Robert's usual tone. Was he simply mouthing what Paul was signaling?

"Father Robert, I sincerely hope it doesn't come to that. But if it should, I think all of you would stand a very good chance of being asked to leave the archdiocese."

"And if we would not leave?"

"Then you would be told to leave."

"In that case, your Cardinal would have to deal with our Bishop Di Giulio! We are, you know, an institute of consecrated life of *diocesan* rite. We belong to Bishop Di Giulio. Our Bishop was appointed by—indeed, sits in the shadow of—our Holy Father. Bishop Di Giulio gave us— our Congregation—canonical status, and he approved of our establishment here. And here we shall remain until, or if, called by him."

Feeling defeated, Koesler rose without further word and made his way out of the old, and now otherwise deserted, bank building. If nothing more, he felt he had enough material for his report. And once he made the report, he could sit back and once more wait for news and rumor to lead to the inevitable final chapter.

For now, he would return to the relative calm of his parish, collect his mental notes of this meeting, and compose his report. And then torture himself as to whether he had done everything he possibly could. He felt he'd never know.

CHAPTER
19

In a good and close friendship, as with a working marriage, people can grow so sensitive to each other that they can communicate on nonverbal levels.

So it was with Inspector Koznicki and Lieutenant Tully.

It was late Thursday evening, well after their shift was officially over. They were seated at a table in a nearly empty Greektown restaurant, nursing cups of decaffeinated coffee. Each had worked long, hard hours on entirely separate cases. They had not seen each other since early this morning. Yet Koznicki could sense that Tully needed him, needed a trusted sounding board. And so they had agreed to meet at the restaurant.

Koznicki was talking. "I do not think the prosecutor's office ever has been handed a more painstakingly put together case."

"What was the bottom line?" Tully was genuinely interested in the Morgan case; it did involve the family of a fellow officer.

"Drugs," Koznicki responded.

"Drugs." Tully shook his head. "Always drugs."

"The Morgans kept considerable money in their home, rather than in the bank. For some old-fashioned reason, they did not trust banks. It was their misfortune that someone they considered a friend knew that."

"How did it happen?"

"Howard—the 'friend'—was sure the Morgans had left on vacation. Actually, they'd been scheduled to leave early in the day. But Mrs. Morgan's sister was taken to the hospital with a heart attack. So the Morgans left, not on vacation, but for the hospital."

"So," Tully conjectured, "Howard cases the home, makes certain they're gone, and goes in."

Koznicki nodded. "He had to ransack the place. While he knew they kept large sums in the house, he had no idea where. The couple returned from the hospital while he was still going through their things. They surprised him. He had a gun." Koznicki didn't need to complete the picture. Drugs and guns, the curse of many big cities, foremost among them Detroit.

"Any holes in it?" Tully asked.

"That is what I spent the major part of this day on. We have gone over every detail from every possible angle. There are no holes in the case. We believe we have enough for Murder One. The defense will undoubtedly contest that charge. But, whatever else happens, Mr. Howard will be going away for a long, long while."

Tully nodded curtly.

"And your day, Alonzo? What happened to your theory about the woman run down by the car?"

Tully hunched his shoulders, then drained the cup. "Dead end. Quigley broke the case today. Coincidence, eh? Her name was Garcia, Mary. Thirty-eight, five kids. Husband's José. Unemployed four years. Drank up their ADC money. They fought all the time. Should have split up long ago. This time he mixed booze and hash. Almost killed himself. Should have; would've been better that way. Instead, he

291

got home somehow. Went after her with a butcher knife. She got out. But he got her later on.''

"His car?''

Tully shook his head. "Lost his car long time ago. Borrowed a cousin's car. That's what took us so long. The husband was the prime suspect from day one. But he set up an alibi by terrorizing his kids—and he didn't have a car. But the guys kept on it and today they found the car. Tire prints match perfectly. Then, after hours of interrogation, the cousin finally talked. Once we had the guy in custody, the kids, one by one, started talking. And that was the end of José.''

"And no help to you.''

Tully held up the empty cup; a waitress refilled both their cups.

"No, no help. My brain's fuzzy, Walt. I gotta give it a night's rest and start fresh in the morning.''

"Sounds like a good idea.''

"Somebody out there wants Pat Lennon. Little doubt of that. But who?''

"Someone she wrote about . . . a probability?''

Tully sipped the hot decaf. "That's what I asked her to think about. I talked to her earlier today—by the way, her boyfriend is back from his *Free Press* assignment.''

There was a pause, but Koznicki said nothing. He had wondered about Tully and Lennon. But that was Tully's private life and would remain so unless Tully brought the matter up.

"It's a good thing he's back,'' Tully said. "He's gonna stick close. It's not foolproof but it should provide some protection. Matter of fact, I talked to him for a minute. He wanted police protection for her.''

Koznicki smiled. "You would think he would know better. He must have seen too many movies.''

"Yeah. I told him she could join the folks who are living voluntarily in our cell block because they prefer even that to certain death in the streets. From the first moment we knew Pat, and not McPhee, was the intended victim, I

292

wanted her to hole up in an apartment, or someplace where we could provide tight security. But she was determined to go to work, be on the street . . . and that's take-your-chances time.

"Anyway, when I talked to Pat, she hardly knew where to start. She's covered almost every beat—politics, crime, graft, drugs, the mayor, judges, lawyers, big business, street crime. There are crazies all over the place. And she's written about most of them. If it's one of them, which one?

"But, she promised to give it a lot of thought and see if she could narrow it down. She really hoped that dead lady who turned out to be Mary Garcia would be the key."

"She does not yet know that that case proved to be a dead end?"

"Not yet. I'll call her tomorrow morning and tell her. And see if she's thought of anyone who might be a hot prospect.

"I didn't have a chance to talk to her very long. She was off to cover that 'Miracle on Michigan Avenue' story."

"Speaking of that," Koznicki said, "how is Alice coming along?"

"So far so good." Tully shook his head as if not believing what he'd just said. "She went to the doctor today. A clean bill of health."

Koznicki's eyebrows rose a millimeter. "A miracle?"

"Who knows? The doc says there's a remission of all her symptoms. That's it. He's not into astrology."

Koznicki smiled briefly. "Are you a believer yet?"

"Not hardly. I've still got some problems with that bunch."

"That reminds me: Father Koesler called."

"Your priest friend."

"Yes. Curiously enough, he has been appointed an investigator into the events there."

Tully thought about that for a moment. "Why?"

"There are claims that what has happened to Mrs. Whitehead and your Alice are no less than miracles."

"Hmmm."

Koznicki realized that talk of miracles was foreign to Tully. "You see," he explained, "the Church feels it is her responsibility to make a public pronouncement on whether these are bona fide miracles or not."

"What difference does it make?"

Koznicki searched for an analogy. The complexities of Catholicism were not his field. "When someone dies from other than natural causes, we are expected to investigate the matter and make some sort of official pronouncement: death by accident, suicide, murder; murder in what degree. Perhaps what the Church does is similar to this."

"Uh-huh." Tully was not particularly interested in what the Church called it. All he knew was that Alice might be cured and might not. Only time would tell. For the moment, she felt well. And that's all he knew. But Walt's friend was involved, and for that reason Tully was willing to invest some concern. "When's he start his investigation?"

"Today."

"Hmmm. Is there some time limit?"

"Tomorrow."

Tully chuckled. "Who do they think he is, Superpriest?"

Koznicki smiled. "His is a preliminary report. A more extensive investigation will follow immediately."

"What's the hurry?"

"It is odd. Particularly when you consider that the wheels of the Church historically grind very slowly. On the other hand, these occurrences have attracted a lot of publicity. That may explain the urgency."

"Yeah, that's probably it." Tully downed the remainder of his coffee. "Well, I better get home to my 'miracle baby' and see for myself how things are goin'."

As Koznicki watched Tully leave the restaurant, he reflected on Detroit's Homicide Division. Koznicki had formed most of its personnel and was almost entirely responsible for its high esprit de corps. He was justly proud of what he'd built. But he knew full well that it would not be his forever. There was pressure for him to move up to the rank of commander. As such, he would no longer have day-to-day contact with the men and women of Homicide.

More often lately he had pondered his successor. There were several homicide officers who would be excellent in the position. One was Alonzo Tully. But Koznicki knew Tully well. He knew that Tully was accustomed to setting goals for himself. And he knew that Tully was home. The position of homicide lieutenant was precisely his goal, and it had proven completely fulfilling.

Tully shouldered easily the responsibility for the men and women of his squad. With little interference from whoever might be the inspector, he was, by and large, his own boss. He would never willingly give up his prerogative of hitting the streets and solving those puzzles. The fictional detective who gloried in finding out "whodunit" was mirrored in reality by Alonzo Tully.

One day, Koznicki knew, he would offer the inspector's job to Tully. But it would be no more than pro forma. Tully, to the end of his career, would wend his way through the streets, alleys, and homes of Detroit, paying vigilant attention to the silent but infallible secrets of the scene of the crime. He would follow the clues and build his case until he put the bad guys away.

Well, Koznicki thought, God bless him.

**FRIDAY
JULY 28**

CHAPTER
20

Joe Cox was dreaming. He was aboard a cruise ship. The manifest content of his dream undoubtedly sprang from his recent excursion up Lake Huron in the Mackinac Race.

Cox's fantasy ship had numerous decks filled to capacity with vacationers. On each of the five passenger decks Cox had a girlfriend—one per deck. The REM phase of his sleep was filled with action, as Cox raced from one deck to the next, trying to keep each relationship separate.

For most men this would have been a nightmare. Cox was enjoying every moment of it.

Preliminary to his pleasant dreams, he'd had a pleasurable evening. After a busy day of accompanying Pat Lennon on her appointed rounds—and, for all he knew, protecting her—they had enjoyed a romantic evening, and lovemaking made all the richer by their mutual period of continence.

Lennon, too, had found their tender, intimate time fulfilling and relaxing. So relaxing, indeed, that despite all her concerns, she fell asleep easily. But sex cannot erase reality indefinitely. So, very early this morning she was wide awake. She could hear Joe's regular, deep breathing and she lay quietly lest she disturb him.

As she watched night give way to day, her mind was busy sifting what Zoo Tully had asked her to consider—possible assailants. There were so many. In her position, if she did a good job, she would make enemies. She did and she had.

There were entire categories of people who could have had motive, but she could not bring herself to picture any of them actually driving the killer car. Elected officials, appointed officials, men in government, the legal field, and so on. If she could not imagine them actually executing the murderous deed, she certainly could picture them hiring a hit man.

Then there were those who could well have driven the car. Men who would not have given away the pleasure of murdering her.

All in all, it was not a pleasant exercise. But, she agreed with Zoo, one that was necessary.

Yet, of all those who paraded through her memory, no one stood out as a prime suspect. She tried to doze, without success; the cast of bad guys kept moving across the screen of her imagination.

The sun was about to make its appearance. It looked as if it might turn out to be a pretty nice day. She could use one.

Zoo Tully had been awake for a little over an hour.

Alice had been waiting up for him last night, bright-eyed and bushy-tailed. She felt great. And, after having felt like death warmed over for months, her exhilaration was difficult to contain. So she hadn't. They had made love virtually throughout the house. Just like, Tully had been tempted to say, the good old days. Except that it was even better than the good old days.

And here it was, almost morning. The bedroom ceiling was dappled with rays of the sun glancing off leaves in the heavily wooded neighborhood.

Tully had awakened to find Alice snuggled against him, her head on his shoulder, her arm across his chest, and one of her legs draped over his. At this stage of the summer it might have been too warm for the close body heat. But it was a balmy morning with a gentle breeze stirring the lace curtains. Besides, he was so happy to have Alice back he wouldn't have minded if the heat had been oppressive.

He hoped Pat Lennon had done her homework, although he didn't envy her. If he had to compile a list of people who would be happy he was dead, or, better, people who would be happy to kill him, it would be almost a comprehensive directory of the local criminal scene. The only nice thing about his list was that a good majority of those on it were in prison. Tully had to believe that, given her type of work and given her competence at it, Pat's list might well be close to as comprehensive as his.

Alice's breath was gently stirring the hair on his chest. He looked down at her and smiled. She had returned. But he hadn't forgotten how she'd done it.

The Mad Monks of Michigan Avenue.

Not for a moment did he believe it was a miracle. Like the rationalists, he philosophically denied the possibility of miracles. After that, it was a matter of finding a reasonable, natural cause for what had happened.

So, how did they do it? He ran the affair through his consciousness once more. The old monk, the priest: Hundreds came to him, all seeking something—a job, health, sight, peace of soul, whatever. After observing him at work, even briefly, the routine was clear: Listen to the problem, get a whatchamacallit—a relic—from the Big One, read from the card the Big One gave him, bless the client, and that's it.

A simple enough scam. People feel they're not alone anymore: God's in their corner due to the priest's prayer and the blessing with the relic. Maybe with that extra confidence, they go out and actually improve their chances. They feel better. They land the job. They patch things up at home.

And all the while, the money pours in.

But—and here was the tricky part—how in hell did the priest know when to try something extra?

From all he'd heard, the routine had been identical with the Whitehead woman. And with his own eyes he saw that the routine was the same for Al. Tully would have entertained the hypothesis that the Whitehead dame was set up for this—how, he couldn't be sure. That would be the province of some expert—maybe in parapsychology. In cahoots with the doctor, maybe.

He would have been willing to entertain such a hypothesis if not for Al. He knew she had approached the priest out of the blue. There had been no setup. It was reasonable to assume, then, that Whitehead had been in the same boat as Al. She had come in, just like everyone else, hoping for something that would help her.

Obviously, the guy couldn't pull this trick—whatever it was—on everybody. Nine-tenths of the people who came to him got the ecclesiastical version of a bum's rush. Tell me your problem, I'll give you my blessing, then scoot. There are boxes all over the church where you can leave your donation.

How did he know when to try for the big gamble? And a big gamble it seemed to be. What if the priest had encouraged Whitehead and Al to go for a healing—a miracle—and nothing had happened? If he had tried for a "miracle" and nothing happened, that could well have ruined the rest of his routine. If you can't do the big one, maybe you can't do the little one. And the line of clients dries up. And the donations stop. And the little band of monks pack up their belongings and get outta here. Maybe they go out of business altogether. An enormous gamble. How did he know when to try for it?

And the Big One—Brother Paul—something was definitely wrong there. He seemed to intimidate nearly everyone. Maybe it was just instinct, but after all these years on the force and being a student of human behavior, Tully was prone to trust his instincts. In fact, if it weren't for Brother

Paul, Tully would have been willing to write off the monks, forget about them and simply enjoy a healthy Alice. And to hell with how she got that way.

But Brother Paul bothered his police antennae. Tully wasn't sure what to do about Brother Paul, but something.

"How did he know?" Pat Lennon said loudly as she sat bolt upright in bed. "How did he know!" she repeated, this time more as an exclamation than a question.

Her utterance happened to coincide with a crucial moment in Joe Cox's dream. As he dashed from deck to deck, keeping his many girlfriends happy, complications festered on the Promenade Deck. Buffy's husband turned up.

This was a classic example of a dream turning into a nightmare, with the hitherto peaceful sleeper transformed into a momentary maniac, crying out, and tearing at the bedclothes. Cox, in his dream-cum-nightmare, had just hurried down from the sun deck and Heather. He dashed into Buffy's cabin and was ripping off his clothing, for the umpteenth time, when the unexpectedly fully-clad Buffy announced that her husband was in the closet, loading his gun.

"Oh, Joey," Buffy shrieked, "oh, Joey, he's here! He knows! He knows all about us! Oh, Joey, you're dead meat! You're history!"

Thus, when Pat exclaimed, "How did he know!" she took the words right out of Joe's somnolent brain.

Limbs thrashing in search of traction to get the hell out of that stateroom, Cox was incoherent. He was babbling something like, "Oh, no! Please, don't! I'll be better! I'll be good! No, please!"

Pat poked him. "Joe, wake up! You're having a nightmare."

"What! What? What!"

"Wake up!"

"What happened?"

"I figured it out, Joe!"

"What? Figured what out?"

"Who tried to run me down."

"You mean the guy who got Pringle?"

"Yes. It's got to be. It's got to be him."

Pat went on to explain, in some detail, her dealings over the past few days with the Congregation of St. Stephen and particularly with Brother Paul. "It was when I mentioned a Church investigation—that's when a kind of subtle change came over him. He didn't want that investigation."

"Few people do," Cox reasoned. "Banks don't like investigations; neither do mayors or corporations or legislators, or the cops. And especially, nobody likes the IRS."

"The point is, Joe: As far as I know, I was the first one to think of there being one. As soon as that priest told that woman to forget doctors and live by faith alone, I saw the possibility—no, the probability—of litigation. He tells that to enough people and one of them decides to believe in miracles instead of doctors and gets sicker and dies, and the Church gets sued out of its gourd."

Cox pondered that for a moment. All right as far as it went, but . . . "Why pick on you?"

"Because it was my idea. I was going to write about it. I *did* write about it. Don't you think it's a bit of a coincidence, Joe? This was not the first miracle; it was the second. How come the Church waits to begin its investigation until after I write that the priest advised this woman to abandon medicine?

"What if Brother Paul can see all this coming? He's no dummy. Matter of fact, from all I've been able to see, he seems to be running that operation. It doesn't take a genius to figure out that when I write my piece the archdiocese is going to have to react. So he goes after me that night. It's his first chance to get me. Either he's lucky and gets me before I can write the piece or, by killing me, he gets the news media to turn in on itself: My murder is a bigger story than a Church investigation. And, in any case, I am no longer around anymore. You know as well as I, Joe, that it would take any other reporter several days to catch up with the story. I was just plain lucky to be prepared for this story and I've had an inside track from the very beginning."

"Well, I can't argue that that doesn't give him a motive—and a pretty strong one. But do you think—"

"Wait, Joe. I saved the best for last. Yesterday, when you went to get the car; when we were about to leave the monastery, when he was getting rid of me, he told me to retreat to my high-rise."

The significance struck Cox immediately. "He said that!"

"He said that. And how did he know, Joe? How did he know? Our reclusive brother doesn't stay home *all* the time. He's a busy little rascal. And he plans ahead.

"From the beginning, I caused him more problems than any of the rest of the media 'cause I was on top of the story. He had to have cased me. He knew what kind of car I drove. And he knew where I lived. The last person you'd think would be out casing somebody, planning a crime, would be a brother or a priest. But who's to stop him if he's top dog in that monastery? He can slip out whenever he needs to. And who knows him? Who can spot him? All anybody ever sees is the habit and that hood."

"Sounds good to me."

Without leaving the bed, Pat leaned over, picked up the phone, and began dialing. "This is the part, in the movies, where reporter goes after murderer and gets captured or worse. This is the part, in real life, where the reporter calls the cops, comes in one step after the police, gets the story, and also gets to live . . . uh, Sergeant Moore, this is Pat Lennon . . . that's right, of the *News*. I've got to talk to Lieutenant Tully . . . when will he be in? No, now; I've got to talk to him now! . . . Okay, I'll wait for his call, but get him now, please. I don't know how much time we've got."

Pat headed for the shower with a word for Cox to get her, no matter what, should Tully call.

Cox wondered about this Tully. Since when had he become the entire police force? Why did it have to be Tully? As an astute reporter himself, he felt questions flood his inquisitive mind. However, there was no time for them now.

Later.

CHAPTER
21

It had gotten so that William O'Brien automatically looked for the monks at twenty minutes before opening time. Although he didn't, he could have set his watch by their arrival.

And here they were, right on time. But, no, it wasn't "they"; only he. Only Brother Paul. Odd, but of no great consequence. Father Robert had become a presence—a revered presence—but nothing more. Brother Paul was the one with whom business was done. And if nothing had changed anyone's mind, this was to be the day of the significant loan to the Congregation. Mr. O'Brien was ready for it. The next few moments would tell whether the Congregation was similarly ready.

O'Brien unlocked the door and greeted Brother Paul.

"It's so kind of you. We really appreciate your courtesy."

"Think nothing of it, Brother." Truthfully, O'Brien had had just about enough of this obsequiousness. It also would be appreciated if the good Brother would pull that damn hood back so his face could be seen. With the exception of an occasional blind person wearing dark glasses, O'Brien could think of no one he did business with—besides this Brother, of course—whose eyes he could not read. And even with smoked glasses, a person's features were discernible. With Father Robert and Brother Paul, their identities were ciphers. However, while he would give a lot to see some eyes sometime, O'Brien was a devout enough Catholic to go along with the peculiar demands of religious life.

After leaving the bag containing yesterday's receipts with a teller, O'Brien ushered Brother Paul into his office. The manager, knowing well the outcome of such invitation, did not bother offering coffee.

After settling himself, Brother Paul said, "I'm almost afraid to ask, Mr. O'Brien, but . . . is it all right to arrange for the loan today? You know, the loan we spoke of?"

O'Brien smiled. Underneath it all, the good Brother was as naive as all the other religious who came seeking a loan. O'Brien guessed that religious men and women were so accustomed to receiving gifts that they felt the same sort of gratitude for a loan as for a gift. They did not advert to the fact that banks are in business to loan money at interest. And that one of the safer loans to make was precisely the one at hand. The Congregation of St. Stephen was one of the bank's better accounts, with money coming in increasingly by the day. O'Brien had had no cause till now to give it much thought, but at this moment he'd be willing to state that miracles were one of life's better collaterals.

"Yes, Brother, it's all set and ready to go. Five hundred thousand dollars. "

He laid out a series of legal documents on his desk. "If you'd care to read these and then sign them where I have marked Xs in red. . . ."

"Oh, it won't be necessary for me to go through them, Mr. O'Brien. It's legal language I'd never understand. But I know I can trust you. I'll just go ahead and sign them."

As Brother Paul proceeded to do so, O'Brien said, "I hope Father Robert is all right. We sort of miss his presence."

"Poor man." Brother Paul shook his head. "This has been a trial for him. But he's . . . well, just tired. The other Brothers and I felt he should get all the rest he can now. You understand."

"Yes, of course. You're undoubtedly correct." O'Brien noted the final signature had been made. He retrieved the documents.

Brother Paul leaned back. "Now, Mr. O'Brien, I wonder if it would be convenient for you to find some way to get this money, plus another half-a-million from our account, to a Chicago construction firm?"

O'Brien inclined his head slightly and tried, again without success, to see into the cowl. "A Chicago firm?"

"Yes. Complo Builders of Chicago. You see, Mr. O'Brien, Mr. Complo has been a friend of the Congregation almost from our beginning. He is a fine Catholic gentleman, husband, and father—eight children. And, blessedly for us, he has expressed his willingness to supervise the architectural engineering and the erection—the entire construction of our new monastery—as well as to act as a consultant for no more than the overhead costs.

"You must know, Mr. O'Brien, that we know nothing about construction. But God has sent us Mr. Complo. As we trust you, so do we also trust Mr. Complo. He has promised to consult with us about the details of the new monastery. So we want to transfer the funds to Mr. Complo's bank, and they will handle the whole thing." Brother Paul sounded as though he was smiling. O'Brien had no way of knowing.

"Yes, of course we can do that, Brother."

How like religious to fall into gravy like that, thought O'Brien. A construction firm that will handle a major building project for overhead costs because the CEO is a Catholic. Well, hell, even *he* had been bending a few rules for the sake of the "good" Father and Brothers.

"Well," Brother Paul leaned forward, "how can we do this?"

O'Brien fell into a benign but didactic attitude. "Oh, it's

very easy, Brother. We simply wire-transfer Fed Funds—that's Federal Reserve Funds, Brother. It's the same thing as sending cash."

"Can you do that? I mean, without involving anyone else?" Brother Paul knew the answer. Indeed Brother Paul knew all the details to this transaction at least as well as O'Brien.

"Yes, of course, Brother. I am authorized to have access to the wire-transfer department. This whole transaction will be completed before . . . before you get to your monastery."

Brother Paul enveloped in both his hands O'Brien's right hand, pen and all. "Thank you ever so much, Mr. O'Brien. We surely are grateful to you. And you can be assured that we will keep you and your good family in our prayers. Not only now, but when we move into our new monastery. Now, here, Mr. O'Brien"—Brother Paul extracted a piece of paper from deep inside one of the pockets of his habit and handed it to the banker—"is the address and phone number of Mr. Complo's bank."

O'Brien glanced at the paper, pursed his lips, and nodded. "Very good, Brother. I know this bank well. It's one of the most prestigious in Chicago. You have nothing to worry about. Your money is in good hands."

"I'm sure that's true. Again, we can't thank you enough. But you will never be out of our prayers."

A few more effusive expressions from both parties and the monk was gone. The banking day had now begun and William O'Brien, true to his word, got busy transferring funds.

Zoo Tully skidded his car into the bank's parking lot, narrowly missing a sensible black Ford driven by an elderly blue-haired woman, who had a lot to say to this whipper-snapper who had almost ended her life, though not prematurely. With all the street noise, Tully could not hear what the lady said. And he was just as glad he could not read lips. He screeched into the only empty parking place, which was reserved for the handicapped. Tully felt strongly about these spaces being used by anyone but the handicapped, but this was an emergency.

He half expected the bank to be in a state of pandemonium. He had convinced himself that Brother Paul had come here this morning to rob the place.

There did not seem to be an emergency. But, in fact, this entire morning had been an emergency.

It had started languorously enough with Al waking up cuddled in his arms. After their long abstinence, they enjoyed making love, as it turned out, night and morning.

He was shaving when the call came from Angie Moore with an urgent call-back for Pat Lennon. So, of course, he cut himself. And the day began snowballing from there.

He agreed with Pat all the way. It didn't hurt that he already suspected Brother Paul of some sort of evil. When Pat got to Brother Paul's admonition that she get back to her high-rise, she didn't have to spell out the implications. By that time, Tully was well ahead of her.

After the call, he left home as expeditiously as possible and drove directly to the monastery. He had considerable difficulty gaining admittance but finally was able to convince the monks that (a) he was a police officer, and (b) this was an emergency.

The one he wanted—the Big One—was out and no one seemed to have any clue as to when he might return. Father Robert and the other monks were only slightly more communicative than sphinxes. Eventually, he was able to get one of them, Brother Francis—in Tully's quick evaluation, the most guileless of the four—to check Brother Paul's cell. Returning wide-eyed, Brother Francis announced that Brother Paul's few belongings were gone. What could that mean?

Tully was pretty sure what it meant. And by the time he was able to drag out of them where it was Brother Paul had gone—to the bank—Tully was even more sure of what it meant.

From the monastery, Tully sped to the bank. And now

here he was, slightly more than an hour after Brother Paul had left this same spot.

Proceedings were hectic at the bank. Everyone seemed busy and someone was in the office with the manager. Tully's ID, his air of resolute authority, and his assurance that he was going to speak to the manager here and now or at police headquaters—also now—gained him immediate audience with William O'Brien.

O'Brien's greeting was affable, though he could not imagine why a police officer was so insistent on seeing him. His wonderment increased tenfold when he glanced at the calling card and read, under Tully's name, *Homicide Section*. What in the world would homicide want with—

"Did a Brother Paul come in here earlier this morning?"

"Why, yes. About, oh . . ."—consulting his watch—"about an hour-and-a-half ago."

"What was his business?"

O'Brien hesitated. "Really, Lieutenant, that does fall into the privileged information category."

"Mr. O'Brien, I can go get some papers that will ensure your cooperation. In the meantime, you—your bank—may be out some money. I've got a sneaky feeling a *lot* of money."

"There must be some misunderstanding. Brother Paul is a religious, a Roman Catholic Brother!"

"And Rasputin was a monk."

"Oh, I fear you are badly mistaken, Lieutenant. In any case, there was nothing suspicious about today's transaction. The bank merely made a short-term loan to the Congregation and transferred a sizable amount of money to the corporation that will be handling the contruction of a new monastery."

"How much money was transferred?"

"The total came to one million dollars."

Tully whistled softly. "Want to check that out?"

"No need, Lieutenant. The money is in one of the most reputable banks in Chicago."

"Do me—and yourself—a big favor: Check it out!"

Tully's tone made it considerably more than a suggestion.

The Lieutenant's self-assurance was beginning to shake O'Brien's confidence in what was—even for a bank—a major transaction. But he tried to appear unruffled as he looked up the Chicago number and dialed it. He was put through promptly to the manager. They exchanged pleasantries. Then:

"Frank, a little over an hour ago, I wired Fed Funds to one of your accounts. Could you check that for me? Yes; it was Complo Builders. Yes, that's right."

O'Brien began to perspire, despite the fact that the bank's air-conditioning was working so well that Tully felt chilly.

"Something wrong?" Tully asked.

"What? No; no, of course not. It's just that . . . well, I expected Complo Builders to be a rather significant account. It should have been familiar to Frank. It . . . it wasn't."

"Hmmm."

After a short interval the Chicago manager returned to the phone.

"Yes, Frank. You mean . . . But, I . . ." O'Brien was perspiring profusely. "But that would mean . . ." Now his color was not at all good. "It what! What was that, Frank? That's . . . that's . . . All right, Frank, thank you very much. What? Oh . . . yes, see you at the convention next month." O'Brien hung up. He did not look as if he might still be living next month.

But Tully could not afford to wait around to see if O'Brien would make it to the convention. "Well? Well!"

O'Brien had lost his elasticity. He sagged. He was staring at the desktop but seemed to be seeing nothing. "It's a shell corporation," he muttered.

"What?" Tully almost shouted. "Speak up, man!"

O'Brien looked at Tully. "It's a shell corporation," he repeated. O'Brien's transformation was remarkable. When Tully first met him just a few minutes ago, O'Brien had resembled a helium-filled balloon. Now, he was completely deflated.

"It's called a shell corporation," O'Brien continued tonelessly, "because it's empty inside. Anyone can incorporate. And, apparently, Brother Paul, a/k/a John Reid, did, d/b/a Complo Builders."

Tully wanted to make certain of every detail. He detected a spoor and he was eager for the pursuit and capture. "So, Brother Paul is also known as John Reid—they are one and the same person. And . . ."

O'Brien took up the uncompleted thought. ". . . and d/b/a—he was doing business as Complo Builders. As I said, anyone can incorporate, and Brother Paul . . . that is, John Reid, did . . . as Complo Builders."

"That's why your friend in Chicago—Frank—didn't recognize the account when you gave him the name."

"Because it was a shell corporation consisting of just one person—John Reid. John Reid incorporated several months ago. Then he opened this account in the Chicago bank with a couple of thousand dollars in it. And that's what's in it now: a couple of thousand dollars."

"What!"

"Shortly after I transferred the funds to Chicago, John Reid phoned Chicago, identified himself, and had all but two thousand transferred to a Swiss bank."

Once more, Tully whistled softly. "A million bucks!" There was awe there.

"Such a simple plan," O'Brien said. "But . . . a religious Brother! He and the priest—Father Robert—they seemed so sincere, so genuine! I suppose they're all in this together?".

"Uh . . . we don't know. Probably just Brother Paul . . . uh, I guess we might just as well get used to calling him John Reid. We think he's in it alone. That ought to restore some of your faith in mankind," he added. "But Reid's emptied out at the monastery. I think he took them, too. Either he's history now or he's trying to get out of town. Either way, we gotta get him. Fraud against a federal institution. Not bad for starters. Then we'll see if we can't nail him for attempted murder."

"Attempted—oh, my!"

"I gotta use your phone." Tully did not ask; he merely pulled the phone close and proceeded to dial. As he waited for an answer, he glanced at O'Brien, whose appearance continued to deteriorate. "You okay, man? You look really bad."

"I don't feel . . ."

"Why don't you go home or go to the doctor or something."

"I won't be needed . . . ?"

"Not right away. We'll need you later. But you go take care of yourself now."

"If you say . . ." O'Brien shook as he slowly rose from his chair. As he staggered from his office, his assistants gathered and supported him as if he were a dying elephant. They would get him to a doctor.

Meanwhile, back in O'Brien's office, Tully made phone contact. "Angie?"

"Zoo?"

"Angie, we gotta move!"

The tone and the economy of words told Sergeant Moore that Tully wanted the ensuing done last week. She grabbed a notepad.

"We got a guy wants to get outta town bad. Get this on the LEIN and NCIC. *Now*."

This insured general broadcast over the police Teletype. The Law Enforcement Information Network carried police emergency news statewide. The National Crime Information Center went nationwide.

Tully closed his eyes and concentrated. " 'Be on the lookout for John Reid, alias Brother Paul'—damn, Angie, you know I've never seen the guy without that goddam habit. Damn, damn, damn! Well, we gotta go with that; it's all we've got. Let's hope he's still wearin' the goddam habit. Then, it's: 'Be on the lookout for John Reid—a/k/a as above—approximately six-two, 220 pounds. May be dressed as religious order monk in gray habit. Wanted for bank fraud and suspicion of attempted murder.' "

"The Lennon case?"

"Yup."

"And bank fraud! He's been busy!"

"Angie, cover the tunnel and the bridge—and make sure there's some uniforms checkin' the Greyhound Terminal. Get somebody over there now. And don't forget the Amtrak station in Dearborn and the Canadian Rail station in Windsor. And call what's-his-name at Metro—Charlie—used to be with the Department; he's head of security there now. He'll get his deputies all over the airport.

"And besides LEIN, give a personal call to the Wayne County Sheriff and the State Police. We gotta close up as many holes as possible.

"And contact all the international air carriers; have them check their passenger lists for all flights leaving the country. Start with the flights to Switzerland; he's got a Swiss bank account. And don't forget the flights out of Toronto, just in case he's already crossed the border.

"Check the connecting flights to Kennedy, too. We don't even know if Reid is his real name, and he may use another alias . . . but we gotta go with what we have. Of course he doesn't know we're on to him, so he may not try to hide his trail. In which case, he'll just take a connecting flight to Kennedy and then a flight to Zurich.

"And Angie, get on your horse and meet me at Metro. I'm cuttin' out right now. Check out the best way of gettin' to Switzerland from here about this time. I'll be in touch with you on the road."

He did not wait for her response. He knew she'd do everything he asked and more.

He started to leave O'Brien's office, cursing his luck that he'd never seen Brother Paul well enough to make a positive ID, when he stopped abruptly. There was one man who might know, might have seen him. But what were the odds of reaching him right now?

He had to try.

He got the number from information and dialed.

No one who knew Tully would have described him as a man of prayer. Although on rare occasions, he had come close to praying. He experienced one of those occasions as he dialed. He continued his own private form of prayer as the phone rang. It rang nine times before the receiver was picked up. "St. Anselm's."

"Father Koesler?"

"Speaking."

Tully smiled. Wow, he thought, it does work!

CHAPTER
22

As she sped toward the airport, Sergeant Moore alternated keeping her eye on the traffic and giving flight information over the radio to Tully. She had taken I-94 toward Romulus; Tully had swung northwest to pick up Father Koesler, then south on Telegraph Road toward I-94 and Metro.

Should they meet at the International Terminal? No; it wasn't noon yet; Reid wouldn't want to wait around for the Pan Am or British Airways flights to London; their departure wasn't scheduled until this evening. He wants to be outta here.

Let's see: The connecting flights to Kennedy leave from the Northwest Terminal. But Pan Am and TWA have connecting flights from their terminals too. . . . Which one? Wait: Something was buzzing through Tully's mind.

Chicago.

Chicago? Yeah, Chicago. That tour to Europe that he and Alice had planned to take and then she got ill. It was a package deal, and . . . the flight had left from Chicago! With a connecting flight from Detroit on . . . American Airlines.

"The L.C. Smith Terminal, Angie; we'll try American!"

It was just a hunch, but the more he thought about it, the more he was certain he was right. Sure, Reid—or whatever his name was—didn't know they were on to him, but obviously, he had something planned. He would want to give himself as much lead time as possible to get out of the country . . . get into international air space. He would take as few chances as possible. Instead of flying to New York and trying to make the 1:45 Concorde—which was an iffy connection in the time he had—or waiting around for the evening flights to Europe, he'd fly to O'Hare, catch a late afternoon flight: Zurich, or Brussels, Amsterdam, Paris, or Frankfurt, and be off and away long before anyone gave him—or that route—a second thought.

He'd have to give his real name for any transatlantic flight, of course; you had to present your passport when checking in; but he could use any name on a domestic flight, thus obliterating that part of the trail. And he wouldn't have to make a reservation in any case; if one flight out of Chicago happened to be sold out—which was doubtful in First Class, which he would certainly be traveling . . . or, maybe not; maybe he wouldn't want to call attention to himself . . . but, it didn't matter. The point was, if one of the international flights was sold out, he could take one of the others . . . or even, if worse came to worst, stay over and catch a flight the next day. After all, who'd be looking for him in Chicago?

Yes, he'd bet on it—he *was* betting on it: the SOB was going to Chicago . . . if he hadn't already gone.

Tully had the door open before the car had screeched to a full stop in front of the terminal. Moore's car was already there, the sergeant standing by the door, clutching the OAG . . . the huge guide that listed the flights of scheduled airlines all over the world. In times past, the OAG had been the travel agents' bible; nowadays computer reservations systems had taken over.

Tully introduced Koesler to Moore. En route, Tully had explained the situation to the incredulous priest. Tully had solemnly assured him that the bank fraud at least was a lead-pipe cinch. And the assault and attempted murder was the next best thing to a sure bet.

Koesler, whose precious daily routine had been smashed to hell-and-gone, was very upset. Not only had his parochial schedule gone down the tube, but his almost-completed report on the congregation of St. Stephen, which was due at the Chancery today, included no mention whatever of bank fraud or attempted murder.

Tully, Moore, and Koesler now stood beneath the video terminal displaying departure times and gates for American Airlines.

"Okay," said Tully, "Flight 393 to Chicago, leaving at noon from Gate B–10, and it's on time—or so it says." He turned his wrist. "Twenty-five minutes. They should be just about ready to board. Let's go."

The three started walking briskly through the terminal toward the passageway that would lead to Gate B–10.

Koesler knew they were looking for Brother Paul. But it was all so confusing. Detroit's airport terminals were by no means the largest in the world. But they were big and, even during morning hours, crowded. Koesler tried to be as vigilant as possible.

As they walked, Tully explained, "This is pretty much guesswork. For sure, Reid will try to get out of the country. How he's going to do it is up for grabs. We're trying to block him in every possible way."

"See the security, Zoo?" Moore broke in. "Charlie came through for us."

"I knew he would," Tully said. "I don't know how often you've been to Metro, Father, but you may notice there are more than the usual number of airport security officers around. More sheriff's deputies too. The State Police are specially watching the expressways for ground surveillance. We're casing the bus and rail stations, and we've got the Windsor Tunnel and the Ambassador Bridge covered. But, in the end, the bottom line is, we're lookin' for a phantom. Outside of the other monks—and they are not cooperating at all—you're the only one we know of who's actually seen Reid's face. Walt Koznicki told me about your investigation yesterday. You're our ace. The problem is, where to play you."

"Play me? I don't understand."

"To keep this tiny little advantage, we have to get you to the most likely spot where Reid is apt to try to make his escape. But where is it? That's where the guesswork comes in."

Koesler, whose head was swiveling like a surveillance camera, said, "So, this is it. How come here?"

"My guess," Tully said. "Purely my guess. He could be anywhere, and he could be headed anywhere. But the money is in a Swiss bank. So, my guess is that's where he's headed.

"Now, there are lots of ways to get to Switzerland. Angie's travel agent says the best way of getting there is Swissair. But Swissair doesn't fly out of Metro. So she checked on connecting flights. There are lots.

"But there is one particularly lovely flight. It'll take him from Chicago, where the money was, to Switzerland, where the money is, aboard Swissair. And the American connecting flight is where I'm going to play my ace"—Tully pointed one elongated index finger at Koesler—"you, Father."

"What if he decided to wear his habit?" Koesler asked.

"Makes the job easy for us," Moore answered. "Everybody's looking for a guy in a gray monk's habit."

"But," Tully said, "it's not healthy to assume that bad guys are out to make our job easy. The big thing, far as I'm concerned, is he doesn't know we're onto him. And, come to think of it, if it weren't for Pat Lennon, we wouldn't be onto him yet. She's the one who gave me the tip that put me on his trail. I didn't expect to find bank fraud, but that was helpful.

"Thing is, if he knew we were half a step behind him, he would be sorely tempted to just get the hell out of here.

But he doesn't know. That's why I think we'll get him . . . it's just a hunch, but—"

"But," Moore said, "when Zoo Tully has a hunch, put good money on it."

Koesler was all but overwhelmed by the sheer number of people in this concourse. They were passing by more like fish in a tank rather than ships in the night. People meeting travelers; people deplaning, searching for loved ones or hurrying toward an exit; people almost at a run, obviously late for a flight or for meeting an arrival; hundreds of people just waiting—bored, bored, bored.

Ahead, on the left, he could see the gate numbers jump by twos on the even side: 6, 8, and, their destination, 10.

Tully, Moore, and Koesler slowed markedly as they neared Gate 10. Reid would not know Moore; he might conceivably recognize Tully; he almost certainly would identify Koesler after their meeting yesterday. If Tully's guess proved correct and John Reid was indeed taking this flight, the next few minutes were crucial, and there was no predicting the outcome. Luck, now in making an arrest without anyone's being hurt, was still very much needed.

One thing was clear at first glance: This was a popular flight. A planeful of people were waiting in the gate area. Seated in the unupholstered, bolted-down chairs, pacing restlessly, reading paperbacks, conversing with friends and/ or relatives who were seeing the traveler off. But, a religious habit?

There was a nun in a white habit. Koesler recognized it instantly as that of the Maryknoll Missionary order. There was a priest who was approximately Koesler's age. They did not know each other, but they nodded and smiled at each other. Oh, the incomparable camaraderie of the priesthood! No one but a priest could fully appreciate it.

But, no gray habit. Brother Paul, if he was here, had disappeared, perhaps forever. If he was here, he was John Reid, and in his layman's guise he had thrown an extra challenge at them to find him.

With no set plan, the three slipped into a sort of practical search configuration, with Koesler in the point position and Tully and Moore behind to his right and left.

Koesler moved slowly, only inches at a step, in order to try to take in each and every person in this vast congested area. The only consolation was that, sooner or later, everyone emplaning would have to pass, single-file, through the boarding gate. But the sooner they could identify Reid the better for all of them.

Assuming he was here.

The check-in agent began speaking over the microphone in the peculiar childlike singsong cadence that seemed to be a required course in airline personnel school.

"Good morning, ladies and gentlemen. We *will* now begin boarding *at* Gate 10 for Flight 393 *to* Chicago. We *will* begin boarding those *with* small children or those who *may* experience some difficulty in boarding."

There was a general stir throughout the area. A couple of people with babies stepped up to and through the gate. They were followed by a woman hunched in a wheelchair, being pushed by an attendant. Koesler looked sharply at the attendant.

A ragged line began to form, stretching from the gate out into the concourse.

Koesler continued to pour his every ounce of diligence into the search. But no John Reid.

The priest began to doubt himself. Did he really remember Brother Paul all that well just from yesterday's meeting? That was foolish; of course he remembered. But there were so many people here, all moving this way and that. So many people. He reminded himself that he was looking for a tall man, almost as tall as himself . . . within an inch, anyway. So he confined his search to eye-level height.

"We remind you, ladies and gentlemen: This *is* Flight 393 *to* Chicago, *now* boarding through Gate 10. We *will* now board passengers holding seat numbers 1 through 8. Please *have* your ticket *and* boarding pass ready *for* the attendant *at* the gate."

More activity. Not many first class passengers, evidently. But more people getting in line.

"Now, ladies and gentlemen, we *will* be boarding passengers holding seat numbers 20 through 32. We remind you at *this* time that FAA regulations allow *only* two carry-on items *per* person, and that *all* carry-on luggage *must* be able to fit *under* the seat or *in* in the overhead bin."

It's him!

Oh, my God, Koesler thought, there he is!

Dressed casually in a white, short-sleeved, open-collared shirt and black trousers. Hatless. Peculiar: From a cord around his neck hung a huge ornate metal cross—as if he could not quite relinquish his religious persona. Strikingly handsome man. Looked as if he could light up a room with his smile, but also looked as if he seldom tried.

Tully and Moore sensed it. They moved up to brace Koesler. "You made him, didn't you?" Moore said.

Koesler nodded.

"Where?" Tully asked. "Which one?"

Koesler stammered, something he seldom, if ever, did. "H . . . he . . . he's in line now, about tenth from the front . . . see? In the w . . . wh . . . white shirt and black pants. Th . . . the . . . the cross . . . see it? On a cord around his neck, lying against his chest . . . see it?"

"It's okay, Father," Tully reassured, "we got him. You just stay right here."

Tully nodded to Moore; both had heard Koesler clearly. They moved forward slowly, seeming to follow some prearranged strategy, though Koesler had not heard them discuss it. Quite clearly they operated together. Maybe they had executed a similar maneuver previously. The priest watched them move ever so casually toward their prey.

Reid was now about eighth in line. He began to look around, his head pivoting slowly, in an owl-like circumference. Too late it occurred to Koesler that he should have taken a seat or, better, left the area entirely. Reid caught sight of him, seemingly startled as the tall clerically garbed man came into his vision. In that instant he knew who

Koesler was and in the next instant guessed why he was here. Of course: Koesler—the only one who could identify me.

He wouldn't be here alone; there must be someone with him. Cops. Where?

Reid's eyes were fiercely alive, darting here and there. That black guy. He was in the chapel with the girl who got cured. He was in the singles bar with the reporter. A cop. He had to be.

With one eye on Tully, Reid tried to bulldoze his way up the line, drawing irate comments for his pains. He was unaware that Moore had moved up almost even with him on his blind side.

"Oh!" Moore cried out, feigning a twisted ankle, as she fell against Reid, forcing him out of line.

He was about to shove her aside when she suddenly displayed her badge and ID and said, firmly, "Police! You're under arrest!"

Moore thought her reflexes were fast, but she learned something from Reid, who, in a split second, wrapped his left arm around her neck, spinning her and gripping her against himself as a shield. His right hand drew the knife from its camouflaged sheath in the vertical bar of his pendant cross. He pressed the blade to her throat as he maneuvered her between himself and Tully.

Some screamed, some shouted; all backed away, leaving Reid plenty of room.

"Back off, cop! Back off, or she's dead!" Reid retreated toward the gate leading to the plane, dragging Moore with him.

Tully, who had drawn his gun, was now immobilized. An almost extraneous thought crossed his mind: *You go all your life without drawing your weapon, then in one week it's hardly ever out of your hand.*

Moore's shoes were not spike-heeled, but neither were they flats. As Reid dragged her toward the gate, in one motion she lifted her right leg higher than was called for and with all her strength brought her heel down on Reid's instep.

He howled in pain and relaxed his grip for just a moment. For just the moment she needed. She slipped out of his grasp, fell to the floor, and rolled away from him.

He was now without a hostage. Nothing stood between him and Tully's gun but his knife. He edged menacingly toward Tully.

Tully smiled for the first time in a long while. It was not a pretty smile. "In the immortal words of Clint Eastwood, 'Make my day!'"

Reid's shoulders sagged. He almost smiled. He dropped the knife.

No sooner did the knife clatter to the floor than Reid was overpowered by a potpourri of airport security personnel, sheriff's deputies, and Detroit police. All of them had been in the vicinity and, in the short period that Reid had held Moore hostage, the cohort had closed in. Now, just a few moments later, Reid had been cuffed, Mirandized, and led off. His knife had been carefully retrieved by one of the officers and taken away as evidence.

Tully hastened to Moore, who had been largely ignored during the officers' brief scuffle with Reid. She had dragged herself to one side and was seated on the floor, leaning against the wall, trying to calm herself.

Tully knelt at her side. "How you doin', Angie?"

She looked at him, grateful to be alive to talk to anyone. "I've been better, Zoo. That was kind of dumb, wasn't it—getting taken by that turkey!"

Tully shook his head. "He was fast, Angie. It could've happened to anybody. Anyway, you did good. And we got him and—wait a minute: What we got here?"

Blood was staining through the right shoulder of her blouse. He traced the flow, brushing aside her hair till he found the cut. It was just below her right ear.

"He cut you, Angie. Not bad . . . must've got you when he let go and you fell away from him." He pressed his handkerchief firmly against the gash, trying to stanch the flow. He didn't want to alarm her, but actually the cut was deep. He was surprised that Reid could inflict so serious a wound with such a relatively small knife.

Tully lifted her to her feet. "I'll get somebody to take the priest home. I'm gonna get you to a hospital. They may have to take a few stitches, but don't worry: you'll still be able to wear your bikini."

It was over.

Almost.

CHAPTER
23

Father Koesler was running a little late, extremely rare for him. After this morning's excitement at the airport, it had taken him a while to calm down. Little by little the day had gotten away from him. Mary O'Connor had to postpone his final two appointments of the day or he would not have made it to dinner at all.

Proprietor Moe Blair met him just inside the door of the Wine Barrel. "The others are here already, Father. I'll take you to the table."

"Thanks, Moe." As they made their way through the restaurant, Koesler said, "Moe, remember you asked me about those monks—the Congregation of St. Stephen? Well, as it turned out, I did have a chance to look into it."

Blair smiled. "I know. I read about it in the paper."

"Oh, that's right. . . ." Koesler had forgotten that Pat Lennon had interviewed him on that very subject. Things had been happening so fast for him these last couple of days, he hadn't even had the leisure to read the papers. "Anyway," he went on, "from what I've seen of the outfit,

I wouldn't put much faith in it. Of course, the archdiocese intends to pursue the investigation. Or, maybe, I should say intended. I'm not sure there'll be any need to go on."

"I know. Radio and TV news is full of the bank fraud story. I agree with you: I think this is the end of that group."

"But more important, how is Betsy?"

"Oh, she's fine. Thing's all cleared up."

"What was it?"

Blair chuckled. "What it always is when the doctor doesn't know, a virus."

They reached the table, where Koesler was welcomed by Koznicki and Tully. The officers had drinks. Blair took Koesler's order of a Chablis.

The policemen raised their glasses in salute. "Welcome, Father, the hero of this morning's arrest," hailed Koznicki.

Koesler waved a hand. "Oh, no; no, I was along for the ride. Lieutenant Tully and Sergeant Moore were the heroes. By the way, where is the sergeant?"

"She has been admitted to the hospital," Koznicki said. "She was in shock. Then, after she was stabilized, she was in some pain. They want to keep her in observation overnight."

"That's too bad," Koesler said. "Her life was really on the line this morning."

"She's a pro," said Tully. "Not exactly all in a day's work, but she knew what to do and did it. But this little party is in your honor, Father. We couldn't have done it without you."

Koesler's wine arrived. "Kind of you, Lieutenant, but I merely identified him."

"Your identification was vital," Koznicki said. "If he had gotten out of Detroit—and he was only a few steps away from doing just that—we might never have caught up with him."

Koesler looked puzzled.

"If we had not arrested him in Detroit," Koznicki explained, "we would have had no idea which direction he had taken. He might have gone to New York, Chicago, any number of cities, before catching a flight to some country with which we have no extradition agreement. More than likely we would never have gotten him.''

"By the way," Koesler toyed with his wine glass, "I didn't think of it at the time—with all the excitement—but later, I wondered about your making that arrest. Weren't you out of your jurisdiction?''

"We were in what's called 'hot pursuit,' " said Tully. "That gave us the right. Besides, we have an agreement with the state police that makes it legal for a Detroit police officer to make arrests anywhere in the state of Michigan. Not many people know that.''

Koesler was impressed. Then another thought occurred. "But I was not the only one who knew what he looked like. The other monks . . .''

Tully shook his head. Koesler had sensed from the beginning that while this was a victory celebration of sorts, Tully's heart was not in it.

"Something's going on there," Tully said, "and I'm not sure what. But we're getting nothing out of those guys retroactively.''

"They're not cooperating?" Koesler was puzzled. "But . . . but they're Catholic monks. This man committed a crime, a federal crime. I can't believe the others would not cooperate with the police.''

Tully shrugged. "I'm just telling you what's happening. I can't explain it any better than you can.'' After a moment of silence, he continued. "They seem . . . terrified of him. It's the only explanation that makes any sense. But, why . . . ? We just don't know.''

"Terrified? But he's locked up," Koesler said, ". . . isn't he?''

"Yeah," Tully replied, "but not for long.''

"Not for long?''

"We feel we have a very sound case against Reid," Koznicki said. "Although anything can happen, we really believe we will get a conviction for bank fraud. But even with a conviction, Reid is not looking at much time.''

"Oh?"

"Maybe five years," Tully said. "With good time, he probably wouldn't do more than . . . oh, twenty months. So, if for some reason those guys are afraid of him, they've got a right to be: He's not gonna be in the lockup all that long. But, why would they be afraid of him?"

"I don't know," Koesler said, thoughtfully. "But what happens when you put them on the stand in court? Then they'd be under oath. Then they'd have to tell the truth."

"They'll never see the stand in court," Tully said. "It's clear they're not involved in the bank fraud. That was a gig by Reid alone. And even though I'm certain Reid tried to kill Pat Lennon and got her friend by mistake, we don't have a shred of evidence to bring him to trial for that. So, possibly the monks could testify to an attempted murder charge—but they'll never have to."

Koesler was beginning to understand why Tully was not deliriously happy. Reid was most likely going to prison, but not anywhere near long enough to satisfy Tully's sense of justice.

Sensing that the subject had reached an impasse, Koznicki shifted the conversation. "Well, Father, your commission from the Cardinal admitted you to the inner sanctum. How was your first attempt at an investigation?" His tone was not far removed from that of an indulgent father toward a son who had tried something new.

Koznicki intended the change of subject to lighten the conversation. On the contrary, as the priest considered the question, he seemed to be weighing a matter of some gravity.

"Well," Koesler said, "I got my report in to the Chancery on the way here tonight. I didn't go into much detail. Just enough to tell the next batch of examiners that in my opinion I don't think there was anything genuinely miraculous going on. The priest, Father Robert, had an interesting explanation of how it felt to . . . what?—work a miracle, or at least to rouse enough emotion to trigger a psychic cure— a psychosomatic cure. I have no idea which of these took place. But I didn't feel there was enough clear indication that it was a miracle to call it one."

"Well, that is understandable," Koznicki said.

Koesler seemed to draw further inside himself. "But there's more," he said, after a pause. "More that I didn't touch on in my report. It's not tangible or definitive, maybe just a feeling, but . . ."

Koznicki grew more sensitive to his friend's evident distress. "Perhaps if you were to tell us what you really think, it will help you deal with the matter."

"The talking cure." Koesler smiled. "Well, why not? It's worked before." He sipped the wine, as he considered a course of presentation. "There was something about that priest, Father Robert. . . ."

"Yes . . . ?" Koznicki prodded.

"It wasn't any one thing, just a bunch of odd, curious, out-of-the-ordinary things that started me thinking and wondering."

Both Koznicki and Tully had the strange sensation that Koesler was about to impart something of vital importance to their investigation. Tully particularly sharpened his attention.

"Well, as you very well know, Inspector, I was at sea when I was appointed to conduct this initial investigation. So, before I got into it, I tried to reduce my involvement to its least common denominator. Which was: What I could do was evaluate my brother priest, in this case, Father Robert. After all, we are about the same age, he being a little older. We both came from the same preconciliar era. We were trained almost identically. We share the unique character of the priesthood.

"It may sound silly to call it unique. All I can say is you'd have to experience it to understand it. For instance, this morning at the airport, I spotted another priest, and we nodded and smiled at each other. Now, this is not like a couple of soldiers or a couple of anyone else meeting as strangers yet sharing something in common. I could have sat at a counter with that priest, had coffee, and immediately begun conversing as if we were long-lost friends.

"Well, that's the sort of thing I brought to my 'investigation.' If nothing else, I could evaluate a priest. And . . . I don't quite know how to say this, but . . . it wasn't there. There was no spark, nothing between us. I know; I know that's not much to go on. But there are specific instances.

"There was . . ." Koesler hesitated. "Well, I don't suppose there's any point in going into them now. They were very technical sorts of things."

"Surely, Father," Koznicki said, "you cannot mean that all priests are alike. Or even that they are cordial with one another. Or, God forbid," he chuckled, "that they all agree with each other."

Koesler smiled. "No, I couldn't mean that."

Koznicki smiled in return. Then, more for Tully's sake than anything else, he continued, "These days, more than ever before, parishioners are deeply concerned over which priest will be assigned to their parish. Years ago it did not much matter who the priest might be."

"I guess that's pretty much true, Inspector," Koesler replied.

"One might be a better preacher. Another might be better at administration. But the theology was just about the same no matter who the priest was. Of course," he added, "that would have to have been pre–Vatican II."

"It is far different today, is it not, Father?" Koznicki said. "Today's priest might teach anything from that fine old war horse, *The Baltimore Catechism*, to Liberation Theology."

"Yes . . ." Koesler hesitated again. ". . . but . . . but that's not exactly what I had in mind."

As it happened, Tully couldn't have cared less about the distinctions Koznicki was making. However, he found himself intensely interested in what Koesler was intimating. "What is it? What do you have in mind?"

Koesler felt somewhat self-conscious. "It's an impression, just an impression I came away with."

"What impression?" It was like pulling facts from a rock.

Tully was growing impatient. He was sure he knew what conclusion Koesler had reached, but he could do nothing until the priest said it.

"My impression," Koesler spoke slowly, deliberately, "my impression was that Father Robert was not a priest."

"Not a priest!" Koznicki exclaimed. "But . . . but how could that be?"

Koesler waved his hand as if admitting he could not completely satisfy the Inspector's objection. "It's just an impression. Nothing I could prove in any definitive way. But some of the things he did . . . some of the things he said . . . well, I just came away with the overpowering feeling that he was not a priest. Or—perhaps more precisely—that he was not who he claimed to be. And that leaves me with a dilemma."

"A dilemma!" Tully clearly was eager. "What sort of dilemma?"

"Well, to pull off what the real Father Robert did—"

"The real Father Robert!" Tully interrupted.

"Yes, the real Father Robert. His was a master stroke of manipulation of Church law. He would have to have been a genius, at least when it came to Church law. And the Father Robert I talked with the other day made a serious canonical blunder. There's that. And there were other things—those technical errors I alluded to before."

"I think I know what you're driving at," said Tully, "but I want to hear you say it."

"Well," said Koesler, by now extremely self-conscious, "the conclusion that I reached—and it's just a personal conviction—is that I doubt very much that the person called Father Robert is a priest. I have no idea what they might have done with Father Robert. He has to have been real; no one else could have unified this little group and got them through the maze of Canon law and off the ground—but I can't see any Father Robert anywhere in that group."

"Say that again, Father," said Tully.

"What?"

"I have no idea what they might have done with Father Robert." Koesler had no idea why he was asked to repeat it.

"You got a good look at their living quarters. Tell me what you saw," said Tully.

"Well, gee . . . let's see. Ummm, it's all very, very simple—spartan, I'd say. Each one has a cell, a small cubicle to live in, enclosed by plasterboard partitions. And in the cells—what?—just a lumpy bed, a chair, a small table, and . . . on the wall of the cell . . . uh . . . nightclothes, an extra habit, and a discipline."

"A what?"

"A discipline. Very monastic. A ritual whip. To use as a reminder of the necessity to do penance."

Tully was clearly excited. "No carpet?"

"No . . . no carpet."

"No carpet, lots of kneeling, a terrazzo floor, a whip, a knife, and no Father Robert," said Tully.

It was Koesler's turn. "What?"

"You gentlemen must excuse me," said Tully, as he stood, "I gotta go."

"You're leaving before dinner?" Koesler said.

"I gotta go. The way I feel now, I couldn't keep it down if I ate it." Tully turned to leave, then turned back. "Father, I like you so much I could almost become a Catholic!" Then he left.

Koesler and Koznicki looked at each other wordlessly for some moments. "You know," Koznicki said finally, "for Alonzo, that was rather effusive."

SEVERAL
DAYS LATER

CHAPTER
24

Tully visited the Wayne County Jail as infrequently as possible. His job could be depressing enough without enduring floor after floor of raucous, malodorous, obscene, angry losers. But today's call was as much pleasure as business.

As always, he deposited his gun at the desk and, as always, a deputy sheriff took him through a series of formidable doors that were unlocked before them and locked behind them. Finally, Tully was situated in one of the miserable little interview rooms containing a small table and two chairs. Shortly, John Reid was ushered into the room. Tully made no move to rise, offer his hand, or extend any greeting. Nor did Reid greet Tully. Each heartily disliked the other and both knew it. Yet they would conduct their business with a sort of distant civility.

Briefly, Tully considered and rejected opening with a meaningless pleasantry. Instead, he asked, "Was it worth it?"

Reid returned Tully's steady gaze, eye to eye. "Worth what?"

"The million. A million bucks isn't worth what it once was."

Reid smiled without any humor. "Oh, a million, tax-free, properly invested, isn't bad. Besides, it was going to be lots more than that. Time ran out."

Tully noted that Reid shied from admitting responsibility for any failure on his part. Rather, he blamed it on "time."

"Still," Tully said, "its seems like a lot of trouble for even somewhat more than a million. Hell, guys play a little ball these days for millions."

"Yeah, but they sweat more than I did. It's not that hard to set up a dummy corporation. Anybody can incorporate, open an account, open a numbered Swiss account. It wasn't tough. In fact, it was sort of fun."

"I didn't mean that," Tully said, "I meant the murder."

The smile was gone. "There wasn't supposed to be any murder. That wasn't part of the original plan."

Tully tilted his chair onto its two back legs. " 'Not part of the plan.' Reid, we've been building quite a file on you. You mess up pretty regular. Snafu could be your middle name."

For an instant, naked fury transformed Reid's countenance. He looked preternatural. Then he checked himself again. But he made no reply.

"Why the murder?"

Reid was smug. "I was temporarily insane."

"That's your plea. But it's not going to hold water. Just between us, what drove you to 'temporary insanity'?"

"That fool, Robert. He wouldn't go along. He just plain refused. No matter how hard I tried to . . . uh . . . persuade him."

"Yes, the beating."

Reid waved a hand, seeming to dismiss the matter. "You wouldn't have anything on me but the bank job if you hadn't found the body." He snorted. "Finding the body. No more than a fluke!"

"No fluke, Reid. Good detective work from an unlikely source: Father Koesler."

"Koesler." Reid repeated the name as if sometime in the future he might seek revenge.

"If Koesler hadn't seen through your bogus Father Robert, you might just have gotten away with that one. We had you on a platter for the bank case and I wanted you for the attempt on who you thought was Lennon." Reid smiled briefly. Tully noted that. "But we might never have suspected anything more if Koesler hadn't been suspicious that your substitute wasn't Father Robert or even a priest.

"It was a sweet bit of deduction on Koesler's part. He wondered what you'd done with Robert, and then he mentioned the whip. That's when I remembered the 'bum' whose autopsy I happened to watch a week ago Saturday. His body was covered with contusions—from your whip. His knees carried markings I thought strange at the time—but they match perfectly with your terrazzo floor. And finally, his throat was cut with the knife you used on Sergeant Moore. It even had a flaw in the serrated edge that matched the cut on the real Father Robert."

Reid's lip curled. "Convenient that you knew where to find the body."

"We would have found it even if I hadn't seen it in the morgue. Once Koesler demonstrated that the real Father Robert was missing, we would have gone looking. And the first place we would have looked was where we actually found him—in the morgue.

"And, speaking of convenient, it was lucky—since you say you didn't plan it—it was lucky you found a replacement for the real Father Robert."

"One of the original group," Reid said. "In the dim lighting of that chapel, plus the fact that anytime that priest got close to people he was wearing the cowl, one old man can look pretty much like another. Besides, your case against me would be no more than circumstantial if you hadn't gotten the others to talk."

It was Tully's turn to smile. "Strange: the kid I shot was on the center table at the morgue. The real Father Robert was on one side. And a woman I thought figured into the Lennon case was on the other side.''

At the mention of Lennon, once again Reid smiled his mirthless grin. Once again, it was noted.

Tully continued. ''There were plenty of witnesses as far as the woman's killing, but they were all afraid to talk—until we got the guy on circumstantial evidence. Once they were convinced he couldn't hurt them, they talked.

''Same thing with the Brothers. You had 'em scared stiff. Until, with circumstantial evidence—that is lots stronger than you think it is—we could put you away. They knew if we got you for the bank fraud alone you'd probably be out in less than a couple of years. They were convinced you'd come get them then. But once we showed them what we had on you and that you'd go up for life with no parole, they started to talk.

''You terrorized them and then you scared them shitless by forcing them to watch you kill the priest after you'd tortured him. They're eyewitnesses, Reid. And their testimony is icing on the cake.''

Reid sighed. ''Tully, you say this and I say that. What the hell are you doing here anyway?''

Tully tipped his chair upright. ''I want you to tell me about your attempted murder with the car.''

Reid smiled broadly, almost genuinely. ''Lieutenant, you think you've got me for Murder One. What more do you want?''

I want to put you away so deep for so many things that some future governor won't be tempted to commute your sentence, thought Tully. But he said only, ''Tie up loose ends. Close the file on a pesky case. Oh, and speaking of closing files on cases, we've got you for beating up some dame while you were AWOL from the monastery on a date. Shame on you! It could only have complicated your grand plan.''

''You got her? Out of the woodwork?''

''She ID'd you from your picture in the paper and just showed up today. Surprise!''

"Well, here's one for you. Did she tell you where I met her?"

The question surprised Tully. He shook his head.

"In Murray's singles bar." He let that sink in a moment. "While you were making your move on the Lennon broad." A pause. "If things get dull, I may just let your live-in know about your roving eye. How is the lovely lady, anyway? Still enjoying her miracle?"

"She's doin' fine, sleazeball. And if we can't survive you, we don't deserve to be together. Matter of fact, now that you mention it, Alice is doing fine . . . and so is Mrs. Whitehead. And so is the Congregation of St. Stephen."

Reid's eyebrows raised in an unspoken question.

"The Archdiocese of Detroit is doing everything it can to discredit them—the miracles debunked, the fact that there isn't a real priest among them. Still the crowds keep coming—and the contributions keep pouring in."

Reid laughed. "One born every minute."

"Maybe. They seem to think they're doin' the Lord's work.

"Now, about that attempted murder—and, hey, lucky for you it's likely to stay at an attempt: The McPhee girl is stabilized. The docs think she's gonna make it."

"Who cares?" Reid tipped his chair back, matching the former nonchalance of Tully. "Look, Tully, you haven't got a thing—nothing—or you wouldn't be asking me about it, you'd be telling me about it. I don't care what happened to—what's her name?—McPhee. And if whatever happened to her should have happened to the Lennon dame, I'm sorry the guy goofed up. It was Lennon who screwed up everything by calling for that Church investigation. If she hadn't done that, I could've pulled it off."

"You 'could've pulled it off'!!" Tully's voice dripped sarcasm. "You are a walking, self-destructing jerk, Reid! You are a first-class screw-up. You've done it all your life. We've got a psychiatric evaluation on you, says you're attracted to failure like a moth to flame. You 'could've pulled it off'! You couldn't knock over a kid's piggy bank and get away with it. Face it, Reid: You're a loser! Just a goddam born loser!''

As he delivered this verbal abuse, Tully stood and looked down at Reid and watched as, once again, Reid's facial appearance changed into a hard mask of hate and pent-up destruction.

Suddenly Reid leaped to his feet. Almost in the same motion, he swung his heavy wooden chair over his head, screamed a curse and, with animal strength, swung the chair at Tully's head.

Tully found room to flatten himself against the wall, and not an inch more. The chair missed him by a hair, splintering against the wall.

It was the sound of the chair crashing that alerted the deputy. With all the shouts, yells, and hubbub going on throughout the floor, the guard would have paid no attention to Reid's verbal outburst in the general din. It was the unexpected explosion of the chair that caught his ear.

It took only an instant for the deputy to get the door open. Although he was a huge man, and although Tully pitched in with the desperate strength of one whose life was threatened, it took every ounce of their combined force to subdue the enraged Reid.

However, once he was restrained, Reid tried, not altogether successfully, to return to his structured civility. By this time several more deputies had arrived. They were no longer needed, but they would stay with the prisoner until he was securely back in his cell.

Tully left in the manner in which he'd arrived: through the series of successively unlocked then relocked doors. His gun was returned and he slipped it back in its holster. He then took stock of his clothing. Disaster! The struggle with Reid had been so brief that Tully hadn't expected such extensive damage. His summer suit was wrinkled, soiled, and torn in several places. His only comforting thought was that he was in an appropriate part of town to look like a bum. He'd have to return home, shower, and change. And probably bandage some cuts he would become aware of only when the shower spray hit them.

For the last time before his inevitable court appearance, he thought about Reid.

Now that the bank had recovered its money and the rest had been returned to the monks' account, Reid was literally observing his make-believe vow of poverty. Tully was very familiar with Reid's court-appointed attorney, Al J. Calhoun—Big Al, the criminal's pal.

When every other alternative defense was fruitless, Big Al traditionally relied on "temporary insanity." He hardly ever got it to work and it certainly wouldn't work in Reid's case. Brother Paul had bought the big one. Murder One. Life with no parole.

In his heart, Tully knew Reid had driven the car with which he had, over and over, savaged an innocent, helpless woman. Probably they would never be able to nail Reid for that one. The woman—the eyewitness—who swore she would never forget the face of that driver, had failed to identify Reid in a show-up.

As Jack Kennedy, among others, had said, life is unfair.

What gave it a semblance of fairness in this case was that Pat Lennon had gotten the story earlier and in greater detail than anyone else in the media. And she and the recovering Pringle McPhee would be free to go and come as they wished for the rest of their lives. And John Reid would not.

As for Tully, he was headed home for repairs. Alice would be there to greet him, and together they would put her miracle to the test. By now, neither of them doubted that the miracle would continue to pass.

LATER,
THE SAME DAY

CHAPTER
25

Junk mail!

Father Koesler, although not a gambler, was almost willing to bet that priests had the dubious distinction of receiving more junk mail than anyone else in Christendom.

He had just finished a very light lunch and had a few minutes remaining before his first appointment of the afternoon. A few minutes during which to get a little more caught up. What with the excitement of the past few days—his investigation of the monks followed by his unexpected involvement in the police investigation—he had fallen behind in his parochial duties. Thus he tried to utilize every spare moment, as he was now, in plowing through the mountain of mail on his desk.

There was a soft knock at the door. He looked up to see the always deferential Mary O'Connor smiling and holding a plate on which was a large glass of iced tea.

"Thanks very much, Mary," Koesler said. "That looks terrific. But I expect Mrs. Rozicki any minute now. And it wouldn't do for me to be sipping tea while dealing with the head of the Christian Service Commission.''

"She won't be here," Mary said. "She called just a few minutes ago and canceled her appointment. 'An emergency,' she said. 'A family emergency.' She didn't go into details, so neither did I."

So like Mary not to intrude into another's privacy. It was also true, thought Koesler, that in the near future, she would know what Mrs. Rozicki's problem was. That's the way this parish functioned. There were few absolute secrets. And those that were shared with two or three "close" friends eventually reached Mary O'Connor's ears.

Koesler was not sure why events seemed always to follow this course. Maybe it was a combination of Mary's genuine care and concern, along with her ability to *really* keep a secret.

"Then," Koesler said, clearing a small space on his cluttered desk, "bring on the iced tea. And thanks again."

The glass was placed on his desk. He selected another envelope and began to slit it open when something out of the ordinary happened. Mary sat down opposite him. She smiled mischievously, rare for her.

The priest was puzzled and his expression said so. "Mary . . . ?"

"Are you going to tell me about it?"

"About what?" He knew what.

"The Congregation of St. Stephen."

He shook his head. "You've read all about it in the papers."

She shook her head. "I want to get it from the horse's mouth." Then, feeling as if she had been indeliberately irreverent, she added, ". . . as it were."

Koesler shrugged. "The papers pretty well told the story, especially the *News*." Briefly he reflected on how totally Pat Lennon had dominated this news event.

"But not your part in it," Mary protested. Typically, he had downplayed his role to the inquiring media. Reading between the lines, however, she knew he had contributed much more than had been reported.

"What can I tell you?"

As it turned out, Mary had a suggestion. "It said in the paper that you were the one who first doubted that 'Father' Robert was a real priest. And that was what got the police started on the murder investigation."

"I guess that's so. But it wasn't such an unusual conclusion for any priest to reach."

"How did you do it?"

"Well, it wasn't any one thing, Mary; it was a series of peculiar, questionable things the so-called priest did that made me wonder, then doubt, then be pretty sure that no genuine priest—particularly the specific sort of priest Father Robert was supposed to be—well, a real priest just wouldn't do those things.

"For instance, right off the bat, there was the corporal—the linen cloth on which the priest puts the chalice and the host—"

Mary nodded.

"That's right," Koesler acknowledged, "you've washed and ironed enough of them to be as familiar with them as I am. Remember how they're folded?"

Her hands and arms moved in an ironing and folding pattern. "Four times," she said. "Up, down, then left, then right. You fold the corporal in on itself."

"Exactly. The idea is, if there's a particle of the host on the cloth it'll stay in the cloth and not be spilled on the altar or the floor. Did you ever see a priest open a corporal like he was shaking out a dish towel?"

"No!" Shocked: "Did he do that?"

He nodded.

"A momentary weakness, a distraction . . . ?"

"I tried to make allowances for him, but it wasn't easy. I've never seen any priest—young or old—do that. But, as I said, it wasn't just a solitary incident. After that, he read the opening prayers from a card."

Her brow furrowed. "Is that so odd?"

"How many times have you seen me or any other priest *read* the opening prayers?"

"But . . . wasn't he saying the Mass in Latin?"

"Just like he has been, in the new form, for the past twenty years. The identical prayers day after day. And Latin should be practically the mother tongue for an extremely conservative priest.

"And that brings up the next unusual occurrence that made me wonder if he were a priest at all.

"After they took me back into the monastery, we got into a discussion about miracles. Which was to be expected, I suppose, since the occurrence of the alleged miracles there was the reason for the Church's investigation.

"Anyway, the discussion turned out to be sort of academic. If you can believe it, we were arguing about whether a miracle more nearly resembled a sacrament or a sacramental. You remember: the old distinction between *ex opere operato* and *ex opere operantis*."

"Vaguely." As was the case with Catholics exposed to an enormous amount of parochial and graduate religious education, Mary had been sufficiently touched by scholasticism to be familiar with a significant number of Latin phrases.

"The odd thing about our 'discussion,'" Koesler continued, "was that 'Father' Robert took no part in it. It was entirely between me and a couple of the brothers who had had some seminary training. When pressed, Robert simply cited some Scripture passages. A device that might be described uncharitably as 'Protestant,' or, more correctly, as postconciliar. Surely not preconciliar, or typical of a conservative spokesman.

"Besides," Koesler was working up to what, for him, passed for animation, "there was something going on between 'Father' Robert and 'Brother' Paul. It didn't seem that Robert was coming up with those texts spontaneously. Paul was sending him signals. Almost like in baseball when a catcher signals to a pitcher. And Paul was doing much the same when Robert was blessing people.

"It made me wonder who was running this show—Robert, the ostensible leader, or Paul, maybe the actual leader.

Paul impressed me as sort of a . . . well . . . gray eminence. The power behind the throne. The power behind Robert.

"Then, the final straw was Canon law."

"Canon law?" Mary gave Koesler an opportunity to sip his tea. He took it.

"Just before I left the monks, things were getting a bit dicey, even hostile. I mentioned that if the controversy about a claim to miraculous powers were not settled and if push came to shove, the Cardinal might order their congregation to leave Detroit.

"At which point, Father Robert got a bit angry and claimed that the only order they need obey would be one from Bishop Di Giulio, their Italian benefactor."

"And . . . ?"

"And that's not true. When I was talking to Cardinal Boyle, I wondered why, with all this controversy and trouble, why he didn't just tell them to leave. The Cardinal replied that it would be poor form and bad public relations. He didn't say he couldn't do it, for the simple reason that he *can* do it. When a congregation such as this takes up residence in a diocese, it's under the direct jurisdiction of the local bishop."

"Maybe," Mary said, "Father Robert didn't know that?"

"That's the very point! The genuine Father Robert was a genius when it came to Canon law. He manipulated it masterfully to get his little Congregation officially recognized by the Church and then got it cut loose so he could establish it anywhere in the world he wanted to locate it.

"The real Father Robert made no mistakes when it came to law. The real Father Robert would have known very well that the local bishop had every canonical right to demand that he and his Congregation had to leave."

"That was rather clever of you to bring up the idea that the Cardinal could tell them to leave."

"Not really, Mary. Before I went to see them, I not only had a talk with the Cardinal, but I also phoned Inspector Koznicki. And both of them suggested I pay attention to

351

the law involved . . . although I don't think either one could have foreseen how their suggestions would work out.''

"So," Mary said, "that's how you knew that the man posing as Father Robert was an impostor.''

"Maybe, 'know' is a little strong for the way I felt when I was interviewing the monks. I'm a slow learner, as you know, Mary. Let's just say the seed was sown then and in the space of a day it grew enough for me to suspect the truth.''

"Is it true, then," Mary asked, "that the one who posed as Father Robert was really one of the original Brothers, as it said in the papers?''

Koesler nodded. "Uh-huh. Brother Alphonsus. He and the real Father Robert were about the same age. In the chapel's dim light—which was contrived by John Reid— it was nearly impossible to tell them apart.''

"But what made the Brothers go along with the plan? They are good, religious men, aren't they?''

"Sure. But because they're monks doesn't mean they can't be scared to death. Literally scared *of* death—death and torture. Reid tormented and abused the real Father Robert—as he did in effect later to Father Robert's stand-in. He forced the Brothers to witness Robert's death and made it explicit that this—and worse—would be their fate if they ever said a word to anyone.''

"Okay, one more question and then I'll let you get back to your work.'' She said it facetiously, knowing that she could never have kept him from his work if he hadn't wanted to tell her all about his adventure. "How did they know where to find Father Robert's body?''

"They didn't. Not at first. Lieutenant Tully accepted my hypothesis right from the start . . . maybe because he wanted so badly to get Reid on a murder charge . . . anyway, before he talked to me, the Lieutenant first thought it might be possible that Reid had somehow hidden the body someplace in the building. If they'd had good refrigeration, say a large freezer . . . ''

Mary shuddered. "What a horrible thought!''

Koesler smiled. "You've got to have a strong stomach"—knowing his was among the queasiest in captivity—"for this sort of thing, Mary."

"Anyway," Koesler continued, "at that point, Lieutenant Tully asked me to describe everything I saw when I was taken on a tour of the place. So I told him the monks' accommodations were very . . . uh . . . spartan, as you'd expect—as I expected from my memory of the Trappist monastery in Kentucky.

"Each of them had a cell, a small cubicle to live in, enclosed by plasterboard partitions. And in each cell there was just a lumpy bed, a chair, and a small table—and on the wall of the cell, hooks holding nightclothes, an extra habit, and a discipline."

"A what?"

"That is exactly what Lieutenant Tully asked. It's very monastic, very ancient, and mostly symbolic. A discipline is a sort of ritual whip one is supposed to use on himself as a reminder of the necessity to do penance."

Mary wrinkled her nose. "People actually used them?"

"Uh-huh. You weren't supposed to draw blood."

"Even so, it sounds disgusting."

Koesler shrugged. "That's the way it was. And, to a much lesser degree, that's the way it still is.

"Anyway, it was at this point that Lieutenant Tully began putting it all together. Or so he told us later. The combination of the cut that John Reid inflicted on Sergeant Moore's neck, and the damage that a whip could cause—even one that was meant to be used only in a ritualistic way—got him thinking about the body of the presumed bum he had viewed in the morgue. Even to the knees."

"The knees?"

"The knees," Koesler repeated. "The Lieutenant remembered that the vagrant had peculiar marks or scars on his knees. At first, he thought it was because the man had been crawling around in alleys and the like. Or . . . *or* the marks could be the impression of the terrazzo floor on his knees.

"Tully knew there was no carpeting in the public part of the monastery. And when I told him there was none anywhere else in the building, he saw the possible relationship between the man's knees and the floor he must have knelt on so often and so long. And, as it turned out, the marks matched. As did the notch in the knife wound in the neck of both the vagrant and Sergeant Moore. The 'vagrant' was the real Father Robert.

"Later—when they were finally convinced that John Reid would never be able to threaten or harm them again—the real monks were more than willing to testify against him."

Mary became aware her mouth was hanging open. She closed it. "Amazing. Amazing."

"But . . . but how does the monastery stay open? The paper said that Church authorities determined there was nothing truly miraculous going on. And you said the Cardinal could tell them to leave. And by now everyone knows there is no real priest there." She frowned. "I don't understand."

Koesler finished the tea and gave every indication he'd enjoyed it. "Yes, the Cardinal told them to leave. And, canonically, they have to go. But my understanding is that they are no longer terribly concerned with Church law. On the one hand, they are still being financially supported handsomely. And, on the other, they are convinced that they are doing God's Will no matter what the Church does. So the Cardinal can tell them to leave all he wants; it doesn't have any effect in civil law. The police aren't going to throw them out. The only effect is in Church law. Which should be enough—except that they no longer give a damn about Church law."

"Amazing," Mary repeated.

"Yes, it is.

"And now, if you don't mind, Mary, I'm going to get back to work or my chances of getting through this pile will also be amazing."

Mary retrieved the now empty glass and started to leave. She turned back, and said, "Anyway, nothing should get in the way of your work now.'' She meant it in the sense that there were no further appointments this day.

Evidently, he took her statement in a larger sense, for he replied, ''You're absolutely right. I have the distinct feeling that I will never ever again be roped into any sort of police investigation.''

Mary smiled as she left the priest's office. From time to time she would gamble a bit—a lottery ticket, a Bingo game. But under no circumstances would she lay money on this one.

ABOUT THE AUTHOR

William X. Kienzle was ordained to the priesthood in 1954 and spent twenty years as a parish priest. For twelve years he was editor-in-chief of the *Michigan Catholic*. After leaving the priesthood, he became editor of *MPLS Magazine* in Minneapolis and later moved to Texas where he was director of the Center of Contemplative Studies at the University of Dallas. Kienzle and his wife, Javan, live in Detroit.

Look for William X. Kienzle's newest mystery
starring Father Koesler and Zoo Tully—

MASQUERADE.

A mystery writers' conference brings together
an unusual collection of authors: a rabbi, a
nun, a monk, an Episcopal priest. They all write
mysteries, but they also have something else in
common: each of them happens to despise
the sleazy televangelist who is also on the guest
list.

If Father Koesler had any misgivings about acting as a consultant at the conference, they
disappear when murder upsets the entire
agenda, and Koesler is faced with a very pious
group of suspects.

Be sure to read all the Father Koesler
mysteries by William X. Kienzle
available in Ballantine paperback!

ASSAULT WITH INTENT

Four clumsy assassins stalk the seminaries of
Detroit. Who's behind this quartet of killers? Father Koesler, clerical sleuth extraordinaire, had
better find the answer quickly as he himself is
now the number-one target.

DEADLINE FOR A CRITIC

The venomous critic Ridley Groendal is dead.
Who did it? The playwright? The violinist? The
author? The actress? Each had a dark, long-
time link to the victim. And Father Koesler,
who'd known Groendal since their school days,
wants to know what happened.

DEATHBED

Father Koesler goes undercover as a hospital
chaplain to follow the tracks of four people
whose rancor toward someone is so great it
could translate into violence. The object of their
wrath: an indomitable, unsinkable nun who
almost single-handedly keeps the inner-city
Detroit hospital open.

DEATH WEARS A RED HAT

The first one is recovered beneath a cardinal's
red hat. The next few specimens are found
perched on the shoulders of church statues
throughout Detroit. They're all human heads,
heads that once conceived the most monstrous
crimes in the city. Father Koesler begins a terrifying quest into ancient rituals of revenge for the
critical clue to these macabre murders.

KILL AND TELL

Father Koesler has heard some shocking news in the sanctity of the confessional: yet a new murder victim will soon breathe his last. The honor-bound Father can't breathe a word, but as the sleuthing priest, he steps into action.

MARKED FOR MURDER

The older prostitutes of Detroit are the victims. Mutilation and branding are the methods. A man in the black garb and white collar of a Catholic priest is the suspect. Father Koesler may never forgive himself for what he's about to uncover.

MIND OVER MURDER

The Monsignor's Cadillac is found in the parking lot. Inside are traces of blood and a shell from a .32 automatic. All that's missing is the Monsignor. Father Koesler stars in an unforgettable Motor City mystery.

THE ROSARY MURDERS

It begins on Ash Wednesday, when someone pulls the plug on the hospital respirator of an elderly priest. Then a nun is brutally murdered in a bathtub. In swift, terrifying succession, men and women of the cloth fall prey to a savage killer who leaves a macabre calling card—a plain, black rosary entwined in the fingers of his victim. The introduction to William Kienzle's indomitable sleuth, Father Robert Koesler.

SHADOW OF DEATH

A cardinal is brutally murdered in his own church. Another is slain in the Vatican. On a trail from Detroit to Dublin to Rome, Father Koesler plunges back into his own haunted past—and becomes an unholy candidate for assassination.

SUDDEN DEATH

Hank "The Hun" Hunsinger, superstar tight end for the Pontiac Cougars, is murdered by ingenious and macabre means in his own shower. Himself a religious football fan, Father Koesler unearths a secret every bit as astonishing as a winning eighty-yard touchdown pass with three seconds to go.

Title	SBN	Price
ASSAULT WITH INTENT	33283	$3.95
DEADLINE FOR A CRITIC	33190	$3.95
DEATH BED	33189	$3.95
DEATH WEARS A RED HAT	35669	$4.50
KILL AND TELL	31856	$3.95
MARKED FOR MURDER	35397	$4.50
MIND OVER MURDER	35667	$4.50
THE ROSARY MURDERS	35668	$4.95
SHADOW OF DEATH	33110	$3.50
SUDDEN DEATH	32851	$3.95